GINNA GRAY

COMING HOME

PINNACLE BOOKS
WINDSOR PUBLISHING CORP.

PINNACLE BOOKS are published by

Windsor Publishing Corp.
850 Third Ave
New York, NY 10022

First Pinnacle Printing: October, 1994

Printed in the United States of America

Chapter One

She sat in the dark, alone.

On the outside she appeared composed and relaxed, her expression calm as she stared out the window at the glittering sprawl of Houston's skyline, but her utter stillness had a taut quality.

Evelyn Delacorte Ketchum was a woman who possessed immense wealth and power and the intelligence to use both. These days, almost no one intimidated her and very little frightened her . . . but she was frightened now.

Mist blurred the moon, creating an eerie nimbus around it. Down the hall an elevator pinged, and the soft tread of crêpe-soled shoes passed by her door, squeaking against the tile floor. From outside came the distant wail of a siren and the muffled *whop-whop-whop-whop* of a Life-Flight helicopter landing somewhere nearby. The bouquet of yellow roses on the table—one of Rourke's thoughtful gestures—had opened, and their sweet scent wafted through the darkness, mingling with the sharp odors of disinfectant and antiseptic that permeated the hospital.

Evelyn was only remotely aware of any of it. She

felt numb, frozen inside, as though she would shatter if she made the slightest move.

However, beneath the icy fear, anger was building. How could this be happening? There was far too much left to do, too many plans yet realized. She wasn't ready.

For the first time, Evelyn wished that she were young again. Not that fifty-one was such a great age. Nor did she really mind getting older—at least, not because of wrinkles and graying hair. She had waged a semisuccessful battle against those for years. Her business was founded on fighting the outward effects of time and enhancing a woman's appearance. No, what she hated was the weakness that age brought, the draining away of youthful vigor and energy, the limits on her physical body. Most of all, she hated the sense of time running out.

The door opened and light poured in from the hall.

"Hell, Evelyn. What're you doing sitting in the dark?"

She turned her head and saw Rourke Fallan silhouetted in the doorway. The corners of her lips twitched into something resembling a smile. "Nothing, really. Merely contemplating my mortality."

Rourke tensed, and Evelyn instantly regretted the remark. He was sharp and intuitive, and he knew her better than any living soul on earth. The comment was out of character, and she knew he had caught the note of bitterness in her voice.

He flipped the switch beside the door and the lamps on either side of the sofa flooded the sitting room of the VIP suite with light. Stepping inside, he closed the door behind him.

As always whenever Evelyn encountered Rourke,

she was struck anew by his masculine appeal. Though he was not male-model handsome, there was something about him that made a woman catch her breath and stare.

He was Irish, and he possessed the dark good looks and mysterious brooding qualities of his Celtic ancestors. Over six feet tall, with the lean, hard body of a man who kept himself in excellent physical condition, he somehow appeared both elegant and tough. He was the only man she knew who could wear Savile Row suits and scruffy jeans with equal panache.

His hair was black as coal, his eyes the brilliant blue of sapphires. At thirty-eight, Rourke Fallan was a man in his prime.

Evelyn gazed at him. She appreciated beauty in all its forms. Rourke's dark good looks and that aura of keen intelligence and vitality he exuded were qualities she had always admired in the past, but for an instant they were an affront, and she experienced a rush of bitter resentment.

She quickly shook off the feeling, recognizing it for what it was; a natural—if irrational—reaction to her situation.

"By the way, thank you for the roses. They're lovely." She glanced at the extravagant bouquet and smiled. The gift of flowers was typical of him. Rourke was a man acutely attuned to women, and he knew how she detested these yearly physicals the insurance company required.

Leaning back against the door, Rourke crossed his arms over his chest. "Something's happened. What's wrong?"

Evelyn opened her mouth, but he did not wait for an explanation.

"Someone tracked you down, didn't they? Damn it! As far as the rest of the world is supposed to know, you're vacationing. I left strict instructions that all business matters requiring immediate attention were to be directed to me until you returned.

"Who was it? One of our people? Or one of the bankers? And how the hell did they find you? I made all the arrangements myself. You're even checked into the hospital under an assumed name, for Chrissake. Outside of the two of us and Dr. Underwood, no one is suppose to know where you are. Hell, even Alice thinks you're up at the mountain cabin."

Alice Burke had been Evelyn's secretary for twenty years. A plain, quiet woman in her early forties, she had never married and had no family. Her job at Eve Cosmetics was her whole life, and she was as loyal and devoted as Rourke. For Evelyn to do anything without Alice's knowledge was next to impossible.

"Calm down, Rourke. As far as I know, no one knows my whereabouts."

"Then what's the trouble? Something is bothering you."

"Yes." She looked away from that vivid gaze, experiencing a numbing pressure in her chest. Rourke was the executive vice president of Eve Cosmetics and her second in command. Aside from that, he was her friend and confidant and the person whom she trusted most in the world. She was going to need his help.

"Sit down, Rourke. I have something to tell you."

He frowned, but did as she'd asked. When seated, he stretched one arm along the back of the small sofa and watched her. His curiosity was palpable, but he waited with the patience of a hunter, quiet and still, a man in complete control of his body and his emotions.

"I'm afraid I've had some bad news. From Dr. Underwood."

Rourke stiffened. "Something showed up on one of the tests?"

Evelyn looked at him then, and his eyes narrowed. "Wait a second. Why am I suddenly getting the feeling that you didn't come here merely to have a routine annual checkup?"

Her weak smile fluttered again. "You're right. There was more to it. To tell you the truth, lately I've been feeling . . . not ill, exactly, but . . . well . . . excessively tired. So I had Dr. Underwood run some extra tests." Imperceptibly, she gripped the arms of the chair tighter. She met Rourke's gaze and drew a deep breath. "He found that I am suffering from acute myeloblastic leukemia."

"Jesus!"

Rourke was unaware of whispering the expletive. Or of flinching. For several seconds all he could do was stare. Evelyn gazed back at him, her beautiful face cool as marble.

Her composure scared him. Life flooded back into Rourke's numbed senses and he shot off the sofa. Before Evelyn could protest or evade, he grabbed her hands and snatched her up out of the chair and into his arms.

She held herself stiff, instinctively resisting the intimacy, but he pretended not to notice. "God, Evelyn, I'm sorry. I'm so sorry. If you want to cry, go ahead. Rant and scream if you want to. Pound your fists. I won't mind. Hell, you can bay at the moon, for all I care. God knows, you're entitled."

"No, I'm all right, Rourke. Really."

To hell with that noise, he thought, and held firm when she tried to pull away. He knew all about her fierce pride, but this was not the time to let dignity get in the way.

After only a few seconds, she moaned and gave in, sagging against him. Gripping his suit lapels, she buried her face against his chest.

She wept quietly, barely making a sound, but Rourke felt the tremors quaking through her. His face grim, he rubbed his hands up and down her back and said nothing.

She felt so damned fragile in his arms. He would bet his next bonus they were the first tears she had shed since learning of her illness. He didn't doubt for a minute that they would be her last. Sighing, he felt a mixture of admiration and anger, and marveled, not for the first time, at the indomitable strength and iron will in this slender, elegant woman.

When at last she calmed, she stepped back, and he handed her the handkerchief from his breast pocket.

"Thank you." She sniffed, then grimaced and blotted her eyes. "I suppose I needed that."

"What is Dr. Underwood's prognosis?" Rourke asked gently. "Can this type of leukemia be cured? How do they treat it?"

Evelyn finished dabbing at her eyes and handed the handkerchief back to him with a mumbled thanks. Tightening the sash on her robe, she turned back to the window.

Absently, Rourke noted that even now she was the picture of perfection. Her mahogany-brown hair framed a face of classic beauty, the silver wings at her temples giving emphasis to high cheekbones and mesmerizing pale-green eyes. At the moment those eyes were red-rimmed from the bout of crying, but there was only the slightest tracery of lines at the corners, and her skin was porcelain smooth.

"You know how doctors are. You can't pin them down. He intends to start transfusions of blood and platelets immediately. Also anticancer drugs. And antibiotics, because of the high risk of infection. This type of cancer is particularly virulent, but he's hoping we can get it into remission. If not . . ." She waved her hand vaguely.

He studied the stiff set of her shoulders, that exquisite profile. "Is there anything I can do for you?"

Evelyn did not respond at once. Then she lifted her chin. It was an unconscious gesture, one that Rourke had witnessed thousands of times, but now there was a poignancy to it that clutched at his heart.

Squaring her shoulders, Evelyn turned from the window. "Yes. You can check me out of here. While you're doing that, I'll pack my things."

She marched into the bedroom. Rourke followed. "You're leaving? But what about your treatments? Shouldn't you stay in the hospital for those?"

"I'm sure Dr. Underwood would prefer that, but I'm afraid he'll have to arrange for me to have them on an outpatient basis. At least for the time being." She pulled out a Gucci bag from the closet and spread it open on the bed.

"Evelyn—"

"You know as well as I do that staying here right now is impossible. If the press gets wind that I have a health problem, the sharks will start circling." She turned from placing a stack of silk nightgowns into the suitcase and shot him an ironic glance. "Ones both in and out of my family."

"But—"

"Rourke, please. Don't fight me on this. I promise you, I'm going to do everything I can to lick this thing. Believe me, I don't want to die. But in case it comes to that, I am going to take steps now to safeguard my business. I didn't work for twenty-seven years building my company to let it be destroyed by grasping relatives."

Rourke wanted to argue, she could see it in his eyes, but after a brief hesitation, he firmed his mouth and nodded. "Okay. I'll go take care of the paperwork."

When he had gone, Evelyn clutched the bedjacket she was holding tight against her chest and closed her eyes. There had to be a way. There had to be someone who could step into her shoes and keep the wolves at bay. There *had* to be.

Rourke strode down the hall toward the elevators, his mind whirling. Leukemia. Jesus Christ! She could die.

It didn't seem possible. Evelyn Delacorte-Ketchum, founder, majority shareholder, and president of Eve Cosmetics, was too vital to die. She was always so full of life and energy. Hell, the woman was a dynamo. She put in long hours at the office and at home, flew all over the world to their various labs and plants, and kept her finger on every aspect of the operation.

Evelyn had a stunning knack for business and high

finance. Combined with an artistic flair for fashion and style, that made her a formidable force in the business.

She also had the uncanny ability to sense trends in the cosmetic industry. She seemed to know what the public wanted before they did, what would endure the test of time and what would be a passing fad. Eve Cosmetics never failed to profit from her shrewd foresight.

Evelyn was what every woman of the nineties strove to be, and so few ever were—a woman who did it all, who had it all.

At the same time that she had been building her company into a thriving, multimillion-dollar concern, she had also been a wife to Joe and a mother to three stepchildren. Evelyn was indeed a remarkable woman. A brilliant and extraordinary woman. Which was one of the reasons Rourke had stayed with her all these years.

Who would replace her? Which one of Joe Ketchum's relatives would inherit the reins of Evelyn's vast, worldwide company? She had not chosen a successor. Hardly surprising. At age fifty-one, who worried about dying? She'd probably thought she had years to find a solution to that particular problem.

Now that time could very well be mere months. Maybe less.

The night clerk's eyes lit up when Rourke entered the admitting office.

"Mr. Fallan. What a pleasant surprise."

Sondra Yount had been on duty four nights ago when Rourke had checked Evelyn into the hospital. Each evening she had either contrived some excuse to visit Evelyn's room while he was there or else waylaid him in the halls. She was blonde and blue-eyed, in her mid-twenties, with a pretty face and a spectacular body, sensuous and ripe with promise. So was the look in her eyes.

Rourke had considered asking her out to dinner, maybe taking her back to his place later, but he was no longer interested.

"My shift will be over soon," Sondra said, shooting him an under-the-lashes look. She stood up and came around the desk, gliding toward him with a sinuous sway of her hips.

Rourke's nostrils twitched. *Christ. The woman was as subtle as a bitch in heat.* "I'd like you to get Mrs. Smith's discharge papers ready, please. She's checking out."

"Tonight? Oh, I'm afraid that's impossible." Sondra smiled and smoothed her palms down the front of her dress. "We only admit patients on the night shift. All discharges are done during the day. However, if there's anything else I can do for you . . ." Her gaze slithered over him, and her lips parted.

"Miss Yount. This is a hospital, not a prison. Mrs. Smith is free to leave whenever she pleases. And she wants to leave now. I suggest you prepare her discharge papers."

"But . . . but I can't. Not without Dr. Underwood's approval. He has to sign them, and I don't know where he is."

"Then find him."

Sondra grew flustered. "I'll try, but I don't think—"

"Tell him if he's not here in half an hour, he is dismissed from Mrs. Smith's case."

"Ye-yes, Mr. Fallan. Of course. Right away."

"Good. I'll be back in thirty minutes."

Rourke left the woman bustling around the office and sought the solitude of the deserted and darkened sun room at the end of the hall. Winding his way through the wicker chairs and lounges, he walked to the glass outer wall.

The sun room overlooked a small parklike area. Rourke stared out at the misty night, oblivious to the clipped hedges and flowerbeds and manicured lawn, the benches under the trees, artistically illuminated by concealed landscape lights. Through the mist, their hazy glow gave the place a surreal look.

If Evelyn died, the impact on Eve Cosmetics would be staggering. The mere news of her illness was going to throw bankers from California to Florida into a tailspin. The enormous loans to begin construction on Eden East and Eden West had been granted largely on the strength of Evelyn's reputation. As the projects progressed, they were going to need additional financing. Whether or not they got it was going to ride on who took over the reins of Eve. Not a comforting thought.

None of the other board members had approved of building the two sumptuous beauty spas. The new ventures meant pouring profits back into the business, and Evelyn's stepchildren and the rest of her husband's family resented anything that cut into their dividends.

They had all voiced their objections at every board meeting since Joe Ketchum died. Evelyn had listened and mulled over their suggestions and opinions, then done as she pleased. With fifty-five percent of the stock, she had control of Eve Cosmetics firmly in her hands.

As far as Rourke was concerned, Evelyn's family was not only greedy, but short sighted. Opening the spas was a sound move and a logical expansion of the business. To compete with Lauder and Arden and all the other giants in the industry, Eve Cosmetics could not remain static and merely continue to sell a product. They had to be innovative.

Rourke massaged the back of his neck. Damn, he needed a cigarette.

The instant the thought registered, he snorted. "Yeah, sure. Fat chance." Shortly after coming to work at Eve twelve years ago he'd quit smoking . . . at Evelyn's suggestion.

"It's a disgusting habit," she had stated in that pleasant but commanding way of hers. "It's also bad for your health. You have the potential to go far in this company, Mr. Fallan. However, if you ever hope to work closely with me, you'll have to give up cigarettes. I cannot abide the nasty things."

He had quit that day. Cold turkey.

Over the years since then he had made many such changes, he recalled with a wry chuckle. Some big, some small, but all were aimed at one thing—reshaping and refining Rourke Patrick Fallan into a polished man of sophistication and class, a man destined for success.

The man who should be Evelyn's successor.

Outside the sunroom, two nurses cut across the lawn, hurrying through the mist to disappear into the building on the opposite side of the postage-stamp-sized park. Thrusting his suit coat back, Rourke jammed his hands into his trouser pockets and rocked back on his heels, his eyes narrowing.

Personal ambition aside, he was the best person for the job. The only sensible choice, really. And he deserved it. In the past twelve years, he'd worked his tail off helping to build the company into what it was. He knew almost as much about running Eve Cosmetics as Evelyn.

There was just one problem. To be president, you had to own stock in the company and have a seat on the board. The way things stood now, only family members or their spouses could do that. Evelyn was determined to keep Eve Cosmetics and all its subsidiaries strictly in the hands of her family.

Over the years Rourke had received offers from other firms—lucrative offers with unlimited possibilities. He had stayed on at Eve out of loyalty to Evelyn . . . and because he had known that time would eventually force a change.

Evelyn had no children of her own and no other living blood relatives. Despite their faults, she loved her stepchildren, and she was absolutely loyal to all the Ketchums—though at times he wondered why—but she was far too shrewd and too protective of the business she had built to leave control of it to one of them.

That left only him. After all, who else was there?

Chapter Two

Gazing out the side window of their car as the long line of vehicles crept toward the Dorothy Chandler Pavilion, Sara Anderson wondered why she hadn't had the good sense to open a limousine rental. It certainly would have been more profitable and less stressful than the business she had chosen.

Everybody knew that anyone who was anyone in Hollywood arrived at the Academy Awards in a limousine. Not just any old limousine, either, but a full-blown stretch limo, one of those block-and-a-half-long jobs that scream, "Get out of my way, peasant." Anything less marked you as an insignificant nobody, and in a town where image was everything, that was the kiss of death.

It was an ostentatious, ego-pandering overindulgence, of course, but she had no real problem with it. Sara understood the importance of image.

Early in life she discovered that people responded to the persona you projected, not what was inside.

If you didn't let people see you sweat, they never knew you were nervous. Stand up to a sadistic bully without flinching and deny him the pleasure of watching you cower in fear and that sometimes defused his viciousness. If you appeared successful, or well bred, or self-assured, or strong, or competent, or delicately feminine, or vague, or helpless—whatever—people assumed you were and responded to you accordingly.

Sara had taken that knowledge and made it work for her through a less than perfect childhood and adolescence. As an adult, she had combined what was by then a well-honed skill with her innate sense of what worked and what didn't, along with a flair for style and color, and opened her own image consulting firm. She had figured the Los Angeles–Hollywood area was a veritable gold mine for someone with her special skills, and she had been right.

Not that it had been easy. Even after almost two years, she still had to frantically tread water at times to keep from going under. Especially now, with the mounting costs of her mother's care eating up every spare dollar.

Things were beginning to look up, however. Word about Reflections and Sara's ability was spreading. Granted, at the moment, the volume was hardly more than a whisper, but if things went as she hoped tonight, tomorrow she and her service should be the hot topic on the Hollywood grapevine and new business would soon be pouring in.

"Oh, gawd! There's that bitch Madelene Ketchum," Cici Reynolds groaned. "Shit. If I'd known we were in line behind that barracuda, I'd've had our driver ram her limo."

Cici's agent, Lennie Herskowitz, leaned forward from the rear facing seat and patted his client's hand. "Cici. Sweetheart. Relax. Don't get yourself all worked up over Madelene. Just stay calm and play it cool. The cameras are going to be focused on you a lot tonight. I want you to use that to your advantage. And make sure you remember everything Sara has taught you."

Cici made a face. "Will you relax, Lennie? I'm not going to screw up. But you can't blame me for fantasizing a little about kicking that old has-been's arse up around her shoulder blades. Madelene Ketchum is a certified, gold-plated bitch."

"I know. But tonight we've got more important things to worry about. Like you winning the Oscar."

Cici made a rude sound. "Yeah. Right. I've got about as much chance of winning as a hooker has of meeting the Queen of England."

"Cici. Sweetheart," Lennie cajoled, in his Hollywood-sincere voice. "You may be the dark horse, but that doesn't mean you aren't in the running. You know this crazy town. The Academy members adore voting for the underdog."

"Can the crap, Lennie. We both know the most I can hope for tonight is to attract the attention of the studio brass and maybe make enough of an impression that they'll at least let me audition for the part of Emma. That's what these past few weeks have been about, remember?" Assuming an indifferent air, Cici crossed her legs and looked out the window.

Sara glanced sideways at her client. Cici didn't fool her. The actress's hands were clasped together so tight her knuckles were white, and her shapely leg swung in a jerky rhythm. She was wound as tight as an eight-day clock. Oh, she wanted that Oscar, all right, Sara thought. Cici was ambitious and competitive; she wanted it all.

Sara could find no fault with that. She and Cici Reynolds might be opposites in most ways, but they shared that merciless, all-consuming need to succeed.

After what seemed like an hour of stops and starts, at last their limo glided to a stop before the cordoned-off red carpet leading to the entrance of the pavilion. One of the attendants sprang forward and opened the passenger door, and Cici picked up her evening bag from the seat.

"Well, boys and girls. Looks like it's time to haul ass and get this show on the road." Her eyes flicked to Sara, and her smile held challenge and a touch of malice. "And you better hope this goddamn overhaul of yours works, because if it doesn't, you can kiss that fat fee of yours goodbye. There's still time for me to stop payment on your check, you know."

It was a threat Cici had issued at least once every day for the past month. Sara's stomach cramped at the thought of what losing that much money would do to this month's profits, but she merely smiled and quietly admonished, "Please watch your mouth, Cici. A lady never uses that kind of language."

Cici paused before climbing out of the limo and flashed her cocky grin. "Don't worry, Teach. I haven't forgotten all that crap you've been drilling into me. I'm a damned fine actress, remember? When I step out of this lead sled, I'll be so goddamn refined I'll make Princess Di look like a fucking bag lady."

Sara didn't so much as blink at the vulgarities. She knew Cici used them to goad her. The actress needed Sara's help, but that did not stop her from resenting the necessity.

Accepting the white-gloved hand of one of the

attendants, Cici extended a long, shapely leg from the door of the limo and stepped out.

A gasp went up from the crowd. It was followed by a groundswell of murmurs and exclamations as the dramatic change in her appearance registered. Cici, ever the consummate actress, paused to smile and wave, turning slowly to give everyone, especially the flashing and whirring cameras of the press, a good look at the newly remodeled Cici Reynolds.

Almost no one noticed Sara or Lennie until the three of them started up the carpeted path toward the entrance. Then the murmurs and whispers followed in their wake like a rustling wind.

"Who's that with Cici?"

"Dunno. The woman looks familiar, but . . .

". . . don't recognize . . ."

"You think she's an actress?"

". . . never seen her in anything . . ."

". . . maybe a relative . . ."

". . . don't look anything alike."

"Naw, she's nobody . . ."

Sara bit back a grin. That opinion suited her to a tee. The last thing she wanted was to draw attention away from her client. For that reason, tonight she had deliberately played down her own looks and opted for a simple gown and hairstyle.

Actually, if Cici hadn't insisted and the opportunity to perhaps pick up new business were not so great, Sara would not have attended the awards ceremony at all. She suspected the actress wanted her to witness the unveiling of her new image so that she could chew her out if the revamping did not produce the desired effect.

Cici Reynolds was Sara's newest client, and the

biggest name celebrity she had worked with so far. She was also her biggest challenge.

In her first movie, Cici had played a giggly, dumb blonde with such flair she had been instantly type-cast. Since then, the only parts she had been offered were bimbos or sluts.

The actress's abominable taste and lack of style had not helped. Cici had landed in Hollywood straight from the tough streets of Chicago. She had natural acting talent, but her idea of glamor was bleached platinum hair, four-inch heels, and clothes two sizes too small, cut down to her navel and up to her ass.

Hollywood had given a collective gasp when the Oscar nominations had been announced and Cici's name had been on the list. The role that had earned her the nomination had been yet another gum-popping, wisecracking ditz who wiggled and bounced her way through the movie in a tight dress. However, clever dialog and a unique and funny fast-paced plot had set the role apart from the run of the mill and given Cici the chance to display a perfect sense of comedic timing and turn in a stellar performance.

Cici had thought the nomination would open new doors for her. Word was out that Opal Studios would be ready to go into production on *The Collingswood Affair* as soon as they found the right actress to play Emma, the central character. Cici wanted that part. She would have sold her soul for it, but when Lennie had broached the idea with the producers, they had laughed in his face.

Cici Reynolds? Play a classy lady like Emma Collingswood? Sure, it was a comedy-drama, but holy shit, *Cici?*

As a sop, they had offered her another bimbo role and shown Lennie the door.

That was when he'd brought his reluctant client to Sara.

The first thing she'd done was take the actress to an excellent stylist and have her "Dolly Parton" hair cut to a fashionable shoulder length and returned to its natural light brown, with the addition of subtle golden highlights. Sara toned down Cici's makeup, instructed her on attitude and decorum, threw out her unbelievably tacky wardrobe, and took her shopping.

Cici, naturally, had fought her every step of the way.

Inside the pavilion, her client's changed appearance created even more of a stir among the other actors and film people. Sara could not have been more pleased. It was precisely the reaction she'd hoped for.

When they were seated, several people stopped by on the pretext of wishing Cici well, but it was obvious they really just wanted a closer look. Maxine Rhodes, one of the top three gossip columnists in the country, was more open.

"Cici, darling! What have you done to yourself? You look simply gorgeous!"

"Why, thank you, Maxine." Cici's smile and manner were so gracious, her voice so well modulated, you'd have thought she was a Junior Leaguer. "Actually, you're seeing the real me. I simply got bored with the trashy look. It was fun for a while, but it got to be tiresome. To tell you the truth, I'm ready to move on to meatier roles, and people weren't taking me seriously because of the way I looked."

"Well, darling, you look sensational now. And I must say, the change was a very wise move on your part. I'm sure when the studio brass see you tonight they'll be impressed."

They were. Within five minutes, Aaron Lewis, the head of Opal Studios, and producer David Blessing stopped by.

"Cici. Darling. How are you?" Aaron took Cici's hands and leaned down to kiss the air somewhere in the vicinity of her left ear. When he drew back, his eyes flickered over her, his expression a mix of admiration and amazement.

"I'm fine, Aaron. A bit nervous, of course, but holding together."

Introductions were made and the two men expressed delight in meeting Sara and greeted Lennie with hearty friendliness, as though less than a month ago they had not practically laughed him out of their office, but their attention returned at once to Cici.

"You look gorgeous, darling. Truly lovely. Doesn't she look lovely, Dave?" He glanced at his colleague, then back at Cici. He strove for a blasé charm, but Sara saw the calculation in his eyes.

David Blessing's face wore the same look of suppressed excitement and conjecture. "Yes, indeed. You look terrific, Cici. Really terrific."

Sara bit back a smile. She could almost hear what both men were thinking. She had read the book on which the screenplay for *The Collingswood Affair* was based. Sara had purposefully modeled Cici's new look after the main character—her hairstyle, her makeup, everything, right down to her pink painted toenails. Even the dress she wore tonight, which had been made especially for her, was a loose interpretation of one that had been worn by the heroine. Aaron Lewis and David Blessing were looking at the perfect Emma, and they both knew it.

"Why, thank you. It's so sweet of you to say so." All trace of Cici's midwestern twang was gone. So were her hard edges. Her smile and cultured tone were soft and gracious as a genteel breeze on a warm summer night, and the effect on both men was apparent. They exchanged another speculative look and a subtle nod.

"We just stopped by to wish you luck, my dear," Aaron continued, patting her hand. "We'll be rooting for you."

"Yes," Dave echoed. "You deserve to win."

"You're both so sweet," Cici simpered. "I'm just thrilled to have been nominated."

The orchestra began to warm up, and Aaron glanced at his gold Rolex. "Ah, the festivities begin. We'd better get back to our seats." He bestowed another air kiss and started to straighten, then bent down again. "Oh, by the way, Lennie. Why don't you and I do lunch next week and we'll talk?" His gaze flickered briefly to Cici. "We might be able to work something out, after all."

Stunned, Cici watched the two men walk back up the aisle to their seats, but she barely had time to exchange an ecstatic look with her manager before the house lights dimmed and the orchestra struck up the overture.

"Holy shit, do you believe that?" she whispered in Sara's ear. "They bought it! The hair, the la-di-da talk, the dress! They fucking bought it!"

As the emcee walked onstage, Sara could feel Cici vibrating with excitement next to her. She smiled, remembering how her client had objected to everything Sara had done or suggested over the past few weeks, particularly the dress.

"You expect me to wear this to the awards? It doesn't even show any cleavage, for Chrissake."

"That's right, it doesn't. That's one of the reasons I chose it," Sara had replied calmly, as she'd circled her client, looking for a flaw in the fit.

The elegant gown was royal blue silk crêpe with a subtle tracing of gold embroidery across the blouson bodice and down one sleeve. The neckline draped delicately across her collarbone and dipped low enough in the back to be tantalizing but not vulgar. The pencil-slim skirt fell to her ankles and had a discreet slit up one side to just above her knee. In it, Cici looked sophisticated and classy and breathtakingly lovely.

"Shit, can't we at least have it taken in some? It's too goddamned loose across my butt."

"No."

"Why the hell not?"

Normally, Sara would have cajoled or reasoned, but she'd had it up to her eyeballs with Cici's constant complaints, so she decided to lay it out in terms that the actress would understand. "Because the part you covet so much calls for elegance, and that's what you have to show the producers. Trust me, tits and ass play hell with elegance every time."

The crude statement, coming from Sara, stopped Cici cold. She lowered her lashes partway and fixed Sara with an assessing look. A moment later, docile as a lamb, she wrote out a check for the dress.

After that, she had gone along with Sara's suggestions with only an occasional token complaint.

Cici was so keyed up and fidgety, she was about to come apart at the seams. A couple of times while the obscure awards were being given out at the beginning of the ceremony she became so impatient Sara was afraid she was going to lose it and stand up and screech at everyone to "get the goddamn show moving."

Mercifully, they didn't have long to wait. Of the four big acting awards, Best Supporting Actress was presented early in the program. Sara suspected it was done that way to keep everyone from falling asleep.

The emcee cracked a couple of stale jokes before introducing the presenters. Sitting between Sara and Lennie, Cici gave up all pretense of indifference and clutched their hands in a death grip as Gene Hackman and Glenn Close made their entrance.

At the podium, the pair exchanged the usual rehearsed repartee while Cici squirmed and muttered obscenities under her breath. After what seemed an interminable time, they finally read off the nominees.

When they read Cici's name and the television camera zeroed in on her, she managed to appear composed. She even whispered something to Lennie and smiled for the benefit of the viewers, but her grip on Sara's hand became excruciating.

Gene gallantly handed the envelope to Glenn. After a bit of fumbling she broke the seal and pulled out the card. Her eyes widened as she read the name, and she gave the audience a coy look. "And the winner is . . ."

Cici closed her eyes and dug her nails into Sara's palm. "Oh, shit, oh shit, oh shit."

". . . *Cici Reynolds! For* In Your Dreams!"

Chapter Three

Rourke followed Evelyn into the foyer of her penthouse apartment and nudged the door shut with his shoulder. He cocked one eyebrow and hefted the cases. "Shall I take these to your bedroom?"

"No, just put them down anywhere. Mrs. Chester will put everything away when she arrives in the morning." She turned and headed down the hall. "Come with me to the study. We have work to do."

"Now? It's getting late. Shouldn't you get some rest?"

"No. I'll be doing plenty of that before long. More than I care to think about. Right now, I have some decisions to make, and I want your input."

Rourke watched her walk away. On the short drive from the hospital she had barely said a word. He had thought she was still upset or perhaps feeling the effects of her illness. He should have known that agile mind was busy.

Eve Cosmetics was Evelyn's number-one priority. With the possible exception of Joe Ketchum—and Rourke wasn't completely sure about that—it had always been the most important thing in her life. She had adored her husband and loved her stepchildren, but the company was her baby. Over the years she had poured blood, sweat, and tears into the business to make it what it was today. It was her creation, the child she'd never had. And like all mothers, she was fiercely protective.

Rourke strolled after Evelyn, shaking his head. *Lady, you are one helluva woman.*

Evelyn was already pouring a Scotch when he entered the study, mere seconds behind her. She handed him the drink, accepted his thanks with a nod, and turned back to pour her usual club soda with a twist of lime. Sipping the Scotch, Rourke ambled around the room.

He had always thought of this place as totally Evelyn's. Technically, the rambling old house on the Ketchum ranch, fifty miles or so to the west of Houston, was her primary home. Thanks to Joe, it belonged solely to her now. However, the ranch house had been lived in continuously by Ketchums since it had been built in the 1860s, and every succeeding Ketchum wife had left her mark on it.

For the twenty-five years that she and Joe had been married, Evelyn had lived with him there without complaint, commuting back and forth daily between the Ketchum Cattle Company headquarters and the Houston offices of Eve Cosmetics, either by chauffeured car or by helicopter.

Evelyn had bought this place two years ago, shortly after Joe's death. She claimed it was more convenient, especially on those nights when she worked late, but Rourke figured she had simply wanted a place all her own on which she could put her stamp.

He suspected also that she wanted to escape now and then. Despite whose name was on the deed, Joe's brother, Will, and his two sons, Chad and Paul, and Paul's wife, Monica, all lived in the ranch house.

The whole apartment reflected Evelyn's character, Rourke thought, but no room more so than the study. Pale-blue silk wallpaper above pecan wainscoting, floor-to-ceiling bookcases, polished oak floors, and an Adam fireplace combined solid strength and tranquil beauty. The furnishings were eighteenth-century period pieces, all with elegant lines and the rich patina of quality and years of care. The soft blue and cream of the floral print draperies and oriental rug, the delicate crystal and porcelain pieces scattered around, a profusion of plants, and the blurry romanticism of the painting above the mantel—all quietly proclaimed it to be a woman's domain. The overall effect was subtle, and that, too, was typical of Evelyn—a mere touch of feminine gentility and refinement to soften the underlying power.

Rourke had always liked the little hideaway. He found it restful and soothing.

Deep in thought, Evelyn turned from the armoire that served as a bar and sat down, bypassing the desk in favor of one of the Queen Anne chairs before the fireplace. Rourke settled on the sofa. A comfortable silence fell between them, broken only by the tick of the mantel clock and the clink of ice cubes against glass.

Evelyn sipped her drink. With a whisper of nylon, she crossed her legs and looked at Rourke. "How is construction proceeding on the spas?"

"We've had a bit of trouble with a couple of the California subcontractors, but so far, Eden West is right on schedule. The site in Florida caught the edge of Hurricane Grady. There was no structural damage, but the rain delays have put Eden East a bit behind where we wanted to be."

"Is there any way of speeding things up? I'd like to have these projects well along before news of my illness gets out."

"I don't think so. Not without sacrificing quality, and I doubt you want that."

"No, of course not. The spas have to be not merely first class but opulent. I want them to be luxurious almost to the point of decadence. Quality must be given top priority."

"Then the answer is definitely no."

Evelyn pursed her lips. One salmon painted fingernail tapped the side of her glass. "How long do you think we can keep my condition a secret?"

"For now it shouldn't be a problem. We can come up with a plausible story to cover you when you have chemotherapy sessions. Should you reach a point where you have to be hospitalized, it'll be a whole different ball game. If it comes to that, I'll probably be able to keep a lid on things for a couple of weeks. A month at the outside."

Her eyes widened. "Really? I'm impressed. That's longer than I expected. How on earth will you manage it?"

Rourke's gaze locked with hers. Determination deepened his voice and gave it a hard edge. "Don't worry, I'll manage.

"Yes," Evelyn murmured, studying him. "I'm sure you will."

The silence stretched out again. After a while, Rourke asked, "Are you going to tell your family?"

"Not yet. Not until I have things arranged the way I want them."

"Not even your stepchildren?"

"Especially not my stepchildren." Her eyes held droll amusement. "I might as well make a public announcement as tell Madelene. You know her first thought would be to milk the situation for publicity. She'd probably call a press conference and turn the whole thing into a drama. I can see the headlines now." Raising her hand, she pretended to block out a caption in the air. *"Grief-stricken movie star Madelene Ketchum flies to bedside of dying stepmother."* Evelyn made a droll face. *"She,* of course, would get top billing."

"Of course." Rourke chuckled and lifted his glass in a wry salute. Evelyn loved her stepchildren, but she never let that blind her to their shortcomings.

She rose and returned her empty glass to the bar. From there she wandered over to the French doors. For a time she stood with her arms crossed, looking out at the small terrace garden and the lights of the city beyond, fuzzy through the misting rain. Rourke watched her and waited.

"I can't put it off any longer," she said finally. Pitched low, her voice was heavy with resignation. "I'm left with no choice. I have to pick a successor."

"Yes," Rourke agreed just as quietly. He felt a rush of relief. A tug of excitement. At last, it was out in the open. Ever since she had told him of her condition the matter had hovered between them, charging the air like invisible heat lightning.

"But who? Which one of them do I choose?" She made a disparaging sound and looked up at the sky. "Naturally, one of Joe's children would be my preference, but can you honestly see Chad running Eve Cosmetics? Or Madelene? The only thing my stepson is interested in is the Ketchum Cattle Company. If you can't rope it, brand it, or string a barbed wire fence around it, a thing has no value to Chad. Maddie's even worse. She barely knows a world exists outside Hollywood."

Evelyn turned away from the French doors and began to pace the length of the room.

"What about Kitty? She's bright enough."

Rourke had no qualms about playing devil's advocate. He knew it was probably the quickest way to bring things into focus and settle the matter. He and Evelyn had never discussed who her successor would be—there had been no need—but they were both aware that not one of the board members was an acceptable candidate to head Eve Cosmetics.

At the moment she had her back to the wall, so she was fighting the obvious, but he knew Evelyn. She had the rare ability to put sentiment and emotions aside and make tough decisions based on logic and an intelligent and pragmatic appraisal of the situation. Self-deception simply was not her style. No matter how unpalatable a truth, she faced it, then did whatever was necessary. He was confident that she would in this situation, too, once all the facts were laid out and examined logically. Until then, he could be patient.

"Yes, I agree. The problem is, she doesn't. Growing up in this family, especially in Madelene's shadow, hasn't been easy for Kitty. She's painfully insecure—about her looks, her intelligence, her abilities. You name it. What's worse, she has even less interest in the business than her sister. Merely getting her to fly home every month for a board meeting is a struggle. All she wants is to write her plays and to make it on her own in New York."

Rourke thought of his first few years in Houston and wondered how anyone could call living on a fat quarterly dividend check "making it on her own." He kept the thought to himself, however. If Evelyn had a blind spot, it was Kitty.

Madelene had been fourteen and Chad ten at the time of Evelyn and Joe's marriage, but Kitty had been only four. Evelyn had raised her and loved her as though she were her own daughter. Of the three stepchildren, she was by far closest to Joe's youngest child.

"So . . . what about one of the others?" he suggested. "How about Lawrence?"

It was hopeless. They both knew it. Nevertheless, for the next half hour they considered, discussed, and dismissed every person who held a seat on the board of directors of Eve Cosmetics.

Lawrence Tremaine, Madelene's fifth husband, was a brilliant tax attorney. He looked after his wife's interests and was an asset to the company, but he was ultraconservative and unimaginative. He lacked both the drive and the insight needed to head a worldwide firm.

On the surface, Joe's nephew, Eric, Will Ketchum's youngest son, seemed a logical choice. Eric had worked for Evelyn since graduating from college, six years ago. For the last two he had been the marketing and promotions director. He liked his job and he was good at it, but he was not executive material. No one knew that better than Eric himself. A playboy with a frivolous nature, he was, much to his father's disgust, more than content to leave the running of the company to Evelyn and Rourke.

The only person who came close to having the skills necessary to hold the reins of Eve was Will. However, even had he not been seventy and crippled from the stroke he'd suffered the previous year, Evelyn was unwilling to hand over her company to her brother-in-law.

"Granted, after thirty-five years of running Ketchum Oil, Will's got a lot of business experience, but somehow I don't think it would translate to directing a cosmetics firm," Evelyn said, when Rourke brought up his name. "For one thing, his method of operation is to run roughshod over anyone who gets in his way, particularly women. In this business, that would be suicide." She shook her head, her expression adamant. "No. I'd sooner close the doors than hand my company over to Will Ketchum."

She dismissed Paul, Will's oldest son, for many of the same reasons. Though he'd been the acting head of Ketchum Oil since his father had fallen ill, he was merely a younger version of Will, only not as smooth—or as clever.

Paul's wife, Monica, was a featherbrained creature who didn't know a profit-and-loss statement from a grocery list—and what's more, didn't care. As long as she had her credit cards and that little fireball sportscar she tooled around in, she was happy. She was so far out of contention her name never entered the discussion.

When the choices had been exhausted, Evelyn stopped pacing and returned to her chair. Leaning her head against the high back, she closed her eyes and exhaled. "What am I going to do? Not one of them has what it takes."

"There is a solution. You may not be crazy about it, but it will work."

Evelyn lifted her eyelids partway. "Oh?"

"You could let the company go public. That way—"

"No. Absolutely not. You know my feelings on that score. I didn't like the idea when Will and Paul brought it up a few months back, and I don't like it now. I will not have strangers getting their fingers in my business."

Rourke ran his thumb through the condensation on his glass. The obstinate set of her jaw concerned him, but his gut told him the time was ripe. "It doesn't have to be strangers, you know." He felt rather than saw her tense. "In fact, going public could be the best thing for the company."

"Oh? How so?"

Rourke looked up, straight into her eyes. They were narrowed slightly and wary, and for the first time since he'd known her, mistrustful. He regretted that. "The others would be sure to sell off at least part of their stock. Especially Chad and Paul. They're always scrabbling for money to keep the ranch and the oil business afloat. I could buy up a block of the stock they offer. Then you could vote me onto the board and make me president."

Evelyn considered him in silence, her mouth pursed. "Even if they sold only a small portion of their stock, you're talking about a great deal of money. Do you have that much?"

"What I don't have, I can get."

For twelve years he had socked away every bonus

he had earned and earmarked it for just that purpose. For a split second he considered admitting as much, taking the gamble that openness would weigh in his favor, but he knew the admission could just as easily cost him everything he had ever worked for. Evelyn appreciated honesty and determination—more so than most—but where her company was concerned she could be unyielding. First and foremost, her instinct was to hold on to what was hers, and to that end she was as ferocious as a tigress protecting her young.

She looked at him for another long moment. "So," she said at last in a flat voice. "You're turning on me now, too, are you?"

Rourke did not so much as bat an eyelash at the rebuke. His voice was even and calm, only mildly chastising. "Of course not. I'm merely offering a possible solution to the problem. I happen to think it's the best solution, but the decision is yours. And you know full well that you have my complete loyalty, whatever you decide."

For several more moments they regarded each other, a silent standoff between two strong, determined people.

Finally she sighed. "I'm sorry, Rourke. No one is going to sell their stock. When Joe financed my business twenty-seven years ago, that was the only condition he made—that it always remain in the family. It's a tenant the Ketchums have always held to—what's theirs remains theirs—and it has served the family well for a hundred and thirty–odd years. They've managed to hold onto their fortunes while all around them others were going under. Joe put up his own money to back my business, but the stipulation was still included in the company charter and spelled out clearly in the articles of incorporation, the same way it is in all Ketchum ventures. To change it would require a majority vote of the shareholders."

"Which you control."

"That's true. But even if I wanted to let the company go public—which, as you know full well, I don't—I wouldn't, because I promised Joe. And I trust his judgment.

"He was the one who held the Ketchum family fortunes together for the past forty years. Will is smart but he has a wildcatter's mentality; he's always looking for a gusher. If he so much as sniffed oil, he'd risk everything to get at it. Thank God, John Ketchum recognized the differences in his sons and left Joe in control.

"Joe was worried about his family, about their ability to survive, left to their own devices. That's why he willed five percent of his half of Eve to me, to ensure that I would have complete control. Not merely so I could safeguard what I've built, but so I could look after his family for him."

She shook her head. "I'm sorry, Rourke, I won't allow the stock to be sold out of the family. You must know that I'd like nothing better than for you to take over for me and run Eve. But I won't go back on my promise to Joe. Not even for you."

Stifling his disappointment, Rourke shrugged as though her decision were immaterial to him. It wasn't over, he told himself. Nothing had changed. "Then what will you do?"

She sighed. "I don't know yet, but I'll think of something. I have to."

"I'm sure you will. You always do." He stood up

and stretched, rubbing the back of his neck. "Me, I'm fresh out of ideas, so I think I'll call it a night. Don't bother, I'll see myself out," he said, waving her back down when she started to rise. "Let me know what you decide."

He called "Goodnight" over his shoulder, and Evelyn responded in kind. She watched him stride out the door, her mind already drifting away to other things. He had barely disappeared when he stuck his head back inside. Concern darkened his handsome features.

"Are you going to be all right here alone?"

"Of course. I'm fine."

"You sure?"

"Perfectly."

"I could get Mrs. Chester to sleep in the guestroom instead of the maid's quarters. She'd be a lot closer there."

"I don't need anyone with me. I'm not an invalid yet."

"How about if I—"

"Rourke."

"Yeah?"

"Go home."

For several minutes after Evelyn heard the front door close behind him, she remained in the chair, her head resting against the high back. Ah, well, it was foolish to feel disheartened by Rourke's suggestion. It wasn't as though she was surprised. From the beginning she had been aware of that burning ambition of his. Beneath that smooth exterior and effortless charm he hungered for more . . . more challenge, more power, more success. If he could, Rourke would own the world.

Evelyn chuckled, not in the least disturbed by the thought. She understood ambition that strong. She shared it.

It had been that fierce need in him that had caught her attention when they first met. Whenever she thought about how he had strutted into the Eve offices so long ago, wearing those awful gaudy clothes and flashing that cocky grin, she had to laugh. The brazen devil had actually had the nerve to try and fast-talk her. *Her!*

Oh yes, he had been a brash one, all right, but beneath his cockiness she had glimpsed that crackling intelligence, that fire. So she had played a hunch.

In twelve years, she had never once regretted it.

He had been an apt pupil, eager and determined, learning everything she could teach him with a quickness and depth of understanding that had surprised even her.

To Rourke's credit, he had learned on his own as well. As astute and observant as he was bright, he had gradually knocked off his rough edges and acquired manners and polish as he hauled himself up the ladder of success. By sheer dint of will, Rourke had turned himself into a man to be reckoned with, a man who was the epitome of stylish charm and intelligence who understood power and knew how to use it.

She admired that. She admired him.

Evelyn sighed and ran her fingers through the silver hair at her temples. The truth was, she couldn't be more fond of Rourke, or more proud of him, if he were her own son. There had even been a time when she had harbored hopes that he would marry one of her stepdaughters.

It was not to be, of course. And it was for the best, really. In her heart she had always known that. Madelene was too wild and promiscuous for Rourke's discriminating taste, and Kitty was too submissive and insecure. Rourke needed a strong woman, a woman of intelligence and depth, with a will and drive that matched his own.

Still . . . it was too bad. He was the perfect person to step into her shoes as president of Eve.

Realizing that her thoughts had come full circle, Evelyn got up from the chair and walked through the apartment to her bedroom, turning out lights as she went.

It was a relief just to be home, she realized, entering the spacious room. Her eyes swept with pleasure over the fourposter bed and the elegant Philadelphia highboy, the lovely settee in soft shades of peach and coral and seafoam green. After four days of anxiety, of being poked and jabbed and x-rayed and scanned, of pacing that determinedly cheerful but sterile suite of hospital rooms, being among her own things again gave her a kind of peace.

Or perhaps it was merely the relief of finally knowing what she was facing.

She glided into the dressing room and through it to the monstrous closet beyond. Half an hour later, freshly showered and dressed in an ivory satin nightgown and matching robe, she walked back into the bedroom.

She went to the small writing desk beside the window. Her current diary, a ledger-sized volume bound in dark blue leather, lay on the desk top. Smiling, Evelyn ran her fingertips over her initials and the year, embossed in gold on the front.

Recording the events of her daily life, her feelings, was a therapeutic ritual she had performed for forty-one years. The practice had been suggested to her by a kindly minister at the time of her parents' death. To the frightened, grief-stricken ten-year-old she had been at the time, it had been her salvation. Over the years the exercise had gotten her through many difficult times. Even now it continued to help her sort out her problems and see things more clearly.

Taking a seat at the desk, Evelyn opened the book to the first blank page, plucked the pen from the gold desk set, and began to write.

Today I learned that I have leukemia. Leukemia. Cancer. Oh, God. The mere word gives me chills.

Dr. Underwood tries to be cheerful and encouraging, but there is something in his eyes . . .

Am I going to die? My soul cries out at the thought. I don't want to die! It's too soon! I'm not ready! There's so much more I want to accomplish. I have so many plans. It can't end now.

But it might. No matter how much I rail against the fates, that's a possibility I must face.

There's so much to do, and so little time. I have to protect my business. But how? How? What can I do?

I've gone over it and over it in my mind, but the result is always the same. The plain fact is, there's no one among my family I can trust to follow my wishes. Even if there were, none of them is capable.

If only Joe and I could have had children of our own. As it is, there is no one to preserve what I've worked so hard and so long to build. No one at all . . .

Unless . . .

Dear heaven, I hesitate to even think it. Still . . . it

is a chance. A slim one, to be sure, but still a chance. The only one I seem to have.

Am I crazy to even consider it?

Probably. If I do this, it will stir up all manner of things that are best left alone. Oh, God, it's such an extreme step, a last-resort act of desperation.

But then . . . I am desperate.

Evelyn stopped writing. She gazed into the distance and nibbled the end of the pen. Making an aggrieved sound, she closed her eyes and caught her lower lip between her teeth. For several seconds she remained utterly still, her face taut.

Finally her eyelids lifted. She stared at her reflection in the windowpane. A glint entered her eyes and she jutted her chin and picked up the pen again.

Yes. Yes, I will do it.

On the West Coast, Sara Anderson let herself into Reflections' suite of offices in the prestigious Winthrop Tower in the heart of downtown Los Angeles. The four-room suite cost her the earth but an imagemaker's image was all-important and the building had just the right cachet.

The single lamp that was always left burning in the reception room at night cast a dim pool of light over the oriental rug and elegant furnishings. The thick carpet absorbed Sara's footsteps as she crossed the room in a whisper of silk, her long gown swirling around her ankles with each tired step.

In her office she did not bother with the main switch but merely flicked on her desk lamp. Tossing her beaded bag onto the desk top, she sank down onto the leather chair, propped up on both elbows, hung her head, and massaged the tight muscles in her nape with both hands.

"Rough night?"

Sara started at the question and looked up to see Brian Neely slouched in the doorway that separated her office from his. He stood with one shoulder propped negligently against the doorframe, his poet's face and spaniel-brown eyes full of warmth.

He wore his usual after-office-hours attire of faded jeans and a ratty sweatshirt, and his overly long, sun-streaked blond hair was tousled, as though he'd been running his fingers through it. A resigned smile tugged at Sara's mouth. At thirty-three, Brian still clung to the flower-child look he'd had as a teenager. The sad part was, she admitted with a twinge of despair, it suited him. Brian drifted with the tide, blithely shrugging off anything that smacked of responsibility.

She gave him a wry look. "A long one, at any rate. I didn't expect to find you here so late."

"Yeah, well . . . I had some paperwork to catch up on." He pushed away from the door and ambled into her office. Hitching one leg, he perched on the corner of her desk, picked up her gold-handled letter opener, and began tossing it end over end, catching it by the tip every third revolution. "So . . . our little dark horse took home the big one. Who would've thought it? The oddsmakers are probably ruining their knickers about now."

"I take it you caught the awards ceremony on TV."

"Yeah. Long enough to watch Cici win, anyway. Which reminds me. What're you doing here, beautiful? I thought you'd be out partying with our little Oscar winner and drumming up new clients."

"I thought so, too, but apparently Cici changed her mind about giving Reflections an endorsement. Once she had that statuette in her hot little hand, she decided it wouldn't be smart to let everyone know I was responsible for her new look."

"She actually said that?"

"Not in so many words, but after being introduced as her cousin from Chicago a few times and having my arm pinched black and blue, I got the message."

"Why, the ungrateful, doublecrossing little bitch. What about your agreement? You gave her a cut rate in exchange for her passing on a good word about Reflections. I can't believe she'd go back on a promise."

Sara spread her hands wide. "Hey. That's showbiz."

The attempt to shrug off her disappointment fell as flat as her smile. They both knew exactly how much she had been counting on Cici's patronage.

On the surface, Reflections was doing well. After only two years in business, Sara had among her clients the entire on-camera news team of a local TV station, two minor politicians and their wives, a pro athlete, and several up-and-coming entertainment personalities.

Even so, getting a business off the ground was an expensive proposition and overhead was high. Reflections wasn't in the red, but last month's profit margin was so thin she could feel her creditors breathing down her neck.

"Yeah, you're right. Screw the little bitch. Who needs her?"

I do, Sara thought, but she merely chuckled, and the look of relief that flashed across Brian's face saddened her.

Tossing the letter opener back onto the pile of unopened bills, he leaned across the desk and hooked his fingers under her chin. When Sara met his gaze, he flashed his melancholy smile. "It's getting late, beautiful. How about we knock off for the night and I drive you home?"

"Thanks, but there are a few things I want to do here first. You go on. I can get a taxi."

"You sure?"

"Mmm."

"Okay. Suit yourself." He pushed off the desk and headed for the door, but two steps away he stopped and turned back. "Oh, I almost forgot. Dr. Ardmore called three times after you left this afternoon. He wants you to call him first thing tomorrow."

"Oh, Lord," Sara groaned, and buried her face in her hands. "That's all I need. I'm a week behind paying for Mother's care. If Cici's check doesn't clear, I won't have enough to cover the fee. And I wouldn't put it past her to stop payment, now that she's riding high."

"Hey, don't worry about it. So you're a little late. What're they going to do, put your mother out in the street?"

"They might." With a sigh, Sara leaned back in her chair and raked the fingers of both hands through her hair, pushing the silky sable-brown pageboy away from her face. Damn it, the high cost of her mother's care, on top of everything else, was breaking her back financially.

The flash of resentment had come out of nowhere,

and Sara was immediately ashamed. It wasn't her mother's fault. She couldn't help being ill. And it had been Sara's decision to place her in the exclusive nursing home.

There were cheaper facilities around, but none of them came close to offering the level of care of Clarewood House. Abruptly Sara clenched her jaw and straightened her spine. Damn it! No matter what it cost, her mother was going to have the very best care available. God knew she deserved that much, after the hell her life had been.

"Hey, don't worry about it." Brian turned and headed for the door again. "Everything will work out. You'll find a way. You always do." With a wink and a wave, he sauntered out as though he hadn't a care.

Which, Sara realized, he probably hadn't.

The old familiar heaviness settled in her chest as she watched him go. How typical of Brian to blithely dismiss the matter with an airy, "Sara can handle it."

She supposed by now she ought to be used to it. Brian had been leaning on her for fourteen years. Nevertheless, it still saddened her to realize how weak he truly was.

Problems, responsibilities, or complications of any sort made Brian panicky. His method of dealing with them was to simply deny their existence—or pass them off to someone else, usually her. When that failed and life pressed in on him too hard he simply ran away, disappearing to God only knew where for weeks at a time.

It was a lifelong pattern that seemed destined to repeat itself over and over.

It had been Brian's inability to cope that had

wrecked their brief teenage marriage. At the time of the divorce Sara had still cared for him; she simply could not be married to him.

But then, neither could she bring herself to cut him out of her life. For the past fourteen years, one way or another, she had continued to look after him. No matter his faults, Brian was a sweet and dear man, and he had no one else. She shuddered to think what would become of him without her. Their marriage might not have lasted, but their friendship had. No matter how fed up she sometimes got, she could never abandon Brian.

Any more than she could abandon her mother. Or Jennifer, her secretary-receptionist, who had been unwed and seven months pregnant when Sara had hired her.

Sighing, Sara leaned back in her chair and closed her eyes. If things didn't pick up soon, she might be reduced to sacking groceries at the local supermarket to support them all.

Evelyn arrived at the Houston corporate offices of Eve Cosmetics at nine the next morning.

"Good morning, Alice." Stopping beside her secretary's desk, she picked up her mail and began to riffle through it.

"Why, good morning, Mrs. Ketchum. Welcome back. I didn't realize you were returning today. How was your vacation?" Alice Burke smiled up at Evelyn, her ordinary face lit with pleasure.

"Fine, thank you. I got a lot of rest, which was exactly what I needed. Now I'm raring to go again."

"Would you like some coffee?"

"Yes. That would be lovely, thank you. Oh, and would you buzz Rourke and ask him to come to my office, please?"

Only moments later he tapped on her door and stuck his head inside.

"You wanted to see me?"

"Yes. Come in, please."

"I was hoping you would stay home and rest today. I guess I should have known better."

Ignoring his pointed look and the note of censure in his voice, Evelyn motioned him toward the chair before her desk. When he was seated, she leaned back in her chair and looked at him steadily. "I want you to handle a personal matter for me."

"Sure."

"A very delicate personal matter."

"No problem."

She stared at him for a moment longer, then picked up a folder and handed it to him across the desk. "In there you will find information concerning a man named John Edgar Anderson and his wife, Julia Marie. The Los Angeles address listed is over thirty years old, so they may not still be at that location. If not, I'm hoping it will at least be a starting point that will help you trace them. I'd rather not bring a private detective into this, but if it becomes necessary to do so, keep my name out of it."

"All right." Rourke looked up from leafing through the folder, his brow creased. "If you don't mind me asking, who are these people?"

"Mr. Anderson is a plumber and a part-time preacher. As far as I know, Mrs. Anderson is a housewife."

"Why do you want to find them?"

"It isn't Mr. and Mrs. Anderson I'm interested in locating. I want to find their daughter, Sara."

She paused a beat, her gaze never wavering from Rourke. "Sara is my daughter. Immediately after her birth I gave her up to the Andersons for adoption."

Chapter Four

A child. Evelyn had a daughter. Christ!

Rourke stared out the window of the company jet. The spring sun blazed silvery white, reflecting off the airplane's metal wing. Below, the California landscape shimmered in rich earth tones of umber, sienna, and ocher. A small flotilla of clouds glided lazily across the sky in the distance, seemingly the only thing moving in a somnolent world.

He couldn't believe it. It had been over four hours since Evelyn had dropped her bombshell, but he was still too stunned to take it in.

"Sara is my daughter."

Rourke shook his head. That had been the last thing he had expected her to say. He had sat there, unable to move, staring at her like a shell-shock victim, until at last she'd prodded him with a terse, "Well?" She lifted one elegant eyebrow. "Have you nothing to say?"

"You're serious, aren't you?"

"Quite serious."

"How old is this . . . daughter?"

"Sara was born when I was nineteen. I was in

college at the time, but I had to drop out. I had no family—at least, none that I could turn to—no money, no way to take care of myself, let alone a baby."

"How about the father? Couldn't he have helped you?"

Evelyn gave him a level look. "There was never any question of that."

"I see."

"I doubt it. But that doesn't matter. The important thing is, I have a daughter. I want you to find her for me and bring her here."

He frowned, an uneasy suspicion beginning to curl inside him. "Why? What could you possibly hope to accomplish by making contact with her at this late date?"

Evelyn propped her elbows on the padded arms of her chair and steepled her fingertips. "If I'm lucky, I'll find an heir to step into my shoes."

"Oh, come *on,* Evelyn. You *can't* be serious. For Chrissake, you don't even know this woman. She doesn't know you. Chances are good she won't want to. Anyway, what makes you think she would be even remotely capable of taking over a company like Eve? Or even interested?"

"I don't know, of course. And I won't until I meet her." Evelyn's chin lifted and her face took on an obdurate set. "But if there is any of me in her—any at all—she'll be interested."

A muscle ticked in Rourke's jaw as he drew his gaze away from the sunlit world beyond the plane's window. Every time he played that scene over in his mind he became more frustrated. Damn it! He had used every reasonable argument he could think of, but he hadn't been able to budge her. He couldn't believe a woman as sensible and intelligent as Evelyn could hatch such an impractical scheme.

Sighing, he pulled his hand down over his face. Which, he supposed, just proved how desperate she was. Hell, he guessed he would be, too, in her situation.

Earlier he had shed his suit coat and now he ran a hand beneath his loosened shirt collar and massaged the back of his neck. It disturbed him that she had not confided in him before now. He would have sworn that he knew her inside out. Yet in all those years he had never dreamed that she had been keeping such a secret.

What the hell was he going to do now? In a matter of seconds, with one simple statement, almost twelve years of planning and working his way toward the top had gone down the toilet.

There were some who would say that he had already climbed higher in the company than he'd had any right to expect. And maybe they were right. He had to admit, whenever he thought back on the brash hotshot he'd been twelve years ago, it was a wonder to him that Evelyn had hired him at all.

He had been twenty-six when they'd met, working as a sales rep for a packaging company. Wesley Containers had been strictly a small-potatoes outfit, and accounts like Eve Cosmetics had been way out of their league. Thinking only of a huge commission, he had called on them anyway and managed to finagle an appointment with Harry Sills, the marketing director. To Rourke's delight, he had barely begun his pitch when Evelyn had walked in.

A wry grin tugged at Rourke's lips as he recalled how shamelessly he had interspersed his sales presentation with fulsome compliments and flashed his most dazzling smile. To his credit, not all his praise had been insincere. At thirty-nine, Evelyn Ketchum had been at the height of her beauty, and her success had been well known.

She had not been impressed, but she had stuck around. Remaining in the background, she had let Harry state their requirements and ask all the questions. Not until Rourke quoted a price and delivery schedule did she utter a word.

"That's an excellent deal, Mr. Fallan," she interjected. "On paper, at any rate. But tell me . . . how much of the order do you plan to farm out?"

"Why, none. I assure you—"

"Please, Mr. Fallan. I'm not a fool. Your firm hasn't the capacity to fill a standing order of that size at those intervals."

To his astonishment, she had proceeded to rattle off facts and figures. She had known, down to the last printer and cutter, exactly what equipment his company had and the maximum volume they could turn out with it. Not surprisingly, she had rejected his bid.

Then she had turned around and stunned him with the offer of a job.

Even now, Rourke winced when he remembered how close he'd come to rejecting the opportunity of a lifetime.

Partly out of embarrassment and resentment over being outsmarted, and partly out of plain old male chauvinism, he had reacted with condescension.

"Me? Peddle women's cosmetics and frou-frou?" His chuckle had dripped disdain. "No offense, Mrs. Ketchum, but . . . I don't think so. I'm doing okay where I am."

"Are you?" She smiled. "I'm offering you a job, Mr. Fallan, because you and I are so alike."

He had laughed aloud at that, unable to fathom what a bold schemer like him could possibly have in common with a stylish and sophisticated woman like Evelyn Ketchum, but she had gone on, unfazed.

"People like us are never satisfied with just 'doing okay.' We want to make it to the top. We want to succeed. And in such a big fashion no one will ever doubt it. I'm not quite where I want to be yet, but I'm on my way. Come to work for me, Mr. Fallan, and I'll take you with me."

She could not have said anything more guaranteed to win him over. With clear-sighted shrewdness, Evelyn Ketchum had zeroed in on what drove him. Ambition.

The chance she presented had been irresistible to the young man he had been twelve years ago. The hunger that had been with him all his life was suddenly gnawing at his insides like a sharp-toothed animal. With the offer, she had opened the door on a whole new world of possibilities. Until then, his ambition had been limited in scope by the narrow vision of his past—a past of poverty, ignorance, and hopelessness.

Rourke had been born in a four-room shack in East Texas. It was a land of red dirt and tall pines, of rolling hills and sultry heat and lush beauty. A land of simple folk, set in their ways, where, for the most part, the standard of living fell far below that of the rest of the country. In those piney woods, with few exceptions, a man either raised a few cattle or cut timber. The Fallan men for three generations back had been loggers.

It was a life of hard, back-breaking work and low pay. Deep in the forest, year after year, a logger strained his muscles, sweating his life away in the torrid heat of summer and shivering in winter's dank chill.

For most, it was the only life they knew, the only one they would ever know. Exhaustion and constant poverty had a way of draining away ambition and hope.

As a boy, Rourke had listened to his uncles and his grandfather recount tales of the hellacious labor they performed day after day. They talked of maiming accidents and disfigurements, of broken bones and crushed limbs, of fingers lost to a saw blade or a shifting load of logs. The man who reached thirty whole was a rarity. Rourke's own father had been killed by a falling tree when Rourke was three.

As soon as he was old enough, as was expected of all the males in his family, Rourke spent his summers working on the logging crew with his grandfather and three uncles. He hated every minute of it.

Whenever he thought about spending the rest of his days in the stifling woods in back-breaking labor, he felt sick. There had to be something more to life. Something better.

The night Rourke graduated from high school his grandfather presented him with a new pair of logger's boots. Later that same night, after the others were asleep, Rourke stuffed his meager belongs into a pillowcase, walked down the dirt road to the highway, and stuck out his thumb. He left the new boots sitting beside his cot.

He arrived in Houston with thirty dollars in his jeans and his heart pounding with excitement. He loved everything about the city—the towering buildings, the bustle, the aura of power. To his naive eighteen-year-old eyes, all the well-dressed men and women carrying briefcases looked successful and important. He made up his mind on the spot that someday he would be one of them.

He managed to find a job at a fast-food restaurant, working for minimum wage and all the hamburgers he could eat. The hours were long, the work was hot, boring, and repetitious. Still, it beat felling trees.

Over the next year Rourke held a variety of jobs, usually more than one at a time. He worked as a delivery boy, a meter reader, a waiter, a cab driver, a shoe salesman, a department store clerk. The jobs kept a roof over his head and his belly full, but he wanted more. The desperate yearning and fiery ambition that had made him flee the East Texas woods still burned inside him.

He watched the people who were his idols, observing their mannerisms, the way they conducted themselves. He listened to them in elevators and restaurants, on the streets, noting the way they spoke, the things they said, how they said them. Gradually, it came to him that what they all had in common was an education.

At the first opportunity, Rourke enrolled in college. He fit his classes around his various jobs, going mostly at night. He studied business administration and finance and marketing, keeping always in mind the image of the suited executives striding around town with their briefcases, exuding an aura of power and money.

In English class he learned correct grammar and diction, and by listening carefully to his professors and emulating their speech, he painstakingly rid himself of his East Texas twang.

While in his second year of college, Rourke met Clyde Bates. Clyde was the kind of man who would never go unnoticed in a crowd. A flashy dresser, he wore a diamond ring on each hand and walked with an arrogant swagger. He came into the department store where Rourke was working looking for a replacement for his favorite tie, which had been permanently stained with red wine. Rourke immediately turned on the charm and attempted to flatter him into buying a sportcoat and pair of slacks as well.

Clyde listened to his pitch in amused silence, then said, "You work on commission, don't you, kid?"

"Well . . ."

"It's okay. I understand. I'm in sales myself." He looked Rourke over shrewdly. "But you know, you're wasted here. Outside sales—that's where the real money is. You're a good-looking kid with a gift of gab. With the right training you'll go far."

Rourke's heart began to hammer. "How do I get that?"

"As it happens, my company is looking for a bright young man. I'll put in a word for you, if you want."

Within a week Rourke was working as a sales trainee at Wesley Containers and was assigned to Clyde during his internship.

He was a natural. Soon he was racking up impressive sales. At twenty-one, Rourke was a well-built, personable young man, and his dark good looks and startling blue eyes did not go unnoticed.

"You got it made, kid. The women love you." Clyde laughed and slapped Rourke on the back. "It's the secretaries who run things. Worm your way into their good graces, and you'll have no trouble getting in to see the boss. After that, the rest is easy."

In Rourke's eyes, Clyde was the epitome of success. He admired the older man's trendy clothes, his flashy jewelry, and his flashier car. As soon as he was making enough money, he began to emulate his benefactor in every way.

In less than two years, Rourke's sales had topped Clyde's. By the fifth year he was the company's top salesman. He was earning decent money, he had a nice apartment, great clothes, a big car. He routinely dated beautiful women. Yet he wasn't satisfied. He just didn't know why.

Then he met Evelyn. She had known.

"People like us are never satisfied with just 'doing okay.' We want to make it to the top." With those few words she had cut to the heart of his discontent, and he had known it, too.

Just making money, having material things—though nice—would never be enough for him. He wanted power, position, respect. He wanted it all.

True to her word, Evelyn had shown him how to get it.

He had started at Eve as a division sales manager.

He had known that he had been lucky to catch Evelyn's attention, but he had also known that if he failed to live up to her expectations, his career would dead-end before it began. Evelyn was a business-woman right down to her fingertips.

There had been other young men in the company with more experience, better backgrounds, fancier educations, but Rourke was clever and quick, and his rise through the ranks had been meteoric. Under Evelyn's deft and expert guidance, he had learned the subtle intricacies of business and finance that could not be taught in a classroom.

She had shown him how to run an international business, how to manage a huge labor force, how to market a product, how to get and maintain a strong-hold in a competitive field. She taught him diplomacy and the fine art of negotiation; when to compromise, when to stand firm; when to yield, when to charge straight ahead and when to maneuver. Thanks to Evelyn, Rourke developed into the topnotch execu-tive he was meant to be.

Three years ago she had promoted him to execu-tive vice president.

He had benefited from his association with Evelyn in other ways as well. Just as she had recognized the hunger and potential in him, he had quickly realized that Evelyn had that elusive something called class. Her quiet dignity and understated elegance, the calm, self-assured way she conducted herself, made Clyde Bates seem like a sleazy hustler.

By observing her carefully, Rourke learned the value of restraint and classic understatement, in his attire, his choice of automobile, his abode. He ab-sorbed the subtleties of good taste and manners and courtesy like a dry sponge.

Rourke knew exactly how much he owed Evelyn. Under her guidance he had acquired polish, turned his street savvy into knowledge, his brash charm and cunning into smooth sophistication and business acumen. Thanks to her he had money, position, and power; all the things he'd yearned for as a wild youth.

Still . . . it was not enough.

The intercom pinged, drawing Rourke's attention. A instant later the pilot's disembodied voice came through the speaker.

"We're starting our approach, Mr. Fallan. Please fasten your seatbelt. We'll be landing at LAX in about ten minutes."

Rourke clicked the belt together and turned his head to stare out the window again.

You're probably worrying for nothing, he told himself. The chances of this woman being what Evelyn is looking for are poor to zip. You may not even be able to find her. Hell, she may not be alive. Anything could have happened in thirty-two years. Even if she is alive, chances are she's married to some poor working slob and has three or four kids and a house in the suburbs.

The address turned out to be a small, post–World War II stucco house in an older section of Los Angeles.

A few sprigs of grass dotted the tiny patch of ground in front, like spotty peach fuzz on an adolescent male face, testimony that a lawn had once grown there. A tricycle, several plastic toy dump trucks and race cars, a partially deflated wading pool, along with assorted other toys littered the hard-packed dirt yard.

Picking his way up the cracked sidewalk, Rourke

eyed the clutter with mixed emotions. The presence of small children probably meant the Andersons no longer lived there, but he didn't know whether to feel relieved or disappointed.

In the yard next door an elderly, birdlike woman was watering a bed of petunias and eyeing him curiously.

The front door was open. Through the sagging screen, Rourke could see that the interior of the house was as littered as the yard. There was no one in sight, so he knocked on the screen door, making it rattle. While waiting, he glanced around.

It was an aging working-class neighborhood. At one point the place had probably been an enclave of modest but neat homes. Here and there, like next door, where the old woman wielded her garden hose, some were still well maintained, the exteriors crisply painted and surrounded by well-tended lawns and flowerbeds. But the area was slowly giving way to urban decay.

Down the street a rusting automobile sat on blocks in a front yard with weeds growing up around its wheelless axles. Most houses had peeling paint and missing roof tiles and at least a few broken and boarded windows. Street lights were smashed, porches sagged, mailboxes and house numbers hung askew, and litter was everywhere.

It was difficult to imagine a daughter of Evelyn's growing up in such surroundings, even when the neighborhood had been at its best.

"Yeah. Whadda you want?"

Rourke swung around. Through the screen door, he found himself facing a young woman with a toddler straddling her hip. She was as unkempt and unattractive as her front yard.

Barefoot, dressed in baggy shorts and a faded and stained T-shirt, she wore her bleached blond hair in a stringy ponytail scraped back from a face bare of makeup. She was at least thirty pounds overweight. Most of the excess flesh had settled in her thighs and pot belly. The child riding her hip had a runny nose and dirty feet. But then, Rourke thought, glancing downward, so did the woman.

Could this be Sara? She was about the right age, as far as he could tell.

"I'm looking for the Edgar Anderson family. I was given this address and told that they lived here at one time."

"Ain't nobody here by that name." The woman eyed him suspiciously. Her small eyes were a muddy hazel, close set and surrounded by stubby lashes.

"Do you know how long ago they moved? Or if they left a forwarding address?"

"Nope. Me'n my old man, we just rented this place a few months ago."

"I see. Then could you give me your landlord's name?"

She shrugged. "I dunno it. Some dude comes by on the first of the month and collects the rent."

He asked several more questions, but the woman was no help at all. Finally, resigned to spending several boring hours at the Hall of Records, he thanked her and turned to go.

"Yoo-hoo! Oh, young man!"

Pausing in the act of unlocking his rental car, Rourke looked around and saw the old woman next door scurrying toward him. She arrived out of breath and flustered, her wrinkled face alive with curiosity.

"Did I hear you say you were looking for the Andersons?"

"Yes, ma'am. Sara Anderson, actually. Do you know where I might find her?"

"Oh my, yes. Why, I've known that child since she was in diapers. Such a dear girl she is, too. Mind you, now, Sara's been gone from this house for years. And who can blame her for that, seeing as how things were and all? But Sara's a good daughter. Yessir, she's always looked after her mother, no matter what."

The old lady sighed and shook her head, her expression turning mournful. "Poor Julia. Poor, poor Julia. Such a terrible thing . . ."

Her words drifted away and a faraway look came into her faded old eyes. The bony hands, which had been fluttering like a bird's wings the whole time she chattered, came to rest on her sagging breasts and crossed over her heart. Age spots dotted them like splatters of brown paint.

Rourke waited for her to continue. When she didn't, he cleared his throat. "Uh, excuse me, ma'am . . ."

The old woman blinked. "What? Oh, land's sakes, where're my manners?" she exclaimed, flapping her flowered apron. Her scent drifted to him on the draft of air, a musty mix of lavender and menthol rub and old age. "My name is Hattie Blankenship. I live right next door. Have for nigh on to forty-six years."

Rourke introduced himself and explained that he was trying to locate Sara on behalf of a friend. It was all the encouragement the garrulous little woman needed.

"Well, now, isn't it a good thing I stopped you? You just come along to the house with me and I'll get you her address." Spry as a cricket, she scurried across her manicured lawn, rattling on every step of the way.

"The Andersons lived right here up until about a year ago. 'Course, for the last five years, since Edgar passed on, Julia was alone. Not that that was such a bad thing. Humph! If you ask me, that was the only peace the poor woman had since she married Edgar Anderson. It's just a darn shame that poor Julia didn't get to enjoy her freedom longer. If you ask me, it was her husband's treatment of her that brought on her problem. Now, I don't mean to talk ill of the dead, mind you, but mercy me, the stories I could tell you about that man!"

She led Rourke into the spotless little house and hurried over to a desk, where she began to search through an address book. "Now, let me see . . . I know it's here somewhere."

"I take it Mrs. Anderson has passed on, too."

Hattie Blankenship looked up from her search. "Oh, no. Though God knows, you can't help but think she'd be better off if she had. Julia has Alzheimer's, you see," she confided in a hushed voice. "Has spells where she's right out of her head. Got so bad about a year ago, Sara had no choice but to sell the house and put her in a home."

Rourke was still digesting that when she straightened, waving a white card. "Here it is. I haven't had much call to phone Sara since she moved her mother out, but I knew I had it somewhere. From the time she first left home, when she was just a girl, she always made sure I had her number so I could call her if . . . well . . . you know . . . if things got too bad over at her folks' house. Sara was always good that way."

Fleetingly, Rourke wondered what she meant by that, but then his attention focused on the slip of cardboard she handed him. "This is a business card."

"Yes. Sara owns her own company," Hattie said proudly. "Of course, I knew that girl would amount to something one day. She always was a gutsy little thing. Smart as a whip, too. Her home address and phone number are written there on the back," she added, with a flutter of her bony hand.

Rourke glanced at the flowing script on the back of the card, then turned it over again and stared at the crisp, embossed lettering:

REFLECTIONS
Sara Anderson
Image Consultant

At six o'clock that evening, Rourke walked into the suite of offices in the Winthrop Tower.

The young woman behind the receptionist desk looked up. Her eyes widened and her professional smile altered to one of blossoming interest. "Yessir. May I help you?"

"I'm Rourke Fallan. I called earlier."

"Oh, yes, of course, Mr. Fallan. I'll tell Ms. Anderson you're here."

Rourke did not bother to sit. While he waited, he looked around. The reception room was decorated in shades of cream, pale green, and faded raspberry, with a surprisingly harmonious mix of antique and modern furnishings, a lot of plants, and soft watercolor paintings. The overall effect was inviting, restful, and in excellent taste.

"Ms. Anderson will see you now, Mr. Fallan."

She sat behind an elegant rosewood desk, her head down, absorbed for the moment in the papers she was reading. She wore her hair parted slightly off center in a silky pageboy that at present had swung forward, hiding her face. It was the same rich mahogany color as Evelyn's, Rourke noted, but longer, brushing the tops of her shoulders.

Under Evelyn's tutelage, Rourke had learned the value of playing his cards close to his chest. He made it a practice, especially when walking into an unknown situation, to conceal his thoughts and emotions, but when Sara Anderson looked up, his self-possession almost shattered. For an instant his step faltered and his expression registered shock. He felt as though he had been kicked in the gut.

"My God. She's the image of Evelyn!"

Chapter Five

Sara's first thought when she looked up at Rourke Fallan was, *"My word. What a stunning man."*

That was quickly followed by, *"Why is he staring at me that way? He looks as though he's seen a ghost."*

The look vanished almost before she completed the thought, and he strode forward to introduce himself, his expression pleasant and professional.

Sara rose, extending her hand to him over the desk, returning his polite smile and the courteous greeting.

"I want to thank you for seeing me on such short notice."

"You said on the phone that you had an urgent matter to discuss with me. One that wouldn't wait. However, Mr. Fallan, I do hope you understand that we had to squeeze you in. I'm afraid I can only give you a few minutes. I have a client coming in shortly."

"So late?"

"Many of my clients are public figures who keep odd hours. I try to work around them."

"I see. Very well, I'll be brief. Does the name Evelyn Delacorte-Ketchum mean anything to you, Ms. Anderson?"

"No, not that I—oh, wait. Isn't she the woman who owns Eve Cosmetics?"

"Mrs. Ketchum is the major shareholder, yes. She's also the founder and president of the company." He withdrew a business card from his pocket and handed it to her.

Executive Vice President. Sara was impressed, but not overly so. She was, after all, an image consultant in Los Angeles.

"As you can see, I work for Mrs. Ketchum. I am here on her behalf. She would like to meet with you privately, Ms. Anderson."

"Meet with me? Why would Evelyn Ketchum want to meet with me?"

"I'm not at liberty to say."

Sara gazed at him in amazement. How odd. "When does she want this meeting to take place?"

"As soon as possible. The company jet is waiting at the airport right now to fly us to Houston. We can leave whenever you're ready."

"What? Now, hold on. I thought you were talking about setting up a meeting here, in Los Angeles. I can't go flying off thousands of miles on the spur of the moment without even knowing why."

"All I can tell you is this is an extremely confidential matter of the utmost importance, the nature of which only Mrs. Ketchum can disclose."

Sara gave a dazed chuckle. "I'm sorry, but that's just not good enough. In case you haven't noticed, Mr. Fallan, I have a business to run. My schedule is crammed for several weeks."

The whole thing *was* intriguing, though. Why on

earth would a woman like Evelyn Delacorte-Ketchum want to meet with her?

One thing was certain—she was not in need of Sara's professional services. The woman routinely made everyone's best-dressed list.

"Can't someone take over for you for a couple of days?"

"I'm afraid not. I offer a service, Mr. Fallan. It is my advice, my expertise, my . . . taste, if you will, that clients are buying. Reflections is still fairly new, and while I'm doing well, I cannot afford to neglect the business. Not even for a day."

"Ms. Anderson, please believe me; you're making a mistake. This is a very serious matter."

"What is, Mr. Fallan?"

He answered her with a regretful look, and she smiled ironically and spread her hands wide. "There you have it, then. I'll admit, you have aroused my curiosity. But I'm sorry. As intriguing as I find your proposition, without further information, I'm afraid I must decline." Smiling politely, she rose and again offered her hand. "Now, if you'll excuse me, it's almost time for my next appointment. Good evening, Mr. Fallan."

She had turned him down flat. Rourke wasn't sure what he had expected, but it sure as hell hadn't been that. The mere mention of Evelyn's name usually had people stumbling all over themselves to be accommodating.

Evelyn was not going to be pleased.

The elevator doors opened and Rourke made a beeline for the bank of telephones in the lobby of the

Winthrop Tower. He inserted his credit card and punched out the number of Evelyn's private line, the one that rang directly through to her office, bypassing even Alice. Only a handful of people had the number.

She answered on the first ring.

"It's Rourke," he said, without preamble. "I've found her."

There was a beat of silence. He thought he heard a sigh, but he couldn't be sure, and when she spoke, her voice was as composed as ever. "Good. Excellent. Have you spoken with her?"

"Yes. But I've hit a snag. She refuses to fly back with me. Says she can't afford the time away from her business."

"She has her own business?"

He winced at the eagerness in Evelyn's voice. "Yes. The firm is called Reflections. She does image consulting. But it's nothing big. As far as I can tell, the whole company consists of just her and a receptionist. So don't get your hopes up."

"I'm not a Pollyanna, Rourke," she rebuked quietly. "Still . . . you have to admit, it *is* a good sign."

"Yeah. I guess. But if she won't meet with you, it hardly matters one way or another."

"Offer her money."

"What?"

"If she's concerned about the effect her absence will have on profits, then we eliminate the problem by compensating her for her losses."

"How high do you want to go?"

"Whatever it takes."

Rourke sighed. "Okay. You're the boss. I'll call

you after I've made the offer." He was about to hang up when she stopped him.

"Rourke?"

"Yeah?"

Several seconds of silence followed. "What is she like?"

Rourke grimaced. He tipped his head forward and massaged the throbbing just above his eyes with the thumb and first two fingers of his right hand. He was tempted to lie. Hell, he could say the woman was a complete washout. She would accept his word.

"I wasn't with her with long enough to form a definite opinion, but she seems intelligent. She's certainly poised and articulate, but then, in her line of work, I suppose that's to be expected." He didn't add that she was beautiful.

This time he was sure he heard the sigh. It was one of relief.

"Don't worry about a thing, Mr. Killibrew. Andre knows his business, and I've explained to him in detail exactly what I want. Now here's the address of his salon. He'll be expecting you tomorrow morning at ten."

"Well . . . if you're sure . . ."

"You're going to look terrific, Mr. Killibrew. Trust me."

Smiling encouragement, Sara clasped her client's elbow and escorted him out. "Believe me, this will do wonders—"

Two steps into the reception room she came to a halt. "Mr. Fallan."

He was sitting in the waiting area, calmly flipping through a magazine.

"Your receptionist had already gone when I returned, so I made myself at home. I hope you don't mind."

"No. No, of course not. I'll be right with you."

She forced a smile to hide her irritation. Didn't the man take no for an answer? It had been an exhausting day filled with back-to-back appointments, and she still had to drop by the nursing home and visit her mother. She was tired, she was hungry, her feet hurt, her back hurt, and she had the beginnings of a headache. She wanted to go home and take a long, hot soak, then have an early night, not rehash this man's ridiculous request.

After seeing Mr. Killibrew out, Sara returned with every intention of cutting the interview short. She remained standing and crossed her arms over her midriff, hoping he would get the message. "I haven't changed my mind, Mr. Fallan. So if that's why you've come back, you're wasting your time. As I explained, I can't afford to take the time off."

"What if I made it worth your while financially?"

"You mean hire me?"

"Something like that. We propose to pay you for your time. I assume you bill your clients by the hour. What is your rate?"

When she told him he smiled. "We'll pay you five thousand if you will come to Houston for one day."

"Five thousand?" Sara stared at him. "Are you serious?" That was more than twice what she could make if she worked the whole twenty-four hours. It was tempting . . .

Then she thought of her schedule for the next few

weeks and what a daunting chore it would be to rearrange it, and what Jennifer's reaction would be if she asked her to do so. Her receptionist was a jewel and a dear friend, but meek acceptance was not part of her makeup. Sara shook her head. "I'm sorry, Mr. Fallan. That's a very generous offer, but—"

"How about if we make it ten thousand?"

"Ten!"

Dazed, Sara sank down in the chair opposite his. Ten thousand dollars? What in heaven's name was so important that Evelyn Ketchum would pay that kind of money just to talk to her?

For the life of her, Sara could not imagine. She searched Rourke's face, but found no answers there.

Sara had to find out what was going on. Her curiosity would eat her alive if she didn't. Besides, the plain truth was, she could use the money.

A quick mental calculation of how many months of nursing-home care ten thousand dollars would provide made her eyes widen. Suddenly a few disgruntled clients and an irate receptionist seemed a small price to pay.

Rourke Fallan was a man who got things done, Sara quickly discovered. He would have hustled her off to Houston that night if she hadn't balked.

"I can't just fly off on such short notice. I have to notify my employees. My secretary will have to rearrange my schedule, and I'll need to brief my assistant about several things he'll have to handle for me. Also, I need to contact my mother's doctor. She isn't well, and I keep him apprised of where I can be reached at all times. Which reminds me, I'll need telephone and fax numbers from you in case he needs to contact me."

When she would not budge, Rourke accepted the delay graciously, but the next morning he took charge like a whirlwind. He picked her up at her apartment bright and early in a rented Cadillac and drove her to her bank. Exuding that air of absolute authority cloaked in exquisite politeness which seemed to be a part of him, he obtained an immediate audience with the bank president—a man with whom Sara could usually not even get an appointment in under a week. In mere minutes Rourke made arrangements for an immediate transfer of ten thousand dollars into Sara's account, and in the process he had the officious manager and his assistant practically falling over themselves to accommodate him.

While Sara's mind was still spinning over the speed and efficiency with which he'd accomplished the matter, he drove them to the airport, where he escorted her aboard a sumptuous corporate jet with the Eve Cosmetics company logo—an apple with a bite out of it—painted discreetly on its side.

Inside, the jet was decorated in shades of mauve and silvery blue and looked more like someone's living room than the cabin of an airplane. Sofas and overstuffed chairs replaced the regulation seats. A partners' desk sat beside one window, and a bar-cum-galley occupied the front wall, which separated the cabin from the cockpit. Through a door toward the rear, Sara could see an elegant bedroom and a small but luxurious bath.

Rourke courteously settled her into a comfortable easy chair, and Sara sighed when he took one on the opposite side of the cabin. She was relieved to have some space between them at last.

The instant she had opened the door to him that morning she had felt the impact of his masculinity. It had hit her like a shock wave following a bomb explosion. Sudden. Forceful. Stealing her breath away.

He had stood there on her doorstep, so tall, so powerful and compelling. And so close. The sight of him had caused Sara to draw in a sharp breath, and with it, his scent. The heady aroma had gone straight to her head and made it spin—dark, and dangerously enticing, a mix of aftershave, soap, starched linen, and potent male.

His smile and soft, "Good morning, Ms. Anderson" had been perfunctory and polite, but as she'd gazed into those vivid blue eyes and that chiseled face, her heart had skittered and thumped in her breast.

The effect he had on her was unsettling and puzzling. It was more than just his looks. She dealt with good-looking men every day in her line of work—many of them more classically handsome than Rourke Fallan. Gorgeous men were thick on the ground in Hollywood. Sara appreciated male beauty as well as the next woman, and a few of those specimens had made her pulse flutter, but none had ever affected her the way this man did. Just the sight of him did strange things to her insides, and when he was close, little frissons of sexual excitement danced over her skin and interfered with her breathing.

What was it about him that stirred her so? She had never reacted to any man so strongly before, certainly not in such an overtly sexual way. And there was no point in denying it—that's what it was.

Sara tipped her head forward. Through the silky fall of her hair, she glanced sideways at him. Even now, just looking at that strong profile made her nipples pucker and harden.

He began to fasten his seatbelt, and as her gaze slid down his chest over the perfect fit of his custom-tailored gray suit, her heart skipped crazily. Good Lord. Even his hands were sexy. Large and well shaped, with broad palms, long, blunt fingers, and well-kept nails, they moved with a masculine grace she found mesmerizing. The backs of his hands were lightly dusted with black hair and his wrists were wide and strong, his skin dark against the crisp white of his shirt cuffs.

Was he married? Sara scanned his hands for a wedding ring, but the only jewelry he wore was the wafer-thin gold watch that glinted now and then from beneath his left sleeve. Not that the absence of a ring necessarily proved he was single. Many married men conveniently did not wear wedding rings.

There was something about Rourke, though, something intangible but strong, that told her he was unattached. Beneath that smooth, professional exterior, those impeccable manners, was tough, undomesticated pure male. She would bet money on it.

Not that it mattered to her one way or the other, of course. After today, she would never see him again. Which was probably just as well, since it was obvious she did not have the same effect on him. When he bothered to look at her at all, his gaze was as impersonal as that of a judge.

"You'd better buckle up, Ms. Anderson."

Sara started. Her gaze flew to Rourke's. A light flush tinted her cheeks and she looked flustered and alarmed. He wondered what she had been thinking. Had she begun to suspect the reason behind Evelyn's request to see her? Had she been calculating how much she could squeeze out of her natural mother?

The look of vulnerability vanished almost before he could blink, and as he watched, Sara straightened her shoulders and lifted her chin and that look of elegant calm that she habitually presented to the world settled over her features.

Oh, yes, she was her mother's daughter, all right, Rourke thought. Classy right down to her fingertips, regardless of her humble upbringing. And beautiful.

Perhaps even more beautiful than Evelyn, he realized with a small sense of shock. Until now, he hadn't believed that was possible.

Rourke didn't doubt that behind that lovely face, Sara also possessed her mother's keen intelligence. Whether or not she had her mother's character remained to be seen.

"I'm sorry. I was woolgathering." Sara flashed him an apologetic smile. "I didn't realize we were ready to take off."

Rourke watched her fumble along the sides of the chair for the straps. She located one of them, but when the other remained elusive, he unbuckled his seatbelt and went to her rescue. "Here, let me help."

"Oh, no. That's all ri—" Sara bolted upright when he reached round her shoulders. Her hair flew out like a rippling curtain, and a strand caught the button on the sleeve of his suit coat. "Ow! Oh, dear!" Instinctively, she raised her hands to her stinging scalp and at the same time tried to pull away.

"Be still," Rourke ordered. "You're going to hurt yourself." To ensure that she obeyed him, he wrapped his arm around her shoulder and held her against his chest. With his other hand, he reached around in front of her and worked to free her hair from the button.

The shiny strands felt like silk between his fingers. With her face pressed against his chest, the crown of her head nestled just below his chin, and the smell of floral shampoo drifted to him. He felt her start as his forearm brushed against her breast, but in their position, the intimacy could not be avoided. She held herself stiff, but he could feel the fine tremor that ran through her . . . and the warmth that spread along his arm from the point of contact.

"There. You're free," he murmured, but he did not release his hold on her.

Lifting her head from his chest, Sara looked up into his eyes. Their faces were so close he could see each individual lash that circled her dazed green eyes . . . and the pulse that fluttered at the base of her throat. Her breath feathered across his throat in erratic little puffs.

"Th-thank you," she whispered.

He stared into her eyes. Slowly his gaze lowered to her lips. "You're welcome."

His voice came out low and raspy, and he felt her tremble. The reaction sent his blood roaring through his body. His nostrils flared, like those of a primal male catching the scent of woman. He saw the knowledge flicker in her eyes, the sudden flare of apprehension.

What the hell was he doing? Gritting his teeth, Rourke released her and pulled back. "Are you all right?"

"Yes. I'm fine. What a silly thing to happen."

"No harm done." He returned to his seat and buckled up. When Sara had done the same, he pressed a button on the speaker mounted in the bulkhead beside his chair and informed the pilot they were ready. Without looking her way, he picked up his briefcase and snapped it open.

Sara spent the entire trip staring out the window, trying to pretend he wasn't there.

At two o'clock, Sara and Rourke arrived at Evelyn Ketchum's Houston apartment.

He pressed the doorbell, and a muted chorus of chimes sounded on the other side of the door. Sara shifted from one foot to the other.

"Are you nervous?"

She shot Rourke a look of mild surprise. "No, not at all. Is there any reason why I should be?"

"No. I suppose not. You seemed restless is all."

Of course she was restless. Who wouldn't be, in her place? She was burning up with curiosity and anxious to get the meeting under way.

In addition, she admitted truthfully, being in close proximity with Rourke, as she had been for the past six hours, had an unsettling effect on her. He made her feel edgy and out of breath and her skin got all prickly and hot when he looked at her.

Sara sighed. Chemistry. You never knew when it would strike . . . or why.

In this instance the feeling was uncomfortable and unwelcome, particularly so since she was not at all sure that Rourke even liked her. On the flight here, he had scarcely spoken to her. He had spent the whole trip working on the papers he carried in his briefcase.

After that foolish incident when she'd caught her hair on his coat sleeve, he had barely glanced her way. She might not have even been on the plane, for all the attention he paid her.

There had been that moment when something hot had flared briefly in his eyes. At the time, she had thought he was experiencing the same strong attraction she was, but after thinking about it, she realized now that it had probably been anger. Physical attraction had a way of addling your brain and skewing your judgment.

The door was opened by a big, raw-boned woman who greeted Rourke with a smile. When her gaze switched to Sara, her eyes widened with what looked like shock; but with the decorum of a well-trained servant, she composed her features and escorted them into the living room.

Evelyn Ketchum rose when they entered, her gaze at once zeroing in on Sara. Throughout the introduction Sara was aware of her hostess's intense scrutiny and wondered at its cause.

The woman was impressive. Sara knew that she had to be in her fifties, yet she could easily pass for forty—in certain lighting, even less. Her skin was flawless, and the silver wings of hair at her temples merely added a touch of drama to that serenely beautiful face. Even more striking than her looks and elegant slenderness, however, was the aura of quiet strength and power that surrounded Evelyn Ketchum.

There was something hauntingly familiar about her as well, but Sara could not quite put her finger on it. She finally decided the impression came from having seen her picture in newspapers and magazines.

"I want to thank you for agreeing to meet with me, Sara. Do you mind if I call you Sara?" Evelyn asked, when they were seated.

"No. Not at all. As to my being here, you have Mr. Fallan to thank for that. He made it difficult for me to refuse."

Evelyn glanced at Rourke and smiled fondly. "Yes. I can always count on Rourke."

Her gaze swung back, and once again Sara experienced that probing look. She felt like a bug under a microscope and had to consciously fight against the urge to squirm.

"I'm sure you're wondering why I asked to see you."

"Yes. Yes, I am."

"Ever since Rourke called last night to tell me that you had agreed to come I've been trying to think of a way to explain it to you. I finally realized that there's no easy way to put this, so I'll just say it straight out."

She paused and glanced at Rourke again. Then she drew a deep breath. "Sara . . . I am your mother."

Chapter Six

The statement drew a startled laugh from Sara.

"I'm sorry," she said, recovering her composure. "I don't mean to be rude. But you see . . . I'm afraid you have the wrong Sara Anderson. My mother is in a nursing home just outside of Los Angeles."

She thought about the ten thousand dollars Rourke Fallan had deposited into her account that morning and had to bite back another chuckle.

"It's true that Julia Anderson raised you. And I understand that you think of her as your mother. So you should. But I am your birth mother, Sara."

The urge to laugh left Sara in a rush. She stared at Evelyn Ketchum, her chest growing tight. "But . . . that would mean . . .

"No. No, that . . . that simply can't be. This is a mistake. You must have the wrong Sara Anderson. That's the only explanation."

Evelyn and Rourke exchanged a look. "Are you saying that the Andersons never explained that you were adopted?"

"Of course they didn't!" Panic and doubt swirled inside Sara, making the denial come out harsher than she intended. "Why would they? I *wasn't* adopted. My parents would have told me if I had been."

But would they have? Would her father have? The questions flickered through her mind before she could stop them, but Sara did not want to know the answers.

How silly. Of course they would have told her. She shook her head and struggled to slow her rapid breathing and suddenly caroming heart. She could not accept this. She wouldn't! The woman was mistaken. She had to be. This was all just one big bizarre mixup.

"Apparently they didn't. Because the Andersons did adopt you, Sara. You are my child."

"No—"

"If you want proof, I have it." Evelyn picked up a folder from the end table beside her chair and opened it, withdrawing several papers. "Here is a copy of your birth certificate. It has my thumbprint and your footprint on it. This is the private adoption agreement between Edgar and Julia Anderson and myself, which we all signed three months before your birth. Here are the final adoption papers." As Evelyn spoke, she placed the papers on the coffee table, spreading them out for Sara's inspection.

Sara glanced at the documents as though they were a coil of hissing snakes, but she made no move to touch them. "Documents can be forged."

"Yes. They can. But these are quite genuine, I assure you. They are copies, of course. The originals are locked in my safe. However, if you would like to have an expert check them out, you may."

The tightness in Sara's chest squeezed harder—so hard she could barely breathe. An icy knot had lodged in the pit of her stomach and she was shaking inside. She could feel herself teetering on the edge of hysteria, her composure fragile as a frayed thread.

That frightened her almost as much as this woman's ridiculous claim, and she snatched at her poise, wrapping it around her, slipping back behind the protective cloak of the image she had perfected for herself—calm, chic, in control.

She happened to notice that she was clutching the arm of the sofa so tight her fingers were bloodless, the tips digging deep into the silk upholstery. One by one, Sara forced them to relax.

She sent Evelyn an accusing look. "Why are you doing this? Even if I am your—" She glanced at the papers on the coffee table and quickly looked away. "If I am who you say I am—which I don't believe for a minute—why drag me here now and tell me this? What's the point?"

"Not to harm you in any way, I promise you. I know you're upset, Sara, and I regret that, but I had no choice."

Evelyn spoke calmly, her lovely green eyes steady on Sara. Watching her, Sara experienced a hysterical desire to laugh and cry all at the same time. She refused to believe any of this . . . but Evelyn Ketchum obviously did. Yet whatever she felt about seeing for the first time the woman she believed to be her daughter, it did not show, either in her expression or her voice. Her beautiful features remained composed and unreadable. She sat in her elegant Queen Anne chair, her hands folded in her lap, her shapely legs crossed, one swinging gently with a sibilant hiss of nylon.

"Actually, I brought you here to discuss a gift I wish to give you."

Sara was an expert judge of fashion and value—it was part of her business to know quality and workmanship, to judge overall style and effect. Everything about Evelyn Ketchum—her impeccably coiffed hair and perfect but understated makeup, the diamond rings that adorned her graceful hands, her pampered skin and manicured nails, the chic little designer dress and Italian pumps, the simple but elegant strand of pearls at her throat and the matching earrings—all shouted money and good taste. And most of all . . . power.

"A gift? What kind of gift?" Sara eyed the older woman with suspicion.

"You are my only child, Sara. As such, you are entitled to inherit at least a part of Eve Cosmetics."

"What's the matter? Suddenly feeling guilty after all this time?"

It was not Sara's nature to be nasty or sarcastic, but her nerves were strung so tight the need to lash out was reflexive. Evelyn Ketchum did not so much as blink.

"No."

The denial came without hesitation, her tone not in the least ruffled. She regarded Sara without a trace of remorse or anger, and Sara's frustration level climbed even higher.

"Then why would you give me a part of your company?"

"I have my reasons. They're unimportant. Suffice it to say I am prepared to gift you with some shares."

"If that's what you wanted, all you had to do was

include a bequest in your will. Why this meeting? Why stir this up now?"

"Because I don't want to wait until I'm dead to give you . . . I suppose we can call it your birthright. Since you will be a part owner in Eve Cosmetics, I think it would be prudent for you to learn about your inheritance in order to make intelligent decisions regarding your holdings."

She raised an elegant eyebrow. "As a business-woman, I'm sure you realize that an asset such as this brings not just benefits, but responsibilities."

"Yes. Of course," Sara murmured, a chill of disbelief settling over her. Didn't the woman *feel* anything? If what she claimed was true, this should have been an emotional meeting. How could she just sit there talking about business and stock shares and responsibility? God, was she made of ice?

"Good. I'm glad you agree. For that reason, I'd like for you to move to Houston and start familiarizing yourself with the company. If you are willing do that, I will gift you immediately with four percent of the stock. The rest will be yours upon my death."

"Four percent? Are you serious?"

"Very."

"But that's—"

"Enough to make you a moderately wealthy woman. In addition, I will put you on the board of directors and give you a position with the company."

Under normal circumstances, the ambitious side of Sara's nature would have had her turning cartwheels at such a windfall, but she was still reeling from the bombshell that Evelyn had dropped. She struggled to maintain her dignity, but her heart thundered and her breath came in harsh pants, as though she had been running.

Anger and a host of other emotions roiled inside Sara. Across the width of the Chippendale coffee table she returned Evelyn Ketchum's steady gaze, feeling as though she might fly apart at any second from the pressure in her chest.

She had to get out of there, she thought in a flash of panic. Oh, God, she wished she had never come.

"I see," she finally managed in a tight voice. "That's a very generous offer, Mrs. Ketchum. Perhaps when you find your daughter she'll even be grateful. But none of this has anything to do with me."

She delivered the rebuff with just the right note of indifference, then spoiled it by adding, "However, let me just say that if I *were* your daughter, I'd tell you exactly what you could do with your shares. And the rest of your offer.

"You've got brass, lady, I'll say that for you." With each word, Sara's voice grew harder, harsher, shaking with the force of her feelings. Her eyes blazed and she flung out her arm in a wild gesture. "Do you really think you can just give a baby away like so much unwanted junk, just leave her to whatever fate dishes out, then pop up thirty-two years later and play mama bountiful?"

"I had my reasons for giving you up, Sara. I won't discuss them with you. I understand that you're upset, but that does not change the fact that you are my daughter. As such, you are entitled to an inheritance.

"I feel I must point out that should you accept what I am offering, the financial benefit to you will be enormous, far surpassing anything you could hope for through your own company."

That was a truth Sara could not deny. It didn't take a genius to figure out that four percent of a company like Eve Cosmetics would amount to a small fortune. What she could not accept was that her life up until now had been a lie. A hideous, unfair sentence handed down because this woman hadn't wanted to be bothered.

"That may be true, but it has nothing to do with me. No matter what you say or how many phony documents you trot out, I am *not* your daughter."

"How can you even doubt it?"

Rourke had sat quietly, not uttering a word until now. He'd have bet money that Sara had forgotten he was even there.

He had watched with interest as the tense little drama had unfolded, watched Sara's elegant composure shatter with a few words from Evelyn, watched her struggle to deny the obvious and tamp down on the emotions that were tearing loose behind that beautiful face. She was a tough little nut; he'd give her that.

She looked soft and fragile, as delicate as thistledown—almost too delicate, too fine, to survive against the harsh realities of life. Yet she had absorbed the shock of Evelyn's announcement and forcibly held herself together. Most women would have been screaming hysterically by now.

He hadn't meant to speak at all, but it was painful to watch her struggle against the truth.

"Open your eyes, Ms. Anderson," he said with deliberate bluntness. "All you have to do is look in a mirror to see the truth. For God's sake, you're the spitting image of Evelyn."

Sara's gaze swung to him. Finding a target for her raging emotions, she ignored his comment and let fly, her words snapping with anger. "You knew about this, didn't you? You knew why she wanted to see me. Why didn't you tell me?"

"It wasn't my place. Besides . . . would you have come with me if I had?"

"No. And I'm not staying now. This entire thing is absurd, and I don't have time for it. I'm going home. Either you can have your pilot fly me back to Los Angeles, or I'll take a commercial flight. One way or the other, I'm leaving."

Her face remained composed, but Rourke could see the panic swirling in her eyes, and he experienced a swift pang of sympathy. She could not take much more. Her emotions were raw, her nerves stretched tight and shrieking.

"You're overwrought and not thinking clearly."

Sara's lips tightened. Rourke knew that to the younger woman's ears, Evelyn had probably sounded maddeningly indifferent. Just the opposite was true. Anyone who knew her well could see that Evelyn was strung as tight as piano wire. That distant, slight bored tone was the one she unconsciously used whenever she was uncertain or nervous. Just as her daughter hid behind that ladylike poise. He wondered if either of them realized how alike they truly were.

"I refuse to take no as your final answer until you've had time to cool down and consider the whole thing with a clear head," Evelyn said, flicking an imaginary fleck of lint off the skirt of her dress. "I'm sure once you've thought it through, you'll feel differently—perhaps not about me, but at least about my offer."

"I don't *need* to think about it. I keep telling you, I'm not who you say I am! I'm *not!* I'm—oh, what's the use? This is crazy and pointless." Sara jerked to her feet and stumbled blindly for the door.

The sweet scent of floral shampoo wafted to Rourke on the breeze she created as she swept by—the same scent that had tantalized and distracted him earlier on the plane.

"Sara."

She had barely taken three steps. From where he sat, Rourke had an excellent view of her profile. He watched her jaws clench, and he knew she wanted desperately to ignore the call. However, though it was soft, Evelyn's voice held that unmistakable note of command that came from years of holding the reins of power. It was impossible to disobey.

Sara stopped but stared straight ahead, refusing to turn around. "What?"

"I will give you ten days to reconsider. During that time, a return ticket to Houston will be held for you at the Los Angeles airport."

"Don't hold your breath waiting for me to use it," Sara snapped, and bolted out the door.

Seconds later the outer door slammed. The sound echoed through the apartment, angry and accusing. Evelyn looked at Rourke. "She's upset. Go after her, Rourke. See that she gets to the airport safely."

He nodded and was on his feet before she finished speaking.

When he had gone, Evelyn closed her eyes and released a long breath, sagging back in her chair. Her heart raced and her stomach knotted and gnawed. Slowly her eyelids lifted, but she remained motionless, her lips pressed tightly together, staring at the spot on the sofa where her daughter had sat.

Rourke caught up with Sara at the elevator. She paced in front of the doors, slowing her agitated steps every few seconds to give the lighted button another vicious jab. Arms crossed over her midriff, she hugged herself tightly, as though trying to physically hold herself together.

"Ms. Anderson—"

Sara whirled on him, and Rourke cursed silently at the raw pain in her eyes. She looked as vulnerable and distressed as a lost child. He'd have bet money it was a condition this woman seldom allowed to occur, one she sure as hell didn't want anyone to witness.

"Go away." She glared at him and tried to blink away the telltale moisture swimming in her eyes.

Rourke ground his teeth. Damn it to hell. He'd always been a sucker for a woman in distress. And somehow, fragility in a strong woman got to him the most.

After the scene he'd just witnessed, he had no doubt that Sara Anderson was every bit as strong as her mother. Evelyn had had the advantage of surprise this time, but if the two ever met again, Rourke was willing to bet that Sara would hold her own.

"Are you all right?"

"Of course. I'm fine," she insisted too quickly.

She didn't look fine. She looked pale and brittle as old parchment, as though she would crumble at the slightest touch. He watched her struggle to get a grip on her nerves and recapture her cool image. Squaring her shoulders, she schooled her features and brought her chin up at a determined angle. The mannerism was so identical to Evelyn's that Rourke caught his breath.

"Are you sure? Maybe you should—"

"I said I'm fine. I've simply had enough of that . . . that farce," she snapped, sending a dagger glare at Evelyn's door.

"I see. Very well, then I'll take you to the airport."

"Forget it. I'll get there on my own."

She turned away and tapped her foot. Rourke saw her jaw work and knew she was clenching her teeth. She cut him a sideways glance, her eerily familiar green eyes smoldering. "Didn't you hear me? I don't need your help, Mr. Fallan. I don't want it. Just get lost, will you?"

The elevator pinged and the doors slid open. "Not likely," he drawled, and before she realized his intent, Rourke grasped her elbow and hustled her inside.

"What do you think you're doing? Let me go!" She tried to jerk free, but he merely tightened his hold and punched the first-floor button.

"I brought you here. I'll see that you get back safely."

"My, my. How gallant," she jibed.

He quit staring at the floor indicator above the doors long enough to slant her a smile, the kind that usually had women eating out of his hand. Sara returned it with a look cold enough to frost over hell. "Yes. Isn't it?"

Tightening her mouth, she stared straight ahead.

He could feel her shaking. Her features might be set, but she could not disguise the fine tremors that vibrated from her arm into his fingers. The quaking reaction twisted Rourke's gut into a knot.

Her skin felt soft as satin. And warm. Rourke glanced at her out of the corner of his eye. She stared at the floor, her head tipped down. Her silky pageboy had slid forward, partially obscuring her face and baring a strip of tender skin at her nape. The mahogany fall of hair was shiny as a beaver pelt. On a waft of stale air-conditioned air he caught again that clean smell of floral shampoo, and his nose twitched.

The elevator doors opened, and with his hand still on her elbow, he led her through the elegant little lobby.

Outside, the limo that had whisked them from the airport only a short while ago sat waiting at the curb. Norman Tucker, Evelyn's chauffeur, was leaning against the front fender, but when he spotted them, he snapped to attention and opened the rear door.

At the car, Sara jerked to a halt and pulled her arm from Rourke's grasp. "I'm sure your driver knows where to go. There's no need for you to escort me, Mr. Fallan."

"It's no trouble."

"Perhaps not, but to be blunt, I've had about all I can take of your employer—and you. I've fulfilled my part of our bargain. As far as I'm concerned, our business is completed."

She slid into the back seat and slanted him another look. "Goodbye, Mr. Fallan."

Rourke could have stopped her. He could have overridden her objections and insisted on escorting her and she couldn't have done a damned thing about it. Hell, he could have charmed her into accepting his company if he'd put his mind to it. But she looked so damned fragile. He doubted she could tolerate any more right then.

After a brief hesitation, he braced a hand on the top of the car and bent down.

Her eyes widened at his sudden nearness. She flinched back, her nostrils flaring, awareness quivering through her. The skittish reaction was oddly exhilarating and erotic, and sent Rourke's blood coursing through his body to settle, hot and heavy, in his groin.

Her lips looked incredibly soft. Her unblinking eyes swirled with apprehension and reluctant excitement. For an instant he was tempted to dip his head and kiss her, but sanity reasserted itself. "Have a good trip, Ms. Anderson."

He straightened, gave a nod to Tucker, and stepped back.

Sara stared straight ahead, refusing to look at him, her delicate chin in the air as Tucker drove down the shallow U-shaped drive in front of the building and pulled out into the traffic zipping by on San Felipe Street.

Rourke watched the limo drive away, his eyes narrowed against the blazing Texas sun.

Would she use the plane ticket?

If she did, a lot of carefully laid plans were going to go right out the window . . . his own included.

One thing was certain; Evelyn's stepchildren and the other members of Joe Ketchum's family were not going to be pleased. Not pleased at all.

Twenty-four hours ago Rourke hadn't been, either. But now . . . now he was no longer sure exactly how he felt about Ms. Sara Anderson's sudden emergence in their lives.

Chapter Seven

When Sara arrived in Los Angeles, she took a taxi to her apartment, picked up her car, and headed for Clarewood House. She did not linger even long enough to go inside and check her mail and answering machine.

Whether or not her mother would be capable of conversation was by no means a certainty. There were days when she was not. More and more as time went by.

It didn't matter; Sara had to try.

For three hours, alone in the luxurious cabin of the Eve Cosmetics Company jet, she had stewed. It was true. Intellectually, she knew that. Evelyn Ketchum had irrefutable proof. Why would the woman lie? What possible purpose would it serve? An intelligent and successful woman like Evelyn Ketchum would not simply give part of her fortune away to a stranger for no reason.

Even so, deep down, a tiny part of Sara clung to the idea that Mrs. Ketchum had made a mistake. Before she could accept the woman's claim, she would have to hear the words from Julia Anderson's mouth.

The first person Sara saw when she entered the nursing home was Helen Van Nyes, the head nurse in charge of her mother's wing. The middle-aged woman flashed a bright smile when she spotted Sara.

"Why, Ms. Anderson. We didn't expect you today. Mr. Neely was in just this morning to bring your mother's account up to date."

"Good." Sara smiled. She'd known she could depend on Brian. As long as someone else made the decisions, he could be relied upon to carry out instructions to a T. Brian simply could not deal with the pressures or responsibility without falling apart.

"How is my mother today?"

Nurse Van Nyes beamed. "Actually, I'm glad you decided to visit. Julia is having an exceptional day. She's been perfectly lucid all afternoon, ever since she woke up from her nap. She'll be delighted to see you."

"That is good news." Nurse Van Nyes had no idea how good.

With Julia, you never knew what to expect. She drifted in and out of reality at the blink of an eye. Sometimes she seemed to be living in the past, convinced she was back home in Iowa on her parents' small farm. At other times she thought she was back with her husband in the shabby little house in Los Angeles, and she was somber and nervous, her eyes flickering this way and that.

More frequently these days, though, Sara's mother simply wasn't there. For hours she sat perfectly still, her mind adrift, her blank eyes focused on some distant world where nothing and no one could reach her.

Sara's nose twitched as she hurried down the hallway. Clarewood House was elegant and impressive. The furnishings were lovely antiques, the color scheme soft rose and dusty blue. Beautiful oriental rugs covered a great deal of the marble and wood floors, and original oil paintings adorned the walls. The windows were draped in lace and silk, the dining tables in crisp linen. Fresh flowers filled vases in the main rooms. Every effort had been made to give the look of a luxurious private home, but the smells gave away the establishment's true purpose. Nothing could disguise the sharp odors of disinfectant and antiseptics and alcohol that permeated a nursing home or hospital.

Pausing outside her mother's room, Sara crossed her fingers, sent up a silent prayer, and stepped inside. Julia sat in an easy chair beside the window, gazing out, an open book in her lap.

"Hello, Mom."

"Sara! Why, darling, what a lovely surprise." Her eyes lighting up, Julia Anderson smiled and held out her work-worn hands. Sara took them, and knelt before the chair.

"How are you today?" Her anxious gaze searched her mother's face, and Julia smiled.

"I'm fine, dearest. Truly I am." For the moment, the look in her eyes said. That her mother was aware of her illness during these moments of lucidity amazed Sara and wrung her heart. It seemed to her that it would be more merciful if she did not know that her mind was slowly deteriorating.

Reading the sadness in Sara's gaze, Julia gave a

determined smile and squeezed her daughter's hands. "So, what are you doing here? I didn't expect to see you today. Brian was here earlier, and he said you were out of town on some sort of mysterious business."

"Yes. I was. Actually . . . that's what I want to talk to you about."

"Oh?"

Sara stared at her mother's hands. She rubbed her thumbs back and forth over the knobby bones and brown age spots, absently noting the stark difference between Julia's roughened skin and the pampered softness of Evelyn Ketchum's.

"Mom, do you know—" Sara pressed her lips together, unable to come right out and ask what she so desperately needed to know. "Can you . . . can you tell me again about the night I was born?"

Julia chuckled. "Goodness gracious, child, don't you ever get tired of hearing that story?" She pulled one hand free and smoothed the silky fall of hair away from Sara's face, her expression soft with love. "You were born in the middle of the afternoon on Valentine's Day. I used to call you my little Valentine. Remember?"

Sara nodded. She remembered, too, that her father had had other names for her.

"You were the most beautiful baby. Just like a little angel. When they put you in my arms, I thought my heart would burst with love. And right from the start you were such a good child, the best behaved in the nursery. All the nurses on the maternity ward said so. I was so proud of you. I still am."

It was the same story Sara had heard all her life, but this time she noticed that her mother gave no

details—none of the personal revelations or anec-
dotes about the trip to the hospital or the labor or
delivery that most women talked about. On reflection, Sara realized that whenever she had coaxed
Julia into recounting the tale, she had always done so
in general terms.

"Did it hurt much?"

"Hurt?"

"When I was born. Where were you when you
went into labor? How long did it take? You've never
told me."

Julia turned her head and stared out the window.
"I . . . I don't remember. It was a long time ago."

A terrible sadness settled over Sara as she gazed at
her mother's averted profile. *Oh, Mom. Most women
remember for all of their lives every detail of the birth
of the children.*

"Mom . . . does the name Evelyn Ketchum mean
anything to you?"

Relieved by the change of subject, Julia turned
back. "Evelyn Ketchum? Hmm . . . Ketchum . . .
Ketchum . . ." She shook her head. "No, I don't
think so. Why do you ask?"

"How about Evelyn Delacorte?"

She hit a nerve with that one. The look that flashed
in her mother's eyes sent Sara's heart plummeting
and brutally smashed her last slender hope.

"I . . . I don't know. I don't remember." Julia's
hand trembled. She pulled it from Sara's grasp and
plucked at her cotton robe. Her gaze darted around,
looking anywhere but at her daughter, finally settling
on the satin house slippers Sara had bought for her
the previous week.

"Mom, look at me. Look at me." Sara cupped her

mother's cheek and turned her head until she had no choice but to look her in the eye. "I met with a woman named Evelyn Ketchum this afternoon in Houston. Evelyn Delacorte-Ketchum."

Julia made a distressed sound and tried to pull her chin from Sara's grasp. Her eyes filled with tears and her lips wobbled pathetically. Sara felt as though she'd been kicked in the stomach.

"She's my natural mother, isn't she? Isn't she, Mom?" she prodded, when Julia merely stared at her with tears dripping over her lower lashes.

"Why'd you have to go and talk with her? You weren't supposed to meet her. Not ever."

"Oh, Mom." Sara caught her lower lip between her teeth as pain shuddered through her. It was true. It was all true.

"I wanted a baby so much. So very much. And Edgar wanted a son. He blamed me. Said it was my fault. All my fault." Remembered pain swam in Julia's eyes.

"And so you adopted me," Sara prodded gently, when she did not go on.

Julia nodded. "Edgar had read about couples who adopt a baby, then have children of their own. He was hoping that would happen for us—that's why he agreed to the adoption."

"I see," Sara murmured, closing her eyes again against the hurt. And she did. A lot of things were clear now. Painfully clear.

Julia was staring out the window when Sara opened her eyes. She studied her, a bleak despair weighing down her chest. "What I don't understand is, why didn't you tell me?"

Sara waited for an answer, but her mother continued to stare out the window, her restless fingers constantly plucking at her robe. "Mom? Did you hear what I said? For God's sake, why didn't you tell me?"

Julia turned her head and blinked. "I couldn't. It was a secret. Willie made me promise not to tell."

"Willie? Uncle William?" A knot of dread tightened in Sara's stomach. Her mother's brother had been dead for over twenty years.

"Uh-huh. He said Papa'd whip us both if he knew we'd gone swimming in the creek after he'd told us not to."

"Mom, no. Not now, please. Come back. Listen to me—"

"Ssh, you'll wake up Amber."

"Amber?"

"My baby doll. *Rock-a-bye baaa . . . bee, in the tree top. When the wind blows . . .*" Cradling in the crook of her arm the book she'd been reading, Julia rocked back and forth from the waist, crooning the lullaby in a high-pitched little girl's voice.

Sara sat back on her heels, her shoulders slumping. "Oh, Mom."

Julia didn't hear her. She just kept rocking and singing.

Finally, feeling as though she were a hundred years old, Sara climbed to her feet and left the room, left the woman she had called mother all her life, crooning a lullaby to an imaginary doll.

In the ladies' room off the lobby, Sara splashed her face with cold water and let it run over her wrists. She stared at her pale reflection in the mirror.

Oh, yes. So many things were clear now. Like why she was nothing like either of her parents—not in looks or personality or any other way. Why she had always had this . . . this need to make something of herself, why ever since she could remember she'd wanted something different out of life than they did. Something more. Why she had always felt like a misfit in her family.

And most of all . . . why her father had despised her so much.

Sara grimaced. No. Not her father. Thank God. That was the only good thing to come out of all this—to learn that Edgar Anderson's blood did not run in her veins.

For years she had hated him. God, how she'd hated him. And for years she'd felt guilty for it. Now, at least, that burden was lifted.

She had no idea who her real father was, but he had to be better than the brutal fanatic who had raised her.

That was what tore her apart inside. Sara thought of her childhood—the fear and the pain and the sheer emotional wretchedness of it—and wanted to hit something. Oh, God, it had been bad enough all those years when she had thought she'd been born into that life, but now, knowing she had been thrust into it by a cruel twist of fate, it was so much worse.

She had been cheated. Betrayed. Not once, but twice. First, by the woman who had borne her and given her away, and then by the one who had raised her and lied to her.

Sara stared at her face in the mirror, studying it, for the first time seeing with her eyes what her mind had never let her see before. No wonder she had thought there was something familiar about Evelyn Ketchum; she had been looking at her own face in about twenty years. Rourke Fallan had been right; she was the image of his boss.

The image of her mother.

After a long soak that did little to soothe her troubled thoughts, Evelyn walked into her bedroom. A cloud of moist air roiled out of the bathroom behind her, redolent with the scents of floral soap, lotions, and talc, the tantalizing bouquet of her newest line of bath products to compliment the new perfume, Original Sin, which they would be launching soon.

Tightening the belt on her ivory satin robe, Evelyn sat down at the writing desk beside her bedroom window. She moved slowly, with the regal grace and composure that was second nature to her, but the hand that reached for the gold pen and opened her diary trembled.

I met her today. Sara. My daughter. How strange it felt to look into the face of this thirty-two-year old, poised young woman, this stranger, and know that she is the baby I carried all those years ago.

How strange, too, that this was my first sight of her.

I did not look at her when she was born. I couldn't. I do remember lying on the table, sweating, panting with exhaustion and pain, my eyes squeezed shut, listening to her newborn cries—cries that grew fainter as the nurse carried her out of the delivery room. Out of my life.

I remember, too, the terrible jumble of feelings that had swamped me. Sadness, regret, rage, guilt . . . but most of all . . . relief. Blessed relief.

It was over at last. That was all I could think about. I could finally put what had happened behind me and get on with my life. I was free once again to pursue my dreams.

And the child—a girl, I'd heard one of the nurses say—would be much better off with someone else.

Was that thinking merely an excuse I used to quiet my conscience? I've asked myself that question many times, before and since Sara's birth, yet when I search my heart, I can honestly say, no, it was not.

Sara disagrees, and I cannot convince her otherwise, not without revealing things from the past that would only hurt her more.

She is so bitter, so angry. At first I thought it was because she felt cheated out of the lifestyle my money would have given her, but I was wrong. I sense there is something more, something deeper troubling her.

The whole time I carried Sara I was filled with resentment and anger. I never wanted her. I even resented the occasional maternal stirrings that gripped me when she moved in my womb, or when I saw new mothers with their babies. Even so, I did truly want her to be happy. I felt that she would be better off with the Andersons. At least she would have parents who loved her. That is not something I am sure she would have had with me.

The admission shames me, but at least I cared enough to make certain that she never had to endure a childhood totally devoid of affection. Of being raised by someone who was merely doing their "duty." How well I know how much it hurts to be made to feel that you are just an unwanted responsibility. It's true that I may not have loved her, but at least I spared her that.

* * *

"Well? What happened? What did Evelyn Ketchum want to talk to you about?" Jennifer demanded, the instant Sara entered the office the following morning.

Her secretary was so eaten up with curiosity she was about to burst. Her amber eyes sparkled and her small pixie face was even more animated than usual, making the freckles across her nose even more noticeable. Even her mane of riotous red-gold curls seemed to crackle.

"Yeah." Perched on the corner of Jennifer's desk, Brian flashed a coaxing grin. "C'mon, gorgeous, spit it out. We're dying to know what was so urgent that she'd pay you ten thousand dollars just to meet with her." This morning Brian wore the regulation business suit that Sara insisted upon during office hours, his shaggy hair combed neatly, but he still managed to look like a melancholy poet from the nineteenth century.

"I would hardly call it urgent. Mrs. Ketchum has been in possession of the information she just gave me for over thirty years." Sara strove for an indifferent air, but the bitter edge to her voice was discernable even to her own ears.

"Uh-oh," Jen muttered. She and Brian exchanged a look, eyebrows arching skyward.

Sara headed for her office with her two employees on her heels. They waited while she dropped her purse into the bottom drawer of her desk and settled into her chair, but that was as far as Jen's patience would stretch.

"Well? Are you going to tell us? Or do we have to get a rubber hose and beat it out of you?"

Sighing, Sara looked up. Aside from being her

employees—and in the case of Brian, her ex-husband—they were her best friends, and the closest thing she had to family, other than Julia. They cared about her, worried about her. They deserved the truth. "It seems that after all these years, Mrs. Ketchum finally saw fit to inform me that she is my mother."

The announcement had the impact of a bomb exploding in the room.

"Your *what?*"

"You've got to be *kidding!*" her two friends squawked in unison, their expressions incredulous.

Sara shrugged. "That's what she claims."

"But . . . but there must be some mistake. Julia and Edgar—"

"Adopted me, according to Mrs. Ketchum. She even has the legal documents to prove it. When I returned last night, I went to see Mom at Clarewood House." Not looking at either Jennifer or Brian, Sara needlessly straightened the lamp on her desk and the gold pen-and-pencil set. Her mouth worked, then tightened at the corners. "She verified it," she murmured in a dull voice.

"Good grief." The stunned murmur tumbled from Brian's lips as he sank into one of the delicate chairs in front of Sara's desk.

"Oh, Sara," Jen whispered, and plopped down beside him. She stared at Sara across the desktop, her eyes big as saucers, her mouth agape, for the first time in her nineteen years at a loss for a smart-ass retort.

Their shock did not last long. Within seconds they were peppering Sara with questions.

Her friends listened, unbelieving, as she poured

out the whole story. They were supportive and sympathetic, and both seemed to understand her anger, but when she told them she had no intention of accepting Evelyn's offer, they did not respond at all the way she'd expected.

"Have you lost your frigging mind?" Jennifer bellowed, shooting up out of the chair. She faced off at Sara with her hands planted on her hips. At five-feet-one and ninety-seven pounds, her amber eyes almost shooting sparks, she reminded Sara of a feisty terrier on the attack. "The woman offers you a fortune on a silver platter, *plus* an important position in her company, and you turn it *down?* Shit, Sara! I always thought you were such a clever businesswoman, but that's just plain stupid."

Sara jutted her chin. "It was a conscience offer."

"So? Who gives a rat's ass? There's no law that says you have to forgive her if you accept it, is there?"

"Jen's right, sweetheart. You're angry—and who can blame you? But for Pete's sake, don't let pride stand in your way. Part ownership and a seat on the board of a company like Eve Cosmetics is too big an opportunity to turn your back on, no matter what."

"That's right. Plus, if you take her up on her offer, you'll get to work around that gorgeous hunk who lured you to Texas yesterday."

Brian frowned at that. Sara pretended not to notice. Their marriage and the teenaged puppy love they had once shared had ended years ago. Brian dated other women all the time and he certainly harbored no lingering romantic feelings for her. Because of her hectic workload, her own lovelife tended to be a hit-or-miss proposition, but she had not lived like a nun since their divorce. At least one relationship had been serious enough for her to consider marriage—not for long, but she *had* considered it. Brian had never been bothered by the men in her life, but for some reason Rourke Fallan made him bristle.

The mention of Rourke Fallan brought a scowl to Sara's brow that rivaled Brian's. Jennifer's comment had sent a tingle whispering over her skin and caused her heart to give a little bump. It was crazy, but even in the midst of all the turmoil the previous day, she had been aware of him, drawn to him.

It annoyed her that she was so attracted to the man. God! He was Evelyn Ketchum's assistant!

What was more, he had made it fairly obvious that he wasn't interested in her. He had come to fetch her because Evelyn had wished it, and he had been polite and courteous. At times he had even displayed a remote sort of charm, which Sara suspected had been a mere hint of his true ability to beguile. On the outside he was correct and businesslike, but behind that smooth professional image, those polite smiles and diplomatic gestures, the blue-eyed, black-haired executive exuded an aura of sensuality and raw masculinity that was almost palpable. Sara had no doubt at all that his effect on women was lethal.

Yet with her, she sensed in him a taut restraint.

Sara had a gut feeling that Rourke Fallan didn't really like her. Nor did he want her in Evelyn's life.

Chapter Eight

Rourke pretended not to notice when Evelyn glanced at the mantel clock again for what had to be the hundredth time in the past hour.

The ten days were almost up. In another few hours they would be. And no sign of Sara.

"We seem to be having a problem with distribution in southern Italy."

Evelyn was so preoccupied, it took a few seconds for Rourke's comment to register. Blinking, she looked at him, and he could see her struggle to bring her thoughts back to the business they had been discussing. "Yes. Yes, I know. Customer service tells me we've had over a dozen calls from disgruntled retailers in that area during the past month. I want you to check into it and see what's going on over there."

"I'll get right on it." Rourke scribbled a note to himself, adding the request to his list of things to do. "Anything else?"

Evelyn did not answer, and after a moment, he looked up and saw that she was staring at the clock again, and his mouth thinned. She had been so certain that Sara would come.

"Why don't you just forget about it, Evelyn? It doesn't look as though she's coming," he said gently.

Jerking her gaze from the clock, she sent him a quick look and took the next folder from the neat stack on the corner of her desk. "Perhaps she went to the office. Even though we met here at my apartment the first time, it would be a natural assumption that I would be at work during the middle of the afternoon."

"If she had shown up at Eve, Alice would have called."

Resentfully, to be sure, he thought with a hint of a smile, and in that miffed voice she used whenever Sara's name was mentioned, but she would have called. Alice could be counted on to follow orders no matter what.

Evelyn had not yet confided in her secretary as to Sara's identity, and Rourke knew she would not unless Sara accepted her offer and it became necessary. However, for the past ten days, Alice had had a standing order to contact either Rourke or Evelyn immediately should a Ms. Sara Anderson show up at the corporate offices of Eve Cosmetics.

The request had aroused both curiosity and pique in the oh-so-efficient woman. She had been Evelyn's confidential secretary for twenty years. That there was something afoot of which she had no knowledge was obvious, and she took it as a personal affront.

Evelyn did confide her condition to her secretary, however. Because of her need to be away from the office for the frequent and regular chemotherapy sessions, she'd had no choice.

Alice had taken the news badly. Rourke had always known that she was devoted to Evelyn. Nevertheless, he had been surprised when she had broken down and sobbed uncontrollably. Though she was at least ten years Evelyn's junior, anyone witnessing her crushing grief would have thought she was a mother facing the possible loss of a beloved child. It had taken his and Evelyn's combined efforts to calm her.

However, once it had been done, she had applied herself to protecting Evelyn and her privacy with more diligence than ever. No one but the three of them, either on the staff or outside the company, had a clue as to Evelyn's whereabouts when she disappeared for the twice weekly therapy sessions, as she had done that morning. For those with the temerity to inquire, Alice invariably came up with a perfectly believable answer.

The chemotherapy often left Evelyn too weak and debilitated—and, Rourke suspected, too nauseated—to return to the office. However, being the dedicated workaholic she was, she insisted that on those days she and Rourke work together afterward at her apartment, as they were doing today.

"There's still time," Evelyn insisted. "Sara will show up. Actually, I expected her to wait until the last minute. In her place, I'd do the same thing."

"Maybe so, but I wouldn't get my hopes up if I were you."

"Of course not. You know me better than that." She opened the folder and pushed her dark-rimmed reading glasses farther up her nose. "Now, about the Eden West project . . ."

Rourke was concerned, and over the next several hours the feeling did not abate. They worked diligently, but he noticed that Evelyn's gaze kept darting from the clock to the door. She was counting on

Sara, all right, he thought. Whether she admitted it or not.

By noon they had gone over all the urgent business that was pending and were about to break for lunch when Mrs. Chester, Evelyn's housekeeper, tapped on the door and stuck her head inside.

"Sorry to interrupt, Mrs. Ketchum, but you did say to tell you right away if Miss Anderson arrived. Shall I show her in?"

Evelyn darted a look at Rourke that was part relief and part triumph. "Please do, Mrs. Chester."

"Would you like me to leave?" Rourke asked, when the housekeeper had gone.

"No, stay. You already know about Sara and what I'm planning, so it doesn't matter." One corner of her mouth twisted wryly. "Plus, I may need a witness."

Smiling encouragement, Rourke settled back to wait. He was surprised to discover that he was anxious to see Sara again. The prospect actually created a tight knot of anticipation beneath his breastbone.

Which surprised him. He liked women. He liked women a lot. But it had been a long time, if ever, since a woman had interested him quite as much.

He didn't have long to wait. Seconds later Mrs. Chester escorted Sara into Evelyn's cozy study.

"I'm so pleased you changed your mind and used the plane ticket, Sara," Evelyn said, when the door closed behind the housekeeper.

"If you had let us know, we would have had you picked up at the airport," Rourke added.

Sara slanted him a cool look. "I managed, thank you."

"So I see." He nodded and smiled politely, stifling the urge to sigh. The abrupt statement squashed any hope that her attitude had softened. She seemed calmer, more in control, but her tone was as hostile as it had been ten days ago.

Once they were seated, Sara came straight to the point. She crossed her legs, smoothed her skirt, and looked Evelyn right in the eye. "I've come to discuss your offer. But you should know that *if* I decide to accept—and that is a very big if—I will insist upon certain conditions."

"Conditions?" Evelyn raised an elegant eyebrow.

"That's right. You came to me, remember. Either you agree to my conditions or we forget the whole thing.

Rourke bit back a grin. He'd figured that this time Sara would come out swinging, and he was right.

"I see," Evelyn murmured. "And just what are these . . . conditions?"

"First of all, I want to know what's going on. And don't feed me that line about wanting me to have my birthright. There's got to be more behind this sudden spurt of generosity than that. For the past thirty-two years you haven't even wanted to know if I was alive, so your maternal concern doesn't quite wash."

She threw the statement down like a gauntlet, her gaze steady, her chin jutted. She was delicate and feminine, and on the outside she appeared calm, but beneath that controlled facade she bristled with challenge and confidence and righteous ire. Rourke watched her, fascinated.

Leaning back in her high-backed desk chair, Evelyn pursed her lips and studied Sara, her expression unreadable. Sara stared right back.

Rourke's gaze slid back and forth between one pair of identical green eyes to the other, watching with interest the silent battle of wills. God, did they have any idea how alike they were? How evenly matched? It was like watching a tennis game between two top-seeded players.

"You're very bright," Evelyn said at last. "And you're right, of course, there is more to my offer than that. The fact is, I'm looking for a successor."

Ah, very clever, Rourke thought. Hit your opponent with a surprise shot, keep her off balance.

That the statement had stunned Sara—which he was sure had been Evelyn's intention—was evident. She gave an involuntary start and her eyes widened, but Evelyn allowed her no chance to comment.

"You see, no one in my husband's family—neither his children nor his nephews—is capable of running Eve Cosmetics. Nor are any of them interested, really, though a couple would no doubt like to gain control. All they really want is to be able to sell off their shares and take the money and run. I, on the other hand, am adamant that ownership of Eve Cosmetics and all its subsidiaries remain wholly within the family. I refuse to allow what I have worked most of my life to build to be taken over by outsiders or frittered away.

"If, as I suspect, you have inherited my drive and business sense, and you demonstrate a facility for leadership, I plan to leave control of the company in your hands when I die."

"Control? Are you *serious?*"

"Very."

Rourke's gaze switched to Sara. A small smile tugged at his mouth. She aced you with that one, sweetheart, he thought. Now the ball's in your court.

Sara shook her head. She must be dreaming.

Things like this just didn't happen. Not to people like her.

Apparently they did, though, because Evelyn Ketchum was watching her, waiting for an answer.

Sara swallowed hard and tried to think over the booming of her pulse. She had come here expecting, at most, to walk out with a modest share in the company and a job. The possibility of someday running Eve Cosmetics sent an almost unbearable excitement percolating through her system. Oh, Lord, the challenge would be exhilarating—beyond her wildest dreams.

She'd be damned, though, if she'd let Evelyn see how much she wanted what she was offering. Regrettably, her initial flare of excitement had no doubt shown in her eyes, but there was nothing she could do about that. Schooling her features, she matched Evelyn cool stare for cool stare.

"What makes you think that I would follow your wishes once you're gone? What's to stop me from agreeing to do as you ask now, then doing as I please later? I could vote to go public and sell off the company the first chance I got. I could take my money and run, just like the rest of your 'loving' family, and there wouldn't be a thing you could do about it."

Except for an infinitesimal narrowing of her eyes, Evelyn showed no reaction to Sara's goading. They stared at one another in a silent battle of wills as the air around them vibrated and hummed with challenge and raw emotions.

"You could," Evelyn said, after what seemed like an interminable amount of time. "But if you're half as smart as I think you are, you won't. I'm counting on you to have the good sense and business ability to recognize that retaining control of Eve Cosmetics is the smartest decision."

"You may want to sell out just to strike back at me, but you won't. I'm handing you the business opportunity of a lifetime, Sara. You won't throw it away just for the sake of revenge. There is too much of me in you for that."

The statement incensed Sara. It was hateful to her that so much as one drop of this woman's blood ran in her veins. "You can't be certain of that. And you don't know me at all."

Evelyn shrugged. "Perhaps not. But from what I do know, I'm willing to take that chance."

"If I accept your offer, my secretary and my assistant come with me. I won't leave them high and dry."

"Very well. Eve has a full and competent staff, but I'm certain we can find something for your people to do."

"They'll work for me, as they always have, or you can forget the whole thing." Sara lifted her chin at a pugnacious angle and met Evelyn's steady gaze head on. She knew she was being belligerent and pushy, maybe even unreasonable, but she didn't care.

"Very well," Evelyn agreed. "Anything else?"

"Yes. I want to know what happened thirty-two years ago. Why did you give me away?"

Evelyn stiffened. It was the first crack in her composure that Sara had witnessed, and she felt a spurt of satisfaction.

"That is something I won't discuss with you, Sara."

"Why not? Surely I have a right to know."

Evelyn merely looked at her with those cool green eyes as calm as a placid lake, and Sara's ire rose.

"Can't you at least tell me who my father is? Or don't you know? Were there so many—"

"That's enough." Rourke's voice sliced across her words like a sharp knife, low and taut and icy with anger. The look in his eyes sent a little quiver of alarm down Sara's spine, but she lifted her chin, refusing to back down.

"It's all right, Rourke." Evelyn raised her hand to stave off any further defense from him, her gaze all the while on Sara. "I suppose you are entitled to some information. Yes, I knew your father."

"What was his name?"

"That I won't say."

Sara's jaw worked. "But I was right, wasn't I? You weren't married."

"No."

"Is that why you gave me away?"

"I put you up for adoption for several reasons, Sara. I was young and alone and couldn't take care of you. And I will admit, at that stage of my life I didn't want a child; I was ambitious, just as you are. I had plans for my life, plans I would never have been able to achieve had I had the responsibility of a child.

"Not all of my reasons were selfish, however. I also wanted you to have a good home and a mother and a father who would love you as you deserved to be loved."

A snort of laughter burst from Sara. "Oh, really?" She sat forward in her chair, her eyes blazing. "Shall I tell you about the 'loving' parents to whom you gave me? Edgar Anderson was a vicious bully who took pleasure in abusing his wife and child—all in the name of the Almighty, of course.

"He hated me from the moment I was born. He

called me things like 'Satan's spawn' or 'child of lust,' or 'Jezebel's daughter.' I never understood why, until I met you. Obviously he could not abide having an illegitimate child in his home, especially one bearing his name.

"He was always screeching Scripture at me, especially when he was knocking me around or laying into me with a belt. *That's* the kind of good, loving family you gave me."

Sara had the satisfaction of seeing Evelyn flinch, but it wasn't enough. Not nearly enough. She wanted to heap abuse on the woman, lacerate her with sharp words until she experienced all the pain Sara had endured.

Her face stiff as stone, Evelyn looked at Sara. "I'm sorry. I didn't know."

"You should have made it your business to know what kind of people they were."

"I thought I had. I met with them several times before you were born. Julia was a pleasant, mild-mannered woman and he was a minister. Naturally, I thought they would be kind."

"Kind? Oh, that's rich. Edgar Anderson didn't have a kind bone in his body. He got an almost orgasmic pleasure out of whipping me and hearing me scream. When I realized that he enjoyed it, I learned to grit my teeth and take his abuse without a whimper. It used to drive him crazy.

"The 'wonderful' life you planned for me was so awful, at seventeen I eloped with a boy who lived down the street just to get away from home."

Rourke's head jerked up. "You're married?"

"I was. To Brian Neely, my assistant. You met him the morning you first brought me here. The marriage lasted less than a year." Sara shrugged. "We were just a couple of kids, both trying to escape unhappy homes. We thought we could by clinging to each other, but it didn't work."

Sara looked at Evelyn, her eyes full of silent accusation. If she hoped to see her squirm, she was in for a disappointment.

"I'm sorry you had such a difficult life, Sara. Please believe me, that's not what I wanted for you. However, I must say, you seemed to have survived quite well. You're lovely, intelligent, articulate." Her gaze flickered over Sara. "You obviously have marvelous taste and a sense of style. You even have your own business. Who knows? Had your life been easier, you might not have gotten as far as you have."

The statement incensed Sara. She thought of the fear and dread that had never left her as a child, and how hard she had worked to get through college and keep a roof over her head and watch out for her mother and Brian at the same time, and she gritted her teeth to keep from screeching at the woman. "That's it? You excuse yourself and what you did by suggesting it was *good* for me?"

"I don't have to excuse myself, Sara. I did what I thought was best at the time. For you, and for myself. It was a judgment call. From the information I had, it should have been a good one. I regret that it turned out badly, but since it was not through malicious intent on my part, I can hardly be held to blame."

Sara couldn't argue with the cold logic of the statement. It wasn't logic, however, but raw emotion that was eating away at her insides. She felt as though there were a hole in her heart you could drive a tank through, and with every word this woman spoke, it got bigger.

"Just answer one question: if you had it all to do over, knowing what you do now, would you make the same decision?"

Evelyn considered the question only the briefest of moments, her gaze never wavering. "Yes."

The reply hit Sara like a fist to the chest, the brutal honesty taking her breath away. She felt the color drain from her face, and for a moment she couldn't breathe. She had expected abject denial, which she would not have believed, of course, but at least it would have been a sop to her feelings.

"And if one of your stepchildren or someone else in your husband's family had the ability and the interest to take over your business, you would never have contacted me, would you?" she asked in a shaky whisper.

"No."

The second blunt answer brought another wave of pain, but Sara absorbed this one without flinching. "I . . . I see. Well, at least you're honest."

"I know I'm not your ideal of a loving mother, but I won't lie to you, Sara, or sugarcoat anything. Ever. You can count on that.

"I do admire you for what you've managed to make of your life under harrowing circumstances. I know it's not what you want to hear, and I'm not offering it as an excuse, but perhaps you did gain strength from the experience.

"And now, if you will allow me, I would like to help you realize your full potential." Evelyn leaned forward in her chair, the subtle move lending urgency to her soft voice. "I may not have been part of your life until now, Sara, but what I am offering you is the result of those thirty-two years, the thing into which I have poured almost every ounce of my energy and effort. It can all be yours . . . if you want it."

Rourke almost laughed. *If* she wanted it? Hell, she wanted it so badly he could taste it. The tug of war going on inside Sara was visible in her face. Watching her, Rourke had the feeling she would like nothing better than to spit in Evelyn's eye. And in a way, he couldn't blame her. However, Sara was ambitious, and the possibility of someday being the majority shareholder in Eve Cosmetics was too good to pass up for something as fleeting and worthless as revenge, unless you were a fool. He didn't think Sara Anderson was a fool.

"You've heard my offer, Sara," Evelyn said at last. "So what is your decision?"

"I don't know. I . . ." Sara twisted her fingers together in her lap, her troubled gaze darting around. Abruptly, she stood up crossed to the French doors with stiff steps. Keeping her back to the other two, she stared out.

The Texas sun bathed the terrace garden in glaring light. Far below, beyond the waist-high brick wall surrounding the terrace, the rounded tops of ancient trees stretched away into the distance. Here and there, glimpses of glittering blue swimming pools and manicured lawns and the bright array of flowers surrounding the magnificent mansions of River Oaks, Houston's "old money" neighborhood, peeked through the green boughs. In this neighborhood, all was glittering and pristine and perfect.

Sara saw none of it. She was experiencing so many emotions at the same time she didn't know exactly what she was feeling . . . except that it hurt. It hurt so much. A knot of pain had lodged beneath her breastbone and wouldn't go away. She wondered if it ever would.

The hurt child in her wanted to turn and walk out, let the woman whistle in the wind for an heir, but the practical, intelligent woman she had become knew that sort of childish revenge would never ease the pain that filled her being.

And the bottom line was—Evelyn Ketchum owed her.

Drawing a deep breath, Sara squared her shoulders and turned, her gaze leveling on Evelyn. "If I accept your offer, I won't make any promises," she said, with a lift of her chin. "When the stock is mine, I'll do with it whatever I choose. If you can't live with that, then say so now, and I'll go back to California."

Evelyn frowned, but after a moment she nodded. "I suppose I will just have to rely on your good sense and business ability to see that retaining control of Eve Cosmetics is the smartest decision."

Rourke held his breath. Sara's face remained set, but he saw the agitated rise and fall of her breasts, the muscles working in her throat as she stared at Evelyn and struggled to swallow the knot of anger and hurt. At last her chin came up in that characteristic way.

"All right. I accept your offer."

Rourke released his breath and settled back in his chair, his eyes on Sara's face. All things considered, the second set was a tie.

Chapter Nine

Until that moment, Evelyn had not known how anxious she was. Relief poured through her, leaving her weak and quivery inside. Outwardly, she managed to hold onto her composure and respond with a smile and a quick nod.

"Good. I'm glad. For what it's worth, I think you've made the right decision, Sara. Now, then, I suppose the first order of business is to get you settled. There is so much I need to teach you, it would be convenient if you stayed here. I have plenty of room, and that way—"

"No," Sara snapped. "I won't live under your roof."

The bitterness in her face gave Evelyn pause, and something flickered in her breast, something very close to pain, but she immediately smothered it. She understood Sara's enmity and accepted it as part of the price she must pay.

Green eyes stared into green eyes, defiance and pride and a host of choking emotions hovering between them.

"If I may make a suggestion," Rourke interjected.

"Sara could use the company apartment. At least for the time being, until she's gotten her feet wet. It's only a few blocks away. Later, Alice can help her find a place of her own, if she wants." He turned to Sara. "Alice Burke is Evelyn's secretary, and an absolute jewel. You'll find she's an invaluable source of information and help. Whenever we want something done, we turn it over to Alice."

Evelyn sent Rourke a grateful smile. He could be tough as nails when he had to be—he wielded power like a man born to it—but when an occasion called for finesse and tact, no one had a lighter hand. "That's a wonderful idea, Rourke."

"The company keeps a fully furnished apartment for visiting clients and high-ranking employees who are in town on business," Rourke explained. Sara still looked angry and doubtful, but he went on undaunted, his voice smooth and full of confidence and charm. "It's conveniently located, and since it sits empty most of the time, you might as well use it. It's quite nice, and I'm sure you'll be comfortable there."

"What about your clients?"

"No problem. If someone important comes into town, we'll put them up at a hotel."

"Well . . . I suppose that would be all right."

"Good. Then it's settled," Evelyn said. "First thing tomorrow, I'll get Alice started on locating apartments for your employees."

"My secretary has a two-year-old daughter, so she'll need a good day-care center as well."

"No problem," Rourke said. "We have one on the premises. All of our factories and offices around the world have complete child-care facilities. It's free to our employees." Surprise flickered across Sara's face.

Rourke smiled, slowly, smugly. "Evelyn insisted on it years ago—long before it became the politically correct thing for big companies to do."

Sara's gaze flew to Evelyn, her eyes wide with confusion. She clearly did not want to believe his claim.

"It's just good business," Evelyn explained, wondering, even as she spoke the words, why she felt compelled to downplay any altruistic motives on her part. For the first time since they had met, she felt she had gained a modicum of respect from Sara—grudging though it was. "Most of our factory workers are women. So are many of our office staff. Many have dependent children. If those children are nearby and being cared for in a happy and safe environment, our employees are more comfortable, and therefore work more efficiently. We've also had a marked drop in absenteeism since incorporating the child-care program."

"I see," Sara said, appearing more comfortable with the explanation.

Rourke was not. Frowning, he propped his elbows on the arms of his chair and watched Evelyn over steepled fingers. He didn't get it. He had expected her to bend over backward to win Sara over, but she seemed determined to keep a barrier between them. Why?

"I'd like to start your training right away. And, of course, I must introduce you to the rest of the family. The sooner the better, don't you agree, Rourke?"

"Mmm, you're probably right." He glanced at Sara, and stifled a chuckle at the thought of the shock waves she was going to send through the Ketchum clan. "But first, I think we should start by familiarizing Sara with the internal workings of the company. Beginning with—"

"Wait." Sara looked from one to the other. "Before you start planning too far ahead, I should tell you that I can't stay long. A few days, a week at most. I have to go back to the West coast to close Reflections and tie up loose ends there. Also, I'll have to spend some of my time here looking for a nursing home so I can transfer my mother."

"You're going to bring Julia here?"

"Yes." Sara looked at Evelyn, challenge glittering in her eyes. "I want my mother nearby where I can look after her. Do you have a problem with that?"

"No. Of course not.

"You must do what you think is best. However, that doesn't give us much time to get things rolling on this end. Fortunately, Alice can locate a facility for your mother. Just give her a list of your requirements. Rourke, why don't you take Sara to the apartment and get her settled in? Later, you can give her that tour of the offices and the factory."

She turned an apologetic smile on Sara. "I would go with you, but I have a prior engagement. I do hope you understand."

"I'm sure Mr. Fallan and I will manage."

Sara's voice and expression left no doubt that she was happy not to have to bear Evelyn's company, and Rourke winced for her.

He did not need to see the entreaty in Evelyn's eyes to pick up her silent message. He knew she had no appointments that afternoon, and one look at her pale face told him that she was exhausted and needed desperately to rest for a while.

Standing, he turned the full force of his smile on Sara. "Shall we get started, Ms. Anderson?"

Without so much as a word or a glance for Evelyn, Sara rose.

The softly fragrant essence of her—a hint of floral perfume, the whisper of shampoo, the warm, womanly scent of her skin—drifted to him. He stepped close. He put a guiding hand on her elbow and was surprised at the current of heat that zinged up his arm. Sara flinched at the slight contact and her back stiffened like a ramrod. The corners of Rourke's mouth lifted with grim satisfaction; at least he wasn't the only one who felt the strong chemistry.

"Oh, Rourke, one more thing. Please notify everyone that I'm calling a special meeting of the board in two days' time. I want all the shareholders and their spouses here at noon sharp the day after tomorrow. No one is excused."

He paused in the doorway and looked back, and felt a stab of concern. Evelyn looked pale and exhausted, and, for the first time since he'd known her, oddly vulnerable.

And alone.

Rourke frowned. Loneliness and vulnerability were not words he had ever thought of in connection with Evelyn before.

"Don't worry. I'll take care of it."

This was one board meeting he wouldn't miss for the world. The Ketchums would all be mad as hornets at being so peremptorily summoned. Even before Evelyn dropped her surprise on them.

* * *

After Rourke and Sara left, Evelyn remained in her chair, staring into space. She did not move until Mrs. Chester popped her head inside the room. "Could I get you anything before I leave, Mrs. Ketchum? Some tea, maybe?"

With an effort, she pulled her thoughts back to the present. She was surprised when she glanced out the terrace doors and saw that the sun was setting. She turned to her housekeeper with a wan smile. "No, thank you, Mrs. Chester. You run along. I know this is your favorite television night, and I wouldn't want you to miss it."

"You sure? Mr. Fallan said to keep an eye on you, that you weren't feeling well, and—"

"Mr. Fallan worries too much. I'm fine. I'm going to read for a while, then go to bed. Now, you run along."

"Well . . . if you're sure . . ."

When she had gone, with an effort, Evelyn got to her feet and walked slowly to her bedroom. She was tired. So tired.

The wide bed beckoned, and her weary body longed to curl up on its inviting softness, but the troubled thoughts and memories that pulled at her would not allow her to rest. Halfway across the room she hesitated, then stopped. Slowly, unwillingly, drawn by a force she could not deny, she turned and stared at the bookshelves on the opposite wall, her eyes swirling with pain.

No, don't, her mind screamed, but her feet moved of their own accord. With the slow gait of one in a trance, she crossed the room. Clasping her arms protectively over her midriff, she stopped before the shelves and gazed at the books that lined them. Her diaries. The story of her life. Written by her own hand.

There were forty of them on the shelves, forty-one in all, counting the current one that lay on her writing table, ready for her nightly entry. One for each year since her parents' death. The last twenty-seven volumes were the rich, leatherbound journals, embossed in gold with her name and the year. The ones before that, before her marriage to Joe, were the inexpensive kind you get at the dime store.

"What happened thirty-two years ago? Who was my father? You weren't married, were you?"

Sara's questions echoed through Evelyn's mind like an annoying broken record, accusing her, prodding her. Unable to resist, Evelyn gazed over at a book on the top shelf.

The answers were written there.

Evelyn rarely read any of her old diaries. None beyond the last thirty or so. She tried never to think of that period in her life. The last thing she wanted was to read of those painful times.

Some things, however, were stronger than desire or good sense or self-preservation. Even when you know it is going to hurt, like probing a sore tooth with your tongue, you cannot resist.

Evelyn's mind cried *"No! Leave it alone!"* but her shaking hand reached for the top shelf and withdrew the ninth volume in the row.

Clutching the cheap book to her chest, she dragged her exhausted body to the chaise longue beside the fireplace and lay back with a sigh.

The date she sought was etched permanently in her memory. Drawing in a shuddering breath, she steeled herself and with trembling fingers opened the book to the month of May and began to read.

I'm so excited I feel as though I'm going to burst at any moment! Larry Bainbridge asked me for a date.

Evelyn shook her head sadly. Lord, she had sounded so young. So foolish.

I still can't believe it. I keep pinching myself, but it isn't a dream. He really asked me out. Me. A lowly freshman. A nobody. Larry's a senior and the star receiver on the football team, and probably the most popular guy on campus. And he's so handsome, too. And so nice. He could have his pick of any girl in school, and he wants to go out with me! I'm so lucky.

Evelyn leaned her head against the high back of the chaise longue and closed her eyes. What a fool she had been. Oh, God. How could she have been so naive? Such a starry-eyed innocent?

It had not occurred to her to wonder why the biggest stud on campus would be interested in a shy eighteen-year-old. Opening her eyes, Evelyn gazed at the ceiling and caught her lower lip between her teeth to keep it from trembling.

At eighteen she had been so alone and so lonely, her love-starved heart had responded to him without hesitation or question. When she'd waltzed out of her dorm the next evening with her arm through Larry's, she'd been walking on air, her mind awhirl with romantic dreams.

How quickly and cruelly he had shattered those.

Evelyn blinked the sudden rush of moisture from her eyes and resolutely turned to the next night's entry. She stared at the page, her insides quaking. The events of that night had left her soul scarred and altered her life forever.

Even her writing looked different. Shaky. Agitated. All slashing marks and jerky, spiked letters that screamed pain.

He raped me. Larry Bainbridge raped me.

Even now, after all these years, the bald words raked over Evelyn's heart like talons. The hurt was so excruciating she almost cried out. She pulled her gaze away from the jerky handwriting and drew in a shuddering breath. As though it were yesterday she remembered writing those words, hurting and ashamed, wanting to die, tears streaming down her face.

She looked down at the page again and saw that the writing was blurry in spots where her tears had splattered.

"Why? Why did he do that to me? How could he? When he finished, he said it was my fault. That I had teased him all evening. That I had wanted it. But that's not true. I didn't. I swear I didn't! One minute we were just kissing, and then he was holding me down . . . tearing my clothes off.

A hard shudder rippled through Evelyn. Oh, God . . .

I fought him, but it was no use. He's so much bigger than me, so much stronger. And it only made him angry.

Oh, God, he hurt me so much. I feel so dirty. So ashamed. When he pushed me out of his car in front of the dorm, I somehow managed to stumble to the student infirmary. Part of the way, I had to crawl.

The nurse on duty called the dean of women and the president of the university. I thought they would help me, but when I told them what Larry had done, they wouldn't do anything.

They didn't believe me. They both just looked at me in that accusing way, and Dean Kirkland said that Larry Bainbridge was a nice young man, and they were sure he would not engage in such an intimacy without encouragement. They said I had gone out with him willingly and I had no right to cry rape simply because I had gotten carried away in a moment of passion. Both Dean Kirkland and President Howe made it clear that they would not allow me to ruin a nice young man's life with such an unfair charge.

It isn't fair. I was the one who was beaten and raped, but they acted as though Larry was the victim.

I wanted to die. I still do.

Evelyn stared at the last line for a long time, then slowly closed the book.

She truly had wanted to die. The interview with Dean Kirkland and President Howe had left her feeling battered and bruised in both body and soul. She had prayed she would die from the beating Larry had given her, and when her healthy young body had betrayed her by healing, she'd entertained thoughts of suicide. Never more strongly than that awful day, a few weeks later, when her worst fear was confirmed.

The brutal attack on her body, on her spirit, had left her pregnant with Larry Bainbridge's child.

That had been the most frightening time of her life. She'd had no money and no family to whom she could turn . . . at least, no one who cared.

The aunt and uncle who had taken her in after her parents' deaths, her mother's sister, Helen, and her husband, John Strahan, had not loved her. They had done what they'd seen as their "Christian duty" and given her a home, but they had never given her any affection or made her feel wanted. In the eight years she had lived with them she could not remember receiving so much as a hug or a pat on the shoulder, or even a smile. They constantly reminded her that she had a home and food in her belly only by the grace of their charity. And the day she turned eighteen they had made it clear that she was on her own.

Evelyn had bitterly resented the unborn child that had been foisted on her through a vicious act of violence, but beneath her pain and anger she had known that the new life growing inside her was as much an innocent victim as she.

She never once considered keeping the baby. Financially, at that point in her life, she simply had not had the means. Emotionally, she hadn't had the desire. Most important, she had been deeply afraid that she would never be able to give the baby the love it deserved. No matter how wrongly she had been violated, she could not inflict a loveless childhood on another human being.

Evelyn sighed and rested her head against the back of the chaise longue. The leaden tiredness that had become so much a part of her life pulled at her. How different things were now, she thought. At the time of Sara's conception, date rape was not recognized as the violent crime it was. If a woman had sex with a man she dated—or even knew—it was assumed she had done so willingly, no matter how much she might protest otherwise. And she was the one who suffered the consequences. If she chose not to do so, she ran the risk of losing her life in a back-alley clinic at the hands of some quack.

No, Sara, Evelyn thought with a tired sigh, as she closed her eyes and gave in to the terrible weakness that dragged at her. If I had it all to do over again,

I would still do the same. You may not have had a perfect life, or even a good one, but at least you were not totally unloved.

And most important . . . you never had to know that you were conceived not in love, nor even passion, but through a brutal assault. At least I spared you that.

The drive from Evelyn's to the building that held the company apartment took less than three minutes, but to Sara it seemed endless. Being alone with Rourke in the close confines of the car made every nerve ending in her body hum like a high-voltage wire. During the walk from the parking garage, in the elevator, stepping into the small but elegant foyer, he guided her with his hand resting solicitously against the small of her back. Through her clothing she felt the imprint of that broad palm and long fingers like a branding iron.

"Here we are." He stopped in front of the door marked 28B, and Sara exhaled a sigh of relief. Apparently, there were only two apartments on the entire floor, she noted, glancing around as he unlocked the door.

"After you." Once again she felt the touch of his hand at the back of her waist. She gritted her teeth. Tingling warmth burned through her gabardine suit and skittered up and down her spine. However, the minute she stepped from the large marble foyer into the living room, she forgot about the sensation.

The apartment was a penthouse with a breathtaking view of the city, and it was furnished in priceless eighteenth-century antiques that rivaled the ones in Evelyn Ketchum's apartment.

"My word," Sara murmured, turning slowly around in the middle of the room. "I thought you said the company kept a 'small' apartment. This place is enormous. And these furnishings—they must have cost a fortune."

Rourke shrugged. "It never hurts to impress clients."

"Well, this place would certainly do the trick."

"If you don't like it—"

"Not like it? Don't be silly! Of course I like it. I love it. It just so . . . so . . . perfect. And so big." Almost her whole apartment back in LA would fit into this living room.

As casually as she could, Sara raked the toe of her navy pump through the thick pile of the oriental rug and calculated that it was worth more than everything she owned put together. Original oil paintings—some undoubtedly the work of masters—hung on the walls, and pieces of costly porcelain, crystal, and silver decorated the surfaces of the furniture as casually as if they were dime-store purchases. There were so many priceless objects around her, Sara didn't know which one to look at first, and like a child turned loose in a toy store, her eyes darted around from one to another.

Rourke set her small suitcase down on the polished oak floor and leaned back against the grand piano beside the terrace doors. Crossing his arms over his chest, he watched her take it all in, a hint of a smile tugging at his mouth. "I'm glad you approve. Evidently you share your mother's taste."

Sara almost laughed at that. Was he kidding? Even

before her illness, Julia Anderson had not known Queen Anne from Danish modern. The thought had no sooner flitted through Sara's mind than she wondered how Rourke could possibly know what kind of taste her mother had.

She shot him a quizzical look, and he smiled. "Evelyn decorated it herself."

Sara's enjoyment took a nosedive. She looked around, wanting to hate the place. She wanted to pronounce it tacky and overdone, but she couldn't. She loved fine things and beauty. Not even her enmity toward Evelyn could completely dim her appreciation.

"Here, until we can pick up another key from the office, you can have mine." Rourke worked the small brass key from the ring and handed it to her. It was still warm from his touch, and the slight brush of his fingers against hers made her pulse flutter. "Tomorrow, I'll arrange for you to have a company car. In the meantime, if you need anything, I'm just across the hall."

Sara's eyes widened. "You live here? On this floor?"

"Yes. We've always found it a handy arrangement, since entertaining customers and seeing to their needs is part of my job." He crossed his long legs at the ankles and cocked one eyebrow. "Why? Do you have a problem with me being close by?"

"No. No, of course not. Why would I? I, uh, I was just surprised, is all." Sara glanced down at the brass key she was fingering, then took a deep breath and looked back at Rourke. "You don't like me much, do you, Mr. Fallan?"

"I don't know you, Ms. Anderson. I do think,

however, that we're past the point of formalities, don't you? Please. Call me Rourke."

Given the effect he had on her, Sara didn't think it wise to dispense with barriers of any kind, but she couldn't very well refuse. "All right . . . Rourke. It has occurred to me that maybe you feel some resentment toward me . . . perhaps rightly so."

"Meaning?"

"Well . . . you *are* the number-two man in the company. Surely you expected someday to step into Evelyn's shoes. And now here I come out of nowhere and . . ." She shrugged and let her words trail away.

Rourke did not say anything for a few seconds. He simply studied her. Slowly, one corner of his mouth curled up in a half smile. "If that's what's worrying you, forget it. As it happens, I'm ineligible to take over as president. To do that I'd have to be on the board, which requires that I be a shareholder. Eve Cosmetics is a closed corporation. Only family members can own stock. So you don't have to be concerned about my nose being out of joint, Sara."

"Good. That's a relief. To tell you the truth, I was worried about causing hard feelings."

He tipped his head back and chuckled, a warm, masculine sound full of wicked amusement that simultaneously made Sara's toes curl and filled her with apprehension. "Oh, there'll be hard feelings, all right. You can count on it."

"What does that mean?"

"It means . . ." He straightened away from the piano and strolled toward her, his vivid eyes dancing. "You haven't met the family yet."

Chapter Ten

Paul Ketchum stomped on the brake and the Cadillac began to fishtail.

"Son of a bitch!" Amid a spray of gravel and a torrent of scorching language, the car slid to a halt in the drive before the ranch house. He tore out of the vehicle and slammed the door so hard the Caddie was still rocking as he stormed up the veranda steps.

With no regard for the handblown and etched ovals of glass in the center of each, he burst through the double oak doors and flung them shut behind him. The crash and the ominous rattle of glass echoed through the old house.

"What the—" The startled exclamation came from the library to the right of the foyer. It was followed at once by the whir of an electric motor. "Paul, is that you?"

Ignoring his father's shout, Paul stomped down the wide central hallway to the den at the back of the house and went straight to the bar.

"Boy! Did you hear me? What the devil was all that racket about?"

"Aw, hell," Paul muttered.

The electric whir grew louder. Paul tossed back a healthy slug of whiskey and water and turned in time to watch Will Ketchum guide his wheelchair through the doorway.

The old man brought the chair to a halt in the middle of the floor. The stroke he had suffered the year before had taken a terrible toll. Will was shriveled to the point of emaciation, his body so wasted his skin seemed to hang on his big-boned frame. The left side of his face drooped grotesquely and his speech was still slurred. A year ago he had been a robust, blustery man of seventy who had looked ten years younger. Now he looked ten years older.

There was nothing weak or decrepit, however, in those piercing gray eyes. They drilled into Paul like lasers. "Well?"

Paul scowled and took another drink. He gave a raspy exhale and wiped his mouth with the back of his hand. "Well what?"

"You listen to me, boy. Don't go giving me any of your lip. I may be half paralyzed, but I can still whip the tar outta you if I have to. Now, I want to know what's wrong."

"What's wrong?" Paul gave a bark of mirthless laughter and made a sweeping gesture with his hand. Whiskey sloshed over the rim of his glass and dripped onto the carpet, but he ignored it. "I've had one helluva bitchin' day, that's what's wrong! Business is shitty. My life is shitty. The whole goddamned world is shitty. Hell, take your pick."

"Business?" Will growled, zeroing in on the only part of the tirade that mattered to him. His bushy eyebrows beetled, and he leaned forward in the wheelchair. "Something's wrong at the company?

Why the devil didn't you say so right off? It's that down dip well in the Hollister field, isn't it?"

Paul gave his father a sharp look and clenched his jaw. "Yeah, that's it," he muttered. He looked away and rubbed the back of his neck with his free hand. He thought of the chilling phone call he'd received earlier and felt his stomach roil. Compared to that, his problem with the frigging well didn't amount to shit, but it was as good an excuse as any to give the old man.

"The damned water cut on well fourteen is going sky high. We'll soon be pumping more saltwater than oil."

"Mmm. That bad, eh. The other partners in the field are going to want to sink an infill well soon to boost production."

"They already do. I got a call from Smithson today. Ketchum Oil's got sixty days to decide if we're going to kick in or go non consent."

"Do we have the money to go our share of the drilling?"

"Hell no. Shit, Dad, you know what things have been like in the oil patch for the last ten or twelve years. We've barely managed to hold on by our fingernails."

"What about the dividends from that Eve stock Joe left to Ketchum Oil? That should have given us some cushion."

"Yeah, well forget it. With the drop in production, we're barely making payroll."

The old man scowled and fell into a brooding silence.

Paul tossed back the last of his drink and poured another. He swirled the amber liquid in the glass and stared at it, his thoughts returning to that phone call and Bruno Scagliala's veiled threats. He had to come up with the money fast. At least with enough to satisfy the bookie for a while. He couldn't keep stalling him. But how could he get his hands on that much? How, damn it?

"If we had control of Eve, we wouldn't have this problem."

The grumbled complaint interrupted Paul's line of thought, and his jaw clenched. Goddamned old coot. When he got started on something, he was like a dog with a bone; he never let go. Paul cast his father an annoyed glance and snorted. "Oh, yeah, sure. Dream on."

"Damn it!" Will roared, slamming his good fist down on the arm of the wheelchair. "Ketchum money started that company. A Ketchum should be running it!"

"Fat chance, as long as Evelyn's got the controlling shares."

The complaint was an old familiar refrain that Paul had heard for most of his life. On the surface, Will maintained an amiable relationship with his sister-in-law, but privately he considered Evelyn Delacorte to be nothing but a cheap gold digger who had married his brother for his money. Paul tended to agree. Why else would a beautiful twenty-four-year-old woman marry a man twenty-two years her senior?

From the start, Will had disapproved of the match. He had been even more opposed to Joe backing her in Eve Cosmetics. Will believed that a woman's place was in the kitchen and the bedroom, not the boardroom. Evelyn's subsequent success merely galled him all the more.

Paul shared his father's opinions, but at the moment he had other things on his mind. With an impatient sigh, he turned away and began to prowl the perimeter of the room.

Over the hundred and thirty–odd years of its existence, through succeeding generations of Ketchums, the ranch house had undergone many additions and renovations. The large room the family now referred to as the den had at one time been a wide veranda that stretched across the back of the original Victorian structure. The three outer walls contained a continuous row of windows that still gave it an open feel and provided a panoramic view of the ranch yard, but when Paul finally stopped to look out, all he saw was his own reflection.

Irritated, he swung away and flung himself down onto one of the long leather sofas.

He stretched out on the cushions and propped his head on one of the arms. Resting his drink on his chest, he fixed his sullen stare on the ceiling. What the fuck was he going to do? If he didn't come up with the money soon, Bruno was going to sic his goons on him. The creep hadn't come right out and said so, but the threat had been there. Paul swallowed hard. He could still hear that soft, oily voice coming through the phone.

"You owe me, Mr. Ketchum. You owe me big. I'm a patient man, but I do have my limits. This is a debt of honor. You don't pay up, and I gotta take it personal. Now, you don't want me to do that, do you, Mr. Ketchum?"

"Hey, man. I'm a little short right now, but you

know I'm good for the money," he had protested, but that hadn't cut any ice with Bruno.

"You gamble big, you'd better be prepared to pay. Because if you lose, you will . . . one way or another."

Paul barely stifled a groan. Somehow he had to get that money. He had to.

"There has to be a way to force Evelyn out," Will insisted.

Paul shot his father an annoyed glance. "Oh, for Chrissake, forget it, will ya?" he snapped. "The only way that bitch will step down is if she's critically ill or dead."

The words hung in the air, charging the silence.

Slowly, Paul rolled his head on the sofa arm and his gaze locked with his father's.

Across the patio, in the ranch office situated in the right wing of the house, Chad Ketchum stared at the computer screen, his jaw tight. His callused fingers tapped the keyboard, feeding in new instructions. The information on the spreadsheet reconfigured, but it made no difference. The column of figures totaled out the same.

"Damn it to hell." Spitting the words out between clenched teeth, Chad shot to his feet and sent the wooden desk chair careening backward on its wobbly casters. It crashed into the wall, but Chad paid no attention. He prowled the office, cursing under his breath.

They were in the red again. For the third straight month the ranch had lost money.

Chad raked a hand through his sandy hair, all the way down the back of his head, massaging the tight muscles in his nape. He had thought—hoped, anyway—that the money from the shares his father had willed to the ranch would carry them, but it didn't come close to matching what Joe had been pouring into the operation year after year.

Of course, dividends were down right now, Chad thought sourly. Thanks to his stepmother's pet projects. Most of the profits from Eve were being poured right back into those damned beauty spas she was building.

Eden East and Eden West. Chad snorted. Nothing but playgrounds for the idle rich.

His family had been wealthy since his great-great-grandfather had started the Ketchum Cattle Company after the Civil War, and his grandfather had added to their fortune when he'd struck oil on the ranch in the early boom days at the beginning of the century. But no one in his family had ever been idle. Ketchums worked. Even his cousin Paul, Chad's least favorite relative, put in long hours at Ketchum Oil.

God, how it galled him to think of all the money Evelyn was wasting on that foolishness, when the ranch, an operation built on the honest labor and sweat of generations of Ketchums, was floundering. It wasn't right, damn it!

He was going to have to delay repairing the barn and repainting the board fence along the highway. And buying a new pickup was out of the question. Even with those cutbacks he was going to have to kick in some of his personal funds to make ends meet this month.

Man, how he hated doing that. Technically, Ketchum Cattle Company belonged to every mem-

ber of the family. The others were willing to share in
the profits—when there were any—but no one, with
the exception of Evelyn, was willing to kick in their
share to cover losses. Their answer was always to sell
off some of the land.

What he'd like to do, what he fully intended *to* do
someday, was build the ranch back up to what it had
been in its golden years.

Chad's eyes glittered and his mind filled with a
vision. He would restock the place with prime cattle,
build new fences and barns, buy new equipment, hire
back all the hands he'd had to let go. And most of all,
he'd buy back the land he'd been forced to sell.
Someday . . . someday, by God, Ketchum Cattle
Company was going to be what it had once been—a
cattle kingdom a man could be proud of.

To do that, though, he needed money. Lots of
money.

He cursed again and made another circuit of the
room, his scarred and dusty cowboy boots thumping
like hammer blows on the wooden floor.

The telephone shrilled, jarring him out of his day-
dream. He snatched up the receiver. "Yeah."

"Chad?" Soft and hesitant, the female voice quivered with uncertainty. "I . . . I was wondering . . . that
is . . . could I see you tonight?"

Chad remained silent, his gaze fixed on the framed
photograph of his father's prize bull which hung over
the battered old rolltop desk.

"Ch-Chad?"

Swiveling around, he stared at the modern work
station in the opposite corner. The sleekly designed
unit housing the computer and printer looked out of
place in the old ranch office, an anomaly in a room

where steer horns, barbed wire samples, rattlesnake skins, and branding irons decorated the rough cedar walls, and most of the furniture was upholstered in cowhide.

The damning amber figures glowed on the computer screen, taunting him. Chad's jaw tightened.

"Sure. Why not. Where are you now?"

"I . . . I'm calling from the phone booth in front of Skeeter's."

Chad's mouth flattened. Skeeter's was the local poolhall and bar just outside of Hobart, the nearest town to the ranch.

"Don't be angry, darling," she rushed on, sensing his displeasure. "I know I shouldn't have come without calling first, but . . . I . . . I wanted to see you so much. Oh, please, Chad . . . don't send me back to Houston."

He remained silent for several more seconds. On the other end of the line her anxiety was almost palpable. "All right," he said finally. "Meet me at the usual place in twenty minutes."

The foreman's cabin sat tucked among a stand of oak trees a mile and a half from the ranch house. It had been unoccupied for the past ten years, since the decline in the beef market had forced stringent economy measures. A ranch operating with a skeleton crew didn't require a foreman.

She waited for him, her nerves taut, almost sick with anticipation and a nagging fear that he had changed his mind.

Chad was late. Again. At times she wondered if his

habitual tardiness was deliberate, a way of keeping her in her place.

As always, she had driven in the back way, down the narrow ranch road that wound around the gently undulating hills. She had hidden her car in the small tractor barn behind the bungalow and let herself in with her own key.

It was hot in the cabin. The air smelled like the inside of a vacuum cleaner. She had switched on the window air conditioning unit and it rumbled nosily, sending out a stream of musty, frigid air. After stashing a sixpack of Chad's favorite beer in the refrigerator, there had been nothing left to do but wait.

At the sound of his pickup crunching to a halt outside, she stopped pacing and stood in the middle of the small living room, her hands clasped, her gaze on the front door.

The minute he stepped inside, she knew he was in a rotten mood.

In almost one continuous motion, he tossed his Stetson onto the rack of deer horns beside the door, stalked across the room, and jerked her into his arms. His kiss was hard and demanding, almost punishing. She moaned and clung to him.

When at last he raised his head he grabbed her wrist. "C'mon. Let's go to bed."

"A-all right," she gasped, but before she could get the words out, he had already towed her along with him into the bedroom.

He released her and tugged his shirt free of his jeans. "Take your clothes off," he commanded, popping open the gripper snaps down the front of the western shirt.

Nodding, she stepped out of her high heels and

began to do as he ordered, all the while watching him.

He treated her abominably. He never called her. He never sought her out. She had to do all the running. There were times when she wondered if he even remembered that she was alive. It was humiliating. Yet she couldn't stay away from him.

Nor could she take her eyes off him. She had seen him naked hundreds of times, but as she watched him snatch off his clothes, her heart began to pound like a wild thing in her breast.

Oh, God, he's so handsome, she thought. So beautifully made. He had powerful, broad shoulders and the lean, hard-muscled body of a man who spent his life in hard labor. His belly was flat, his arms and legs roped with muscles and dusted with golden hair that was a shade lighter than the thick mane which he wore clipped short and brushed off his face. He had the fair coloring of a blond, but his upper body, except for the strip across his forehead that his hat shielded, was tanned to a dark nut-brown. The gray eyes, so common to the Ketchums, were deep set and piercing. At thirty-six, Chad's face was already weatherbeaten, etched with squint lines around the eyes and deep creases in his lean cheeks. He was rugged and virile, and merely looking at him made her mouth go dry.

Hooking his thumbs beneath his jeans and the elastic waistband on his jockey shorts, Chad shoved them down, and as he bent over to snatch the garments off his feet, the muscles in his thighs and buttocks flexed and rippled. She gasped and snatched off the remainder of her clothes.

Fully aroused and naked, he walked to her and

tumbled her onto the bed, coming down on top of her. Dust billowed around them, but neither noticed. His lips clamped over her mouth and he plunged his tongue inside. He squeezed one of her breasts and rubbed the nipple with his thumb until it peaked. Then he explored her hips, her thighs, her belly, his touch rough and hurried. She moaned and arched against him, loving the feel of his callused hands on her body, and when he thrust his hand between her legs, she opened to him.

Breaking off the kiss, Chad buried his face against the side of her neck. He slid his hands beneath her hips, lifted them, and entered her with a single powerful thrust.

Crying out, she clutched his back and wrapped her legs around him. He smelled of horses and leather, sweat and tobacco. And male. She inhaled the scents deep into her lungs as she took his body into hers, her head lolling back on the pillow, her eyes half closed and glazed with passion.

Chad. Chad. She lived for these moments in his arms. He was an addiction, a craving in her blood stronger than any narcotic.

His body pounded hers, and she met each hard thrust eagerly, her nails gouging into his back and buttocks. Moans and grunts of pleasure issued from their throats. The mattress rocked and bounced. The rusty bedsprings squeaked, faster and faster, until their harsh cries rang out.

Then all was still, and there was only the sound of their breathing.

Sometime later, they lay together on the dusty bed in boneless lassitude. Chad smoked a cigarette and gazed at the ceiling, his thoughts already far from the woman who snuggled against his side with her head nestled on his shoulder.

She would have been crushed to know how right her earlier musings about him had been. They had been lovers for over four years, but he rarely gave her a thought. That he was being cruel and thoughtless never occurred to him. It wasn't deliberate. Chad was simply a man with but one focus, one true interest in life, and that was the Ketchum ranch. Everything and everyone else was incidental, and therefore rarely captured his attention but for brief spans.

Chad's intensity was a basic facet of his nature. His tendency to zero in on a thing extended to whatever activity he undertook. Whether he was rounding up strays or branding calves or stringing fence wire, his concentration was total. He had been known to become so engrossed in a task that he forgot to eat all day. When he finally returned to the ranch house and the smell of food reminded him that his belly was empty, he fell upon the meal with ravenous appetite.

The same was true of other needs—including sex. He could go for days, even weeks, without giving it a thought until some outside stimuli reminded him that his body required sexual gratification. As had happened earlier, that usually came in the form of a phone call from the woman at his side, and at those times he made love to her with the same fierce absorption he gave to every activity. When it was over, for him, it was over, and his thoughts switched automatically back to his one all consuming passion: the ranch.

That she needed and deserved more simply never occurred to him. And it didn't occur to him now.

"I want you to do something for me," he announced out of the blue.

She stirred. "Mmm. All right. You know I'll do anything for you, darling," she mumbled.

"Good. I want you to do some snooping around for me at Eve."

Alice Burke jerked up and stared at him, the expression on her plain face appalled. "Oh, Chad."

Chapter Eleven

The arrival of Madelene Ketchum created a stir among the patrons at Jardines. The upscale little Hollywood restaurant was noted for its dignified atmosphere, but not even its well-heeled, high-placed clientele was immune to a little celebrity dazzle.

Madelene swept through the elegant dining room in true star fashion amid a dramatic flutter of silk and masses of flowing blond hair, trailing a cloud of expensive perfume. With a self-possessed smile on her lips, she held her head high and pretended not to hear the gasps and excited whispers, but Lawrence Tremaine knew better.

Maddie loved attention. She thrived on it. It was as necessary to her as the air she breathed. With every step her mood grew more buoyant and smug. By the time they reached their secluded table in the back corner, she was almost preening.

The maître d' performed his duties with flattering attentiveness, expressing his delight at her presence in their establishment in the most obsequious manner. He hovered as long as decorum allowed, then hurried off with an air of self-importance to see if their dinner companions had arrived.

"You know, darling, you were right," Maddie said, the moment the man had gone, flashing Lawrence her famous smile. "Meeting Morris and Stan here was a good idea. This really is a lovely place. It's chic enough to impress, yet quiet enough to have a private conversation."

"I'm glad you like it, darling." He patted her hand, his smile indulgent, knowing that the reactions of the maître d' and the other patrons, not the ambience, had caused his wife's sudden about-face.

Maddie had wanted to conduct the business dinner at Chasen's or Spago or one of the other "in" places where people in the movie industry went to be seen and get their names in the papers. It had angered her when he had scotched the idea, but he had known that in one of the trendy places Madelene would have been just one of many famous faces. Whereas in a lesser-known but upscale little spot like Jardine's she would cause a sensation.

He was glad that his strategy had worked.

It was important that tonight Maddie's star power appear phenomenal. If they were going to interest the head of Epic Studios and Hollywood's hottest producer in their project, they had to first impress them, show them that Madelene Ketchum was still a box-office draw.

It wasn't going to be easy. Her last movie had been released over two years ago. It had been a disaster, as had the two before that. In Hollywood, three flops in a row was the kiss of death.

Lately Maddie had been getting fewer and fewer offers, and the scripts that were being sent to her were atrocities, vehicles in which, a mere five years ago, no one in town would have dared to suggest that Madelene Ketchum star. The plum parts, the ones she wanted, the ones she would kill for, were going to younger actresses.

"Madelene! Sweetheart! How divine to see you!"

They looked up to see Morris Fleishman, head of Epic Studios, and Stanley Tarlick, owner of Nova Productions, approaching, drinks in hand. Lawrence experienced a spurt of pleasure when he realized that they had been waiting in the bar and had undoubtedly witnessed Maddie's entrance.

"Morris! Stanley!" Madelene jumped up and rushed to greet the men with open arms.

"My dear, you look simply marvelous. Doesn't she look marvelous, Stan?"

"Absolutely devastating," Stan concurred, kissing Madelene's hand. "But then, angel, you always do."

"Thank you, darlings," she simpered. "I love you, too."

Lawrence held back and watched the exchange, revolted by their phoniness. Yet he was conscious of an underlying exhilaration, of feeling incredibly lucky to be rubbing elbows with these artistic people.

Even after three years of marriage, he was still amazed that he, Lawrence Wentworth Tremaine, a conservative, uninteresting—some might even say downright dull—tax attorney, had managed to win a gorgeous, wildly exciting and talented woman like Madelene Ketchum. He couldn't believe his luck.

Like many creative people, Maddie wasn't always easy to live with; she was subject to wild mood swings and temper tantrums, and she was obsessive about her career and absurdly vain. None of that mattered to Lawrence. He admired her intelligence and her devotion to her craft, her enormous talent, which he felt was often obscured by her sexy image.

Throughout the meal Lawrence sat back and watched his wife dazzle the two men. She was irresistible—sparkling, witty, charmingly flirtatious . . . and so beautiful it made his chest hurt just to look at her. On the surface she exuded sophistication and confidence, but he knew that inside she was a jittery mass of nerves.

Tenderness welled up inside him. Yes, he thought, she was selfish and self-centered, but even that he found forgivable—in a way, even oddly endearing. Maddie reminded him of a narcissistic teenager— willful, difficult at times, but pathetically vulnerable and easily hurt. That emotional immaturity roused his protective instincts. Maddie was forty-one to his thirty-three, but he felt decades older than her.

He adored her. Making Maddie happy was his top priority.

It bothered him that she had been married so many times, and that she seemed to have discarded those previous loves with the ease that other people tossed aside a used tissue. The thought of her doing the same to him made him physically ill. No, he vowed, watching her flash her incomparable smile. He would not let that happen. Whatever it took to bind Maddie to him, whatever he had to do to hold her, he would. He was her fifth husband, but he was determined to be her last.

Throughout the meal they made small talk and joked about the latest gossip making the rounds of the backlots, the parties they had attended, who was filming what where. Mostly, Lawrence sat back and listened. He was smooth and polished, adept in the social graces—he was, after all, one of the Philadelphia Tremaines, grandson of Judge Winston Tremaine—but he was a quiet man, reserved by nature.

Deciphering dry facts and figures and manipulating convoluted tax regulations to his clients' advantage—that was his forte. Lawrence wisely left it to Maddie to entertain and beguile their guests.

After dinner, when the dishes had been cleared and the coffee served, the atmosphere around the table underwent a subtle change, as though the waiter's departure had somehow signaled the start of business.

"Well, now." Morris turned to Madelene with an ingratiating smile. "I understand that you have the movie rights to *Night Song.*"

Lawrence looked from the studio head to Maddie. He knew that the question had jerked her nerves tighter, but he was filled with pride at the way she handled herself.

"Yes, I do. As soon as I read the book I knew it would make a blockbuster film and I was determined to be a part of it. I contacted the publisher right away and took an option on the story. Lawrence and I had the deal sewn up long before the book climbed to the top of the bestseller list."

"Mmm. That was very astute of you, Madelene. Very astute, indeed." Morris cast a sideways glance at Stan, and Lawrence wondered what kind of discussions the two had had about the project. "Have you turned it into a screenplay yet?"

"Well . . . no. I—"

"What Maddie would like to do is turn the book over to a studio for development," Lawrence interjected. "She purchased the rights merely as insurance that she would star in the film."

The two moguls exchanged another look. "Star? You mean, play the part of Helen?"

"Yes," Madelene answered instantly. "That is exactly what I mean."

Stan cleared his throat and stared at the pattern he was drawing in the tablecloth with the handle of his spoon.

Sighing, Morris slumped back in his chair. He was a bald, rotund little man with a cherub face and the soul of a tyrant. Morris had the Midas touch. Since he had taken over, Epic Studios had consistently produced one runaway hit after another. In a town where power was everything, his was absolute. And he enjoyed using it.

Above the round, ruddy cheeks, his blue eyes fixed on Madelene without a trace of their former friendliness.

"I'll be truthful with you, my dear. Epic Studios wants this project. We want it bad. Hell, I get a hard-on just thinking about it. Handled right, *Night Song* could be the single most important movie of this decade."

A triumphant look began to light Maddie's face, but it faltered when Morris held up his pudgy hand.

"Which means . . . as much as it pains me to say so, we do not feel it would be in the best interests of the film to cast you in the lead."

"What? Now, see here. If you think—"

"Please. Hear me out. Naturally, we're sensitive to the fact that it is your property and we know how much making the film means to you. We have no wish to cut you out, sweetheart. C'mon, Maddie.

Would we do that to you? In fact, we're prepared to offer you the role of Victoria."

"Victoria? The mother? You want me to play the *mother?"* Madelene shrieked."

Lawrence winced. Oh, shit. Now Morris had really done it.

"Madelene, sweetheart. Don't get excited," Stan urged. "It's a terrific part. And you're perfect for it."

"Perfect. *Perfect!* The woman's in her forties, for Chrissake!"

"So are you," Morris said with deadly calm.

Madelene sucked in her breath. "You son of a bitch."

Hurting for her, Lawrence kept a close eye on his wife, noting with alarm the white line around her lips and the bright spots of color on her cheekbones.

"Now, now, sweetheart, you're looking at this all wrong. Taking the part of Victoria could be the smartest move you ever made. Why, just look at Sophia Loren. She played the mother in *Two Women,* and the role did wonders for her career. Hell, she got the fucking Oscar for her performance."

Stan could have saved his breath. Maddie was still engaged in a silent battle with Morris. She glared at him, those famous gray eyes spitting fire and venom. She was so furious she was shaking.

Morris's expression remained bland. "Come now, Madelene. You didn't *really* expect to play the part of a twenty-year-old, did you?"

Her mouth quivered with rage. "That part is mine. *Mine,* do you hear me?" she insisted, jabbing her chest with a long, crimson fingernail. "It was tailor-made for me."

"Twenty years ago, yes. Even ten years ago you

could have pulled it off. But not today." He remained implacable for a moment, then his expression softened and he reached out and patted her hand. "I like you, Madelene. I really do. I think you're a beautiful and extremely talented actress—one of the best. But sweetheart, this part isn't for you. Do yourself a favor—take the part of Victoria."

"Read my lips, Morris. Fuck off. I do *not* play mothers," she enunciated each word in a tight voice, spitting them out through clenched teeth.

"Aw, c'mon, Madelene. Don't be that way." Stan looked at Lawrence. "Can't we work this out? You're a smart guy, Larry. You must know Morris is right. Talk to her."

"I'm sorry, gentlemen. Maddie has my full support in this."

Privately, Lawrence agreed with Morris and Stan. Though still beautiful, and certainly talented, Maddie was forty-one.

That she was too old for the part, however, was something she refused to accept. Just as she could not accept that there were and always would be younger and hotter stars looming on the horizon—charismatic and talented young women like Julia Roberts, Michelle Pfeiffer, Andie MacDowell, and Jodie Foster. The mere suggestion that perhaps she should not try to compete with women a decade or more younger than she threw Maddie into a rage—one that he knew was fueled by growing panic.

Night Song was a strong story with several juicy roles that could easily garner Academy Awards. Maddie wanted the lead desperately. She was counting on the role to revive her career. Whether or not she was right for it was not the issue. Not for Maddie—and therefore, not for Lawrence.

"I'm sorry, Morris. But those are our terms. If you refuse them, then I'm afraid we'll have to take the project elsewhere."

"You're welcome to try, but you'll find it won't do you any good," Morris replied without a speck of concern. "You see, it all boils down to economics. You, of all people, should realize that, Lawrence. These are hard times. No studio is going to risk the kind of money it will take to make this film—not with Madelene in the lead. Even if we rewrote the script and made Helen older, Madelene is no longer enough of a surefire draw to bank on."

"Of course . . . if you and Madelene were willing to put up a large chunk of the production cost yourself, we might be able to work something out."

Lawrence shot Stan a sharp look. He had made the suggestion with just the right degree of spontaneity, as though the thought had only just occurred to him, but Lawrence didn't think so. He had the feeling that the two men had just gone to plan B.

"Are you kidding?" Madelene exclaimed. "You're talking millions. I don't have that kind of money just lying around."

"Surely you can raise it. After all, you are a shareholder in Eve Cosmetics."

"Well, yes . . . but I don't have that many shares. Only about four percent."

"Still, that stock has got to be worth a bundle."

"What you're suggesting is quite impos—"

"No! No, darling, Morris is right." Madelene shot Lawrence a desperate glance. She switched her attention back to the studio head and smiled confidently.

"It'll take a while, but we can raise what we need. I'm sure of it. We'll look into it right away and get back to you."

The instant the Rolls came to a stop under the front portico of Madelene's Beverly Hills mansion she stormed out in a huff and rushed up the steps. Lawrence followed right on her heels and slammed the door.

"Damn it, Maddie, will you listen to me? You know as well as I do that it won't work."

"Then you'll just have to make it work, won't you?" Maddie snapped over her shoulder, and stomped into the living room. She flung her gold evening purse into a chair and whirled back. "Do whatever you have to. Just get me the goddamned money."

"Maddie, be reasonable. You cannot sell your shares in Eve. It's all spelled out in the articles of incorporation. All right . . . you could sell them to another shareholder, but at the moment, no one else in the family is in a position to buy them except Evelyn."

"Then sell the damned shares to Evelyn!"

"C'mon, sweetheart. Be reasonable. You know that she won't go for that. Your stepmother insists that all of you hold onto your stock for security. And she's right. Those shares provide the only steady income you have."

Madelene gave an inelegant snort. "Some income. The dividends are so low right now they barely cover the taxes and upkeep on this place."

"The amount is a bit more than that, but even so,

that will change when the spas are completed. In a few years, once all the construction loans are paid off, they'll show a tremendous profit."

"A few *years!* I can't wait a few years! And that's another thing. You're suppose to be looking out for my interests. That's why you have a seat on the board of directors. Why did you ever allow her to cut dividends and push this ridiculous expansion through in the first place?"

"Ah, hell, Maddie." Lawrence propped his fists on his hips and looked up at the ceiling, expelling a long-suffering sigh. "Just how was I suppose to stop it? Evelyn will listen to the opinions of others. Sometimes she'll even take advice if she thinks it's sound, but basically she does exactly as she damned well pleases with that company. And she has the clout to back it up."

In a softer, more persuasive voice, he added, "Ah, look, sweetheart. Even if you could sell, I'd have to advise against it. It just wouldn't be wise. You'd have to unload all your stock to raise the kind of money Morris is talking about, and I'm not even sure that would be enough. If you did that and the movie bombed, you'd have nothing to fall back on."

"I don't *care!* I want that part, Lawrence! I've *got* to have it!" Shaking, her fists balled at her side, she glared at him, her beautiful face twisted into an ugly mask of fury.

Lawrence knew the exact moment she decided to try another strategy. One second those magnificent Ketchum gray eyes were spitting fire at him, the next they narrowed slightly and took on a calculating gleam.

As he watched, she tamped down her fury and

relaxed her facial muscles. "I'm sorry, darling," she crooned in a husky voice. "I shouldn't yell at you like a shrew. You know I didn't mean it." A small, sultry smile curved her mouth and her eyelids drooped to half mask. She started for him with a sultry slink and that seductive "come-hither" expression that had bewitched hapless males from the silver screen for years.

"Now, Maddie," Lawrence chided, backing up a step. "Behave yourself." He knew what she was up to, but even while his brain told him to stop her, his body tautened and his breathing grew erratic.

Maddie's smile grew bolder. "Darling, you know I can't do that around you. You bring out the wild woman in me. And besides, you don't really want me to behave." Reaching him, she ran her scarlet fingernails up the front of his shirt, toying with the buttons and lightly scouring his skin through the thin silk as she looked up at him through her lashes. "Now, do you, darling?"

She undid a button, slipped one finger inside his shirt, and raked her fingernail through his chest hair. Lawrence gasped and flinched. He grabbed her wrists, but her clever fingers had already freed three more buttons. Giving a throaty chuckle, she nuzzled the shirt open and pressed her face against his chest. Her swirling tongue expertly homed in on a tiny nipple and flicked mercilessly.

"Maddie, this . . . this won't accomplish anyth— Ahh, sweet heaven . . ."

"You know how much this part means to me, darling," she murmured, trailing her hot mouth over his chest. "I'm counting on you to help me. You *will* help me, won't you, sweetheart? Mmm?" She gave his nipple a savage little nip, and smiled when Lawrence groaned and stiffened. Pulling her hands from his lax grip, she went to work on his belt while running her tongue down his sternum.

"Ma-Maddie . . . sweetheart . . . y-you know I . . . will do all . . . all I ca-can, but—Ahh, Jesus!"

She spread his trousers and slid the backs of her knuckles down his rock-hard cock, straining beneath the cotton knit jockey shorts. "You'll find a way, darling. You're so smart, I know you will. And you know how hot it makes me when you use that clever brain of yours." She slid her hands around him and grasped his buttocks, kneading the taut flesh, flexing her long fingers like a cat, while she rubbed her pelvis against his erection in a slow, circular motion. "Don't you, Lawrence? If you'll just do this one thing for me, I promise . . . ." She stretched up on tiptoe and blew into his ear. "I'll make you a very happy man."

"Maddie . . . sweetheart . . ."

She plunged her hands beneath his jockey shorts and shoved them and his trousers downward. His engorged cock sprang free, quivering and erect, straining. Maddie dropped to her knees before him, her smile feline as she watched a pearly drop of fluid form on the tip of the swollen head. Cupping him with both hands, she leaned forward and delicately lifted the drop with the tip of her tongue. Lawrence's knees nearly buckled, but before he even finished sucking in his breath, she lightly raked his scrotum with her thumbnail. He jerked and groaned.

Somewhere in that minute part of his mind that was still functioning a voice told him to stop her, but instead he grasped her shoulders and waited—trembling, aching.

Maddie mouthed her way up the side of his throbbing shaft. "You will get the money for me, won't you, Lawrence?" She kissed the tip—softly . . . oh, so softly.

Lawrence shuddered and moaned and clutched her shoulders tighter.

"You'll find a way, somehow. Won't you, darling?" She lapped delicately at the staining, rosy head, then blew on the wet skin. "Promise me. Please."

Lawrence made a low sound in his throat and thrust his pelvis forward, but she rocked back on her heels just out of reach, denying his silent plea. Smiling, she wrapped her hand around his cock and worked it up and down. At the same time she rubbed her open mouth back and forth across the tip. "Say you'll do it, Lawrence," she whispered against his yearning flesh. "Promise me you'll do whatever you have to do to get the money."

Tipping his head back, Lawrence squeezed his eyes shut and expelled a hissing breath, his face dark and twisted with exquisite agony. "All right. Yes. Yes! I'll do it!"

Maddie smiled and took him into her mouth.

Chapter Twelve

Eric had something on his mind. Kitty could always tell. The more worried he was about something, the harder he strove to appear lighthearted. Of course, he was by nature an upbeat, easygoing person. That was one of the things she adored most about her cousin. Tonight, however, his gaiety and teasing seemed forced.

Kitty wasn't worried. Whatever was bothering Eric, he would tell her in his own time. He always did. They had been confiding in each other ever since they could talk.

Listening with only half her mind to his recounting of an amusing incident, Kitty gazed warmly at her cousin's profile. Dear Eric. It was so wonderful to see him. He didn't get to New York on business nearly often enough to suit her.

Eric was, and always had been, her best friend. In many ways they were closer than brother and sister. And why not; they were the same age and they had grown up together in the same house. We even look alike, she thought, with a rueful but accepting sigh.

Her sister Madelene had inherited her stunning

looks and talent from their actress mother, Claire Chadwick, but as luck would have it, Kitty, like Eric, favored the Ketchums. They were both tall and lanky, though at six-feet-one, he topped her by four inches, and regular workouts had added considerable brawn to his broad shoulders. They shared the same light, almost-but-not-quite blond hair, the same strong jaw and straight nose, the same gray eyes. In Eric, the combination had resulted in dashing—if somewhat devilish—masculine beauty, but those same features in their feminine version had given Kitty merely a wholesome attractiveness.

". . . ask you, how was I suppose to know?" Eric demanded.

Kitty giggled. "You're terrible! You actually ask her to go away with you for the weekend—right there in front of her husband?"

"I told you—I thought he was her grandfather. The old geezer was eighty-five if he was a day, for Pete's sake. And deaf as a stone." Eric grimaced and rolled his eyes. "How the hell was I supposed to know he read lips?"

"Huh. Serves you right for being such a skirt chaser."

Eric grinned. "It's a dirty job, but somebody's gotta do it."

Squeezing his arm tighter, Kitty pressed her cheek against his shoulder, and giggled again.

It was almost midnight. Parked cars lined the quiet side street. A taxi cruised by, but otherwise, they appeared to be the only people on the block. It was strange how safe she felt with Eric. Normally she wouldn't dream of walking the streets of New York at that hour, but she wasn't in the least worried or fearful. Deep inside she knew that Eric would protect her—just as he always had.

Arm in arm, they strolled down the dark sidewalk, talking and laughing. When they reached her apartment building and started up the steps, Kitty dug into her purse for her key.

"Are you sure your boyfriend won't object to me coming up?"

"Don't be silly. Of course he won't. Anyway, Miles probably isn't even home yet. After the play, he and others in the cast are so wired they usually go out for a drink to unwind."

"Without you?"

Kitty heard the irritation in his voice. Leading the way up the stairs, she glanced over her shoulder and smiled. "There's no need to get defensive on my account. Actually, I usually go with them. I begged off tonight so I could have dinner with my favorite cousin."

Not that any of them would miss her. Everyone else in the little clique was an actor. She was just a backstage gofer, someone who painted sets and mended costumes and helped with makeup and dressing. The others only tolerated her presence because she and Miles were living together. Darla Holt was probably delighted that she had begged off, Kitty thought. The little brunette had a thing for Miles and was no doubt at that very moment making the most of Kitty's absence.

She fought back the surge of jealousy. She hated it, hated feeling insecure. Gritting her teeth, Kitty unlocked her door. She stepped aside and smiled at Eric. "Come on. I'll make us some cocoa and we can talk some more." And you can tell me what's bothering you, she added silently.

A man bounded off the sofa the minute they stepped inside the spacious loft. "Where the hell have you been?"

"Miles! What are you doing here? I thought you'd still be with the others."

"Obviously I'm not. And I repeat—where have you been?"

"Why . . . I went out to dinner with Eric. I told you—"

"It doesn't take four hours to eat dinner."

"Well, no, of course not. But we stopped afterward at a little club to hear some R&B. Eric likes it, too, and since you don't—"

"Never mind that. I need to talk to you."

"Look, maybe I'd better go." Eric started backing away toward the door.

"That would be my choice."

"*Miles!*" Kitty turned to her cousin. "Please stay. He didn't mean that. Really."

"Yeah, well . . . it's getting late. And I have a meeting with a Macy's exec in the morning before I leave."

"But we were going to talk."

He smiled and tweaked the end of her nose. "Hey. No big deal. Don't worry about it, Kitty Cat. It'll keep till next time." He kissed her cheek, waved so long to Miles, and left before she could protest further.

The instant the door closed behind him, Kitty whirled on Miles. "How *could* you? That was insufferably rude." Tears rushed to her eyes and her voice shook with suppressed emotions. She was furious with Miles and terrified of showing it for fear she would lose him.

As always, he sidestepped her complaint by attacking.

"I am the one you're supposed to love, remember?" he shouted in his precise English accent, thumping his chest dramatically. "I am the man to whom you are supposed to give your support! Yet when I have a crisis, are you here for me? No. You're out with your precious Eric. What is it you Yanks call these sort of kinships? Kissing cousins? Sounds bloody incestuous, if you ask me."

Kitty sucked in her breath. "That's a rotten thing to say."

"Oh, really. You want to hear rotten? I'll tell you what's rotten. While you were out gallavanting with your precious cousin, *I* was losing my job."

"What?"

"The play closed." His shoulders slumped. He sniffed and looked away, and his voice dropped to a defeated murmur. "We got the word at the end of tonight's performance."

"Oh, Miles. How awful!" She rushed to him and slipped her arms around his waist, her anger forgotten. Snuggling her face against his chest, she closed her eyes and hugged him tight. "I'm so sorry, darling. Really. I know how hard you worked and how much the play meant to you. But don't worry. Something else will come along. You'll see. It's not the end of the world."

"Oh, sure. That's easy for you to say. You're a Ketchum. You don't have to work like us mere mortals. You only took that bloody backstage job so that you could get some experience and get a feel for the theater."

"Darling, please. Don't be that way. I merely meant that you're such a wonderful actor, you're bound to get another part soon. That's all. Honestly."

"Sorry. I shouldn't be taking my anger out on you. I'm feeling a bit rocky at the moment, is all." Gripping her shoulders, he set her away from him.

Kitty watched him walk to the coffee table and pick up a crumpled pack of cigarettes, a sick sensation fluttering in the pit of her stomach. His uncertain temper and rapid mood swings always did this to her. He kept her on edge, off balance, never quite certain where she stood with him.

It had been that way from the first. Miles was a handsome, virile man. Women threw themselves at him all the time. She had been baffled when he began pursuing her—flattered and excited to be sure, but unable to fathom why, out of the many beautiful young women involved in the off-Broadway production, he would want her. She was, at best, pleasantly attractive. She had freckles and straight, fine hair and a figure that, at twenty-eight, showed no signs of ever being anything but coltish.

It had occurred to her that he might have mercenary motives, but she had quickly dismissed that possibility. No one in the cast or production company knew of her background or financial situation. She had told Miles only after he'd moved in with her, and he had been flabbergasted.

He insisted that he loved her, and she wanted to believe him. The trouble was, she didn't feel loved, and his mercurial behavior did nothing to ease her mind. She spent half her time wondering if she was losing him.

He shook out a cigarette, lit it, and took a deep drag. Tossing the match into the ashtray, he blew a stream of smoke toward the ceiling. "I had *better* get another part. And pretty damned quick, or it's all over."

"What do you mean?"

"I *mean,* if I don't find a steady job soon, my green card will be revoked. I will have to return to England."

"How . . . how long do you have?"

"Not long. A few months." He took another pull on his cigarette and looked at her. "This doesn't have to be a problem, you know. Alan Zimmer loves *Dark of the Moon* and wants to put it into production. He's ready to start casting anytime you say."

"Yes. If I can drum up the necessary financing."

"So why the devil don't you just put up the money yourself? That way, as author and principal backer of the play, you'd have the clout to give me the lead role."

"Miles, please. We've been over all this. I don't have that kind of money. If I did, don't you think I'd have produced one of my own plays before now?"

"Oh, come off it, will you? We both know that with your family connections you could get the money if you really wanted to."

"I tell you, I can't!"

Miles stubbed out his cigarette and headed for the door. "Fine. Have it your way." He snatched the door open, then paused with his hand on the knob and glared back at her. "But if you truly want me to stay, you'll raise the money somehow."

"Miles! Where are you going?" she cried, when he swung away.

"Out."

The door slammed. Stricken, Kitty stood in the middle of the cavernous loft and listened to his footsteps clatter down the stairs. After a moment her face crumbled, and she flung herself face down on the sofa and wept.

Whenever Eric was in New York on business he always stayed at Evelyn's Park Avenue apartment. The doorman and all the security people knew him by sight, but when the night guard in the lobby called out a greeting, Eric was so preoccupied he almost walked right past the man without a word.

"Oh. Hi, Joe. Sorry. I guess I was in another world."

"Hey, no sweat." Joe winked. "She musta really been somethin', huh?"

Eric answered with a grin, and the man's sly laughter followed him into the waiting elevator.

The instant the doors closed, the grin faded. Eric leaned back against the oak-paneled wall and gripped the brass rail, his eyes fixed, unseeing, on the lighted floor indicator above the doors. Damn Miles Bentley. He couldn't stand the arrogant bastard. What Kitty saw in him, he'd never know. The creep wasn't half good enough for her.

It had infuriated Eric two months ago when he'd discovered that the actor had moved in with his cousin. The guy was just using her; Eric was sure of it. But try to tell Kitty that. The one time he had, they'd had a whale of a fight.

On the twenty-ninth floor, Eric let himself into the apartment and walked straight through to the bedroom. He sat down on the edge of the bed. Leaning forward, he braced his elbows on his knees and held his head in his hands. He had to talk to someone. Damn it, he had to talk to Kitty. She would understand. Kitty always understood him.

He should have thumbed his nose at the limey bastard and stayed. That's what he should have done.

Eric groaned and rubbed his eyes with the heels of his hands. Christ! What was he going do?

He straightened and withdrew a piece of paper from his inside coat pocket and unfolded it slowly, as though it were something so vile it was contaminated. His hands were shaking so much he could barely read the typed words. Not that it mattered. Since receiving the message two days ago, he'd read it so many times he knew it by heart.

> *Dear Eric,*
>
> *As you can see by the attached photo, I have fond memories of our night together. It was naughty of you to give me a false name. Imagine my surprise when I discovered your true identity. One can only assume that no one knows your little secret.*
>
> *I must say, that is truly amazing. Secrets can be difficult to keep. And costly. Don't you agree? We must get together soon and discuss it.*

There was no signature. There was no need for one. Feeling sick to his stomach, Eric turned the letter over and stared at the damning photograph. There he was, his face etched with passion, entwined naked on a bed . . . with another man.

Chapter Thirteen

The family was not pleased.

That much would have been obvious to the most casual observer who witnessed their arrivals at the Eve Cosmetics complex. The receptionist and the security guard on duty, however, were too well trained to so much as blink at Madelene's tempestuous theatrics as she stomped across the marble lobby, or Monica's whining, or the sizzling curses of the male members of the family. Even sweet-tempered Kitty was in a snit.

Nevertheless, they had come—every one of them. An hour before the appointed time they began arriving from various parts of the country, by car, limousine, plane, and helicopter.

The world headquarters for Eve Cosmetics spread out over forty-two acres along Interstate 10 on the western edge of Houston. The administration building, a fifteen-story modern steel-and-glass structure, stood sentinel over a sprawling complex of research facilities, experimental labs, manufacturing and packaging factories, warehouses, and freight terminals. The complex was the heart of the cosmetics empire that had factories and offices all over the globe.

By twelve o'clock they were in their places—Eric, Kitty, Will, Chad, Paul and Monica, Madelene and Lawrence—gathered around the long oval table in the sumptuous cherry-paneled conference room that looked out over the manicured grounds in front of the building. The only people in the room who were not shareholders were Alice and Rourke. Will's nurse, Mrs. Walters, sat just outside the door.

The instant Evelyn walked in, the family erupted with a barrage of complaints, all talking at once. The cacophony hit her like a wave.

". . . mind telling me what was so damned important?"

"Ketchum Oil doesn't run itself, you know."

". . . had to cancel a manicure to be here."

". . . need to be at the ranch, not—"

"Lawrence and I are in the middle of important negotiations. Tell her, darling."

Calmly, ignoring them all, Evelyn took her seat at the head of the conference table and let the babble wash over her. When she had arranged her notepad and pencil and settled herself to her satisfaction, she glanced at Rourke, who was in his usual place to the right of her chair.

He shrugged and his mouth twitched. Surely you're not surprised, the look in his eyes said.

Evelyn turned a deaf ear to the stream of protests. Finally it dawned on the others that she would not respond as long as they were shouting, and the clamor gradually faded to a grumble, then to sullen silence.

Only then did she look at them. Her unruffled gaze

circled the table, sliding from person to person, the look in her eyes making them squirm like guilty children. She raised one delicately arched brow.

"Are you are all finished? Good," she said, in response to their nods. Folding her hands on top of the table, Evelyn swept them with another look. "I am well aware of how busy you all are, so I shall make this brief. Certain recent events have brought it home to me that it's time I chose a successor."

The statement produced gasps from several quarters and perked up interest around the table. They all sat up straighter, even Will, their attention riveted on Evelyn, their petty complaints forgotten.

"What events?"

Evelyn glanced at her stepdaughter's latest husband and experienced a flicker of impatience. As usual, Lawrence's legal mind had zeroed in on a minute detail. The trait made him an excellent tax attorney and an asset as a board member, but in this instance, Evelyn could have done without his nitpicking.

After giving the matter a lot of thought, she had decided not to reveal her illness until she no longer had a choice. Once the bankers learned she was critically ill, the company was going to be on shaky enough financial ground without giving any of the family ammunition to stir up mischief.

"What happened? Did you have a close call that reminded you of your mortality?"

"Really, Chad!" Madelene shot her brother an annoyed look. "Must you always be so blunt? The important thing is that Evelyn has made a decision that is long overdue. I think it's great."

"Maddie's right. You're doing the wise thing, my

dear." Will nodded in what was meant to be a sage gesture, but the effect was spoiled by his slurred speech and grotesquely drooping features . . . and by the calculating look he exchanged with his oldest son. "None of us knows what's in store for us, so it never hurts to be prepared. Why, just look at me. If I hadn't had Paul here to take over when that damned stroke laid me low, who knows what would have become of Ketchum Oil? Yes, indeed. You're doing the right thing, my dear."

"Thank you, Will," Evelyn said dryly. "I'm glad you approve."

"Have you made your choice?" Chad asked, scowling.

Evelyn almost laughed. Her stepson's expression revealed how torn he was. Chad coveted the power the position would give him, but at the same time, the very thought of being cooped up in an office, running an international company, horrified him.

"Hell, isn't it obvious?" Leaning back in his chair, Paul shot his brother and cousins a cocky smile. "Other than Dad—and his illness disqualifies him—I'm the only one who has any experience running a large company."

Chad bristled. "The hell you say. What do you think Ketchum Cattle Company is? A lemonade stand by the side of the highway?"

"Playing cowboy can't compare to—"

"Will you two stop it?"

The sharp command, coming from Kitty, struck the two men mute. Her eyes snapped back and forth between her brother and cousin, blazing with emotion and suspiciously moist. "You've been bickering and competing with one another all your lives, and I, for one, am sick of it. For pity's sake, you're both grown men. For once, try to act like it."

While the others stared at Kitty with varying degrees of astonishment, Evelyn narrowed her eyes and studied her youngest stepchild. Something was bothering Kitty. That had been apparent from the moment Evelyn had entered the room. The girl was pale and there were dark circles under her eyes; she looked liked she'd been on a three-day crying jag. And she was strung taut as a piano wire. Evelyn made a mental note to talk to her after the meeting.

"You tell 'em, Kitty Cat," Eric drawled. He slid Evelyn a shrewd look. "Anyway, there's no point in bickering. I'm sure Evelyn's already made her choice."

"Yes, I have." She glanced at Rourke, and without a word he rose and left the room.

"What's going on? Where's he going?"

"Just be patient, Paul."

Before Evelyn could say more, Rourke returned with Sara. The resemblance between her and Evelyn was too strong to miss. As Rourke seated her in the chair he had just vacated and took the empty one beside her, the expressions on the faces around the table were almost comically shocked.

The only person in the room other than Evelyn and Rourke who had known of Sara's existence prior to the meeting was Alice. Evelyn had introduced Sara and explained the bare essentials to her secretary the day before, when she'd brought some important papers to the apartment for Evelyn's signature. Alice had been shocked.

"Why, Mrs. Ketchum, I . . . I can't believe it. I mean . . . I had no idea." Her mud-brown eyes had repeatedly darted to Sara, stunned and fascinated by the uncanny resemblance between her boss and the young woman. "A daughter. You have a grown daughter . . . all these years, and you never told me." She had sniffed and assumed a hurt look, letting Evelyn know how deeply wounded she was by that omission.

Then, beaming like a proud godmother, she had turned to Sara and swooped her into a tight embrace. "I'm so happy to meet you, Sara. Oh, this is just wonderful. Just imagine. A daughter." When she'd released Sara, she'd looked at her fondly, and there had been tears in her eyes. "And such a beautiful one, too."

It had been an awkward moment. The look Sara had sent Evelyn had been a condemning reminder that the greeting had been many times warmer than the one she had extended.

"Who is this woman? What's she doing here?" Will leaned forward and peered at Sara, his good hand gripping the arm of the wheelchair, his nose twitching like an animal sensing trouble.

Evelyn's nerves were jumping. This was the moment she'd dreaded most. She hated to tell them. For almost thirty-three years she had kept the awful secret. She had buried it so deep she'd almost forgotten it. Almost. Now the whole world would know about Sara.

Speculation would run rampant. Many—most, probably—would assume she'd had a flaming youthful affair and been abandoned by her lover. The thought was so distasteful Evelyn shuddered. It was like being violated all over again.

Somehow, though, she would bear the whispers

and conjecture and behind-the-hand snickers. There was no other way.

"Wait a minute! I know you!" Madelene burst out before Evelyn could speak. "You're the woman who was at the Academy Awards with Cici Reynolds!"

Sara nodded. "Yes, I am."

"I knew it! I knew it! That's why you look familiar." Madelene's look of triumph faded and she narrowed her eyes, her mouth tightening. "The rumor around town after the awards was that you were the one responsible for her new look. Is that true?"

"Yes. I am—was—an image consultant."

"Then you're the one to blame for me losing the part of Emma in *The Collingswood Affair*," Maddie spat, bristling. "Cici would never have gotten that part if you hadn't cleaned her up and coached her to act like a lady."

"For Pete's sake, Madelene, will you knock it off? Now's not the time for that nonsense."

"Nonsense? *Nonsense?* I'll have you know I'm talking about my career! This woman—"

"Oh, can it, will you. I don't give a rat's ass about your backstabbing Hollywood games." Chad's gaze swung to Sara. "I want to know who the hell this woman is and why she's here."

Evelyn met her stepson's glare with outward composure and a defiant tilt of her chin. She even managed a smile. "I'd like you all to meet Sara Anderson. My daughter."

Three beats of stunned silence followed, then all hell broke loose.

"Your *what?*" Will exploded.

"Daughter?" Paul yelped. "Since when?"

Chad sat forward, his callused hands gripping the edge of the table. "You *can't* be *serious!*"

Eric and Kitty sagged back in their chairs, thunderstruck, their stunned gazes locked on Sara. Kitty's lips quivered. She looked on the verge of tears.

"Damn it, Lawrence. Don't just sit there," Maddie hissed. *"Do* something, for God's sake!"

Blinking her china-blue eyes, Monica looked from one person to the other. "What? What're you all so upset about? So Evelyn's got an illegitimate kid? So what? What's the big deal?"

"Oh, shut up, Monica."

"Well!" The blonde huffed and flounced back in her chair. Her eyes shot daggers at her husband, but Paul was too busy shouting at his stepmother to notice.

The uproar lasted several minutes. As before, Evelyn rode it out in silence, not moving except to glance at Sara and Rourke.

To her credit, Sara seemed to be weathering the storm. Her expression was as unreadable as the Mona Lisa's. Beside her, Rourke watched the goings on with what looked suspiciously like laughter gleaming in his blue eyes.

"God damn it! Will all of you shut up and let me talk?" Will bellowed. Even slurred, his words carried authority, and the others grudgingly obeyed. Will's good eye bore into Evelyn. "Just what the hell are you trying to pull here?"

"Nothing. I'm quite serious. Sara's my daughter. She was born when I was in college, five years before I met Joe. I gave her up for adoption at the time of her birth."

"Did my brother know about this?"

Evelyn fixed Will with a hard look. "Of course. I never lied to Joe or hid anything from him."

"Not even that you married him for his money?"

Aside from a slight narrowing of her eyes, Evelyn ignored Chad's jibe. In the twenty-five years of her marriage to Joe, she had never managed to form a particularly close bond with his only son, but neither had there been any serious enmity between them. Chad was simply striking out now because he was angry. She could understand that.

"How do we even know this woman is your daughter? She could be anyone. If you think we're going to just meekly allow you to palm off some stranger on us, you're mistak—"

"Don't be a fool." The disdain in Rourke's voice cut like Toledo steel. Paul shot him a furious look, but Rourke's gaze did not waver. "Anyone with eyes can see that Sara and Evelyn are related."

"He's got you there, cousin," Eric drawled, staring at Sara. "The likeness is amazing."

"All right. So what if she is your daughter? What's she doing here? This is a shareholders' meeting, not a fucking family reunion." Paul's face was rigid and flushed an angry red. He looked more a candidate for a stroke than his father.

"Sara *is* a shareholder. I've given her four percent of the stock. We signed the papers this morning."

"What? You can't do that!" Chad's hands slapped the table top and he rose half out of his chair. "That stock can only be owned by family."

"That's right!"

"Yeah!"

"No exceptions!" Will and several others protested.

"This woman may be your bastard, but she's no Ketchum," Paul sneered.

From the corner of her eye, Evelyn saw Sara flinch and Rourke lay a reassuring hand on her wrist. Evelyn turned cool green eyes on her nephew-by-marriage. "She doesn't have to be. She's my flesh and blood, and that makes her eligible to own shares. More so than any of you, in my opinion, since I'm the one who built this company into what it is. Joe merely financed me. But if you don't believe me, ask Lawrence."

"What the hell is she talking about?" Paul and Chad demanded in the same breath.

Every pair of eyes around the table swung to Lawrence. He shifted in his chair as though it had suddenly become hot. "Well . . ." He cleared his throat, and fiddled with his pen, but finally he glanced around and grimaced. "Evelyn's right. The articles of incorporation state that only persons related to the company's founders may own stock in Eve Cosmetics. That was Joe *and* Evelyn.

"Actually, technically speaking, Evelyn had the company in operation over six months before the reorganization. That took place shortly after their marriage. That was when Joe poured money into it. Until his death, they were equal partners, each holding fifty percent of the stock. Therefore, Evelyn's daughter . . ." He glanced uneasily at Sara. "Ms. Anderson . . . has just as much right to own stock as any of you."

"Lawrence!" Maddie squawked. "You're supposed to be on our side!"

"I'm sorry, darling, but that's—"

"The point is, Sara can and does own stock.

Whether or not any of you like it is irrelevant." Evelyn looked at each face around the table to drive home her point. "As of today, Sara will take an active part in running the company. And one more thing. I'll put it to a vote, of course, but before we adjourn, she will have a seat on this board."

Four hours later, sitting in Evelyn's office, Rourke flexed his shoulders and stretched his arms above his head. "It could have been worse, I suppose. At least no blood was shed."

"Not yet, at any rate."

Surprised, Sara looked from Rourke to Evelyn. "What do you mean? They were angry at first, but by the end of the meeting they all seemed to at least be resigned to the situation. Except for Paul, they were even cordial."

"They were merely following Will's lead," Evelyn said.

Her announcement that Sara would join the board and become involved in the day-to-day running of Eve had enraged Paul. Only his father's intervention had prevented an ugly scene.

"If you think I'm going to sit still for this, you're—"

"Now, now, son. Just simmer down," Will had cautioned, putting a restraining hand on Paul's arm.

He'd turned his attention to Evelyn and Sara. The normal side of his mouth hiked up in what was meant to be a conciliatory smile. "Fair's fair. Sara—May I call you Sara, my dear?"

She inclined her head. "Certainly."

"Good, good. As I was saying, Sara is Evelyn's

family, so it's only right that she take her rightful place on the board."

"Damn it, Dad—" Paul flared again, but a quelling look hushed him.

Brimming with the disarming, rough-around-the-edges oil-field charm that he used with such skill, Will reversed his wheelchair away from the table and steered it around to Sara's side. Taking her hand in his good one, he gave it a squeeze.

"We Ketchums put a great store in family, you'll find, and I'd like to be the first to welcome you to ours. Oh, and, my dear, I do hope you'll excuse that little set-to just now. We're not usually so rude. This whole thing just sort of caught us off guard, is all. It wasn't personal. You do understand, don't you?"

Sara had smiled at him, immensely relieved.

Now Rourke was looking at her as though she were a naive child.

"Don't be fooled by Will's rough charm. Or his disability. He's a shrewd old bird. You can bet he's no happier about this than Paul, but Will knows he doesn't have a any recourse. Unlike his son, he's too smart to waste time and energy fighting a battle he's sure to lose. Right now he's regrouping, trying to figure out a way to make this work to his advantage."

"Are you saying that his friendly overture was faked?"

Rourke shrugged. "Not necessarily. Just don't relax your guard too much. Give him half a chance and that old bull will trample you into the ground."

"Why? Surely a man in his condition doesn't want to take over the running of a company the size of Eve?"

"No. But he and the others, want to be able to sell

their stock," Evelyn said. "For reasons I've yet to figure out, they are all constantly in need of money. For months now, they've been trying to force me to allow the company to go public. They'll start working on you next, probably hoping you will be able to persuade me."

"I assume you have a good reason for keeping Eve Cosmetics in the family?"

"Several. First of all, I promised Joe that I would. Secondly, I know the Ketchums. If I were to allow the company to go public, they wouldn't just sell off a few stocks. Huge blocks of stock would be offered, which means there would be several institutional purchases."

"You mean like insurance companies and banks and investment firms?"

"Yes. And they'll want to put their own people on the board of directors."

"Would that be such a terrible thing?"

Evelyn gave her a long look. "Joe always said, "A wise rancher doesn't put a rustler on the payroll." I happen to think that's a wise policy."

"But you won't be selling any of your stock, so you'll still have control. Surely strangers couldn't be any more contentious than that bunch I just met."

"Perhaps not. But I know how to deal with the Ketchums. The point is, I don't want outsiders to get their hands on my company. I built it from nothing, and I will run it the way I please."

"Mmm. I suppose that's fair, after all you sacrificed." Sara's smile did not touch her eyes. "You gave up a child and married an old man for his money to get Eve Cosmetics going. It should be yours. You earned it."

The blow hit low, as Sara intended, but Evelyn's only reaction was an infinitesimal flicker in her eyes. She merely looked at Sara, her lovely face still as marble. Rourke's jaw tightened as he watched them.

Picking up her purse, Sara stood and headed for the door. With her hand on the knob, she paused and looked back. "I hope it was worth it."

Chapter Fourteen

"Why do you let her get away with stuff like that? Why didn't you set her straight?"

Evelyn pulled her gaze away from the empty doorway that Sara had walked through moments before and focused on Rourke.

A frown drew his black brows together. Beneath them his eyes glittered like sapphires. Confusion and curiosity marked his expression, along with a hint of anger.

"That would be difficult. I did marry Joe for his money."

"What?"

"It's true. Oh, he knew it, of course. That was part of our deal. In fact, he was the one who proposed it."

"A deal? Are you trying to tell me your marriage to Joe Ketchum was a business deal? I don't believe it."

It was one of the few times in all the years that she'd known him that Evelyn had seen Rourke truly flabbergasted. The sight brought a touch of genuine amusement to her expression. "It's true.

"I was working in Hollywood at Epic Studios as a

makeup artist when we met. Madelene was fourteen at the time, just a child, but she had already been working in films for five years. Following in her mother's footsteps, I suppose. Joe visited her at the studio, and I happened to be assigned to the movie she was making.

"Almost from the moment we met, he made up his mind to marry me." Evelyn smiled and her expression softened as memories of her husband's determined courtship came rushing back—the flowers, the calls and notes, the romantic dinners, the countless thoughtful little gestures. She recalled, too, Joe's disarming cowboy gallantry and wicked sense of humor, his rock-solid strength and sweetness, and felt a warm ache in the region of her heart.

"I told him I didn't love him, but he said it didn't matter. He loved me and he was confident that I would learn to love him. He was so sure of it, he offered to provide the financial backing I needed to get Eve Cosmetics off the ground if I would agree to marry him.

"I had been in business a little over six months, working full time at the studio, and trying to hustle my line of cosmetics on the side. And every month I was going deeper into the red. I desperately needed that money.

"I had never been in love before, and at that time in my life I doubted that I ever would be. I liked and respected Joe, so . . ." She shrugged. "I had qualms, of course, but I rationalized that we would both be getting something we wanted, so it was fair. A loveless marriage to a decent man whom I liked seemed a small price to pay for the realization of a dream."

She didn't bother to mention that she had also

desperately yearned for children. Somehow, giving up Sara had made her almost panicky to experience motherhood.

Sadly, that was the one dream she had never been able to achieve. Not all the money, power, or wanting in the world could bring it about.

Raising Joe's three children had been a consolation of sorts, and Evelyn loved all three of them dearly, difficult as they were, but it wasn't the same. Even now, deep within her, there was still a hollow ache.

"But you loved Joe," Rourke insisted. "Damn it, I know you did. A person only had to see the two of you together to know that."

Evelyn's smile was wry. "You must remember that Joe and I had been married for fifteen years when you came to work here. Eventually I did grow to love him—he was right about that—but I didn't when I married him. So you see, I couldn't very well take umbrage with Sara for speaking the truth, now, could I?"

Rourke studied her, his eyes narrowed. "Uh-uh. There's more to this than you're saying. For some reason, you *want* to keep a barrier between you and Sara. I didn't think so at first, but I've been watching you, and now I'm sure of it. Whenever it begins to look as though you two might connect, you deliberately do or say something to make her dislike you. You sabotage any chance you might have at a relationship. What's more, you seem determined not to show your feelings for her. What I don't understand is why."

"I don't want a personal relationship with Sara. That's not why I brought her here. And I have no feelings for her one way or another. Aside from gratitude and relief that she might save my company, I feel no more for her than I do for any other stranger.''

Rourke snorted and rolled to his feet. "Yeah, right,'' he muttered as he headed for the door. "And you didn't love Joe, either.''

Sara slammed the apartment door so hard the Waterford crystal chandelier in the foyer shook with a musical tinkle.

Two feet inside the apartment she jerked to a halt. She stood rigid, her hands clenched at her sides, her eyes squeezed shut, her jaws locked. The eight-block walk from Evelyn's had not cooled her temper one iota. She was still furious with herself. So furious she felt like hitting something. God, where had her control gone?

"Image. Image. Image.'' Sara ground out the litany between gritted teeth. Image was everything. Vital. She *knew* that. She was an image consultant, for God's sake. She had perfected her own years ago; composed, and dignified, no matter what fate threw at her . . . even the violent abuse of a fanatic father.

As she'd gotten older, she'd often faced Edgar down with a proud tilt of her chin and a silent stare. The tactic had not always saved her and her mother from his fists, but her calm defiance, which had frustrated and infuriated him, had never shattered. No matter how bad life had gotten, she had never lost control. Why couldn't she hold onto it now?

She wanted to treat Evelyn with cool indifference—the same cool indifference she received from her. She wanted to show the woman that she meant nothing to her. Less than nothing.

For hours at a time she would manage just fine. Just yesterday she had spent the whole day with Evelyn and Rourke, getting an overview of the company's operation. Most of that time she was so fascinated by the myriad details and complexities of running a giant corporation that she could relate to Evelyn as simply the savvy businesswoman that she was. Then, out of the blue, the anger and the hurt would bubble up from someplace deep inside her and she would lash out before she could stop herself.

And, damn it, every time she did, she revealed to Evelyn how deeply affected she really was.

"This is crazy. I've got to get a grip on myself," she muttered. Not simply to save face, either. Intellectually, Sara knew that taking potshots at Evelyn would accomplish nothing, except to create a hostile work environment, and she didn't want that. Even more important, though, she hated being bitchy and vindictive. It was a side of herself that she had not known existed—and she didn't like it.

From now on, around Evelyn she would be composed and professional, she vowed. Nothing more.

Sara drew several deep breaths and released them slowly. She rolled her taut shoulders and shook her arms. "You can do this," she muttered, willing herself to relax. "You've endured a lot worse. Just remember that. It's all simply a matter of control. Mind over matter."

Forcing herself to walk slowly, Sara made her way through the elegant apartment to the master bedroom. With the same deliberate movements, she removed her suit and blouse and hung them in the closet, then stripped off her garter belt and stockings and dropped them into a lacy lingerie bag. The methodical ritual had a soothing effect. By the time she had stripped down to her lacy wine silk panties and bra, the knot in her chest had almost dissolved.

Sara had not brought many clothes with her, but she always traveled with at least one pair of jeans and a comfortable top in which she could relax late at night when she was alone and there was no one to see her. She stepped into the jeans and tossed the roomy sweater over her head just as someone rang the doorbell.

Rourke jabbed the button, frowning. Bracing an arm against the frame, he waited, and wondered what the hell he was doing. The surprised look on Sara's face when she opened the door told him she wondered the same thing.

"Rourke."

"I hope you like Chinese food."

"Well, I . . . that is . . . yes. Yes, I love Chinese."

"Good. I brought plenty." He didn't wait for her to invite him in; he wasn't sure she would. He simply stepped past her and headed for the kitchen, ignoring her surprised expression. He heard the door close and her hurried footsteps following him. She caught up with him as he sat the sack down on the large kitchen island and began removing white cartons. The delicious smells of sweet-and-sour pork, fried rice, San Shao, and numerous other dishes filled the kitchen.

Sara hesitated in the doorway. "Rourke . . ."

"I didn't know what you liked, so I got some of everything. I figured you'd be hungry after the day we've had. I sure am." He shot her a quick look. "You haven't already eaten, have you?"

'Well . . . no. But—"

"Good. I didn't think you'd had time. Take a seat and dig in while it's still warm," he commanded, waving toward one of the stools surrounding the island counter.

He noticed that she had changed. The smart burgundy suit and pale rose silk blouse she had worn for the board meeting was gone. She had traded in her business armor for a baggy sweater and a pair of jeans that were soft with wear and faded almost to white. Most of her lipstick had worn off and her hair was slightly mussed from pulling the sweater on over her head. And she was barefoot.

Rourke fought the urge to smile. He would bet a month's salary the always composed and perfectly turned out Ms. Sara Anderson allowed damned few people to see her looking so comfortably disheveled. He had a sudden urge to see her even more mussed.

Sara shifted from one bare foot to the other, tugging on the bottom of her sweater. She started to speak, then closed her mouth, opened it, then closed it again. Finally, looking bemused, she sighed and slid onto a stool and accepted the carton he shoved across the counter at her.

There were stools on both sides of the island. Rourke started to take one opposite her, but he saw the flash of relief in her eyes and at the last second he changed his mind and sat down beside Sara. He wasn't sure why—pure perversity, probably. For some reason he did not understand and wasn't sure he wanted to delve into, he was feeling ornery as sin tonight. Restless and out of sorts, uncomfortable in his own skin.

He could tell that his nearness was making Sara jumpy. If the rapid rise and fall of her breasts was any indication, she was having trouble breathing, as well. Good. Why should he be the only one feeling off balance?

Before coming over, he had discarded his suit coat and tie and rolled up his shirt sleeves. As he opened cartons and poured wine into the glasses he'd taken from the cabinet, the rolled cuff at his left elbow kept brushing her arm. Each time she jumped, and each time he bit back a smile.

Sara opened a carton of Kung Po shrimp and steam rose, moist and fragrant. Closing her eyes, she breathed deeply of oriental spices. "Mmm, this smells divine." She lifted a shrimp with her chopsticks and devoured it with dainty greed, chewing slowly to relish the delicate flavors. Until that moment, she hadn't given a thought to dinner, but she was suddenly ravenous.

"Yeah, Chin Su's is one of the best Chinese restaurants in town." Rourke deftly scooped up a pile of fried rice. "It's only a couple of blocks from here."

"Well . . . that's certainly good to know," Sara replied, mainly for something to say to cover the awkwardness she felt. The last thing she had expected tonight, after taking that dig at Evelyn and walking out, was to find herself sitting alone in the kitchen in her most comfortable "at home" clothes, sharing an impromptu meal with Rourke.

She peeked at him out of the corner of her eye as she worked her way through several dishes. If he harbored any ill feelings over the way she had talked to Evelyn, it was not evident. He looked perfectly at ease, his strong profile free of tension. Of course, if Sara had learned anything about Rourke in the last two days, it was that he was a master at diplomacy and maneuvering.

Sara tried to block out everything but her appreciation of the food, but all along her right side she could feel his heat. Her eyes kept straying to his muscular forearms below the rolled-up sleeves. His skin was dark against the white Egyptian cotton, his wrists broad and thick. He had large but beautifully made hands, she noticed. Wide palms and long, blunt fingers with well-tended nails. Short black hair dusted his forearms and the backs of his hands, and sparse little tufts sprouted between the first and second knuckles. Sara had never particularly noticed such things about a man before, and she had certain never been aroused by them, but for some reason she found that smattering of hair strangely erotic and utterly masculine. Her fingers itched to stroke down his arm through the short, silky thatch.

Sara frowned, not at all comfortable with the drift of her thoughts. This was ridiculous. She hadn't had those kind of daydreams when she'd been a teenager, for heaven's sake.

"Why did you run out like that earlier?"

The question caught her off guard. Sara shot him a sharp look. "I'd had enough for one day and wanted to leave. And I walked out, I didn't run."

"I tried to catch up with you, but by the time I got downstairs you were gone. I assume you took a taxi?"

She kept her eyes on the fried rice she was poking

with her chopsticks. "I walked. It's only eight blocks and I needed some air."

"That's not a good idea, you know. This is a nice area, but Houston's crime rate is soaring."

She didn't bother to reply to that. Several minutes ticked by in silence. Finally he said, "So tell me. What did you think of the family?"

Sara shrugged. "They're . . . interesting."

"Come on. You can be frank. Evelyn's not here. What do you really think?"

She turned her head and gave him an ironic look. Did he actually believe that she would speak her mind to him? Evelyn's right-hand man and confidant? She might be green when it came to big business, but she wasn't stupid. "I think I'll pass."

He searched her face, and Sara felt her pulse kick into a higher gear. Sweet heaven, he was a fabulous-looking man. Not handsome in the accepted sense, but so rawly masculine that just being near him made her tingle all over. This close, she could see each individual lash surrounding those incredible blue eyes, the tiny crinkles at their corners. Now and then, over the smell of Chinese food, she caught his scent, dark and sexy . . . and tempting.

"Cautious little thing, aren't you?" he said, smiling crookedly. Amusement danced in his eyes, mocking her. "Don't you think you're being a little paranoid?"

Sara tilted her chin. "So you really want to know what I think, do you? All right. Just remember, you asked for it. They struck me as being overindulged, self-absorbed, greedy, and utterly spoiled and selfish. Every one of them."

"Bingo. Give the lady a prize."

Sara blinked. She had expected him to defend them and make excuses, not agree with her.

He grinned at her startled expression and popped another eggroll in his mouth. "They're all that and more," he added, when he'd swallowed. "They're arrogant, demanding, self-serving, and can be real royal pains in the ass. Even Kitty and Eric, who're the best of the lot. But they also have their good points. They're absolutely loyal to one another. They have their differences, but when the chips are down, they hang together as a family. They're all bright and talented, each in his own way. They're also a hard-working bunch, even with all their money. You were right, though. They're interesting as hell. Especially when they're all together."

"Mmm. Maybe. If you like being run over by a steamroller."

Rourke chuckled. "If you're going to stick around, you'd better get used to it, because they aren't going to go away."

What did that mean? Did he think she would cut and run at the first sign of trouble from the Ketchums? She turned her head and gave him a cool look. "Neither am I."

Rourke studied her for several seconds. Finally his mouth curled in a slow smile. "No, I don't think you will."

The look in his eyes made her pulse flutter. Sara forced her attention back to the meal. No matter how attractive the man was or how he made her feel, she had no business mooning over him.

They fell silent again, and the air in the kitchen pulsed with awareness and suspicion. Sara felt as though she were poised on a knife edge.

Though no longer hungry, for something to do, she started to spoon black bean sauce over what remained of her rice, but suddenly her nerves could take no more. She set the carton down with a decisive snap and cocked her head at him. "Why are you here, Rourke?"

"What do you mean?"

"Why are you suddenly being nice to me? Why did you bring me dinner?"

"Does there have to be a reason?"

"There usually is."

"Maybe I simply wanted to make sure you ate dinner. I know there isn't any food in the apartment, aside from a bit of cereal and coffee."

Sara narrowed her eyes and studied him. "And perhaps you're trying to win me over, convince me to forgive and forget and be nicer to your boss?"

"She's also your mother."

"No. Julia Anderson is my mother."

Rourke expelled a sigh. "You're determined to hate her, aren't you?"

"I don't hate her. But she hasn't given me any reason to love her, either."

"How about four percent of a thriving, multimillion dollar corporation?"

"Oh, come on. That's just money. Besides, that wasn't for me. That was for her, and you know it. She admitted that if she could trust any one of that bunch she calls a family she would never have contacted me. On a personal level, I mean nothing to her. She makes that clear every time she opens her mouth."

"Sara, listen to me. The thing about Evelyn is, the more nervous or unsure she feels, the more distant she becomes. It's just her way of protecting herself. You should understand that. You do it yourself."

Hurt and anger gush up inside her again, tightening her chest. She wanted to shriek at Rourke and pummel his chest. She barely caught herself in time. Stay calm. Stay calm, she cautioned. Turning her head, she drilled him with a cool stare and said quietly, "Don't ever compare me with her. I'm nothing like Evelyn. Nothing at all."

"Struck a nerve, did I?" Those vivid eyes studied her. Sara had the unnerving feeling that he wasn't just looking at her, but into her, that sharp gaze slicing like a scalpel, probing her thoughts, her feelings. She had to fight the urge to squirm.

That was something she'd noticed about Rourke. He listened when people talked, to the spoken words and the ones left unsaid. Many times he remained quiet and let the conversation swirl around him, but those eyes, that quick mind were always analyzing, dissecting, absorbing.

"Honey, you're so much like her you could be her clone," he said, ignoring her quick frown. "Not just in looks, although that alone is pretty startling. You've got her brains, her drive, her ambition. That sense of style and class that's bred in the bone. Hell, you've both got that same regal quality that can freeze a man with a look." He grinned. "You've got that look right now."

Sara gritted her teeth. "You're mistaken."

"Hey, relax. I meant that as a compliment."

"I'm not flattered."

Rourke's smile faded. "Well, you should be. Evelyn is a remarkable woman. Look, I understand your anger, but can't you see that this whole thing is as difficult for her as it is for you? Maybe more so. I don't know what happened back then, but I do know Evelyn. You can bet she had a good reason for giving you up."

"Then why won't she tell me what it was?"

"I don't know. We're friends, and I'm probably closer to her than any one alive, but personal things, feelings, she doesn't talk about with anyone. The only exception to that I've ever known of was Joe. Some things—successes, hopes, even the occasional defeat—she'll share, but a blow to her heart or her pride Evelyn keeps to herself. It's just her way.

"So if she seems a little remote don't worry about it. It doesn't mean anything. You shouldn't take it personally."

"Don't take it personally? I'm her flesh and blood, for God's sake! How else am I suppose to take it? And what do you care, anyway?"

"I care about Evelyn. I don't like to see her hurt. I don't want to see you hurt, either." His gaze dropped to her mouth and lingered. Sara's breath hitched to a stop, and she forgot why she was angry.

"Wh—" She cleared her throat and started again. "Why? I'm nothing to you."

"Mmm. Not yet, maybe." Rourke leaned toward her, drawing inexorably closer, staring all the while at her bottom lip.

Sara grew still as a marble statue. Her heart pounded. Her gaze locked on his chiseled lips as they came closer. When his mouth was a mere half inch from hers, he stopped. She could feel his breath feathering over her lips, her cheeks. With every breath she drew in his scent. Her nostrils quivered. Her whole body quivered.

"But I have a feeling that you are going to become very important to me," he whispered against her lips a second before his own settled over them in a searing soft kiss.

Sara's heart skittered to a stop, then gave a bump and took off at a sprint. She felt the exquisite caress in every inch of her body. His mouth rocked over hers with seductive tenderness, rubbing, nipping. His tongue stroked, swirled, enticed.

Heat poured through her, racing from the point of contact with that sensuous mouth to settle like glowing coals in her feminine core. Want clawed at her. Desire burned. She clutched the edge of the counter in a white-knuckled grip. Her bare toes curled around the rung of the stool.

Rourke's fingers speared through her silky hair and cupped the back of her head. "Sara," he whispered, as he lifted his mouth to angle the kiss in a different direction. The small respite broke the spell just enough for her to gather the strength to pull back.

She blinked and looked into his face, just inches away. It was dark with desire, his eyes sizzling blue fire. A fresh wave of longing slammed through Sara, but she made herself pull back a few inches more. "Rourke . . . I don't think this is a good idea."

"Why not? The chemistry is there. We've both known that from the beginning."

"I . . ." She wanted to deny that, but she couldn't, so she ignored it. "There are lots of reasons. For one thing, you're Evelyn's assistant and friend."

Rourke's eyebrows rose. "Does that make me the enemy in your eyes?"

"Not the enemy exactly, but . . ."

"But you don't trust me. Right?"

Her gaze lowered to her hands, still gripping the counter, then darted back to his. "I'm sorry."

Rourke released her, pulling his hand slowly from her hair, watching the silky strands slither through his fingers. "Yeah, well . . . me, too. I guess I'll just have to work on that. So what're your other reasons?"

Surprise widened Sara's eyes. She had expected him to back off, even to get angry, but he was still watching her with that predatory gleam in his eyes.

"I would think that's obvious. I have too much on my plate right now to get involved with anyone. I have to put all my focus, all my energy into learning the business. And anyway, it's just not a good idea. We have to work together."

"First of all, I've watched you in action these past few days, and I think you're a lady who can handle whatever comes your way. As for the other, we're both adults. We should be able to keep our business and personal lives separate." He picked up his wineglass and took a sip, watching her over the rim. "Why don't we just go with the flow and see what develops?"

This time, when Evelyn reached for the diary on the top shelf, it was anticipation, not dread, that made her hand shake. The book was the fourteenth, the last of the cheap cloth-covered journals.

Once again, Sara's remarks had stirred up memories. The nostalgia had tugged at Evelyn for over an hour. She had resisted it long enough to eat and bathe and ready herself for bed, knowing if she delayed she would not have the strength. She could feel her energy waning minute by minute, draining away like water in a leaky bucket.

Hugging the diary to her breast, she climbed into bed, pulled up the satin comforter. With a sigh, she leaned back on the mountain of pillows and closed her eyes. The ferocious lassitude made her arms and legs feel like lead.

She felt bad about Kitty. She had been visibly upset when she'd learned about Sara. Her stepdaughter usually spent the night here at the apartment after a board meeting. Evelyn had intended to talk to her this evening and smooth things over, and also find out what was troubling the girl, but Kitty had stormed out of the boardroom in a huff. Evelyn assumed she had gone to the ranch with Will and Paul.

She sighed. She supposed Kitty felt threatened by Sara. Joe's youngest child had been only four when Evelyn had married Joe and she thought of herself as Evelyn's daughter. She was the only mother that Kitty had ever known. At fourteen and ten, Madelene and Chad had had memories of their mother and they had been enough older to be no competition. Sara, however, was a different story. Kitty was a sweet young woman with a gentle personality, but she had a possessive streak like all the Ketchums.

She also had a tendency to pout. It would probably be best, Evelyn decided, to give her a few days to cool down before trying to talk to her.

Kitty really did not need to worry that Sara would usurp her place. In her mind's eye Evelyn could clearly picture Sara. Her daughter, the unwanted child to whom she had given birth. For thirty-two years she had refused to feel anything for her. Neither love nor hate. She had thought of her occasionally, but never with wistfulness or regret. Evelyn didn't believe in regret. You made a decision, then you lived with it, good or bad. Her thoughts had merely been idle curiosity, a humanitarian hope that the child was well and happy. A futile wish, as it turned out.

Evelyn opened her eyes finally and reached for the diary. She rubbed her fingertips over the cheap cloth-covered volume and smiled. It took a tremendous effort, but using both hands, she managed to pull up her legs. She stuffed pillows beneath her bent knees, propped the cloth diary on her thighs, and opened the book.

January 2nd

Today I started work on the set of Scarlet Harvest. *One of the people I made up was Madelene Ketchum. What a beautiful child she is. I watched her during filming. It appears she inherited not only her mother's looks, but her talent as well. In a few years she's sure to be a big star.*

Evelyn smiled. She had been right. Within four years, Maddie had developed into one of the hottest stars in Hollywood.

She turned the page, and her smile deepened.

January 3rd

Madelene Ketchum's father was at the studio today. He visited with her while I was doing her makeup. He's a very nice-looking man. He's got that lean, rough-hewn western look like those men in the cigarette ads. His hair is going gray at the temples, but it merely makes him look distinguished. It's difficult to tell his age, but since Madelene is fourteen, I'd guess him to be in his mid- to late-thirties.

Resting the book against her breasts, Evelyn chuckled. Joe had been forty-six at the time.

She turned her head on the pillows and looked at the photograph in the silver frame on the nightstand. Joe's gray eyes twinkled at her as though inviting her to share a joke, his grin flashing white in his deeply tanned face. The picture had been taken a little over two years ago, just months before his death. His light brown hair had by then turned completely silver, but it had still been thick and luxuriant, and the deepened lines in his face had only added character and made him even more handsome.

Sara had called him an old man, but Evelyn had never thought of him that way. Joe had been one of those men who seemed ageless. He had been vital and fit and full of life even at seventy-one when, without warning, the massive heart attack had taken him.

Her eyes misted over and she reached out and touched the picture with her fingertips. "Oh, Joe," she whispered. "I miss you so much."

The ache in her throat squeezed tighter. She closed her eyes and let the emotion run its course, until finally she could swallow again.

Slowly, she turned the pages in the old diary, skimming the entries, stopping often to savor a passage, smiling now and then as the words stirred poignant memories.

It struck her as amusing when she noticed that her growing love for her husband was charted so clearly in her writing. Why, she wondered, had she never noticed that before?

March 14th

Today is my wedding day. Oh, God, what if I'm making a horrible mistake? What if . . . No. No, I won't

*think that way. Joe is a good man. He's nothing like
Larry Bainbridge.*

March 15th

*I was so nervous last night I cried before anything
could happen. I thought Joe would be angry, but he
couldn't have been sweeter or more patient and understanding, even after I told him about what Larry did to
me. And about the baby.*

April 5th

*We're home at Joe's ranch in Texas. Paris was won-
derful. Imagine! A honeymoon in Paris, France! Joe is
just full of surprises.*

May 12th

*Eve Cosmetics now has a dozen employees, and
we've bought land outside Houston and are building a
factory, all thanks to Joe. When it comes to getting
things done, he's amazing.*

August 1st

*Joe is the most generous man. And not just with his
money. He supports and encourages me constantly.*

September 10th

*Joe had to fly to California to hire a new companion
for Maddie. We're so busy at Eve I couldn't get away
to go with him. I miss him.*

November 2nd

*It's Joe's birthday. He seemed to like the new cus-
tom-made boots I got him. I hope so. I want him to be
happy.*

November 28th

*I don't know how I got so lucky. Joe has to be the
gentlest, most considerate man in the world.*

Evelyn's smile fluttered often as she continued to
turn pages and found more of the same. "Joe this"
and "Joe that" peppered her writing. Any fool could

have read between the lines, but she had gone on blithely, month after month, never facing the truth. Of course, in her defense, she had been so busy with Eve she'd hardly had time to catch her breath that first year.

Wisely, Joe had not interfered. He'd put up the money, but Eve was hers, and he'd left the running of it in her hands. If asked, he gave advice, and it was nearly always right on target, but when it came to making decisions, he stood back and let her have her head, always there to help if she needed him and always, *always,* cheering her on.

Her feelings for him had grown so gradually, so gently, that she hadn't even noticed. Not until she'd received that telephone call at the office, two days before Christmas.

Joe had left less than an hour before. He had wanted her to go with him, but Evelyn and her staff had been rushing around trying to fill last-minute orders and get them shipped overnight to the customers for the holiday.

It had irritated her no end when her brand new secretary had interrupted to tell her she had an important call. It had been a policeman, calling to inform her that Joe had been in a car wreck on his way home to the ranch and was en route to the hospital by ambulance. In less than a minute, Evelyn was in her car, driving like a wild woman and pleading with God to spare him.

Smiling wryly, she turned to December 24th. The writing was sloppy, almost illegible. She had made the entry at dawn, after spending a hellish eighteen hours at the hospital, first waiting for Joe to come through surgery and recovery, then hovering over his bedside until she had been sure he was going to survive. The words she had recorded in her diary were almost the same ones she had blurted out to Joe the second his eyes opened.

I love Joe. Dear God, I love him so much. If I had lost him I wouldn't want to live.

Remembering the tearful declaration at the hospital, Evelyn hugged the book to her chest, her eyes soft and misty. Joe had patted her hand and said, "I know, honey. I know."

You married an old man for his money. Sara's jibe drifted through her mind, and she smiled. It was true, but she had gotten so much more. What Sara didn't realize—what Evelyn herself had not realized back then—was something that Joe had known all along. It wasn't beauty or physical attraction or even sex that made you fall in love. It was the little everyday things, the small kindnesses and thoughtful gestures: a warm meal left in the oven for you when you came home after working late, being awakened in the morning with a kiss and a steaming cup of coffee, an extra blanket thrown over you on a cold winter night.

Those small gestures were like soft spring rain to newly sown seeds. When a man treated a woman with that kind of care and tenderness, love was sure to take root in her heart.

Chapter Fifteen

The Ketchum Ranch

Paul paced the length of the den, cursing.

"Damn it, boy! Just calm down. We've got to figure a way around this. You can't think straight if all you're going to do is rant."

"A daughter. A goddamned illegitimate daughter. Just out of the blue that way. And Evelyn's taking her into the company. I can't believe it."

"Now, son—"

Paul swung on his father. "And I can't believe you cozied up to the bitch the way you did. Don't you get it, old man? Evelyn's bastard not only has a chunk of our property, she could end up running the show someday if we don't do something about it. You said yourself, Ketchum money built Eve Cosmetics. It belongs to us, damn it. Not to some jumped-up little nobody no one has ever heard of." Paul stomped to the bar and splashed more whiskey into his glass.

"I've got no more use for the woman, or her mother, than you do. You oughta know that. But I keep telling you, boy, you'll catch more flies with honey than vinegar. For now, the smartest thing to do is to act friendly."

"Friendly! Jesus, you expect me to be friends with Evelyn's by-blow?"

"You're damned right I do," Will bellowed, out of patience. "At least until we can come up with a plan. We can't do anything about Sara having the stock. That's a done deal. Hell, if we're nice to her, we might even persuade her to sell us her stock."

"Yeah? And just what would we use for money? Even if we got Sara's stock, Evelyn's still got fifty-one percent." Paul tossed back the remainder of his drink in one swallow, snatched up the bottle, and poured more, sloshing whiskey over the edge of the glass onto the bar.

Will grumbled something and lapsed into silence. His good eye narrowed in concentration. The other eyelid drooped grotesquely. "According to Rourke, those goddamned spas Evelyn's sinking all our profits into are going to be big money makers in a few years. But, damn it, we need money for that down dip well now."

To hell with the fucking well, Paul thought. He needed money to pay off Bruno. Soon, before the creep sent his goons to nail his kneecaps to the floor.

"We've got to figure out a way to force Evelyn to go public with the company."

"Aw, Jesus, not that again. We've been over this a hundred times. There's no way."

"Now, now, boy. There's always a way." Will's mouth twisted in a lopsided smile that had nothing to do with humor. "Maybe not a legal way, but if a man's got the guts—"

The telephone shrilled, and on the first ring Paul snatched it up and barked, "Ketchum Ranch."

"Well, well. Mr. Ketchum. You're just the man I wanted to talk to."

The color drained out of Paul's face. Will eyed him curiously. Turning his back on his father, he tucked the phone against his hunched shoulder so the old man couldn't hear. He gripped the receiver so tight his knuckles whitened. "Bruno," he said in a raspy undertone. "I told you never to call me here. How did you get this number?"

"Now, now, Mr. Ketchum, that's not very friendly." Bruno's oily voice altered subtly. "There are ways of getting what you want. Some are quite . . . shall we say . . . painful. But they're real effective." He paused a beat, then added, "I really don't think you'd like them, Mr. Ketchum."

Fear trickled down Paul's spine like drops of icewater.

Chad's pickup was parked outside the foreman's cabin when Alice arrived. Bringing her car to a halt, she glanced at the truck and caught her lower lip between her teeth. It wasn't a good sign; Chad never arrived before she did.

He was still angry. He had been livid earlier when he'd left the office. Except for the brief, blazing look he'd shot her when Evelyn had introduced Sara, he hadn't even looked her way during the board meeting. Afterward, when he had stomped past her on his way out, his terse "The cabin. Ten tonight" had told Alice at least part of his fury was directed at her.

For the first time since they'd become lovers, Alice was not looking forward to meeting Chad.

She'd known what his reaction would be. All during the previous day, torn between her loyalty to Evelyn and her love for Chad, she had wrestled with her conscience over whether or not to call him and warn him about Sara.

In the end, love had won. Even though she had not been able to reach him, she was still ashamed of the decision.

Chad was pacing the living room. The instant Alice stepped inside, he whirled around and pounced. "Why the hell didn't you tell me?" Before she could reply, he stormed across the room and took her by the shoulders. Alice's eyes widened at his expression. Beneath his habitual tan his face was white with rage, the tiny muscles quivering. "You knew, didn't you! God damn it, you knew and you didn't tell me! Don't deny it. You know everything that goes on in that office."

"I . . . I—"

"Damn you! You let me walk into that meeting and get blindsided!"

His fingers bit into her shoulders like talons, but Alice was so upset she barely felt the pain. She cringed and tried to pull back. "Chad, I swear to you, I only found out about Sara yesterday. And I did try to call you. I *did,*" she insisted in a pleading voice when he snorted. "I called every few minutes until three in the morning. Both your office number and the private line in your bedroom. You weren't in either place."

The hint of accusation in her voice made her wince, but he didn't seem to notice. Almost sick with jealousy, she had tortured herself, imagining him here, in their private hideaway, with another woman. Of course, she could never tell him that. Chad hated possessive women.

His blond eyebrows jerked together, and his expression arrested. "Dandy Girl foaled last night. I was at the barn until dawn. You should have guessed that," he muttered, only slightly mollified.

"But . . . you told me never to call you anywhere but on the office line, and—"

"Never mind. That's not important." He swung away and started pacing again. Alice knew that he had forgotten her already. Pressing her lips together, she hugged her arms tight against her midriff and watched him, relieved that her jealous fears had been groundless and hurt that he could dismiss her so easily.

"I was counting on someday inheriting a large chunk of that stock. The future of the ranch depends on it. *Damn it!*" He swung his arm in a vicious, backhanded arc and sent toppling a tacky old lamp made from welded horseshoes.

Alice jumped and let out a squeak when it crashed to the floor. Chad kept pacing. "I've been patient long enough. Too long. It's time to take some action."

"Wh-what? What're you going to do?"

He stopped and stared at her, his eyes hard. "I don't know yet, but I'm going to get what's mine."

The next day Sara and Rourke resumed their tour of the Eve Cosmetics complex. Rourke was friendly and polite but businesslike. Sara could almost believe those few heady moments of passion in the kitchen the previous night had never happened. Like the perfect host, he was gracious and informative as he showed Sara the research labs, the new products testing building, the manufacturing plants.

"We put every product through the full spectrum of allergy tests," he explained, as he escorted her into the vast dermatology lab. "All Eve products are hypoallergenic. We also test every batch of every product for any impurities that may have contaminated the mix during the manufacturing process."

"Does that happen often?"

"Rarely. Our controls are fairly rigid."

"What happens when it does?"

"The batch is disposed of and the equipment sterilized."

Sara was impressed and amazed. She'd had no idea so much went into manufacturing and distributing makeup. When she admitted as much to Rourke, he looked amused.

"We manufacture much more than just makeup, Sara. We make a complete line of hair products, feminine hygiene products, skin care products, sunblocks, vitamins especially for women, and, of course, perfume. We're also gearing up to produce a whole line of grooming products for men." He shot her a wry grin. "The line will be called Adam, of course."

Sara's eyes twinkled back. "Of course."

"The launch date for the men's line will coincide with the openings of Eden East and Eden West. A month or so before that, we'll begin a saturation ad campaign—television, radio, magazines, billboards, the works."

Sara heard the undertone of pride in his voice and she looked at Rourke with new respect. He wasn't just a greedy executive, looking to expand company profits and boost his own status; he was justifiably proud of the organization and the quality of their products.

"Unlike many cosmetics companies, we do not farm out anything. We manufacture everything that carries the Eve brand. These days, we even design and make our own containers and cartons.

"We have factories and labs around the world. They all report to this office. We do millions—hundreds of millions—of dollars of business every year." He paused to be sure she understood the subtle point he was trying to make. "Eve started this business in her kitchen on a dream, a lot of ambition, and the confidence that she could offer women a superior product. We've now grown into a worldwide company with factories in twenty-three countries, seven research facilities, and a network of employees that numbers into the thousands. Making it all click together is a tremendous job."

And you're wondering if I'm up to it, Sara thought, but she merely smiled and stepped past him when he held open yet another door for her.

Rourke showed her the compression factory, where Evelyn's patented makeup bases, powders, blushes, and eyeshadows were pressed into small pots and compacts and stamped with the Eve logo. He took her through the huge rooms where dozens of stainless steel vats were suspended from the ceiling, filled with liquid beauty-care products waiting to be bottled. They toured the packaging factory, where bottles, jars, pots, vials, and tubes jostled along conveyer belts and were labeled and packaged in the distinctive pearly white boxes with the single bitten red apple on it.

There was a glass-blowing factory, a printshop that made all the inserts that went in with each product, and a design center where teams of artists and writers worked on the packaging and presentation of each new product.

It took two full days to tour the entire complex. By the time they had finished, Sara was exhausted and overwhelmed, her head spinning with all she had seen, all the facts and figures Rourke had tossed out so casually off the top of his head. And this was only one complex. There were almost a dozen more scattered around the globe.

Someday she could be in charge of it all. It was a daunting prospect.

No wonder Rourke had doubts about her ability. For the first time, Sara wondered if she really was up to the job.

Ambition and self-confidence had always been an intrinsic part of her personality. Even as a small child, she had daydreamed of someday being successful, and there had never been a doubt in her mind, not even in the darkest days of her early life, that someday, somehow, she would make it happen. Until Sara had learned that she was Evelyn's daughter, she had always wondered where those traits had sprung from. Neither of her parents—adoptive parents, she mentally corrected—had ever shown any such aspirations. Edgar Anderson, for all his pious preaching, had been lazy. He had worked at his trade only when necessity dictated, and then just enough to eke out a living.

Sara's determination to achieve had served her well. When she looked back at her beginnings, she knew she had come a long way, and she had every reason to be proud of her accomplishments. But what did she know about running an international corporation?

The scope of the operation and the responsibilities that went along with heading a company like Eve Cosmetics was mind boggling. For the first time in her life, Sara felt twinges of inadequacy.

Perhaps, when the time came, she should allow the stock to be sold. She had let Evelyn think that was a possibility mainly to torment her, and in all honesty she had considered going against Evelyn's wishes in order to strike back at her. Now Sara wondered if perhaps it wouldn't truly be best all around. Wouldn't the company be better off with someone at the helm who knew what he was doing? Even if that person were a complete outsider?

The next day, sitting in the first-class section of a commercial jetliner streaking westward toward Los Angeles, Sara was still mulling over those questions.

"What do you mean, she doesn't want to let me renew the option? She *has* to!" Madelene gripped the telephone receiver and listened, tapping the fingernails of her free hand against the desktop, her face tight with fury and fear. "Why the hell *doesn't* it stipulate that I can pick up the option for the same price? It's your job to see to details like that. That's what agents do. If I can't trust you to look out for my interests, then what the hell good are you, Harold?"

She listened again, her lips pressed together in a

straight line. Impatient, Madelene reached into the middle drawer of her desk and pulled a cigarette from the pack she had stashed under a pile of papers at the back.

She was supposed to have quit the habit over a year ago, but occasionally she needed something to soothe her nerves. Lawrence would have a fit if he caught her. Her eyes hardened. She lit the cigarette and took a deep drag. Who the hell cared? She was still furious with Lawrence, anyway.

"So how much does she want this time?"

When he told her, Madelene shot up out of her chair, her eyes wide. *"What? Why, that's double the price we gave her before! What the hell do you mean, she wants to be sure the book is made into a movie? What the fuck does she think I'm trying to do with it? Make paper airplanes?"

She listened a few seconds to Harold Dawson's pleading, then snapped, "All right, damn it, tell her I'll pay it. In the meantime, I've got six more months to run on the current option."

"Incompetent ass." Madelene slammed the receiver down so hard it jumped right out of its cradle and she had to do it again, which did nothing to improve her temper.

"Is something wrong?" Lawrence said from the doorway of her home office.

Madelene jumped and glared at him, quickly stubbing out the cigarette. Lawrence noticed and frowned, but he wisely did not mention it.

"I don't have enough troubles. Now the author of *Night Song* doesn't want to let me renew my option on the book."

"She doesn't have a choice. It's in the contract."

"True, but my brilliant agent neglected to freeze the price. Now Ms. Tolkin wants double what I gave her before. She claims to be worried that I'm not doing enough to get the book made into a movie, but I think a couple of little birds by the name of Morris and Stan have been whispering in her ear." The long, crimson fingernails of both Maddie's hands clacked in a rolling rhythm on the arms of her chair.

"Damn." Lawrence edged farther into the room, watching her, half expecting her to screech at him to get out. Maddie's temper had been explosive ever since they'd returned from Houston a week ago. She had yet to forgive him for saying that Sara was entitled to own Eve stock, even though he had only stated the truth. They'd had a flaming row over it, which had resulted in her throwing him out of their bedroom. So far, she'd shown no sign of forgiving him. "I'm sorry, darling. I know how much the project meant to you. But there'll be other—"

"I agreed to her price." Maddie tossed out the statement like a gauntlet, her eyes defiant.

"You did what? But, Maddie, you can't do that! You can't afford that kind of expense. Not right now, at any rate. Sweetheart, don't you understand? You're having a bit of a cash-flow problem. You can't—"

"Don't tell me I can't!" she snapped. "I'm sick of hearing what I can't do. I can't do anything about Sara Anderson owning part of my family's business. I can't sell my stock. I can't put up money for the movie. I can't play the part of Helen. I can't renew my option. I'm sick of hearing I can't!

"Damn it, I'm going to keep the rights to that book. I don't care what it costs. That part is mine.

I'm not going to let Stan and Morris or anyone else steal it away from me."

"But, darling, the money—"

"Screw the money! I don't care where or how you get it, just get it. Embezzle it. Stick up a bank. Hell, I don't care if you commit murder for it, just *get it!*"

Her voice broke on the last and she blinked furiously at the tears in her eyes.

"Aw, darling, don't." Sitting on the corner of her desk, Lawrence picked up both of her hands. "Don't get so upset. I can't bear to see you like this."

"I've *got* to do that movie, Lawrence." Her voice was small, barely a whisper, and wobbly with the threat of tears. With those magnificent gray eyes glistening with moisture and her chin quivering, she looked like a pathetic child who had lost her heart's desire. Lawrence caved in like a sand castle at high tide.

"Ah, sweetheart, don't cry. Everything will work out somehow." He stood and moved behind her chair and began to massage the tension from her shoulders.

Madelene sighed and rested her head back against his middle. She liked the feel of his hands—strong, competent hands. He made her feel pampered, protected, wanted. She needed that now. Desperately.

"You do love me, don't you, Lawrence?"

"With all my heart and soul," he vowed. "You're my life, Maddie. I'll always be here for you, darling. Always."

She didn't believe him, of course, but it was good to hear. Sooner or later, he would tire of her and want to leave. Everyone did.

Throughout her childhood her mother had left her

over and over to go on location. Madelene had adored her beautiful mother. Periodically, in between making movies, Claire Chadwick-Ketchum had come home to the ranch, sweeping in on them in grand style in a swirl of mink and blond hair and expensive perfume, full of laughter and gaiety, dispensing kisses and hugs and presents like a fairy godmother. For a few weeks or months, she would seem content just to be home with them, but inevitably she grew restless. Then she would be off again, no matter how much Maddie had begged her to stay, or what terrible tantrums she had thrown. Half the time her father had joined her while she was filming. Then her mother had gone away for good.

Madelene had seen the signs in all of her ex-husbands—the restlessness, the waning of affection and willingness to please her—and she had done the only thing she could to protect her pride; she had left them before they could leave her. She knew that eventually she would have to leave Lawrence, too.

The only love she had ever been able to count on was that she'd received from her fans. Panic rose like gorge in her throat at the thought of that love slipping away from her as well. She couldn't bear it.

She closed her eyes and sighed as Lawrence's hands skimmed over her neck. With a skillful, feather-light touch, his fingers threaded through her hair, toyed with her ears, then trailed down to her breasts. They were soft and heavy, growing heavier.

"You want me to be happy, don't you, Lawrence?" Her nipples tightened beneath his exploring fingers.

"Of course I do."

Maddie moaned and rubbed the back of her head

against his belly. She smiled at the feel of his erection pressing against her back. "So somehow you'll get the money I need. You'll find a way, won't you, darling?"

"Maddie . . ."

She arched her back, and he cupped her breasts. She covered his hands with her own and guided them in a slow rotation. "Won't you, Lawrence?"

Lawrence felt his heart crack at the desperate appeal in her voice. He gazed down at his wife, his eyes sad and soft. Her nipples pressed against his palms like hard buttons. He watched her arch her neck and rub against him sinuously as a cat, and lust and pity consumed him. She was manipulating him again, using her beauty and sexy body to get her way, but he couldn't be angry. Poor Maddie. She was so needy, so starved for love and attention. How could he deny her anything?

"I'll do my best, darling," he said with a sigh.

Smiling, Maddie unzipped her flowing caftan and guided his hands inside. He explored her midriff, her belly, then plunged his hand between her thighs. Maddie groaned as he cupped her mound. His finger delved beneath the scrap of lacy panties and flicked over the tender petals of flesh. She was hot and moist, and when he slipped a finger inside her she writhed, her hips thrusting against his touch. She reached up to pull him around in front of her. "Make love to me, Lawrence. *Now!*"

Chapter Sixteen

"Holy shit." Standing in the main cabin of the private jet, Jennifer gaped like a kid at a carnival sideshow. "Would you get a load of this crate? This isn't an airplane, it's a frigging flying mansion!"

She whirled and looked at Sara, her expression changing from awestruck to impish. "I could get used to this. Hot damn, boss. We're picking in tall cotton now."

" 'Picking in tall cotton'?" Sara laughed and rolled her eyes at Brian. "I think that's suppose to be Texas talk."

"So that's what that was. I'm glad you told me. She's been saying things like that all morning. By the way, correct me if I'm wrong, but isn't this the girl who only last week was grumbling about having to move to Texas with all those crude cowboys?"

"Uh hmm."

"Hey. A person can change her mind, you know. As a matter of fact, when we get there, I may even rope one of those rich cowboys and slap my brand on him."

"Oh, Lord. Now she's talking like John Wayne."

"John who?" Jennifer demanded, frowning.

Brian groaned and threw up his hands. "I give up. Who can hold a conversation with a mere child?"

Jen stuck her tongue out at him and went back to checking out the cabin.

Two-year-old Cindy, sitting astraddle her mother's hip, wasn't impressed. She bounced and tugged at Jennifer's French braid and chanted, "Down, down, down." Finally, tired of being ignored, she grasped her mother's face between her pudgy hands and turned her head until they were nose to nose and staring cross-eyed at one another. *"Down,* Mommie."

"Forget it, you little rug rat. You're staying with me."

"Aw c'mon, Jen. Give the kid a break. This is an airplane, not a museum."

"Are you kidding? Turn this one woman demolition crew loose in here? I'd still be paying for the damage when I went on Social Security. Not on your—oh, look! There's a bedroom! Jeez, do you believe it?"

She took off at a lope. Bouncing on her hip, Cindy thought it was a game and squealed with delight.

Sara watched her irrepressible secretary disappear into the rear of the plane. "I do think Jen's okay with the move, don't you, Brian?"

"Are you kidding? She's having the time of her life."

"I hope you're right." Sara sat down in one of the plush armchairs and fastened the seatbelt. "I feel awful about uprooting the two of you like this."

"Hey, are we complaining? We're getting great jobs with benefits and a raise in pay." Brian plopped down in the chair beside her and took her hand. His brown eyes twinkled at her and his melancholy face was full of jovial tenderness, but a closer study of the uncertainty swirling in Sara's eyes wiped it away. "Hey, wait a second. This isn't about Jen, is it? You're jumpy as a caged cat. What's going on?"

"It's just . . . this whole thing happened so fast. It's the chance of a lifetime. As ambitious as I am, I never dreamed of anything this big. But the responsibilities will be enormous. I've got so much to learn. Sometimes I wonder . . ."

"What?"

"You know . . . if I'm really up to all this." Merely saying it aloud made her nerves jump. Unable to sit still, Sara released the seatbelt and shot to her feet. She paced the cabin, twisting her fingers together. "I mean, it's an exciting challenge and a part of me welcomes it, but . . ." She stopped and closed her eyes, pressing her palm against her fluttery stomach. "Beneath the excitement and the energy, I have to admit, I'm afraid."

"Afraid? You? Of what?"

"Of failing. Of not being smart enough or experienced enough, tough enough. Brian, you have no idea of the complexity and scope of Eve Cosmetics. It's overwhelming."

"Hey, what is this? This isn't you." Brian grabbed her hand as she went by and pulled her to a stop. He looked up into her face and squeezed her fingers. "You're a tiger, remember? You can do anything. You always could. Once you put your mind to it and adjust to the pace, you'll eat up this corporate bigwig stuff with a spoon, and you know it. C'mon, gorgeous. Smile. You're gonna make one helluva tycoon."

He gave her hand another squeeze and winked. The pep talk might have helped if Sara hadn't seen the flicker of panic in his eyes. Brian expected, *needed,* her to be strong and confident, capable of taking on any situation or problem. He could not deal with insecurity in Sara.

She drew a deep breath and stifled her anxiety. Shrugging, she gave him a weak smile. "You're right. I guess I just have a case of stagefright. Don't pay any attention to me."

Returning to the chair, Sara buckled up and turned her gaze out the window. She *was* strong and smart and capable. And she wouldn't want it any other way. But once in a while she found herself wondering how it would feel to have someone she could turn to, someone strong and reliable who would always be there beside her to lend a hand or just provide a broad shoulder to lean on once in a while when she was feeling down.

Immediately, in her mind's eye, Sara saw Rourke's dark face and vivid blue eyes.

Jennifer bounced back into the cabin, so excited she was practically shooting off sparks. "Hey, do you believe it? There's a bathroom back there!"

"Most planes have bathrooms, kiddo," Brian teased.

"Not with a marble tub and gold faucets!"

Jennifer's excitement over the company jet had barely begun to subside when they landed in Houston and found Rourke waiting for them with a limo.

"Oh, my gawd, would you look at that car? There's a chauffeur, too!" Jen did a little jig and would have hurtled herself and Cindy down the steps of the plane if Sara hadn't stopped her.

"Calm down." Chuckling, she grabbed Jen's arm. "It's just an automobile."

"Yeah. A little decorum, if you please," Brian echoed, two steps behind them. "I shudder to think what kind of impression your uninhibited behavior must have made on Sara's clients."

"Hey! When I'm working I can la-di-da it with the best of 'em," Jen shot over her shoulder.

"All right, both of you. Behave," Sara ordered, but by then Jennifer had spotted Rourke. It was a toss-up which impressed her most, the man or the automobile.

"Oh, shit. I'm not sure my heart can take this," she muttered, as they started across the tarmac. "The royal coach *and* Prince Charming. And he's even sexier than I remembered."

"Jen!"

"You really think that guy's sexy?" Brian demanded.

"Are you kidding? He's got it all: face, bod, butt. And those eyes. Be still, my heart."

Rourke waited beside the limo, feet planted apart, hands in the pants pockets of his dark suit. The stance held his coat thrust back and revealed lean hips and an impressive broad chest. The wind whipped his dark hair and his tie and plastered his trousers against his muscular legs. He looked thoroughly and uncompromisingly male.

Sara was horribly conscious of his gaze on her as they approached him. The morning after he had fin-

ished showing her around the complex she had arrived at the office to find he had flown to Madrid in
the company jet. She had returned to California that
same afternoon.

"Hello, Sara. Welcome back." His voice was low
and intimate, the look in his eyes warm.

She felt her heart stutter. Rattled, annoyed, she
tilted her chin and forced a cool tone. "Hello,
Rourke. I didn't expect to see you here."

"Now, why is that, I wonder?"

He reached to take her cosmetics bag, but when his
hand closed over hers on the handle, he simply stood
there. Somewhere nearby a plane hurtled down a
runway, jet engines screaming. Heat rose from the
tarmac, and the swirling wind smelled of dust and jet
fuel.

They were close. Too close, Sara realized, tilting
her head back to look into his face. So close she could
see herself in his intense blue eyes.

"I . . . I guess I figured you would be too busy."

"Mmm. I see." The wind whipped her hair across
her face. Before she could do anything about it he
raised his other hand and brushed the strands back,
smoothing his fingertips across her cheek. Sara felt
that touch like four trails of fire on her skin, and she
shivered.

"I'm never too busy for you, Sara." Rourke
smiled, and Sara forgot her friends standing beside
them, the chauffeur and pilot loading luggage into
the back of the limo, the clamoring alarm in her head
telling her to back away. "Don't you know that?"

"Well . . . I . . . ." At that moment Sara didn't even
know her own name. His eyes held her mesmerized,
so blue and intense, probing deep into her soul. They

focused on her as though nothing and no one else existed.

"Believe it, Sara. You've become very important. To the company—and to me." He pulled his fingers from her hair and trailed them along her jaw.

The air backed up in Sara's lungs. Speech became impossible. All she could do was stare.

"Thanks for coming to fetch us." Brian stepped forward with his hand out and his jaw set.

Sara jumped and took a quick step back. "Oh, sorry. Uh, Rourke, you remember Brian, don't you?"

Wry amusement chased across Rourke's face. Without a trace of discomfort, he switched Sara's bag to his left hand and clasped Brian's with his right. "Yes. We met in LA, I believe." He turned to Jennifer with a smile. "And Ms. Potts, isn't it?"

Jennifer nodded, for once struck dumb. When he smiled and shook her hand, she looked as though she were about to melt into a puddle at his feet. Even Cindy had stopped whining and fixed him with an unblinking stare. Sara wondered if the man had some kind of hypnotic power over females.

He grinned at the baby and tugged one of her coppery curls. "And this is?"

"My daughter, Cindy."

Rourke poked the baby's belly with his forefinger and winked. "Hello, Cindy." Giggling, she burrowed against her mother and peeked at him coyly.

Jen's cocky grin returned and her own eyes twinkled at Rourke. "Cindy's a sucker for good-looking men. She takes after me."

"Uh, why don't we get going?" Sara gave Jennifer a nudge toward the back of the limo. Jen was rapidly regaining her composure, and along with it, her sass. It was time to get her out of there before she said something truly outrageous.

Sara started to follow, but Rourke took her arm. "Wait. The limo is for Miss Potts and Mr. Neely. You're riding with me." He tipped his head toward the burgundy BMW parked a few yards away. "Evelyn wants to see you."

"Now? But it's getting late and I just arrived. Can't it wait until tomorrow?"

"No. I'm afraid it can't." He tried to tug her toward his car, but Sara held back.

"Wait. First, I need to get Jen and Brian settled in their apartments."

"Tucker will see to it. And they're both adults. Well . . . okay, I'm not all that sure about Jennifer." He winked at Jen, and she flashed a cocky grin. "But they *are* old enough to take care of themselves. And don't worry about your luggage. Tucker will deliver your things to the apartment later."

"But—"

"Go on, boss. Don't worry about Brian and me. We'll be fine." Brian did not look all that happy about the arrangement, but Jennifer ignored him and whispered in Sara's ear, "Don't be an idiot. If that hunk looked at me the way he looks at you, I'd follow him off a cliff. The man's yummy. Now go."

She gave Sara a shove in Rourke's direction, then stuck her nose in the air and strolled to the limo. "Home, Jeeves," she instructed the chauffeur in a snooty voice. With the dignity of a duchess, Jen climbed into the rear of the limo with Brian. Then she spoiled the whole thing by bouncing on the seat and giggling. "I've always wanted to say that."

Chuckling, Rourke lifted his hand in farewell and steered Sara toward his car. "She's a real character, isn't she?"

"You don't know the half of it."

"A bit young to be a secretary, though. Or a mother, for that matter."

Sara stiffened. "Jen's a terrific mother. And a terrific secretary."

"Hey, I didn't mean she wasn't. Merely that she's young for that kind of responsibility." Rourke opened the passenger door of the BMW and gave Sara a smile as she slid inside. "How did you happen to hire her?"

"When I started Reflections, I advertised in the newspaper for a secretary. Jennifer answered the ad."

"I see." Rourke closed the door and Sara watched him round the car.

"She was seventeen years old and seven months pregnant at the time," she continued, when he slid in under the wheel. "She showed up in my office bold as brass, even though she looked as if she'd been living on the streets for months. Which, it turned out, she had.

"When Jen got pregnant, her boyfriend dumped her, and her parents threw her out of the house when they found out about the baby. She was hungry and frightened and tried to hide it with smart talk. She knew she wasn't qualified for the job even before she applied, but she was desperate."

"So you took her in."

"Well, I couldn't let her go back out on the streets."

Rourke raised an eyebrow at that, but he said nothing. Sara's chin went up a notch.

"Anyway, it was a good decision. Jen is sharp as a whip and a quick study. She had the secretarial skills down pat and was running my office smooth as silk within a couple of months. So if you're worried that she's not qualified to work in the Eve office—"

"I'm not worried."

"Oh. I see. Well . . . good." Self-conscious, she looked around and became suddenly aware of the quiet and the fading sunset, and that she and Rourke were practically alone on this end of the airstrip.

He was watching her, his gaze steady on her face. She shifted and looked away, then glanced back. "Shouldn't we be on our way?"

"In a minute. First . . ."

He reached for her. Grasping her shoulders, he dragged her across the seat and against his chest. Sara barely had time to give a little moan as his mouth took possession of hers.

It was like setting a match to gunpowder. In a heartbeat they were fused together, his mouth consuming hers, her hands fisted in his hair. The blast of desire, of need, shook them both. They couldn't get close enough, couldn't take enough, couldn't give enough. It wasn't dreamy and soft, but greedy and raw and real. Need fueled need, and the heat was intense. The flames shot high. The pressure built. Sara felt ready to explode, her emotions stretching taut to the shattering point.

A frustrated groan tore from Rourke's throat. His hand covered her breast, and Sara echoed the sound. The voracious kiss went on and on. It wasn't enough. Their hands clutched and groped, their bodies strained. Sara greedily absorbed his heat, the feel of his hard body, the taste of him, wanting more. The only sounds in the car were small gasps and moans, the rustle of clothes.

Rourke made a low sound and twisted with her—and the car horn blasted.

"Damn it to hell!"

They jumped like guilty teenagers. Sara made a distressed sound and would have jerked out of his arms, but he tightened his hold. "No. Don't. Stay here."

"Rourke—"

"Ssh. Ssh." He pulled her against his chest again and held her close while their breathing eased and their thundering hearts gradually slowed.

Sara lay against him, her head tucked beneath his chin, shattered, her body vibrating. She could feel the matching shudders wracking Rourke's body. She felt raw, her nerve endings sizzling and sparking like a severed power line.

Rourke's big hand cupped the back of her head and he rubbed his chin absently against her crown. With her nose pressed against his neck, Sara drew in his scent with every breath, absorbed his heat, the feel of him.

They stayed that way for several minutes, but gradually the terrible tension eased and the shaking stopped. And sanity returned. With it came embarrassment, and Sara stirred.

This time when she pushed against Rourke's chest, he settled her back in the seat and released her. Flustered, Sara straightened her clothes and finger-combed her hair, carefully keeping her gaze averted from him. When she picked up her purse and dug into it for a lipstick, Rourke reached out and grasped her chin between his thumb and forefinger and turned her face toward him. She kept her gaze lowered at first, but when he whispered, "look at me, Sara," she slowly raised her eyes.

When their gazes met, he smiled. He rubbed his thumb across her swollen bottom lip. "Well. Now we know what happens."

"Rourke, I . . ." Sara had no idea what to say. She was mortified and appalled. They'd been necking in a car like a couple of teenagers, for God's sake. This, after telling herself for the past two weeks that at the first opportunity she was going to make it clear to Rourke that she wasn't interested.

She almost groaned. Not interested. What a joke. She had gone off like a Roman candle the instant he touched her. If it hadn't been for that horn . . .

"Don't worry about it." He released her chin and rubbed his thumb over the frown line between her eyebrows. "Some things you just can't fight. I know. I've tried. But no more. So buckle up, sweetheart, and fix your lipstick." He flicked the key in the ignition, and after one last long look at her, sent the BMW purring out of the VIP parking area.

Sara was too rattled to argue. She did as he said and stared blindly out the window.

With all that was going on in her life, by rights she should not be able to even think of anything but Evelyn and Eve Cosmetics. Yet, all the while she had been in California, as busy as she'd been, over and over her thoughts had kept drifting to Rourke.

What was it about him? Sara had never in her life been so attracted to a man. It was unnerving. And stupid.

She had no business—no business at all—falling

for Rourke. He was Evelyn's right-hand man, her fair-haired boy. His loyalty was to her.

"Did you get your mother settled at Briar Haven?"

The quiet question made her jump. Sara glanced at Rourke's calm profile and realized he was trying to help her settle. "Yes. At least, I think so. Dr. Ardmore and his nurse brought her here two days ago. I wanted to fly back with them, but he thought the transfer would go better if he handled it alone. Mother is so unpredictable. Sometimes, on her bad days, she gets violent and has to be sedated. Dr. Ardmore knows how much that upsets me." She glanced Rourke's way again. "I appreciate the use of the company jet to move her here. Thank you for arranging it."

"No problem. Anyway, I'm not the one you should be thanking. Evelyn gave orders that the plane was to be at your disposal all week."

"Oh. I see. How thoughtful." Sara knew her voice had cooled by several degrees, but she couldn't help it. She wasn't comfortable with the idea of Evelyn making such a gesture. It was easier for Sara to think of her as cold and unfeeling.

Behind them a truck horn blared, and Sara jumped. Until that moment, she had not paid any attention to their surroundings, but looking around, she realized she did not recognize the area.

When Rourke turned into a strange parking garage and started up the ramp, she sat up straighter.

"Where are we? This isn't Evelyn's building. I thought you said she wanted to see me."

"She does." He parked on the second level and turned off the ignition, but he made no move to leave the car. Propping one forearm across the top of the steering wheel, he turned partway toward Sara. The somber look in his eyes made her uneasy.

"Evelyn's not at home, Sara. She's here. This is a hospital."

Something painful and sharp flared in her chest. She darted a look around. "A hospital? What's wrong? Has she had an accident?"

"She's ill, Sara. Very ill."

Sara stared at Rourke, unable to speak. If asked, she could not have defined the riot of emotions that roiled within her, only that the sensation was painful and frightening. She shouldn't care. She told herself she didn't care. The woman meant nothing to her. Still, her chest felt as though it were being squeezed in a vice.

"Wh-what's wrong with her?" she finally managed.

"I think you should hear that from Evelyn."

"Rourke—"

"C'mon. I'll take you to her."

Before she could protest any further, he bailed out and was around the car, holding the door open for her. Putting a supporting arm around her waist, he led her to the elevated crosswalk that spanned the busy street and connected the parking garage to the hospital. Sara was grateful. Her legs felt watery. Without his help she wasn't sure they'd have held her up.

In silence, she walked quickly at his side, through the soaring lobby and down long hallways, shaking, cold inside, though she had no idea why.

When they entered the bedroom of the VIP suite, Evelyn's eyes were closed. The head of the bed was elevated partway, and she lay perfectly still, with her hands folded over the tops of the covers. She looked small and fragile, and terribly pale.

They must have made some slight noise. They barely reached her bedside when Evelyn's eyes fluttered open. "Hello, Sara."

Instinctively, Sara reached out to touch her, but she caught herself and withdrew her hand before making contact and gripped the metal bed rail. "Hello, Evelyn. How are you?"

"I must admit, I've been better." Her gaze sought Rourke. "Have you told her?"

"No. I figured that should come from you."

Several seconds ticked by as she and Rourke exchanged a long look.

Sara tightened her hands on the rail, her gaze darting from one to the other. "For Pete's sake, will *someone* tell me what's going on?"

"Yes. Of course." Evelyn drew in a deep breath and exhaled it slowly. "Sara, I . . . I have an acute form of leukemia."

The shock was like a splash of icewater in the face. For a moment Sara could not catch her breath. She stared, wide-eyed, at Evelyn's calm face. "Leukemia?" She glanced at Rourke—for confirmation, for denial—and received a grim nod. "How . . . how bad is it?"

"At best, the prognosis is only fair. My doctor is hopeful, and he's doing all he can, but . . ."

The instinct to touch, to give comfort, was too strong, and this time Sara did not fight it. She reached out and took one of Evelyn's cold hands and held it between both of hers.

Surprised, Evelyn started and jerked back, but Sara held on tight. Compassion, grief, and guilty regret welled up inside her as she looked into the light green eyes of the woman who had given her life. "Oh, Evelyn. I'm so sorry. Really. I am. But they're doing wonderful things these days. Discovering new drugs, new treatments. A cure could be—"

Sara broke off as the door pushed open and a white-coated man strode in.

"Well, now, how are we feeling this evening?"

Evelyn arched one eyebrow. "I can't speak for you, doctor, but I feel wretched."

"Still nauseated from the therapy, are you?" He stopped at the foot of the bed and picked up the medical chart. "And running a fever, too, I see. Well, don't worry. That's normal. So are those bruises." He looked up from making a notation on the chart and met Sara's anxious gaze. "Well, well. Who is this?"

Evelyn made the introductions, and Dr. Underwood's face lit up. "A daughter? I was under the impression that you didn't have any blood relatives. This is marvelous. Just great." He replaced the chart and took Sara's hand, giving it an avuncular pat. "If you don't mind, Ms. Anderson, I would like to test you tonight. It won't take but a few minutes to draw some blood."

"Test me? I'm sorry, I don't understand. Test me for what?"

"To see if you're a close enough match to be a donor. Your mother needs a bone marrow transplant," he explained, when Sara continued to look confused. "We've tried chemotherapy for over a month, but we can't get the disease into remission, and time is running out. We're searching for a donor match for Evelyn through outside sources, of course, but we've had no luck so far. You are our best chance."

"I see." And Sara was very much afraid that she did.

"So if you have no objections, I'll run down to the lab and set up the testing and you can drop by on your way out. Mr. Fallan can show you the way. Okay?"

"Yes. Of course. I'll be down shortly," Sara said in a wooden voice.

Dr. Underwood bustled out a happy man.

When the door closed behind him, she turned accusing eyes on Evelyn. "You lied to me. All this business about my inheritance was just an excuse. You didn't bring me here to make me your heir." Her voice came out low and raspy, vibrating with bitterness. "Oh, God! What a fool I've been. I thought you were having pangs of conscience over giving me away, but that wasn't it at all, was it? You brought me here hoping I could—and would—save your life."

Chapter Seventeen

"That's not true, Sara. I found you and brought you here for exactly the reason I gave you; to save my company." Evelyn's face was calm, but for the first time there was an edge to her voice, a flicker of anxiety in her eyes. Sara took grim pleasure in both.

"Oh, really? Are you trying to tell me it never occurred to you that I might be a possible donor?"

For several seconds Evelyn simply looked at her. Rourke's gaze swung from one pair of identical green eyes to the other, watching the silent battle between mother and daughter. They were virtual strangers, bound by blood in one of the closest relationships that existed, yet separated by a lifetime apart and a chasm of hurt and anger so wide and so deep he wondered if it could ever be bridged.

"No, I'm not saying that," Evelyn replied finally. "I told you I wouldn't lie to you, and I won't. Of course, the possibility has occurred to me. But I am well aware that I don't have the right to ask that of you, Sara. And I won't."

"But then, you don't have to, do you? You just let good old Dr. Underwood do it for you. And if that doesn't work, there's always your wonderful family.

"Ah, yes. I'm sure Eric and Kitty would ask me to be a donor. Kitty would probably get down on her knees and beg with tears in her eyes. She made quite a point of telling me that she was the 'daughter of your heart.' Even Madelene would probably shed a few tears, being the consummate actress she is. Chad and Paul . . . wellll . . ." Sara spread her fingers wide and waggled her hand in an "iffy" gesture. "But of course, you can count on good old Will to at least give lip service to the request."

Sara shot her a contemptuous look. "No, you wouldn't ask me to be your donor. You'd just make it impossible for me to refuse."

"Sara . . ." Her eyes flashed at Rourke, and he grimaced at the anger swirling in the pale green depths. "Don't you think you should calm down? Let's discuss—wait. Where're you going?"

"To the lab. Where else?" she snapped.

"You mean . . . you're going to let Dr. Underwood test you?" For once Evelyn's calm demeanor cracked. She stared, amazed.

"Why, of course." Sara's voice dripped sarcasm. "What are we talking about? A little blood, a little bone marrow? How could I possibly refuse, after you've made me a wealthy woman? But then, that's why you've been so generous, isn't it?" Her false smile vanished, and her bitter gaze swung to Rourke. "When you're ready to leave, you know where to find me." Without so much as a look for Evelyn, she stalked out.

Rourke stared thoughtfully after her. Silence swelled in the room, thickening the air.

"She's upset," Evelyn murmured. "But she'll get

over it soon and be back. I've noticed that Sara can't seem to maintain anger long. That's a good trait. Especially in a business executive."

Rourke turned his head and looked at Evelyn. His eyes narrowed. *"Did* you bring her here to save your life?"

One imperious eyebrow went up. "You, too?"

Rourke refused to be intimidated.

Finally Evelyn sighed. "No, I didn't bring her here for that. You, better than anyone, know why I brought her here. But I *am* fighting for my life. Naturally, the possibility occurred to me."

He studied her expression for a few seconds more, then nodded and headed for the door. Before he reached it, her quiet voice stopped him in his tracks.

"Just as I'm sure it has occurred to you that the man who marries Sara will be in an excellent position to take over the company."

Rourke looked over his shoulder and met Evelyn's steady green eyes for a long time.

Rourke found Sara pacing the hallway outside the lab. Her steps were quick and jerky. Arms crossed tight against her midriff, hands cupping her elbows, she was taut as a violin string. Rourke had never seen that cold expression on her face before.

"Finished already?"

Her head jerked up at his approached, her eyes snapping. "It doesn't take long." She pivoted and headed for the exit, her heels tapping angrily on the tile floor. He had to lengthen his stride to catch up with her.

"Sara, we need to talk—"

"No!" She jerked to a halt and swung to face him. Her face was white. "Don't! Don't you *dare!* If you tell me again, after what you just witnessed, that Evelyn only wants what's best for me, so help me God, I'll hit you."

The look on Dr. Underwood's face said it all.

The instant he walked into the sitting room of the suite, three pairs of anxious eyes swung in his direction, but before he ever spoke a word, Evelyn knew.

"I'm sorry," he said, shaking his head. "You were close, Sara, but you just don't share quite all of Evelyn's HLAs."

"HLAs?" Rourke frowned. "Translation?"

"Those are human leukocyte antigens, the proteins in the immune system that recognize and reject foreign tissue. We need a perfect match to do a transplant. Even then, sometimes the patient's blood and the donor's can't always 'live together,' so to speak."

Evelyn closed her eyes and sagged back in the chair. She had thought she'd prepared herself for the worst, but the news crashed down on her like a tidal wave. The fear was suffocating, crushing.

What a fool she had been. She realized now that on a subconscious level she'd allowed Sara's uncanny resemblance to her to foster the hope that they would be alike in other ways.

Dr. Underwood patted her hand. "I am truly sorry, Evelyn. But you mustn't give up hope. We'll continue to search the donor registries. People are getting tested all the time. You never know when a match will turn up."

"Yes, of course, John. Please don't worry. I'm all right. Really."

"What happens now?" Rourke asked.

"We continue treatment and try to achieve remission with anticancer drugs and periodic transfusions of blood and platelets. This tends to leave the patient susceptible to infections, so we'll also keep her on powerful antibiotics."

"Most of which can be done at home." Evelyn's voice was velvet over steel—softly feminine, but unyielding. John Underwood had been her friend and doctor for over twenty years, and he recognized the tone as well as Rourke did.

Resigned, he sighed. "Very well. After we have completed the series of transfusions, you may go home. But not back to work. And unless you agree to go to the ranch, where your family can look after you, I must insist that you have a full-time nurse." He held up his hand when she would have argued. "No. I mean it, Evelyn. I don't want you living alone in that apartment. Understood?"

She had neither the strength nor the will to offer more than token resistance. In truth, as awful as she felt, she did not relish the thought of being alone.

When Dr. Underwood left, a heavy silence descended. Rourke sat on the edge of the sofa, elbows braced on his spread knees, hands dangling loosely between them, his head hung at a dejected angle. Sitting beside him, Sara stared out the window, composed but pale.

Studying her, Evelyn felt a peculiar, unwanted flutter in her chest, and quickly looked away.

Rourke raised his head, his eyes full of sadness and

worry. "Evelyn, I . . . I'm sorry. God, that seems so inadequate, but I don't know what else to say."

"Then don't say anything. It was a chance and it didn't work out. There is nothing we can do about that. What we need to do now is to map out a plan of action."

Evelyn sensed Sara's amazed stare, but she kept her gaze fixed on Rourke. "You said once that you thought you could keep the press off the scent for a few weeks. Does that still hold? The next board meeting is just a little over two weeks away. We'll have to tell the family of my condition then, and once we do, it won't take long for word to leak out. Sara's going to face stiff opposition from the Ketchums. I'd like to give her time to absorb all she can before she has to deal with the news media as well."

"I'll take care of it."

"Good. I want you to use this time to work with Sara. Teach her everything you can between now and the meeting. If something crops up overseas that requires your attention, take her with you. See that she has a thorough understanding of any and all problems."

"You got it. Is that okay with you, Sara?"

Evelyn saw the sudden leap of doubt in her daughter's eyes, watched her conquer it and assume a expression of composure and confidence. She looked from Rourke to Evelyn and held her gaze for several seconds. "Of course. That's what I came here for, after all."

The shot was subtle but deadly accurate. Evelyn acknowledged the hit with a slight nod, and as she watched her daughter leave with Rourke, she felt a rush of pride. *Yes. Oh, yes, she'll do. She'll do just fine.*

Neither Rourke nor Sara spoke until they were seated in the BMW in the parking garage. He inserted the key in the ignition, but instead of starting the engine, he turned his head and studied her. "Tell me something—if you had been a match, would you have gone through with it? Would you have been a donor for Evelyn?"

"Truthfully?" Sara sighed. "I honestly don't know."

She could feel the anger and resentment simmering inside her. She told herself that Evelyn's illness wasn't her problem, but as hard as she tried, she could not deny the faint stirring of blood ties.

Rourke chuckled. "Oh, I think you would have. You might not have wanted to, but you would have."

"Oh, really? What makes you so sure?"

"Because that's your nature. Look at the way you see after Julia Anderson. And your ex-husband. And Jennifer and Cindy. I'll bet you even check in on your old neighbor, Mrs. Blankenship, from time to time, don't you?" The look in Sara's eyes and the flush that colored her face answered for her. Rourke smiled and touched her hot cheek with his forefinger. "You could no more walk away from Evelyn in need than you could fly, no matter how angry or hurt you were. Because, Sara Anderson, you're a born caretaker."

Sara wanted to deny the statement, but she could not, so she settled for a careless shrug. "So? What's wrong with that?"

"Not a thing."

Rourke started the car and backed out of the parking space. As he headed for the exit ramp, he glanced her way again. "It's actually a very attractive trait. Another one you have in common with Evelyn."

Evelyn's whereabouts were known only to Sara, Rourke, Dr. Underwood, and the handpicked staff of the VIP wing of the hospital.

As far as the rest of the world knew, Evelyn Delacorte-Ketchum was enjoying a long-delayed and richly deserved vacation at her mountain retreat. Anyone who wanted to check—and several had—had only to aim a pair of binoculars or a high-powered camera lens on the cedar-and-glass house perched in the mountains above Telluride, Colorado.

Steep terrain, the latest in electronic technology, and a heavily guarded entrance provided privacy and security, but paparazzi skulking around the perimeter of the two-hundred-acre property often spotted a slender woman with elegant bearing and dark hair touched with silver at the temples lounging on the deck or passing by the windows as she moved around inside.

Rourke had handpicked the woman himself. Her name was Eloise Martin. She was a widow from Des Moines who was more than happy to receive a hefty fee to act as stand-in for Evelyn Ketchum. She was ten years younger but had the same general size, build, and coloring, and though her facial resemblance to Evelyn was faint, there was enough similarity of features to make detection impossible from a distance.

The first time Sara saw a grainy photograph in one

of Houston newspapers with the caption "Local Cosmetics Queen, Evelyn Delacorte-Ketchum, relaxes at mountain lodge" she was amazed and amused, and her respect for Rourke went up several more notches.

While Evelyn's double enjoyed a restful two-week paid vacation, Sara worked like a demon. She arrived at the complex every morning before the office staff—even before Alice—and most evenings she did not return to the apartment before ten.

Sara had known that she had a lot to learn, but she had not known quite how much until she actually began trying to absorb and assimilate all the information that Rourke tossed at her.

Eve Cosmetics was a giant corporation with facilities all over the world, but eventually everything passed over Evelyn's desk. Inquiries, reports, and complaints came in every day, not only from the various departments in the Houston complex, but also from the dozens of factories, warehouses, distribution centers, and experimental labs scattered around the globe.

There were reports on new product performance, sales figures, P-and-L statements, growth projections, advertising campaigns, freight cost studies, tax information, trade tariffs, market potential surveys, cost analysis, and more.

Daily there were decisions to be made—which factories to expand, which products to push, which to drop, where to open new distribution centers.

And there were the inevitable nuisance lawsuits—people claiming allergic reactions or grievous bodily harm from using an Eve product. Usually, if an alleged condition or incident occurred at all, it was due to gross misuse of the product.

There were also problems and delays, and accidents—more, it seemed to Sara, than there should be—at the health spas under construction.

All of which had to be dealt with daily. If you did not stay on top of things, you risked being buried in problems.

Rourke saw to it that Sara met with the various department heads separately—accounting, legal, marketing, product development, sales. They were all polite and extremely helpful, each doing his or her best to help give Sara a clear picture of a particular department's role in the operation.

On her own, Sara made it a point to introduce herself to the workers, gathering information from everyone she talked with—the people on the loading docks and in the mailroom, assembly-line workers, secretaries, and office clerks.

One thing Sara did not detect, the thing for which she had been mentally braced, was condescension or resentment from the male executives. In her experience, in spite of the so-called enlightened nineties, most men still subscribed to the notion that women were inferior, especially when it came to business. She had run up against that attitude time after time in her own company's short history. Some men simply could not accept a woman in a position of authority. They did not like taking orders from a woman or having her question their work or their methods. It was an affront to their male ego.

If any of the Eve Cosmetics male executives felt that way, they at least had the good sense not to let it show. When she mentioned the matter to Rourke, he laughed.

"You won't have that problem here. Evelyn won't

tolerate so much as a hint of chauvinism, or that old 'it's a man's world' attitude. Those types were weeded out years ago."

Rourke clearly had no problem working for a woman. If ever a man was secure in his masculinity, it was Rourke Fallan. His admiration and respect for Evelyn came through in everything he said.

However, far from being her lackey—as Sara had, in self-defense, originally tried to pigeonhole him— around Eve Cosmetics he was a force to be reckoned with.

Rourke was liked by everyone. He had the unique ability to maintain a friendly working relationship with his subordinates without letting anyone lose sight of who was boss. He turned his charm on all the women and they responded like fluttery schoolgirls. Among the single females, he was considered a hunk.

However, at no time did anyone doubt his authority. When Rourke gave an order, it was obeyed, instantly and without question. Usually his tone was courteous, but when he encountered incompetence or malingering or just plain poor judgment, his voice and demeanor turned to steel.

There was a lot about Rourke that attracted Sara. In addition to his looks and the animal magnetism he exuded, there was his intelligence, his patience, his fierce drive and ambition. Ironically, one of the things Sara admired most about him was his loyalty to Evelyn.

It was also the biggest obstacle to a romance between them.

The night she learned of Evelyn's illness, Sara realized that Rourke had been aware of her mother's condition all along. She had known then that though he might be attracted to her, his loyalty, first and always, would be to Evelyn.

On the drive home that night, fury had kept her silent. She had sat with her arms crossed, distant and unresponsive to Rourke's attempts at conversation. At the door to the apartment, he had tried to take her in his arms but she had rebuffed him, and when he'd demanded to know what was wrong, she had told him.

"Damn it, Sara, she's my boss," he had snapped. "What do you expect?"

"I expect you to do exactly what you did. That's the problem. Don't you understand? I'm angry, but the devil of it is, I can't honestly fault you for your choice. After all she's done for you, you owe Evelyn your loyalty."

"Why does it have to be an either/or situation? Evelyn may have made some mistakes in the past, and I'll concede that she may be not be handling things well now, but damn it, Sara, she isn't your enemy."

"I know that. But then, we're not friends, either. Nor by any stretch of the imagination could our relationship be called familial. At best, we're uneasy allies. I'm sorry, but that alliance is just not strong enough for me to risk a romance with her second in command. I have to know that the man in my life will side with me in any situation."

Rourke had not been happy with her decision and he had tried to change her mind on several occasions since, but so far, Sara had stood firm.

It hadn't been easy. Though the hurt was still there, her anger had faded since that night and her attraction to Rourke seemed to be growing stronger by the day. She had to constantly remind herself how foolish it would be to let her emotions overrule common sense.

Luckily, the long hours they kept left little time for a social life, let alone a romance. Sara and Rourke worked closely together, often late into the night. Sometimes Alice stayed to lend a hand, but as often as not they were alone. During those evenings together Sara became more aware than ever of Rourke.

The board meeting was scheduled for the last Monday in May. A little over a week before the meeting, early on a Sunday morning, Sara was sitting at Evelyn's desk, her nose buried in a production report, when Rourke strode in through the door that connected his office to Evelyn's.

"I just got a call from Jake Ebersole, our contractor on Eden East. Sometime early this morning the sprinkler system flooded the entire west wing of the main building. Walls, insulation, custom woodwork—all of it, right down to the stud walls, is a total loss."

"But I don't understand. The system was just installed and pressure-tested last week. How could it have malfunctioned?"

"It didn't. Someone bypassed the automatic controls and turned on the main valve manually."

"You mean, it was sabotage?"

"It sure as hell looks that way."

"But . . . why? What possible reason could anyone have for this?"

Rourke walked to the wide expanse of windows along the outer wall of Evelyn's office. Bracing his hands on his lean hips, he stared out at the complex. On weekends the offices were closed, and he had dressed casually in jeans and a chambray shirt, the sleeves rolled up to his elbows. The stance stretched the cotton cloth taut over his broad back and shoulders. "My guess is, someone is trying to back us into a corner."

"What do you mean?"

"That whoever is behind this is trying to put us into a financial bind."

"How? I know this incident will be costly, but we're insured."

He turned and looked at her. "And if the insurance company finds out we're a target for sabotage, they'll drop us like a hot rock. With no insurance, the bank will not only refuse us the additional loans we'll need to finish the spas, they may even call in the loans they've already granted us."

"But this was just one inci . . . dent . . ." Sara's voice trailed off as she remembered all the bizarre mishaps and accidents that had been occurring at the two spa sites the past couple of months. Watching her, Rourke could see her mentally make the connection, and his eyebrows rose.

"Exactly. We'd have a hard time proving it at this stage of the game, but I'd bet money not all of those accidents were accidents."

"But who would do such a thing? And why?"

Folding his arms over his chest, Rourke leaned his hips against the windowsill. "The spas are too far along to abandon. We've sunk too much money into them. We'd have no choice but to finish them. If the banks desert us, the company would have to cough up the money to complete the projects. What with all the nuisance lawsuits and expansions at nearly every installation, cash flow is tight at the moment. The only way I see that we could raise that kind of money is to sell off a big chunk of Eve stock."

"The very thing that Evelyn doesn't want to happen," Sara murmured, frowning. "Do you think she knows that all the troubles at the spas were deliberately staged?"

"We haven't discussed it directly, but knowing Evelyn, she probably suspects. As for who is doing it, there are a number of people who would like to see Eve Cosmetics go public, starting with every single member of the Ketchum clan."

"Are we going to tell her about this latest disaster? She's been terribly ill from the chemotherapy this past week. I'm not sure we should upset her."

Rourke pushed away from the windowsill and strolled over to the desk. Placing both palms flat against the top, he leaned in close and grinned. "Honey, I hate to think what she would do to us if we didn't tell her. Evelyn could be on her deathbed, but she'd still want to know everything that affected her company."

In a heartbeat, his mood shifted. His grin eased into a caressing smile. His eyes softened, heated. "Have I ever told you that you have beautiful eyes?"

A tingle skittered down Sara's spine. He was close, she realized, as her heart began to thump. Too close. "Rourke, I don't—"

"They're so clear and green, a man could drown in them."

His gaze slid down to her mouth and lingered. Sara could feel that look like a touch. Her breath caught and a shiver quaked through her, but she could not look away from those blue eyes, smoldering beneath heavy eyelids. When his head began a slow descent, all she could do was grip the arms of the chair tighter.

His mouth settled over hers in a kiss as gentle as a whisper. A painful constriction knotted Sara's chest. Patiently, insistently, he urged her to open to him. Her lips parted in trembling acquiescence, and when his tongue slipped inside and stroked over hers, she moaned.

It took a few seconds for the sound to register, a few seconds more before she realized that it had come from her.

She pulled back and turned her face away. "Rourke, no," she whispered. "Please . . . don't."

He eased back a few inches, but he did not move away. The look in his eyes made her unsteady pulse flutter even more. It was all there—the hunger, the frustration, the blazing desire. She felt their pull like a physical tug, and she knew that if he chose to push, she would not be able to resist him.

"You're a stubborn woman, Sara," he whispered, trailing a finger down the side of her neck. "But I'm a patient man. When I want something, I find a way to have it, no matter what obstacles stand in the way."

In a lightning-quick change of attitude, he straightened, picked up Sara's purse from the corner of the desk, and shoved it into her hand. "C'mon, let's go. It's not going to be easy telling Evelyn that one of her family is stabbing her in the back, but we might as well get it over with."

Chapter Eighteen

The day of the board meeting arrived all too soon. Sara's head was spinning with facts and figures and operations details, but she knew that her knowledge of the business was still minimal. Even with Rourke there to support her, the prospect of announcing to the Ketchum clan that she was now in charge was daunting. Nevertheless, once all the others were in their places, she entered the boardroom and took Evelyn's chair with every appearance of calm.

The faces around the table registered surprise, but the shocked silence lasted only seconds. Predictably, Paul was the first to react.

"What the hell do you think you're doing?"

Sara looked him in the eye and smiled. "I'm about to chair this meeting."

"The hell you are!"

"What?" Will exploded. "Now see here, young woman—"

"You've got one helluva nerve, lady," Chad joined in. "But you've just shot yourself in the foot. Evelyn may have chosen you as her successor, but daughter or no daughter, she won't stand for anyone usurping her position." He looked around, his gray eyes sharp and demanding as they flashed to the door, then to Alice. "Where the devil is Evelyn, anyway?"

"I . . . actually, I haven't heard from her in several days, but I assume she's still vacationing at the mountain cabin," Alice replied with a hint of apology.

"Good God, she's been there for over two weeks." Paul spat out a vile curse. "She should have been back by now. She knew a board meeting was scheduled for today."

"This isn't like Evelyn, to neglect business," Will muttered. "Not like Evelyn at all."

"If she wasn't going to show up, she could have had the courtesy to cancel the meeting," Madelene snapped. "Lawrence and I don't have time to fly back and forth for no reason."

"You don't suppose she had an accident, do you? She's all alone up there. Anything could happen, you know. Maybe we should call her at the cabin, just to be sure."

"Take it easy, Kitty Cat." Eric put a hand on his cousin's arm and smiled. "There are at least three guards around that place. I'm sure Evelyn's fine. Personally, I think it's great that the old girl is finally kicking back. She hasn't taken a real vacation in years."

"Evelyn isn't on vacation. She's in St. Luke's Hospital."

Sara's quiet announcement got their attention more effectively than a blast from a gun. For the space of a heartbeat there was shocked silence, then pandemonium, with everyone talking at once.

"What?"

"Hospital! Evelyn's in a hospital?"

"What happened?"

"Oh, my God! She *has* had an accident!" Kitty jumped to her feet, overturning her chair. "I knew it! I just knew it. Evelyn wouldn't skip a meeting."

"When was she hospitalized?" Lawrence inquired with his usual pedantic attention to detail.

Sara looked at Rourke for the answer.

"Three weeks ago," he supplied.

"Three weeks!"

"This is outrageous!" Will thundered, and banged his good fist on the table. "Why wasn't the family told?"

"Oh, stop it! What does it matter? I want to know what happened. How badly was she hurt? Is she going to be all right? *Tell* me!"

The anguish in Kitty's eyes created a peculiar sensation in Sara's chest—part guilt that she did not feel a deeper sense of grief over her own mother's illness, and part envy that Kitty did.

Evelyn's stepdaughter looked as though she might break down at any moment. Instinctively, Sara reached out and touched her arm. "Calm down, Kitty. Evelyn didn't have an accident."

"She didn't? Then what's wrong?"

"She's ill. Very ill, I'm afraid. Evelyn has an acute type of leukemia."

"Leu-leukemia?" Kitty swayed. Tears welled up, and she put her hand over her mouth. "Oh, my God. Oh, my God."

"Now, take it easy." Eric eased her down into her chair.

At the other end of the table, Madelene burst into

tears. As Lawrence comforted her, the others muttered words of disbelief and shock.

"C'mon, Kitty Cat, I'll take you to the hospital."

"Not just yet," Rourke interjected. "First, there's the matter of the board meeting."

"Screw the goddamned meeting! How can you even think of business at a time like this? Evelyn is critically ill, for Chrissake! And Kitty is too upset to deal with business. We all are."

Sara studied Eric. He glared across the table at Rourke, his arm wrapped protectively around his cousin's shoulder. From all Sara had heard, Eric was affable and easygoing, yet he looked ready to tear into Rourke. Was it an act? Or did he truly care about Evelyn? If so, she wondered how the cold woman she knew could inspire such devotion.

"I'm not insensitive to the situation, Eric. I'm simply following Evelyn's orders. She asked me to make it quite clear that she won't see any of you until the business of this meeting is concluded. Therefore, I suggest we get on with it. Also—just so you know—Evelyn has left Sara in charge and given her temporary voting rights to her stock."

Ignoring the collective gasp that went up, Rourke nodded to Sara. She drew a deep breath and picked up the gavel.

By the conclusion of the meeting, Sara felt as though she had dragged herself, arm over arm, naked through a minefield.

Dumping her notes and papers on Evelyn's desk, she flopped down in the chair, leaned her head against the high back, and closed her eyes with a sigh. "Merciful heavens, are they always that bad?"

"Mmm, mostly." Rourke sat in the chair across from her. "I did warn you that they were stubborn and spoiled and accustomed to getting their own way."

Sara opened one eye and skewered him with a look. "A coddled two-year-old is spoiled. *They* are impossible." At every turn throughout the meeting she had met challenge, stubbornness, devious attempts at manipulation, and irascibility.

"I'll admit, they were in fine form today. You can't blame them, though, if their noses are out of joint. Evelyn sprang you on them from out of nowhere. And now, before they've even figured out what to do about you, here you are in the driver's seat. The Ketchums are a possessive lot. They don't give up what they consider theirs without a struggle."

"That sounds like a warning."

"Not exactly. But I think you should be prepared for them, either singly or together, to try something."

"You mean to oust me?"

Rourke shrugged. "Or to use you."

"I don't see how they could do either—" The intercom buzzed and she pressed the button. "Yes, Alice?"

"It's Jen. The dragon lady has gone to lunch."

Sara looked at Rourke and rolled her eyes. He grinned. Jennifer and Alice were engaged in a territorial war. With Evelyn out of the office, Alice felt it her duty and prerogative to see to Sara's needs, but Jennifer jealously guarded her position. She and Evelyn's secretary had been hissing and spitting at one another like a couple of cats ever since their arrival.

It had seemed a good idea for Sara to work out of Evelyn's office, since it put her close to Rourke, but now she was having second thoughts.

"There's a call for Mr. Fallan on line one," Jen went on. "It's a Mr. Hackley. He said it was urgent."

Rourke frowned. "I'll take it in here, Jennifer. Hackley is our Eden West contractor," he reminded Sara, as he reached for the telephone.

Within seconds, Sara knew from his expression that Roger Hackley's call was bad news.

"Well?" she said, when he hung up the telephone.

"There's been a fire at Eden West."

"How bad?"

"Bad. Over half the project was destroyed."

"Was anyone hurt?"

"No, thank God. It happened in the middle of the night. No one was on site but the night watchman, and he got out."

"Thank heaven for that." Sara sighed and started massaging her temples. "We're fully insured, of course, but the banks still aren't going to like it. They're already antsy over all the accidents on these projects. And the delays are going to kill us." Her fingers stilled when she took a second look at Rourke's face. "Oh, God. There's more, isn't there?"

He nodded. "The fire was arson."

Eric felt guilty for cutting short his visit with Evelyn. He had used the excuse that he had to attend a boring business dinner with the Neiman's buyer. Evelyn had accepted the story, but she had teased him about the woman being a beautiful blonde.

She had been right, Eric thought. His dinner companion was blond and beautiful. And sexy.

As he gazed across the candlelit table, memories of their last meeting flickered through his mind. It had been a night of fantastic sex. Hot. Mindless. Erotic. Sweat-slick bodies straining together. Pants and ecstatic moans and desperate, lustful murmurs in the darkness. And pleasure. Ah, yes the pleasure—so great it had wrung shouts from both of them.

Eric's eyes traced his companion's perfect features—a finely molded nose, sensuous mouth, silvery hair, and incredibly long lashes, lowered now against high cheekbones in perusal of the menu. Oh, yes, the sensuality and physical beauty were undeniable, but inside . . . inside, Keith Morrison was corrupt and evil.

Watching him, Eric wondered what he had ever seen in the man, why he hadn't noticed the calculation in his eyes, the hardness.

Terror gripped his chest like a vice. It took every ounce of self-control he could muster to sit calmly while the waiter finished taking Keith's order. Eric had declined to order anything. He was too nervous even to think of eating.

What did Morrison want? What would be the price of his silence? There would be a price. Of that Eric was certain. Since that anonymous letter and photo almost two months ago, Keith had been toying with him, sending several more cryptic notes and calling him at the office with taunting little reminders of their encounter and vague threats of exposure. Today, however, was the first time he had requested a meeting.

"Well, well, isn't this nice? The two of us together

again," Keith said with a mocking smile when the waiter moved away. Coyly, he inched his hand across the table until their fingertips touched. Eric snatched his hand away as though he'd been burned. Keith smiled.

"Why, Eric, love, what's the matter? Aren't you glad to see me?"

"Cut the crap and get to the point, will you? What do you want from me?"

"My, my, aren't we testy. And I was hoping we could renew our relationship." Mockery and malicious pleasure glittered in Keith's eyes. "Ah, well, I wanted to handle this with delicacy, but since you insist on being so blunt . . . I want money. Lots of money. Otherwise, I shall be forced to inform your father of his youngest son's homosexual proclivities."

"That's not true. I'm attracted to women," Eric blurted, before he could stop himself. He could have bitten off his tongue when he saw the sudden leap of interest in Keith's eyes.

"Are you really? My, my, how interesting. Still, I doubt old Will Ketchum would be any more thrilled to hear that one of his sons was bisexual. I've been doing some checking on your family, and from all I've been able to learn about your father, he's something of an iron-fisted patriarch with a decidedly macho outlook. I really don't think you want him to see the photos, now, do you?"

"That's blackmail."

"Please. *Blackmail* is such an ugly word. I prefer to call it *information brokering*. That has a nice ring, don't you think?"

"You filthy—" Eric bit back the flood of angry

words and looked away, his jaw working. Beneath the table, his fists clenched. He had to struggle against the desire to slam one into Keith's smug face. He knew if he did, the whole nasty business would be plastered in tomorrow's papers. And Keith would take great pleasure in revealing everything.

Finally Eric's gaze swung back. "All right. You win. How much for you to go away and keep silent?"

"Well, naturally I don't come cheap. But I don't want to be greedy, either. So I've decided to be generous and settle for a mere half million."

"What! Are you *crazy?* I don't have that kind of money!"

"Please. The Ketchums are one of the most powerful families in Texas. Don't forget, I've done my research."

"Then you know that our fortune was made in oil and cattle. Those industries are all but bust. Neither Ketchum Oil nor Ketchum Cattle Company has shown a profit in years."

Keith shrugged and examined a piece of silverware. "Perhaps. But there's also Eve Cosmetics. I know you own one percent of the stock."

"Yes, but I can't sell it. And it doesn't earn nearly enough for me to give you half a million dollars. Especially these days, with company profits being poured into expansions. What you're asking is impossible. I simply don't have that kind of money."

Keith's smile was chilling. "Then, Eric, love, I suggest you find a way to get it."

Chapter Nineteen

When Sara arrived at the office the next morning she discovered that Lawrence had made an appointment to see her at ten. He was punctual to the second and came straight to the point the instant the greetings were out of the way.

"Miss Anderson, we—"

"Please. Call me Sara."

"Thank you. Sara, I've come to ask you—beg you, if I must—to vote to allow Eve Cosmetics to go public. It's what everyone in the family wants, and now that Evelyn is critically ill, there's really no point in waiting, is there?"

"She isn't dead yet," Sara snapped.

Lawrence was immediately flustered and apologetic. "No, no. Of course not. I wasn't implying . . . I didn't mean . . . that is . . . I only meant that, since she won't be able to return to work, there didn't seem much point in continuing the status quo."

Sara was stunned by her own reaction, and immediately she softened her tone. "I understand, Lawrence. I'm sorry. I didn't mean to bite your head off."

"That's perfectly all right. After all, Evelyn is your

mother. You're bound to be emotional where she's concerned. However, I do feel, Sara, that going public is necessary. Evelyn has overextended the company financially, and now with all these accidents, our situation is growing worse. When the banks learn of her condition, we could be in serious financial trouble. If that happens, the value of our stock will plummet. It is imperative that we make this change now, while we still can. Surely you can see that?"

Pursing her lips, Sara tapped the eraser end of a pencil against the desktop and studied Madelene's husband. How much, she wondered, did Lawrence know about the so-called accidents at the construction sites?

"I don't think things are quite that bad yet, Lawrence. I do appreciate your concern, but I'm sorry. Even if I agreed with you, I still couldn't do as you asked. I've given Evelyn my word that as long as she lives I will follow her wishes."

She did not bother to explain that Evelyn had made it clear that if Sara did not, there would be no inheritance.

"I see." Lawrence's hand shook as he straightened his tie. He looked like a desperate man who had just watched his last hope disappear. "Then . . . the company will remain privately owned."

"Yes. I'm sorry."

Lawrence was not the only one who had tried to persuade Sara to change the company's status. One by one over the next several weeks, every member of the family tried his or her hand at convincing her.

Chad, with his blunt, single-minded intensity,

barged into her office and laid out his demand with such a lack of tact she was almost amused.

Will turned on his "good old boy" charm, and when that didn't work, he switched to avuncular concern that she should have such weighty responsibilities thrust on her shoulders. The first Sara found amusing, the second insulting.

Witty, devil-may-care Eric took her to lunch and pitched his request over a superb trout almondine, and he did it with such amusing light-heartedness that Sara was almost persuaded to defy Evelyn's orders.

Bristling with hostility and macho superiority, Paul made another stab at bullying her, and Madelene stifled her resentment of Sara long enough to add her arguments to those of her husband.

Even shy Kitty paid her a visit. Ill at ease and almost sick with nerves, she stammered out what amounted to a plea with such desperation that Sara wondered what was behind it. She had seen Kitty's quarterly checks. The amount was more than sufficient for her to maintain a comfortable lifestyle, even in New York. What possible need did she have for the huge sum her stock would bring?

Though visibly upset over the outcome of the meeting, Kitty managed to surprise Sara as she was escorting her out. Halting at the door, she placed her hand on Sara's arm and fixed her soft gray eyes on her. "Sara, I . . . I want to thank you. Evelyn told me that you tested to be a bone-marrow donor for her."

There was absolutely no reason for her to feel guilty. None whatsoever, Sara told herself. Yet the sincerity in the younger woman's face made her squirm. "You don't have to thank me. As it turned out, I wasn't any help at all."

"The point is, you tried. You cared. And even though it didn't work out, I just wanted you to know how grateful I am that you were willing to help her."

When Kitty left, Sara wandered over to the window. For a long time, she simply stood there and stared out at the complex, her chest tight with a painful pressure that made no sense at all.

"Something interesting out there? Or are you thinking of jumping?"

"What?" Sara turned and saw Jennifer leaning against the office door. "What are you talking about?"

"You've been standing there for the last thirty minutes without moving a hair. I just thought I'd check." Jen cocked her head to one side. "She really gets to you, doesn't she?"

"Who?"

"Kitty Ketchum."

"I don't know what you're talking about. Why would Kitty bother me? Actually, I kind of like her. God knows, she and Eric are the nicest of the bunch."

"Hey, it's perfectly understandable. All these years, Kitty's had the life that should have been yours, the mother who should have been yours. It's only natural that she would raise some pretty strong feelings in you. It's just too bad she's not a bitch like her sister so you could hate her."

Sara's eyes widened. With one simple statement, Jennifer had gotten to the heart of the matter. She tipped her head to one side and studied her young secretary. "You know . . . for such a smart-mouthed little urchin, you sure are intelligent."

Jen grinned. "Yeah, I know. Now, if you want— Oops. I'll get it."

She rushed forward, leaned across the desk, and picked up the telephone. "Ms. Anderson's office. May I help you?" She listened for a moment, a slight frown forming between her eyebrows. "Hold on, please."

Jen pressed the hold button and grimaced at Sara. "It's Mr. Braddock, from Security Bank. He and his associates want to meet with you."

Sara twisted and turned. Making an aggravated sound, she flounced and punched her pillow, but it was no use. She was too tense to sleep.

With a sigh, she tossed back the covers. Slipping into her robe, she crossed the room and stepped outside onto the rooftop terrace.

The warm Houston night enveloped her, moist and soft as velvet. The flagstones still retained most of the heat of the July sun and were smooth and hard beneath her bare feet. With her arms crossed over her midriff, she strolled over to the edge and leaned against the railing. Staring out at the night, she absently massaged her elbows, her fingers rotating against the pointy bones. Far below, Houston sprawled out like a blanket of twinkling lights. Sara barely noticed.

She was too tense, too keyed up, too worried. Ever since the call from Mr. Braddock that morning, she'd been a bundle of nerves.

Immediately after speaking with the banker, Sara

had telephoned Evelyn. She had insisted that Sara and Rourke come to the ranch first thing tomorrow morning for a strategy session before the meeting.

"Come prepared to stay a day or so," she had ordered. "We have a lot of other business to go over as well."

From experience, Sara knew that "a day or so" would more than likely mean a three- or four-day stay at the ranch, not only for Rourke and herself, but for Alice, Jen, and Brian as well. Although Evelyn seemed a bit stronger lately, she was still too ill to work, but she insisted upon being kept apprised of whatever was going on. Because she tired easily, briefing sessions and conferences had to be kept short. It often required days to get through all the business.

Sara smiled, remembering those early brainstorming sessions with Evelyn and Rourke. At first, she had felt intimidated and incredibly ignorant and green. However, she had listened and observed and learned, and now, though she still had a way to go to equal Rourke and Evelyn, she at least had the satisfaction of knowing that she was contributing—such as she had when Evelyn had asked her opinion of Eden East and Eden West.

She had been surprised by Sara's lukewarm, "They're very nice."

"Nice? My dear, a warm bath is nice," Evelyn had said with a slight edge to her voice. "A new pair of shoes is nice. The Edens have to be an extraordinary experience. They have to be a slice of paradise. There are dozens of opulent health spas around. To lure people away from them, ours has to be unquestionably the best."

"Then we will have to offer our clientele something extra. All spas have workout machines and mud baths and trainers, superb food, beautiful and luxurious surroundings. To make the Edens stand out, we have to offer more and better."

"And what do you suggest?" Rourke asked.

"Several things. A qualified person on staff to assist each guest in makeup, hairstyle, and colors best suited to them, the selection of a new wardrobe—from our own boutique, of course."

Rourke looked amused. "You mean an image consultant."

"Yes. Why not? Also, we should have a dermatologist in residence. And a plastic surgeon to give injections of collagen where needed and to counsel on the benefits and advisability of cosmetic surgery. Perhaps even perform minor operations such as eye jobs on site. When a guest leaves Eden she should look and feel like a new woman. Who knows, some of the men might like the service, too."

Evelyn and Rourke exchanged a long look, while Sara held her breath. Slowly, he grinned at her over his steepled fingers. "Well, well, well. So you are more than just a pretty face."

The comment, coming from Rourke, had made her ridiculously happy and filled her with pride.

Sara sighed. It was foolish to allow a man to affect you so much, but she didn't seem to be able to do anything about it.

Strolling down the terrace, she trailed her hand along the rail. Her relationship with Rourke—or rather, her lack of one—was another cause of her tension. Now that she was more familiar with the company's operations, he was leaving her more and more on her own. These days she kept her passport at the office. It seemed to Sara that she spent half her time flying to the company's various offices and factories. Sometimes Rourke went with her, but as often as not he was off in some other part of the country, or the world, on Eve business. Days, even weeks, went by without her seeing him.

He hadn't pressured her for a personal relationship, and she wondered if perhaps it was really that important to him, after all.

For years Rourke had travelled extensively. He was a man who routinely visited Paris and London—Rome, Madrid, Athens, all the glamor capitals of the world. She could not believe that he spent all those lonely nights away from home alone. He probably knew women all over the globe, beautiful, willing women who would be happy to receive his attention and provide him with companionship . . . and share his bed.

It was none of her business, of course. She had rebuffed him repeatedly, after all. Still, she often wondered about the women Rourke dated. They would be beautiful and intelligent and utterly captivating, and far more worldly and experienced than she. Sara hated them all.

Disgusted with herself, she whirled away from the railing and marched back to the French doors.

She glanced at the bed, but she was still too keyed up to sleep, and she walked through the bedroom and into the living room. She sat down on the sofa, curling her bare feet under her, and picked up a magazine. After reading an entire page twice without comprehending a single word, she made an impatient sound and tossed it aside. She sprang to her feet and paced to the terrace door, then back across the room, arms folded tight over her midriff. Halfway through the circuit again she stopped and looked toward the entry. Pursing her lips, she tapped her chin with her index finger, her expression thoughtful.

Was Rourke back from Mexico City yet? He'd had to cut short his business with the plant manager there and fly back to make the meeting with Evelyn in the morning. He still hadn't returned when Sara had left the office.

She glanced at the mantel clock. It was almost eleven. If he was back, he might be asleep. She chewed on her bottom lip. But then again, he might not be, and they really should discuss how they were going to approach the bankers.

Before she could have second thoughts, Sara let herself out of the apartment, hurried across the small vestibule, and knocked on Rourke's door. There was no answer. She waited a moment, then knocked again. Torn between disappointment and relief, she was about to turn away when the door opened.

"Sara." Rourke's gaze darted beyond her around the vestibule. "Is something wrong?"

"No . . . that is . . . may I come in?"

One black eyebrow lifted. His gaze skimmed over her, slowly, taking in everything from her bare toes to her tousled hair, pausing briefly in between at her hips and her breasts, making Sara horribly conscious that she wore only a soft batiste nightgown and robe. His eyes, when they met hers again, were heavy lidded and unreadable, his face dark.

"Sure." He stepped back and gestured her inside, and the skin on Sara's arms tingled as she brushed by him.

She walked into the living room, conscious of his eyes on her. In the middle of the floor she came to a halt and turned. Rourke stood in the doorway, a shoulder propped negligently against the doorframe, one ankle crossed over the other.

Sara was so nervous she hadn't really looked at him until now, and her pulse began to skitter. It was obvious that she had awakened him. His hair was mussed, his face flushed and creased with sleep marks, and he was barefoot.

For the first time Sara noticed that he was dressed in only a pair of trousers. In his haste to pull them on, he had not bothered to button the waistband, and she could see that he wore nothing beneath them. A flush heated her cheeks as she realized that Rourke slept nude.

Oh, Lord, what was she doing? She should never have come here.

She fidgeted for a second, then caught herself. Lifting her chin, she stood straighter and tightened the sash on her robe. "I . . ." Her voice broke, and she stopped to clear her throat. "I, uh . . . I thought we should talk."

Rourke stared at her. Finally he shrugged. "Sure. What did you want to talk about?"

"Well . . . I thought it would be a good idea if we worked out our strategy for the meeting with the bankers."

The statement drew another long stare. Sara twisted her fingers together tighter and fought the urge to squirm.

"You know—because Evelyn's so weak. I thought it would be easier on her if we hashed it all out together before we see her."

More silence. Unable to hold that unrelenting stare, she looked away and tugged the lapels of her robe closer. Why didn't he *say* something? "Also . . . uh . . . there's the, uh . . ."

Rourke pushed away from the door and strolled toward her. The look in his eyes made Sara's heart pound.

". . . the problem with . . . with the freight companies."

"No."

"In case they do go on strike we should—"

"No."

". . . make contingency pla—" Sara blinked. "What?"

"Give it up, Sara. You didn't come here to discuss bank loans or freight problems, or even Evelyn. And we both know it."

"I . . . of course I did."

"In your nightgown? At this hour? Uh-uh, I don't think so."

"Nevertheless, I—Rourke, what are you doing?"

Ignoring the question, he hauled her close. He molded her to him, hips, belly, and thighs, his arms slipping around her. Automatically she raised her hands to brace them against his chest, and her heart skipped and bumped as her fingers sank into the silky mat of hair and made contact with warm, hard flesh.

He tunneled his hand beneath the silky fall of her hair and with a gentle tug tipped her head back. Sara's breath caught at the burning look in his eyes. "Admit it, Sara, it wasn't business that brought you here," he murmured. "It was this."

Watching her, he trailed his fingertips along her nape, up the side of her neck. She quivered at the feathery touch, and Rourke's eyes blazed blue fire. His arms tightened, drawing her closer still.

"Sara." He murmured her name, his voice low and heavy with need. "Sara." He strung kisses along her jaw, over her cheek. His breath filtered through the hair at her temple and feathered over her scalp, warm and moist. Goosebumps rippled over Sara's neck and shoulders, and she shivered.

Rourke made a low sound and nuzzled his face into her hair, against the side of her neck, his lips nibbling and mouthing her ear with increasing urgency. "Sara," he whispered again. "I want you. And you want me. That's why you came. Come to bed with me, sweetheart. Let me love you."

"Rourke, I . . ."

He didn't let her finish. His mouth claimed hers, cutting off any objection she might have made.

Desire slammed through Sara with the force of a runaway train. The heat, the hunger, the fierceness of his need overwhelmed. Inflamed.

Sara's frazzled nerves hummed and snapped like a severed high-voltage wire. She was helpless to resist the attraction that had hovered between them from the moment they'd met. Moaning, she pressed closer. She clung to Rourke and returned the kiss with the all the pent-up passion she had kept tamped down for months. Her hands ran over him, clutching his shoulders, his back, grabbing fistfuls of his hair. Their bodies strained to get closer while their mouths rocked and rubbed and their tongues swirled in an erotic dance of passion.

Desire almost swamped her good sense, but from somewhere she finally dredged up the strength to pull back.

"No. No, I can't do this," she panted.

"Sara, for God's sake—"

"No, please." She backed away, holding one hand in front of her, palm out. "I'm sorry. You have every right to be angry, but I . . . I just can't."

Rourke muttered a curse and swung away. Grasping the fireplace mantel, he hung his head between his braced arms and breathed deeply, struggling to regain control. A shudder shook him, and guilt stabbed at Sara.

"Why, Sara? You want me as much as I want you. You can't deny that."

"No, I can't. But that doesn't change anything."

"What you mean is, because I work for Evelyn, you don't trust me." He looked at her over his shoulder. "Isn't that right?"

Miserable, she shifted under that penetrating stare, but she couldn't deny the accusation. "Yes. I suppose it is. I'm sorry."

He straightened and turned to face her. "What would it take to earn your trust, Sara? I can't—I won't—resign my position with Eve Cosmetics. I've worked too long and too hard to get where I am."

"No. Of course not. I would never ask that of you."

"Do you want a commitment from me? Is that it?"

"No. Of course not. We don't know one another well enough for that."

"That's right. We don't. So what's the answer?"

Sara gave him a wretched look and shook her head. "I . . . I don't know."

Chapter Twenty

Kitty's nerves were eating her alive. Nibbling her thumbnail, she sat in the shadows in the tenth row, hunched down in the seat as though trying to make herself invisible. Her gaze was riveted to the two actors on stage.

The rest of the cast was milling around in the wings or sprawled in the seats or the aisle.

Tom Avery, the director of *Dark of the Moon,* squatted down front before the stage, intently scrutinizing Miles's and Alanna Hart's performance.

So far, Tom seemed pleased with the way rehearsals were going. Kitty wished she had his confidence. Maybe then she wouldn't have a knot in her stomach the size of a fist.

"No, no, no. Alanna. Sweetheart." Tom stood up and clapped his hands to stop the scene. "I need more emotion here. You're losing the love of your life. Your heart is being ripped out. Let me see pain. Pathos. I want you to wring the audience's heart. Miles, come back and do your exit again. Take it from the last line."

"Sure." Miles took his position and schooled his

aristocratic features into a look of infinite sadness. He reached out and touched Alanna's cheek with his fingertips. "Be happy, Viv."

Miles held her gaze a few seconds longer, then turned and walked away, exiting stage left.

"Now, I want you to reach out with one hand and take a step after him." Tom demonstrated the move. "As he disappears from sight, let your hand drop and your shoulders droop. Then let everything you're feeling show on your face. Despair, heartache, the works. And a few tears would be a nice touch if you can manage them. Got it?"

Alanna nodded. "Yes. I think so."

"Good. Now, let's run through it again."

Kitty began a chewing assault on her other thumbnail. When Miles walked off stage, she bit down on her thumb and held her breath, her gaze on Alanna.

"That's it. Perfect! Darling, you're beautiful. Both of you are." Tom clapped his hands again. "All right, people. Take ten. When we come back we're going to run through Act Two one more time."

Several of the actors groaned, but Miles was grinning as he hopped down from the stage and trotted up the aisle to where Kitty sat. "Hello, love. It's going super, don't you think?"

"Yes. You're really wonderful in the part, Miles."

"Thanks, lovie." Beaming, he bent over and bestowed a long kiss on her mouth. "I'm really getting into the part now. Got the old juices cooking, as you Yanks say. The play is going to be a hit. I can feel it in my bones."

"I hope so. If it isn't I may be in big trouble."

"Aw, come on, love. Don't be a gloomy Gus. We can't miss. You've written a smashing play, I'm perfect for the part, the supporting cast is right on the mark. So cheer up." He frowned. "You know how I hate it when you go around with a long face. It ruins my concentration."

Instantly contrite, Kitty reached for his hand. "I'm sorry, Miles. You're right, of course. I shouldn't give in to writer's jitters."

His face cleared at once and he absolved her with a magnanimous smile. "No, you shouldn't, you silly goose." He sat down beside her, then popped right back up again, too wired to sit still.

"I could use some tea. Want some?"

"Coffee would be nice."

"Ugh." Miles gave a mock shudder. "I don't know how you can stomach the foul stuff, but if that's what you want, I'll fetch it. Be back in a sec, love."

Wistfully Kitty watched him stroll away with his fingertips stuck jauntily in the back pockets of his jeans. Miles was on top of the world. He always was when things were going his way.

Kitty sighed. She only wished she could share his euphoria. Of course, it was easier for Miles. He was not burdened with her responsibilities . . . or her guilt.

She gnawed on her bottom lip and looked around the semidarkened theater. She still couldn't believe she'd done it. She'd actually borrowed money against her future inheritance from Evelyn to finance the play.

Once her stepmother's condition had become public knowledge, it had been surprisingly easy to do. There was nothing illegal about the arrangement. And it wasn't as if she were hurting anyone. Anyway, she'd had no choice; she couldn't let Miles be deported. She just couldn't.

Closing her eyes, Kitty pressed her balled fist against her queasy stomach. But, oh, God, she felt so ghoulish about profiting from Evelyn's almost certain death.

Almost as bad as the guilt was the worry. The short-term loan would come due just a few months after the play opened. If Evelyn was still alive then, the only way she could even begin to satisfy the debt would be if the play were an immediate smash hit.

"Hey, Kitty!" Bernie Lewis called from the back of the theater. "Telephone."

"Be right there." Grateful for the chance to escape her thoughts, Kitty scrambled out of the seat and hurried up the aisle.

Entering the stage manager's cubbyhole office she flashed him a smile. "Thanks, Bernie. I won't be long."

"No sweat. Take all the time you want. I was about to take a break anyway." He sidled past her out the door as she reached for the receiver.

"Hello."

"Kitty? It's Evelyn. How are you, darling?"

Kitty's hand tightened around the receiver. "Fine. Just fine. What a lovely surprise. I, uh . . . I wasn't expecting to hear from you. It everything all right?"

"Everything couldn't be better. That's why I'm calling. I have some news. Sara and Rourke will be here at any moment, but I wanted you to be the first to know. I had my routine checkup yesterday. Dr. Underwood called just a short while ago to give me the results of the tests." She paused a moment, and Kitty's heart began to beat double time. "I'm in remission. Well . . . actually, I have been for the past month, but I wanted to be sure it would last before

I told anyone. It looks like, for the time being, anyway, the leukemia is inactive. Isn't that wonderful news?"

Kitty sank down on Bernie's wobbly chair. Propping her elbow on the desk, she cradled her head in her hand and closed her eyes. "Yes." She sucked in a trembling breath. "Yes, that's wonderful."

Evelyn was reclining on a chaise longue, writing in her journal, when Sara and Rourke walked into the ranch den. She looked up at them and smiled, and Sara was struck by how much better she looked. She was still frail, of course. Over the last few months the disease and the chemotherapy had taken their toll and she was far too thin, but today there was a sparkle in her eyes and her complexion had a slight rose tint.

"Come in. I was hoping you'd get here soon." Evelyn closed her journal and put it aside. "I have some good news."

"Well, I could sure use some of that." Rourke bent over and kissed her forehead. "How're you feeling, beautiful?"

"Wonderful. Absolutely wonderful."

The enthusiasm in Evelyn's voice touched off a surge of excitement in Sara. She sat forward in her chair. Without realizing it, she reached out and took one of Evelyn's thin hands in both of hers. "They've found a donor for you, haven't they? Oh, thank God."

Emotion flickered in Evelyn's eyes as she met Sara's eager gaze. Slowly, she lowered her eyes and stared down at their joined hands. Sara felt Evelyn's hand tremble in hers. Then, ever so slightly, it tightened.

When her gaze lifted, her eyes were moist. "No. Not yet. But thank you for hoping."

Confusion overtook Sara. She looked away and would have pulled free, but when she tried Evelyn's grip tightened even more.

"However, my news is the next best thing. I got word from Dr. Underwood this morning that I am definitely in remission. We've thought so for weeks."

"Oh, Evelyn, that's marvelous!" For a brief instant Sara was so excited she forgot the confusing few moments that had just passed and the enmity between them. She lunged forward and gave Evelyn an impulsive hug. "I'm so happy for you."

"Hey, that's great," Rourke echoed. "That's really great."

"Yes. Yes it is, isn't it." For the space of ten or so seconds, Evelyn looked as embarrassed and confused as Sara felt. Then, as Sara watched, she squared her frail shoulders, tilted her chin at a regal angle, and pulled her dignity about her like a protective cape. "As I'm sure you can imagine, I'm very happy about it. But the two of you didn't come all this way to talk about me." She cleared her throat and reached for the pad and pen on the table beside the chaise longue. "We have a lot of work ahead of us, so shall we get to it?"

It was a clear rejection of any further personal discussion, and both Sara and Rourke got the message. The thump of briefcase latches popping open was their reply.

"Now, then, Sara, did you call Mr. Braddock back, as I instructed?"

"Yes. I pleaded a crisis at one of our overseas factories and managed to buy us some time, but not much. The meeting with the bankers is scheduled for a week from tomorrow."

"What's your impression of Braddock?" Rourke asked. "Did you get any sense of where he and the other bankers stand regarding the Eve projects?"

"Well . . . I haven't met him, of course, but on a personal level, I'd say that Mr. Braddock is a terse, humorless man who thinks solely in terms of profit and loss. I doubt seriously that friendship or loyalty or any kind of emotion enters into his decision making."

Evelyn pursed her lips and studied Sara with new interest. "That's a very astute assessment. I've done business with Ted Braddock for twenty-seven years, ever since I married Joe and moved to Texas. He's as dour as they come. Eve Cosmetics is a plum account for his bank, but if he thinks we've become a financial risk, we can't expect him to be swayed by compassion or sentimentality. He'll call in our loans in a New York second before he'll lose one penny."

"Which means, we're going to have to come up with a compelling argument to convince him and his associates to stick by the company a little longer." Rourke looked from one woman to the other. "Any suggestions?"

"He and the other bankers know you, Rourke. They know your reputation and they trust your judgment. Perhaps if you explained to them that you and I are personally training Sara, they'll at least be willing to wait and see."

"Maybe. It's worth a try, but I doubt—"

A tap on the frame of the open doorway cut him off, and Alice walked into the den.

"I'm sorry to interrupt, but the plant manager in Houston just called. The sprinkler system in the packaging department came on during the night and flooded the building."

"Damn it to hell!" Rourke snarled. "I've had about enough of this."

"Alice, tell Joe to get the helicopter ready. Rourke and I will be there in a minute."

"Yes, Miss Anderson. Right away."

"I'm sorry, Evelyn, but we'll have to continue this later." Sara stuffed papers back into her briefcase, and Rourke did the same.

"Of course."

"We'll be back as soon as we can. If not tonight, then tomorrow or the next day."

"Come on, Sara. Let's go."

"Ring me when you know something," Evelyn called after them.

When they had gone, she stared at the empty doorway. After a while, she picked up her journal, opened it to where she'd left off, and began to write.

The saboteur has struck again. Who can it be? One of the family? It almost has to be. Otherwise, the whole thing would make no sense at all. But which one? It's painful to think that any of them would deliberately destroy what I have worked so hard to build, but I must face the facts. One or more of them is trying to force me into an untenable position.

She closed the diary and started to put it back on the table beside the chaise longue, then changed her mind. Settling the volume against her updrawn knees, she reopened it and picked up her pen again.

*My suspicion was correct. Something does seem to
be going on between Sara and Rourke. When they're in
the same room, the air between them fairly crackles.
Very interesting.*

Alice put her hands over her ears as the helicopter
lifted off. The powerful rotors chopped through the
air with a deafening *whop-whop-whop.* Turbulence
plastered Alice's dress against her body and flattened
the grass around the landing pad.

Squinting, she watched the craft rise and slide
away over the tops of the live oak trees, whipping
them into a frenzy. When the helicopter disappeared
from view, she turned away and strolled toward the
corrals.

Heat and the ripe smells of animals, hay, and ma-
nure hit Alice as she entered the barn. It took a
second for her eyes to adjust to the dimness, but she
edged down the central passageway toward the
voices at the other end.

Chad, and Hal Cohen, the local vet, and old Wylie
Toler, who had worked at the Ketchum Ranch since
before Chad was born, were in the last stall. The
three men hovered over the enormous form of Winston, the ranch's prize Hereford bull. The great beast
lay prostrate in the hay, still but for the heaving of his
sides with each tortured breath.

Alice was no country girl, but even she could see
that the animal was in bad shape. Chad sent her a
scowling glance when she eased up to the stall and
braced her forearms on the top rail, but he didn't
bother with a greeting. The expression on his face as

his gaze returned to the downed bull warned her that
he would not welcome conversation.

Alice didn't mind; she was happy just to be near
him, to watch him, even though he was obviously in
a black mood.

The only good thing to come out of Evelyn's illness, as far as Alice was concerned, was that she now
had an excuse to visit the ranch often, which meant
she was seeing much more of Chad. For two months
now, Evelyn had been living at the ranch, which
meant that she, Rourke, and Sara had to commute
back and forth from Houston. Often, as now, it became necessary for them to stay overnight, sometimes even for several days.

Sara usually brought along her personal staff as
well, though Alice didn't know why she bothered.
Brian Neely was all right. At least, he was a good
detail man and he wasn't a pushy interloper like that
foul-mouthed little twit Jennifer. Alice couldn't abide
the creature. Nor her brat. Thank God they all
stayed in the guesthouse with Sara, she mused, as
Chad stroked the bull's neck.

Watching that tanned hand slide back and forth
over the red hide, Alice experienced a twinge of resentment. Never, in all the time they had been together, had Chad touched her with such tenderness.

"It don't look good, Chad." Wylie shook his head,
his watery old eyes fixed on the bull. "It don't look
good a'tall."

Chad ignored the old man's comment and drilled
Dr. Cohen with a stare. "Well? Is he going to make
it?"

As if in answer, a low sound rumbled from the
gigantic animal and his rusty red hide quivered. A

snort and a wheeze followed, then a horrible gurgling that sent a chill over Alice. The animal's eyes rolled as he struggled in vain to stand. A final labored breath hissed out and his great sides heaved one last time. Then he went still.

Dr. Cohen listened to the bull's chest. He sighed and pulled the stethoscope from around his neck and shook his head. "I'm sorry, Chad. There was nothing I could do."

Grim-faced, Chad stared at the dead bull. Alice knew the loss of the animal was a tremendous blow, financially and emotionally. She wanted to go to him and gather him close in her arms, offer what comfort she could, but with the other two men there, she didn't dare. In any case, she knew that Chad would not appreciate the gesture.

When the vet had gone, Wylie doffed his battered Stetson and turned it around and around in his gnarled hands. He spit a stream of tobacco juice into the hay and eyed Chad's stony face. "Well, sir, this is about as bad a misfortune as coulda happened. It purely is. What're we gonna do now, boss?"

Chad shot to his feet and stomped out of the stall. He didn't even look Alice's way. "Tell Charlie and Art to bury him," he snapped over his shoulder, striding toward the door.

Wylie had been around too long to be intimidated by Chad's temper. He strode after him, his bowed legs churning to catch up. Alice followed right behind.

"Now hold on, boy. That ain't what I meant, an' you know it. What're we gonna do without Winston? How you gonna run a ranch without a bull?"

Chad jerked to a halt and turned on him. "I'm

going to get a new one, that's what I'm going to do. I know of a damned good animal for sale up in Tarrant County. A prize winner. I aim to buy him."

"Humph. With what? This ranch ain't got two spare dimes to rub together."

Hovering a few feet away, Alice silently agreed with Wylie, but she didn't dare voice that opinion.

"Don't you worry about that," Chad snapped, jabbing a callused forefinger at Wylie's nose. "I'll get the damned money."

"How? What're you gonna do?"

Chad's face hardened. His flinty look sent a chill down Alice's spine. "Whatever the hell I have to."

Rourke and Sara did not return to the ranch for three days. They arrived late in the evening and spent the next hour briefing Evelyn on the damage.

"This was no malfunction," Rourke informed her. "Just like on the Eden East project, someone bypassed the automatic controls and turned on the main valve manually. It looks like whoever is doing this knows only two tricks. I guess we can be grateful he didn't set fire to the place."

"The damage was bad enough as it is," Sara put in. "The building was completely flooded. We lost all the packing material and there was damage to the machinery and the products that were on line to be packaged. The whole department will be shut down for at least week."

"Mmm. That's going to play havoc with our shipping schedule." Evelyn stared into the distance for several seconds, then looked at Rourke. "Did security find any clues that would help us discover who's behind this?"

"Nope. Not a thing."

"Surely someone saw something."

"It was done in the middle of the night, just like the other incidents. There was only the night watchman there, and he can't be everywhere at once."

Sara opened her briefcase, pulled out several sheets of paper, and handed them to Evelyn. "Here is an itemized list of the damages, along with the estimated costs of repair and what the downtime will cost us."

Evelyn gave them a cursory glance and laid them on the table beside her bed. "I'll look at them later. It's late. Why don't the two of you go get some sleep? You look tired. We'll finish this in the morning."

Neither Rourke or Sara had to be coaxed. He offered to walk her to the guest house but she wouldn't hear of it. It was late, and they were both too tired for formalities.

Rourke was a thoughtful man, Sara reflected wearily as she detoured around the pool and made her way along the brick pathway on the other side. She had learned that in the past when he was at the ranch he usually occupied the guesthouse. Now he stayed in the main house and yielded the guesthouse to her and her staff. He never said so, but she suspected he had made the sacrifice because he knew she was still uncomfortable with the idea of sharing a roof with Evelyn.

A lamp had been left burning in the living room, but Jennifer and Brian had already retired for the night when Sara let herself into the three-bedroom bungalow. As quickly as possible, she showered and slipped into bed.

Tired as she was, she expected to fall asleep instantly, but she could not seem to relax. Her mind was clicking and whirling, wrestling with a dozen different problems at once. For almost an hour, she tossed and turned and punched her pillow repeatedly. She was just beginning to doze off when she was jerked awake again by the smell of smoke.

Chapter Twenty-One

Fire.

Sara's heart leaped up into her throat. "Oh, my God!"

She threw back the cover and dashed for the door. *"Fire! Fire! Jennifer! Brian! Wake up! The house is on fire!"*

Heat and billowing smoke hit her the instant she jerked the door open. Coughing, Sara flung her arm up to protect her face and instinctively shied back a step. The hallway was thick with smoke. At the end, near Brian's room, flames were shooting out of the utility room and licking up the walls.

"Jennifer! Brian!" she screamed, but there was no answer. The only sound was the crackle and pop of the greedy blaze.

Steeling herself, Sara sucked in a deep breath, bent low, and plunged into the hall. She lifted the hem of her long gown and held it over her mouth and nose and groped along the wall with her other hand. The blistering heat grew worse with each step she took. Acrid smoke stung her eyes and made them stream. She could barely breathe. After what seemed like an eternity, she found the door to Jennifer's room and fumbled for the knob. As fast as she could, she opened the door, stepped inside, and slammed it closed behind her.

The smoke was less dense in the room, hanging in an eerie cloud from the ceiling to about three feet above the floor. Hunched over, Sara hurried to the bed and shook Jennifer.

"Jen! Jen, wake up!" The girl grumbled something and slapped at Sara's hand. Frantic, Sara grasped her shoulders and shook her hard. "Damn you, Jennifer, I said *wake up!*"

"Wha—" Groggy and disoriented, Jennifer pushed up on one elbow and blinked. "Sara? What're you doing in here?"

"The house is on fire. We've got to get out. C'mon, hurry. I'll get the baby. You open the window and climb out, and I'll hand her to you."

"Holy shit!" Jennifer shot out of the bed and turned in a circle, flapping her hands, coughing. "Holy shit!"

"The window, Jen! Open the window! And stay low!"

The smoke was getting thicker. Sara scooped the toddler from her crib and cradled her against her breast, stumbling in a crouch toward where the window should be. She bumped into Jennifer, who was struggling to raise the stubborn window.

"It's . . . stuck," she panted between coughs.

Holding Cindy with one arm, Sara lent a hand. They strained with all their might. She was considering breaking out the glass when the window suddenly flew up.

Sara pushed out the screen. "Climb out. Hurry!"

Scrambling to obey, Jennifer swung her long legs over the sill and dropped into the azalea bushes beneath the window.

The smoke in the room was getting thicker by the second. Sara could feel the heat against her back.

When she gained her balance, Jennifer spun around and reached for the baby. "Here. Give her to me."

Cindy woke up and started to cry as Sara passed her through the window and into her mother's waiting arms.

Sara's first instinct was to go back for Brian, but a glance over her shoulder told her that the hall was blocked. Already the flames were licking up the inside of the bedroom door.

"C'mon, Sara! Hurry! Get out of there!"

Sara hesitated a second, then scooted through the window. She landed on the trampled azaleas and stumbled to her knees, but she scrambled up at once and took off.

"Sara! Where're you going? Come back!"

"Brian! Brian, wake up!" she screamed, as she ran along the side of the house. Before she reached it, she could see the red glow coming from his bedroom window, and fear clutched at her throat. *"Briii-uannn!"*

Running after her, Jennifer caught her arm and jerked her to a halt.

"Sara, stop!"

"Noooo! Let me go! I've got to get Brian out."

"He's not in there. Sara, listen to me! Brian's not inside!" The horrendous roar and crackle of the fire almost drowned out her voice. Flames were devouring the house in a greedy frenzy, shooting high into the air as though reaching for the night sky and exploding from window after window, blowing out the panes.

Sara shook her head, her eyes glassy with fear and shock. Jennifer shook her, gestured toward the guest parking area behind the house, and shouted over the roar of the fire, "Look, damn it! See? Brian's car isn't there! He went out on a date and he's not back yet! Now, come on! Let's get the hell outta here before we get ourselves killed!"

Dazed, Sara allowed Jen to tow her along at a run. They had barely gone ten feet when the window behind them blew out and the force of the blast slammed them to the ground.

"I'm sorry, Mrs. Ketchum. There was just nothing we could do. The place was too far gone by the time we got here."

"I understand, Sheriff Petrie. You and the volunteers did all you could. We thank you for trying."

"Yes, ma'am."

Here was one tough lady, Sheriff Buford Petrie thought. Even in the aftermath of tragedy, Evelyn Ketchum was calm and in control, her regal dignity not one whit diminished by the fact that she was wearing a bathrobe and her face was bare of makeup.

He had to admire her composure, even though it bothered the hell out of him. In his experience, that kind of self-control usually masked strong emotions. Buford wondered what kind of feelings Evelyn Ketchum kept locked up inside her.

"I blame myself," Will said from his wheelchair. "That guesthouse was built over fifty years ago. I'm sure the insurance investigators will find the fire was caused by that old wiring. I've been meaning to speak to Evelyn about having it replaced for some time now, but I never got around to it. I can't tell you how sorry I am, Sara. I feel just terrible about this."

She didn't answer him. She didn't appear to have heard a word he'd said.

The sheriff switched his Stetson from one hand to the other and cast a concerned glance at Evelyn Ketchum's daughter. Shock, he thought, noting her glazed eyes. Beneath the smudges of soot her face was white as parchment, and a slight tremble shook her whole body. The little red-haired teenager sitting next to her clutching a sleeping toddler to her breast wasn't in any better shape. "Are you sure you're okay, Miss Ketch—uh, Miss Delacorte?"

She gave him a blank look, as though she didn't know he was addressing her. Then she looked away. "Anderson. My name is Sara Anderson, not Delacorte," she said in a dull voice.

"Oh. Sorry. I didn't know. I, uh . . ." He cleared his throat, shifted from one foot to the other, and worried the brim of his hat. "Maybe you should have a doc check you out. I could drive you into Brenham. They got a hospital over there."

Sara Anderson's incredibly long lashes lifted, and she looked him full in the face. She shook her head as her beautiful green eyes filled with tears. One by one they rolled over onto her cheeks, and Buford felt his heart clench in his chest.

He had always been privately amazed at the folly some men would commit over a woman, but now, looking at Sara Anderson, he understood. There were some women who reached inside a man and touched his soul, who could enslave with just a look.

"I'm sorry. I don't know what's the matter with me," she said in a wobbly voice.

"Take it easy, sweetheart. You're just having a delayed reaction to the trauma." The man standing beside her gave her shoulder a squeeze, and Sara placed her hand over his and sent him a fluttery smile.

"Oh, Brian. I'm so relieved you're all right."

"Hey. I'm invincible. You know that," he said, flashing her an affectionate smile.

"I think the sheriff is right, Sara. You should go to the hospital. I'll have the pilot get the helicopter ready. He can fly you to the Houston Medical Center quicker than you can drive to Brenham." Evelyn reached for the telephone, but Sara stopped her.

"No! I'm all right. I'm not going to a hospital."

"Sara, Evelyn's right. You should have a doctor check you out."

"Will you two leave me alone?" Sara sent Rourke a blazing look. "I said I'm fine. I just have a few minor cuts and bruises, that's all. I don't know why you're making such a fuss!"

"Sara, I'm simply concerned about you," Evelyn replied stiffly.

"Really? Funny, I never noticed. All those years I was growing up in California, I don't recall even seeing you around."

Sheriff Petrie's gaze narrowed and cut back and forth. Rourke was frowning, but it was the cool defiance in Sara Anderson's face as she stared at her mother that caught Buford's attention. Something was going on here.

"Sheriff, if that's all, I think Miss Anderson needs

to get some rest. She's had a close call. I'm sure you can understand that she is exhausted, emotionally and physically.''

"Oh, yeah, sure, Mr. Fallan. I'll get outta you folks' hair. Don't bother to see me out," he said, when Eric started to rise. "I'll just slip out through the back and check on the men." He nodded to the women. "Ladies."

Outside, dawn was breaking over the gently rolling hills. Buford paused on the back porch to settle his Stetson on his head. His gaze narrowed on the smoldering pile of charred timbers beyond the swimming pool, all that was left of the guesthouse. He didn't like it. Something about this whole thing didn't smell right.

Around the rubble, the weary firefighters were gathering their equipment and rewinding hoses. Buford stepped off the porch and strode toward them.

Technically, Sheriff Buford T. Petrie was not a member of the Hobart Volunteer Fire Department, but since the station house was next door to his office, he usually went along on calls if he had nothing else to do. Usually he didn't. Other than busting up the occasional barroom brawl at Skeeter's Poolhall or nabbing one of the locals for speeding, Lasko County didn't have much of a crime problem. Which was just the way Buford liked it.

He'd seen enough violence and mayhem during his ten years with the Houston Police Department to last him a lifetime. He'd come home to Hobart and run for sheriff of Lasko County precisely because it was a peaceful rural area where very little truly bad ever happened.

Now that peace had been disturbed by a fire that

had almost resulted in tragedy, and he had that old itch on the back of his neck. The one he used to get back in Houston when something wasn't right.

"Hey, Buford," Charley Hanes called. "That little gal okay now? She sure was unstrung. Pretty little thing, though, ain't she?"

Charley's curiosity about Sara Anderson didn't surprise Buford. The whole town—shoot, the whole danged country—was curious about this long-lost daughter of Evelyn's who had popped up all of a sudden. Most folks around Hobart had caught glimpses of her being driven through town in that chauffeured limo of Mrs. Ketchum's, but no one he knew of had met Sara, until tonight.

"She's still upset, but I got a hunch she'll weather this okay. She's got a lot of her mama in her."

The folks around Hobart were proud of Evelyn Ketchum and all she'd accomplished. She may have been a Texan only by marriage, but she'd been around these parts long enough that the locals considered her their own.

Buford stopped beside the fire truck and stood with his hands on his hips, surveying the smoking remains of the house. "Charley, I want this whole area cordoned off. See that no one disturbs it. And I mean no one. The insurance investigator should be here soon, but before he touches anything, I'm gonna get the arson boys from Austin down here to go through the ashes with a fine-toothed comb."

The conference with the bankers did not go well. More shaken than she wanted to admit, Sara did not argue when Rourke insisted that she and Jennifer take a few days off to recuperate from their close call. During that period Rourke met with Mr. Braddock and the other bankers alone. Somehow he persuaded them to delay taking action, but he was not encouraged.

"They're nervous about all the accidents. And about the company's leadership." Rourke sent Sara an apologetic glance before turning his gaze back to Evelyn. "Braddock didn't come right out and say it, but he made it clear that he and his associates were concerned about the future of the company, now that you aren't running things. They agreed to wait a while before they do anything, but they won't be put off for long."

"Mmm." Evelyn tapped her chin with a perfectly manicured fingernail, her expression thoughtful. "So it boils down to a lack of confidence in Sara."

"Basically. They're not happy about all the accidents and setbacks, but I think they could weather those if they were more comfortable with the company's leadership. Sorry, Sara, but that's the impression I got."

"It's not as though we didn't expect it. The question is, what do we do now?"

"There is a solution. An unusual one, perhaps, but it will work." Evelyn glanced from Sara to Rourke. "You and Rourke could get married."

"Married!" Sara squeaked. She stared at Evelyn as though she'd lost her mind. "We can't do that!"

For an instant Rourke appeared as shocked as Sara. Then his jaw set, and Sara knew he was furious. His expression was icy, but his eyes blazed with turbulent emotions. "That's a bit drastic, don't you think?"

"Not at all. Think about it. A marriage between you and Sara would solve everything. The bankers know you, Rourke. They know your reputation and experience. They trust you. If you were Sara's husband, you could be on the board and she could make you president of Eve. That should satisfy them."

"But you're talking about marriage," Sara protested.

"It doesn't have to be a real marriage. For appearances you would have to share a domicile, of course, but otherwise the marriage need be merely a formality."

Evelyn's matter-of-fact tone shocked Sara, particularly given that her own heart was banging away like a kettledrum. How could she sit there so calmly and make such an outrageous suggestion? "This is preposterous. I can't do it. I married once for the wrong reason. I won't do it again."

"If you have a better answer to our problems, I'm willing to listen."

"Would it be so terrible if you simply let the company go public?"

"Yes." The reply came instantly. Evelyn's gaze was steady, her expression implacable. "I will never agree to that. I'll let the business go bankrupt first. If you want the inheritance I promised you, it will have to be on my terms."

Sara looked to Rourke for help. "Surely you're not willing to go along with this?"

A tiny muscle ticked along his jaw. His face looked as though it had been carved from stone, but he merely shrugged and said woodenly, "It is a solution."

"Sara, please don't dismiss the idea out of hand.

It's not as though I'm asking you to sacrifice the rest of your life. Once the spas are completed, if it's what you and Rourke want, you can have the marriage quietly annulled. It's really not that big a thing."

Not that big a thing? A bubble of hysterical laughter rose in Sara's throat. Maybe it wouldn't be, if she weren't falling in love with Rourke. The trouble was, despite logic to the contrary and the emotional risks involved, she wanted to marry him . . . but not for this reason.

"Sara, sometimes in big business, when the stakes are this high, you have to make personal sacrifices, do things you would not do otherwise."

"You mean, like you did when you married a man for his money?"

Evelyn did not bat an eye or hesitate a beat. "That's right. And it was the smartest—and luckiest—decision I ever made. Joe Ketchum was a wonderful man, and whether you believe it or not, I grew to love him very much. I'll be forever grateful that I made that choice.

"Now you're faced with a difficult choice. You will have to decide, as I did, if the end is worth the means."

Evelyn wrote in her diary that evening.

Rourke is angry with me. I don't think it's because he abhors the thought of marrying Sara. The heat between those two would melt a glacier, though for some reason, they don't appear to be doing anything about it. No, I suspect he merely resents being pushed into a corner. Perhaps he even intended to propose to her himself eventually and is furious because I beat him to the punch. Whatever, he'll get over it. If I had waited around for him to make the obvious move, the company might have gone under.

Evelyn paused and gazed into the distance. After a while, she smiled and began to write again. *I have to admit, the thought of Rourke marrying Sara pleases me. I couldn't think of a man I would rather have as a son-in-law. The truly wonderful part is, a union between them would be advantageous, not just for the business, but for Rourke as well.* Her smile faltered a bit, and her expression became pensive. She gnawed at her lower lip and wrestled with her conscience. Finally she added, *I must admit, I also want very much for Sara to be happy. Perhaps, if I'm truthful, I want that most of all.*

"Thanks for the information. You've been a big help."

In his office in Hobart, Sheriff Petrie hung up the telephone, propped his booted feet on top of his desk, and studied his notes. Well, well. So that fire wasn't an isolated incident at all. Over the past few months, Eve Cosmetics had suffered several setbacks. Too many to be accidents. He'd bet his best blue tick hound on it.

Buford leaned back in his chair and tugged at his bottom lip. Oh, yeah. There was definitely something going on in the Ketchum family.

Chapter Twenty-Two

Sara locked her hands around the porch railing to keep them from trembling. She stared at the wedding band on her left hand. Lord, she still could not believe that she had done it. She had married Rourke.

Sara Fallan. Mrs. Rourke Fallan. As of twenty minutes ago, that was her name. Bemused, she fingered the diamond-encrusted wedding band again. The exquisite ring had been a shock. Given the circumstances, she had expected a simple gold band. Sara wondered if perhaps the ring, like their new living arrangements, was for appearances.

Over the past few months she had learned that when Evelyn wanted something done, it was done expeditiously. Even so, she marveled at the speed with which Evelyn had arranged the wedding. It had been only a week since the fire and three days since she'd agreed to marry Rourke.

The seemingly spur-of-the-moment decision provided a plausible excuse to keep the wedding small and private. For the Ketchums, attendance had been a command performance. They might have grumbled, but none of them, Will included, had had the nerve to defy Evelyn, not as long as they thought there was a hope of someday inheriting a chunk of her stock.

If they had known that she was going to be Evelyn's sole heir, Sara doubted any of them would have shown up, with the possible exception of Kitty and Eric. Over the past few months she had formed a tentative friendship with Kitty, and Eric didn't have a mean-spirited bone in his body.

He had shown up with a sexy redheaded beauty in tow, full of good wishes and devilish teasing. Kitty brought Miles Bentley, though he did not seem at all pleased about being dragged away from rehearsals of Kitty's play.

Evelyn had not met the English actor before. She was polite, but Sara could tell that she did not care for the man. Neither did Eric. It was the first time Sara had ever seen him give anyone the cold shoulder.

The remainder of the family and Brian, Jennifer, and Cindy had been the only other witnesses to the brief ceremony performed in the front parlor of the ranch house by Judge Wilson Doggett, a friend of Evelyn's. For that, Sara was grateful; she had been more nervous than a first-time bride.

She still was, but beneath the jitters excitement was building. And hope. After all, no matter the reason, she and Rourke were married now. Who knew what might develop from that?

"Are you okay?"

Sara turned her head at the soft question to see Brian standing a few feet away, watching her like a lost soul. Her heart squeezed at the misery in his eyes.

"Hi. And yes, I'm fine." Smiling gently, she reached out and touched his arm. "How about you?"

He shrugged. "What're you doing out here all by yourself? Shouldn't you be inside, celebrating with the lucky bridegroom?" The bitter sarcasm in his voice was unmistakable.

"Oh, Brian," Sara chided gently. "Why are you so opposed to this marriage? It's not as though you love me in that way. And you've never been bothered by any of the other men in my life."

"That's because they didn't mean anything to you. Not really. It's different with Fallan."

"You're right. It is. But I don't understand why it upsets you so much."

"I guess I'm just a selfish bastard."

"What does that mean?"

Brian stared out across the pasture, his expression pensive. Finally he looked back at Sara and grimaced. "I guess I'm afraid that you'll get so wrapped up in Fallan that you won't have room for me in your life anymore."

"Oh, Brian. We've been friends since we were children. We always will be. Don't you know that?" In a burst of emotion she lunged forward and wrapped her arms around him, and as Brian returned the fierce hug, she felt him tremble. "I'll always be there for you, Brian," she whispered in his ear. "No matter what."

His arms tightened, but Sara sensed he was too choked with emotion to speak.

"Well, well, isn't this cozy?"

Sara and Brian sprang apart as Madelene strolled out onto the porch carrying a flute of champagne and leaned a hip against the railing beside them. She raised the glass and gave Sara a feline smile. "Does Rourke know how lovey-dovey you are with your ex?"

"I was just saying goodbye to Sara," Brian said, scowling at Madelene smirk. "If you try to make something dirty out of it, so help me, I'll—"

Sara laid her hand on his arm. "It's okay, Brian. Why don't you go back inside and make sure that Jen doesn't have too much champagne? I'll handle this."

To his credit, for a moment he looked as though he would stand and fight, but after giving Madelene one last warning scowl, he turned and went inside.

Sara turned to her stepsister with a cool look. "Did you want something, Madelene?"

"Actually, I just came out to get a bit of fresh air. It's a bit too cheery in there for my taste. However, there is something you can tell me. I'm curious. How does it feel to be a stand-in?"

Sara raised an eyebrow. "A stand-in? For whom?"

"For Evelyn."

"Evelyn? I'm not sure what you mean. If you're asking how it feels to be running Eve, I have to say it's exciting and fascinating. And, of course, utterly exhausting."

Madelene gave her a pitying look. "You really don't know, do you?"

"Know what?"

"I'm not talking about the company. I'm talking about Rourke and Evelyn. He's madly in love with her. He has been for years."

Sara sucked in her breath. Her hard-won composure shattered like crystal.

"That's a lie!"

"It's true, all right. Ask anyone. He only married

you because you look like your mother. When he
makes love to you tonight, it will be Evelyn he's
thinking of."

"Th-that's not true."

"Oh, but it is, darling. But don't worry. Actually,
you're a very lucky woman. Rourke is a fantastic
lover." Lowering her eyelids halfway, Maddie arched
her back, sinuous as a cat, and ran her palm down
over one hip. "Mmm, the things that man does in bed
are positively wicked," she purred. "Believe me, darling, I know."

Sara felt the blood drain out of her face. Watching
her over the top of her glass, Maddie downed the last
of her champagne. With a triumphant smile, she
sauntered away. "Ta-ta, darling. Have a nice honeymoon."

A wave of dizziness washed over Sara. She was
afraid she was going to disgrace herself by being sick
over the side of the porch. Rourke . . . and Evelyn.
Her mother. Oh, God.

"Can I talk to you a minute?"

"Sure. Fire away."

"In private."

Rourke studied Brian Neely's expression, in-
trigued. It was the first time he'd seen anything that
even resembled determination on his face. Usually he
looked like a tragic character from an eighteenth-
century melodrama.

He took a sip of champagne and nodded toward
the door. "Follow me."

He led Brian down the hall and into the library and
shut the door. "Now, what's this about?"

"I just want to know one thing."

Rourke raised one eyebrow at his belligerent tone. "And that is?"

"Do you love Sara?"

A taut stillness settled over Rourke. His eyes narrowed on the other man and his soft voice was velvet-encased steel. "That, I believe, is none of your business."

"Maybe not. But Sara is very dear to me. I won't stand by and see her hurt."

"That's very admirable, I'm sure, but let me remind you that Sara is no longer your concern. Now, if you'll excuse me, I should go find my wife. It's almost time to leave."

"Did you marry her to get control of Eve Cosmetics?"

Rourke stopped with his hand on the doorknob and looked back at Brian in stony silence for several long seconds. Then, without a word, he went out and closed the door behind him with a soft click.

"There you are. I've been looking all over for you."

The sexy rumble of Rourke's voice in her ear was like a slap. When his hands grasped the rounded curves of Sara's shoulders and began to gently massage, she stiffened and clutched the rail tighter.

"It's time to go if we're going to make Rio by midnight. The chopper is ready to ferry us to Houston. The company jet is fueled up and waiting."

"Very well." Sara sidestepped away, breaking contact with those tantalizing hands. Without looking at him, she headed for the door, her back ramrod stiff.

Rourke put a hand on her shoulder and stopped her. "Sara? Is something wrong?"

"No. Not at all," she replied, still not meeting his gaze. "If you'll excuse me, I'll get my bags."

"They're already on board the chopper. Everyone is out at the landing pad, waiting to see us off."

"Oh. I see. Well, then, I suppose we should be going."

The next ten minutes were the longest of Sara's life. No one knew the real reason behind the hurried marriage but Evelyn, Rourke, and her. She therefore had to run the gamut of good wishes and endure the humiliating rituals of throwing her bouquet and being peppered with rice as she and Rourke raced for the waiting helicopter, all under Madelene's malicious gaze.

Sara was not fond of riding in the helicopter, but at least the noise prevented conversation on the short hop to Houston International. During the flight from Houston to Rio de Janeiro on the company jet, her responses to Rourke's attempts at conversation were remote and terse to the point of rudeness. Finally he gave up and pulled some papers from his briefcase. Several times, out of the corner of her eye, Sara noticed him studying her curiously, but she remained silent and distant.

They arrived in Rio shortly before midnight. Sara was nervous as a caged cat when they were shown into their suite at the hotel. She was also still simmering. While Rourke dealt with the obsequious bellman, she stood in the middle of the living room and glanced around at the plush accommodations, and felt anger well anew. Such a perfect setting for a romantic honeymoon. What a pity Rourke was there with the wrong woman.

The moment the bellman left, he turned to her with a smile. "Sorry about that. Some people try too hard. How about a drink?"

"No, thank you."

"At least have a sip. We have to drink a toast to our marriage."

Sara's hands curled into fists. She wanted to hit him for that.

He went to the drinks tray and lifted a bottle from a bucket of ice. "Ah, good. Exactly what I ordered." He popped the cork and filled two glasses. Carrying both, he strolled her way, his eyes warm. Sara watched him, fury building, and when he handed her a glass, she took it automatically.

Rourke clinked his glass against hers. "To us."

Sara watched his throat move as he swallowed a sip of the wine.

"You're not drinking."

"No." In a move so precise it was an insult, she sat her untouched glass on a nearby table. "If you'll excuse me, it's been a long and tiring day. I'm going to bed."

"Mmm, an excellent idea." Smiling, Rourke put his glass down beside hers and reached for her.

Before Sara could evade him or protest, his arms were around her, enfolding her, molding her to him. She could feel his heat from her knees to her shoulders.

Sara squeezed her eyes shut and gritted her teeth. She wanted to feel revulsion, but her traitorous body responded with a will of its own, going pliant against him, her nipples growing tight and tingly. His scent went to her head like fine wine, clean and masculine and uniquely Rourke.

His hands moved across her back. "I didn't want to rush you," he murmured in that sexy rumble. "But I'll admit, I've been thinking about you—and bed—all day."

"What?" Sara pushed against his chest. Rourke nuzzled her neck and made a sound somewhere between a growl and a laugh and held her tighter. Trailing nibbling kisses over her cheek, his lips sought hers, but Sara hunched her shoulder and turned her head away. "Stop it, Rourke. Let me go!"

"Sara, sweetheart. Relax."

"No!" She jerked out of his arms and back up several steps. "Don't touch me."

"Don't touch you? What the hell do you mean, don't touch you? Damn it, Sara, we just got married."

"That was just a business arrangement. You said it wouldn't be a real marriage."

"No. Evelyn said that. Not me."

"But—"

"C'mon, Sara. There's no way in hell that you and I can be married and share a house without making love, and we both know it. It was a ridiculous suggestion. I don't believe for a minute that you took it seriously, any more than I did. If you really wanted that kind of marriage, you've had three days to say so. When we stood in front of Judge Doggett a few hours ago, you knew full well what would happen tonight, and don't deny it. I saw it in your eyes."

"That was before I knew about you and Evelyn."

Without seeming to move a muscle, Rourke withdrew. His whole body went rigid, and his face looked as though it were carved from stone. His eyes, usually such a warm, vivid blue, turned frosty and suspicious. "What about me and Evelyn?"

The clipped tone confused her, put her on the defensive, and Sara lifted her chin. "You're in love with her."

"Ahhh, I see. So you've heard that old tale, have you? And just which one of the Ketchums do I have to thank for that?"

"Madelene told me at the reception."

"Ah, Maddie. Of course."

"She said everyone knew that you've been in love with Evelyn for years. And that the only reason you married me was because I look so much like her."

"We both know that's not true. Your resemblance to your mother had nothing to do with my decision to marry you."

"It didn't hurt, though, did it?"

Rourke pursed his lips and seemed to consider the question. "Honestly? No. It didn't. Evelyn is a beautiful woman, and so are you."

"Are you in love with her?"

She saw his jaw tighten and she knew the question had angered him, but she had to know.

"If you're asking do I admire and respect her, then the answer is yes. Do I find her beautiful and intellectually stimulating? Yes. Do I think she's classy and sexy and special as hell? You bet. I'll even admit that Evelyn is the standard by which I judge other women. If you or the Ketchums or anyone else wants to twist that to mean I'm in love with her, that's your problem, not mine.

"The rumor about Evelyn and me has been circulating for years, even before Joe died. Some people have gone so far as to suggest that we were carrying on an affair right under his nose. I saw no point in dignifying that kind of garbage with a denial, and I won't do so now. Either you trust me, Sara, or you don't."

"Maddie also hinted that you and she were lovers." Sara's tone, her out-thrust chin, made the statement an accusation.

"Damn it, Sara. What has that got to do with us?"

"Then you *are* having an affair with her."

"No. I am not. All right. Yes. Several years ago, when Maddie was between husbands, we had a brief affair. She offered, and I took. So what? Maddie's a sensual creature, and we enjoyed one another briefly, but it was just sex, and it has been over a long time."

The thought of Rourke and Madelene together made Sara sick to her stomach. The thought of him and Evelyn was even worse. She wanted to believe him, but she could not quite bring herself to risk that kind of humiliation and hurt. If it turned out that Rourke did love Evelyn and was using her as a substitute, she would not be able to bear it.

Her doubts must have shown on her face. Rourke's expression grew harder. "I can see I'm wasting my breath. You don't believe me. Fine. Think whatever you want."

He spun away and stalked out without another word. Sara flinched when the door slammed behind him. She stood in the middle of the floor, staring after him, full of uncertainty and hurt and feeling strangely guilty.

Already she regretted blurting out Madelene's poison. Maddie was a vicious and vindictive person. Sara had known of her reputation even before she'd

met her. Certainly she was not above lying to strike
out at someone, and she'd made no secret of the fact
that she resented Sara.

On the other hand, what if she *had* been telling the
truth? If only she could be sure, one way or the other.

Folding her arms protectively across her midriff,
Sara bit her lower lip to hold back the tears that
threatened and cast a forlorn look around the luxurious sitting room. Under the circumstances, she'd
made the right choice, she assured herself, even while
she fought to control her wobbly chin. The prudent
one, at any rate. It was foolish to risk your heart on
a man who very possibly could be in love with someone else. Especially when that someone was your
own mother.

Sara trudged into the larger of the bedrooms and
slowly peeled out of her clothes. Trying desperately
to forget that this was suppose to be her wedding
night, she went through her nightly ritual of preparing for bed and finally slipped beneath the covers.

She tossed and turned for hours, straining to hear
every sound. The empty suite and the clock on the
bedside table taunted her. She peeked at the lumi-
nous dial every few minutes and wondered where
Rourke was. What he was doing? Was he alone, or
had he sought solace in another woman's arms?

Dawn was beginning to break when she finally
heard him enter the suite. His footsteps neared her
bedroom, and she quickly closed her eyes and feigned
sleep. The door opened. Sara lay still and forced
herself to breathe slowly. Through the screen of her
lashes she saw Rourke standing in the doorway,
watching her. Her heart thudded. She half expected
him to come to her, to slip beneath the covers and

take her into his arms and smother her protests with kisses until she had no choice but to surrender. Part of her hoped he would.

After a moment, though, he quietly closed the door. A moment later, Sara heard the door to the other bedroom click shut. The tension that had kept her wound tight for hours seeped out of her, and with a sigh she relaxed against the pillows. Within minutes she was asleep.

She awoke around noon and found Rourke eating brunch on the terrace. She hesitated in the doorway, but when he looked up and saw her he smiled and waved his hand toward the other chair. "Good morning. Won't you join me?"

"Well, I . . ." She tightened the sash on her robe and shifted uneasily.

"C'mon. There's plenty." Taking her acceptance for granted, he rose and held out the chair, and when she had slipped into it, he poured her a cup of coffee.

"I've been waiting for you to wake up," he said cordially, passing a silver serving dish of cinnamon toast to her. "Since this is suppose to be a combination honeymoon and working trip, I thought we should pay a courtesy visit to the plant this afternoon. While we're here, there are several important customers we should call on also."

"Fine. Whatever you think is best." The Rio de Janeiro factory was one which Sara had not visited before. That was one of the reasons they had come to Rio for their honeymoon.

"Good. As soon as you've eaten and are ready, we'll go."

Throughout the meal, Rourke talked about in-consequential things. Sara watched him warily over her coffee cup. Not by so much as a word or a look did he allude to the previous night and their quarrel.

His change in attitude should have pleased her, but it didn't. Rourke was cordial and pleasant, but it was clear that he had thrown up an invisible barrier between them. There was a distance, a stiff quality to his politeness that had not been there before.

While Sara and Rourke were having brunch in Rio de Janeiro, in Hobart, Texas, Sheriff Buford Petrie was reared back in his chair with his feet propped on his desk, sipping a mug of the sludge his deputy called coffee and reading the report that had finally come in from the arson investigators.

On meeting Buford, all most people saw was a slow drawling bear of a man wearing a battered Stetson and dusty cowboy boots and they dismissed him as a typical redneck hick sheriff. Buford didn't mind. If the truth were known, he actually did all he could to reinforce the impression. When people assumed you weren't a threat, they sometimes revealed more than they would have otherwise.

Few people realized that behind the good-old-boy image, Buford Petrie possessed a shrewd mind and a nose like a blue tick hound when it came to sniffing out clues. When that pesky itch bothered him, he started digging like a dog after a bone, never letting up until he came up with some answers.

For the past week, every since that tragic fire out at the Ketchum place, he'd been itching something fierce.

By the time the sheriff reached the end of the report, a frown had cut a deep line between his eyebrows. "Well, crap," he spat. His hunch had been right. Some son-of-a-bitch was pulling some serious shit. Sheriff Petrie stared into the distance, his eyes narrowing.

His rickety old wooden desk chair creaked and his boots hit the scuffed linoleum floor with a thud. "Not, by damned, in my county, you don't," he growled, and snatched up the phone, punching out a series of numbers.

On the third ring someone picked up and barked, "H.P.D. Homicide. Detective Calhoun speaking."

"Hey, Irish. When you gonna come out and wet a line with me?"

"Buford! Well, how the hell are you, man? How're things shaking out in Hooterville?"

"It's Hobart, you big dumb Mick," Buford growled affectionately at his former partner.

"Yeah, yeah. So, what's up? I know you, Petrie. You didn't call just to invite me to go fishing."

"Well, now . . . since you mentioned it . . . I do have me a problem. One I'm gonna need some help on. And since I'm just a dumb ole country boy and you're such a whiz with those newfangled computers—"

"Aw, hell, not again," Mike Calhoun groaned. "Jesus, Buf! Every time you pull that bucolic bullshit I end up working my tail off for you on my off duty hours."

Buford chuckled. "Just think of it as character building. Now, here's what I have so far . . ."

* * *

With each passing day, Sara's doubts about the veracity of Madelene's claim grew, along with her guilt that perhaps she had misjudged Rourke. Looking back, she realized that she should not have been so quick to believe Madelene. The woman was malicious and spiteful, and she'd made no secret of the fact that she resented Sara. She had worked closely with Evelyn and Rourke for months, and all she had noticed between them was mutual admiration, respect, and absolute trust. Sara blamed her knee-jerk reaction on her emotional state at the time.

She was not happy with the way things stood between her and Rourke, but she had no idea what to do about it.

Every day it was the same; they spent the daylight hours touring the factory or in conference with their top people in Rio. Every evening they were wined and dined by the execs and their spouses or by important customers or business contacts. They were almost never alone. Sara suspected Rourke had arranged things that way.

Alone or in a crowd, he was as scrupulously polite to her as a stranger. The distance between them seemed to be widening, and increasingly, as the days passed, Sara felt a keen sense of loss and sadness.

Their fourth night in Rio, she was surprised and delighted when Rourke suggested they have dinner alone at La Tonga, one of Rio's newest hot spots. She was looking forward to having him all to herself at last, but they had no sooner entered the nightclub than Rourke was hailed by a group of people.

"They're the Mendez family of Buenos Aires," he murmured in her ear, as he steered her toward their table. "They own a chain of department stores in

Argentina and Brazil and they have plans to expand into several other South American countries. Their account with us runs into the high six figures every year. So smile."

Several people at the Mendez table expressed surprise when Rourke introduced Sara as his wife. Carlita Mendez, a sultry brunette in her early twenties, appeared particularly shocked.

After a few minutes of chitchat, Sara and Rourke were about to excuse themselves when Carlita suggested that they join them. Everyone else at the table quickly chimed in an agreement.

The fact that they were supposed to be on their honeymoon provided the perfect excuse to decline the invitation—or at least Sara thought so—but Rourke accepted with little urging.

The following two hours seemed endless to Sara. When Rourke was not talking business with Señor Mendez, Carlita claimed his attention. A blind man could see that the young woman was enamored of him. She flirted brazenly, laughing and flashing her dark eyes and using every excuse to put her hands on him. Rourke did not seem to mind. Occasionally Carlita darted Sara challenging looks, as though daring her to object.

Sara became more and more unhappy, and as the evening ground on, she grew more and more silent. Finally, unable to endure the situation a moment longer, she excused herself and fled for the ladies' room.

She had no sooner sat down before the large mirror than Carlita breezed in.

"Ah, Señora Fallan, I did not know you were here. I did not even notice that you had left the table."

Sara met her gaze in the mirror but she did not reply. I'll just bet you didn't, she thought. You were too busy groping Rourke.

"Ah, but I am glad that you are here. It will give us a chance to talk. How is it you Americans say? "Just we girls? *Si?*"

Without waiting for a reply, Carlita sat down on the next vanity stool and took out her lipstick. She smoothed the crimson color onto her lips and made a moue, turning her head from side to side. "You are a big surprise. I did not think that Rourke was the marrying kind. Nor would I have thought that you were his type."

"Oh? And what do you think his type is?"

"Ah, that is easy. Someone with more fire. More passion. Someone not so . . . so . . . how do you say? So . . . reserved."

"I see." Sara arched one eyebrow. "You mean someone like yourself?"

"Si." Not one iota embarrassed, Carlita gave Sara a sultry look and preened. "Rourke, he is a hot-blooded man. He needs a hot-blooded woman. We have been lovers. We will be again. This puny marriage, it will make no difference."

Sara had been braced for subtle innuendos and catty remarks, but this brazen attack took her breath away. Stunned, she stared at the young woman. Instinctively she fell back on the tactic she had used as a girl when Edgar Anderson had berated and abused her. Wrapping her dignity around her like a cloak, she snapped her evening bag shut, rose, and walked out of the ladies' lounge without a word.

*   *   *

Rourke glanced at his watch and wondered what was keeping Sara. She'd been in that damned ladies' room for almost half an hour.

Carlita's parents, Carlos and Maria, were on the dance floor when Carlita returned to the table.

"Did you see Sara in the ladies' lounge?" Rourke asked, when she slipped into her seat beside him.

"*Sí.* I saw her." She smiled and placed her hand on his thigh beneath the table. "When can we get together, darling? Soon, yes?"

Rourke gave her a steady look. Carlita was spoiled and accustomed to getting whatever she wanted. Slowly but firmly he removed her hand. "I'm married now, Carlita."

"So? You cannot love that cold fish of a woman."

"My feelings for Sara are no one else's business. But speaking of my wife, where is she?"

Carlita flounced back in her chair, her face sulky. "She left."

"Left? What do you mean, she left? Where did she go?"

Carlita shrugged. "She just walked out. I guess she went back to your hotel. She—Rourke! Where are you going? Rourke, come back here!"

Chapter Twenty-Three

He caught up with her at their hotel.

Rourke charged through the heavy plate-glass entrance doors like a stormtrooper. Spotting Sara standing before the elevators, he sprinted across the lobby.

The doors slid open with a ping just as he skidded to a stop beside her and grasped her arm. Sara jumped as though she'd been poked with a cattle prod.

"Rourke! What're you doing he—"

"Save it. We'll talk in our suite," he growled, and hustled her inside the elevator.

He could tell that Sara wanted to argue, but she cast a frustrated glance at the three other passengers and held her tongue. She stood rigid, staring straight ahead, her expression mulish. Rourke didn't give a tinker's damn.

One of the passengers got off on the fourth floor. Rourke and Sara were next, and when they stopped on six, he propelled her out of the cubicle and down the hall, ignoring her futile attempts to free herself.

With one hand clamped around her elbow, he

fished his keys out of his pocket; with the other, he unlocked the door and frog-marched her inside.

The instant the door slammed behind them he released her and went on the attack. "All right. I want to know why you walked out like that. Without a word to anyone. What the hell did you think you were doing?"

Rubbing her elbow, Sara lifted her chin. "I was tired and bored, so I left."

Rourke narrowed his eyes and studied her closed expression. "Uh-uh. I don't buy that. You've got too much business savvy to walk out on a big client that way. Now, I want to know what's going on, and I want to know now."

"I've given you my answer—not that I owe you any explanation. Now, if you'll excuse me, I'm going to bed."

"Oh, no, you don't." He sidestepped and blocked her way. "You're not going anywhere until I have the truth."

"I told you—"

"The truth, Sara."

He watched her struggle to remain aloof, but her emotions were too raw, too near the surface. She was practically vibrating. "All right," she shouted. "If you must know, I'm sick to death of being confronted by your lovers!"

"That's it? That's why you took off?"

"Yes! First Madelene and now Carlita, all in less than a week. I suppose you spent our wedding night with your little hot-blooded señorita."

"Does that thought bother you?"

"Of course it bothers me!"

"Why?"

"Why? Because . . . because . . ."

"Why, Sara?"

"Because I'm your wife!"

He stilled, watching her.

"In name only," he reminded her in a quiet voice. "As long as that's the case, we're both free to pursue our own lives. Wasn't that the deal?"

"That . . . I . . ."

Rourke saw the confusion in her face and pressed harder. "Or maybe that's the problem? Do you want to be my wife, Sara?" His voice dropped to a husky pitch and he stepped closer, his eyes warm and seductive. "Do you want to make this marriage a real one?"

"I . . . Rourke, please . . ."

Sara backed away, but he followed. She bumped into the wall behind her, and he stepped forward and braced his palms flat on either side of her shoulders, trapping her. He smiled at her agitation, the mixture of panic and longing in her eyes. Leaning closer, he touched the side of her neck with his fingertips, and his smiled widened when she shivered.

"Is that what you want, sweetheart?" His gaze lowered to her mouth and lingered. He bent his head and brushed her lips in the softest of kisses. They quivered beneath his. "Mmm?" His mouth touched hers again, lightly, withdrew, and touched again. Then he caught her lower lip and sucked gently.

A helpless moan tumbled from Sara's mouth. Trembling, she pressed back against the wall, her palms flat against the silk wallcovering on either side of her thighs. "Rourke, I . . . you . . ."

"Do you want me, Sara? Do you want to share my life?" His mouth rubbed hers with feather softness, and her breath shuddered past her lips in a zephyr of sound. His teeth nipped her lower lip, then he lathed the tiny hurt with his tongue, and Sara moaned again. "And my bed?"

"I . . ."

"Do you, Sara?"

"Yes. Yes!"

She reached for him, but he grabbed her arms and held her pinned to the wall. He looked into her dazed eyes. His own were turbulent and hot. "Be sure, Sara. Because I warn you, if we make this marriage real, there will be no divorce. Ever. It will be just as we vowed before Judge Doggett—till death do us part. Is that what you want?"

Her breast rose and fell with each agitated pant. She searched his face, her eyes wide. "Yes," she whispered through trembling lips. "Yes, that's what I wa—"

Before she could finish, he snatched her into his arms and his mouth claimed her in a searing kiss that rocked her to her toes.

A low moan poured from Sara's throat. She flung her arms around him and returned the kiss with the same wild passion. The hunger that had been building inside her almost from the moment she'd met him rose to the surface and burst free. Frantic, almost desperate, she ran her hands over his back, clutching, groping, her fingers digging into the banded muscles. She pressed against him, straining to get closer, as though she would absorb him into her body.

Below the surface the uncertainty was still there, the flicker of panic and suspicion, but the yearning was greater. It was hot and fierce, coiling through her like fingers of fire, consuming her. A distant voice in her brain tried to sound a warning, but she stifled it and joyfully gave herself up to the firestorm of passion and need.

Rourke abruptly broke the kiss and straightened. Sara made a distressed sound, but it turned to a sigh when he swooped her up in his arms and strode into the bedroom.

He fell with her onto the bed. They tumbled together across the mattress, kissing, touching, exploring. With frantic haste, hooks, buttons, and zippers were dealt with and clothes discarded. The only sounds in the room were eager moans and incoherent sighs and gasps and breathless pants. Like eager children grabbing what they wanted with both hands, they clutched one another and rolled, hands searching, groping, legs entwined, bodies melded together.

Beneath the pounding excitement, Rourke was amazed—and slightly appalled—at his unrestrained behavior. He had spent painstaking years cultivating his technique with women. He wooed with finesse and sophistication, he seduced with clever words and looks and practiced moves. He had never lost control with a woman before, never gone wild.

But then, he'd never wanted a woman like he wanted this one.

Sara delighted him, inflamed him. In the heat of passion, her ladylike control vaporized. Like a drop of water on a hot griddle, she sizzled and writhed, a completely sensual creature, driven by feelings and needs as elemental as time. She was restless and untamed, and gloriously wanton and free . . . and she was driving him to the edge.

Her skin was hot and smooth and incredibly soft.

Rourke wanted to touch and kiss her all over, to lose himself in the feel and scent of her.

A furnace roared inside him. He tried to find within himself the strength to rein in, regain control, but his desire for her burned too hot.

"Sara," he gasped. "Sweetheart, I wanted this . . . to be romantic and . . . gentle. Ju-just give me a . . . minute to sl . . . slow down."

"No!" He tried to pull away, but she clutched him with both hands. "Don't. Oh, please, Rourke, love me. Love me, now. I can't wait any longer."

The thin thread of sanity snapped, and with it his feeble attempt to regain the upper hand. It was no longer an option. It no longer mattered. He gave himself up to the grinding need, let it consume him.

Heat coiled in his belly, searing heat that burned every rational thought out of his brain. Driven by a need so strong nothing else mattered, nothing else existed, he rose over her and braced on his arms.

"Sara. Look at me. Look at me, Sara." The command tore from his throat, raspy and guttural. And when her heavy eyelids lifted and her smokey green eyes focused on his and clung, he rocked his hips forward and eased into her.

Fully sheathed within her warm body, he stilled and threw his head back. A quiver shook him and sweat beaded his face. Veins and tendons stood out in his arms and neck. Eyes squeezed shut, jaw clenched, he grimaced in exquisite agony. Then he began to move.

Sara met each thrust, writhing and undulating to the ancient rhythm of life, of love. There was power and heat. And pleasure. Pleasure so great he felt on fire. Sara's eyes were smoky with passion. Smiling, she looped her arms around his neck and whispered in a throaty voice, "Rourke. Oh, Rourke."

He picked up the pace. He watched her eyes widen, watched her trim little body arch and tense, and smiled—a tight, savage smile. He drove into her, harder, faster. Hearts pounded and breathing became raspy and labored. The tension built, and Sara thrashed her head from side to side on the pillow. Her back arched.

"Rourke! Oh, God . . . *Rourke!*"

"Yes, baby. Yes!"

With a guttural moan, he gathered her close and took them both over the edge.

They drifted for what could have been moments or years. Rourke was only vaguely aware of Sara's hands roaming absently over his sweat-slicked back, the soft eddy of her breath feathering against his shoulder.

His heart thundered against his ribcage as though it were trying to club its way out of his chest. The sound reverberated in his ears like a jungle drum. He felt wiped out, as though every bone and muscle in his body had turned to hot mush.

Finally, he mustered enough energy to roll off her and onto his back. He looped his arm around her and pulled her against his side, nestling her head on his shoulder. Sara sighed and snuggled against him.

Rourke looked down at the woman he held cradled against him and felt a strange tightness in his chest. Sara looked so beautiful, so fragile. And so incredibly sexy, with her shining hair all mussed, her face flushed and radiant with that special glow that comes from good sex.

His wife. She was truly his wife now. He waited for that cornered feeling, the one that always came over him when he thought of committing himself to a permanent relationship, but none came—only the odd tightness in his chest and an almost painful urge to keep her close.

"Sara."

She stiffened and went absolutely still. Her eyelashes fluttered against his bare shoulder. "Yes?"

"I didn't sleep with Carlita on our wedding night. Tonight was the first time I've seen her in months."

She tipped her head up and looked at him, her pale green eyes cloudy with a mixture of doubt and naked hope. Rourke felt something in his chest crack open. "Then where were you?"

"Downstairs in the hotel bar most of the night. When I left here, I went for a walk to cool down. Afterward, I just sat in the bar and thought. The only woman on my mind—the only woman who has been on my mind since I walked into Reflections last March—is you."

She searched his face, her eyes probing his as though somehow she would find the truth there. "What were you thinking about all that time?"

"Us. This marriage. What I could do to get you to trust me enough to give it a chance." He looked deep into her eyes and touched her cheek with his fingertips. "Will you do that, Sara?"

Her lips fluttered in a weak smile. "It appears that I already have."

"Sara." Unable to resist those trembling lips, Rourke captured her chin and tipped her head up even more for a long, heated kiss. When done, he pulled back and gazed at her tenderly. "You won't regret it, I promise you."

Sara made no reply. Flickering another wan smile, she snuggled her face back against his shoulder.

Rourke rubbed his hand up and down her arm and gazed at the ceiling. She didn't trust him yet. Not completely. He'd seen it in her eyes.

But what the hell. Who could blame her? So far in life, she had been betrayed by every person who should have loved and cherished her. Evelyn, Edgar and Julia Anderson, her ex-husband, they had all failed her in one way or another.

It wouldn't be easy, winning Sara's trust. If she ever discovered the real reason he had married her, it might be impossible.

For the tenth time in five minutes, Paul gave the envelope in the inside pocket of his suit coat a nervous pat. It wasn't enough. Not nearly. Hell, to get even this much money together he'd had to sell his Rolex. And he'd been stiffed good on the deal. He'd only gotten a fraction of what the watch was worth. He was going to have to sell off something else, something his old man wouldn't miss.

He drummed the steering wheel with his fingers and looked all around. He didn't like waiting. Not in this part of town. Especially not at this hour. There were people around this neighborhood who'd cut your throat for a dime.

He checked in the rearview mirror, but all he saw was the empty parking lot, illuminated by the eerie amber glow of a lone halogen lamp. Mist swirled and writhed like an apparition in the circle of light.

A long black car glided slowly into the parking lot. Paul's heart began to pound. Feeling sick, he watched the car roll to a stop a few yards away. Two men climbed out of the front seat and looked around. Both were large and beefy and as menacing as characters in a gangster movie.

When they were satisfied that nothing was amiss, one of the men said something to the passenger in the back seat. An instant later, the rear door opened and Bruno stepped out.

The bookie had swarthy skin, a lean pockmarked face, and deep-set ebony eyes that glittered beneath a prominent brow. He was short and slender, and there was a coldness about him, a stillness, that was unnerving. He looked like a snake in human clothing.

Paul swallowed hard and reached for the door handle.

Bruno puffed on a thin cheroot and smiled around it. "Mr. Ketchum. I was afraid you might not show up."

"I said I'd be here, and here I am," Paul replied with bravado. Inside, his stomach was cramping as though he'd eaten a bushel of green apples.

"And you have the money you owe me?"

"Yeah, sure . . . well . . ." Paul cleared his throat. "I, uh . . . I've got part of it." The two bodyguards took a step toward him when he reached inside his coat for the envelope. "Hey; take it easy. Take it easy. It's only money."

The bookie took the envelope. He looked at it, then at Paul. One eyebrow cocked. "Part?"

"It's, uh . . . it's just a down payment, you understand. I'll get the rest of it to you real soon. You got my word on it."

"Mmm." Bruno pulled the money from the envelope and riffled his thumb over the edges of the bills, making a quick count. He was quiet so long, Paul began to feel sick. "Very well, Mr. Ketchum. I'm not in the habit of accepting installment payments, but since you seem to be trying, I'll give you one more month to come up with the rest."

Relief flooded Paul. He felt almost light-headed. "Thanks, Bruno. I really appreciate it. And you won't be sorry. I'll get you the money. I swear it."

Bruno smiled. "Yes. I know you will." He glanced at his two henchmen. Before Paul could move the burly apes had him, one on either side.

"Hey! Hey, what're you—"

Paul's scream rent the night as the bones in both of his thumbs snapped in two.

The pain was so intense he saw stars—red, glowing dots that pulsed and quivered against the backs of his eyelids.

The goons released him, and Paul fell to his knees on the asphalt. Whimpering and blubbering, he knelt hunched over his broken thumbs, cradling them against his chest.

A pair of shiny wingtips entered his line of vision. "Consider that a friendly warning," Bruno said somewhere above Paul's head. "That's just a taste of what happens to people who welch on Bruno Scagliala."

He flicked an inch of ash onto the ground in front of Paul and turned and strolled back to his car with his two henchman trailing behind him.

Paul began to shake. He rocked back and forth on his knees. Pathetic gasps and mewling sounds shuddered from him. Then he bent from the waist and puked.

Chapter Twenty-Four

As the company jet started its descent, Sara gazed down at the wandering streams and dense woodlands surrounding Houston Intercontinental Airport. Absently, she noted that the landscape was still lush. Soon, though, the vibrant greens of the oaks, pines, and Chinese tallows would begin to fade beneath the relentless August sun. After a lifetime spent in southern California, she was still amazed by the intensity of the Texas heat.

"Hey. Why the long face?"

Sara turned her head and met Rourke's gaze, and her heart gave a little bump. He was so handsome. And, God help her, she loved him so much. She managed a wavery smile. "Oh, it's nothing. I'm just a little sad the honeymoon is over, I guess."

The last four days had been the most wonderful Sara had ever known. It had been a magical space out of time, four glorious days—and nights—of passion, of discovery and surprise and pure happiness. For those four days she had pushed everything else aside as though it didn't exist—all her doubts about Rourke, her anger toward Evelyn, the problems with the company, the decisions she would eventually have to make. Now, however, the time had come to return to reality.

"It isn't over." Rourke leaned across the arms of their chairs and kissed her, a long, lingering kiss that made Sara's heart pound and started the now familiar flutter in the pit of her stomach. He pulled back only inches and said in a husky whisper, "It's just the beginning. "I plan for it to last another fifty years or so."

Sara's first instinct was to doubt, to steel herself against hope and hold back, but his voice was so sincere, the look in his vivid eyes so fiercely intense, she could not. Not completely. He meant it. He meant every word. She stared at him with amazement and felt warmth steal through her and coil around her heart.

There was a slight bump as the wheels touched the tarmac and the plane rumbled down the runway, jet engines whining. Still Sara could not look away.

As he watched her, Rourke's pupils expanded and his face tightened. "Keep looking at me like that and we're going to shock the hell out of the pilot," he growled.

"Oh. I'm sorry. I . . ." Flustered, Sara turned red and started to look away, but Rourke cupped her chin in the V between his thumb and fingers and captured her mouth with his.

This time his kiss was greedy and rapacious, filled with heat and hunger and male dominance. His tongue pillaged her mouth like a conquering warrior, giving no quarter.

The rush of heat was instantaneous. Helpless against the assault and the rioting feelings he aroused, Sara surrendered without so much as a token resistance. She clung to him, freely giving all he demanded, and when he unfastened her seatbelt and hauled her from her chair into his lap, she moaned and curled into him.

She never knew when he undid the buttons on her blouse, but when his hand slipped beneath the silk material and curved around her breast, she shuddered with pleasure. Through the lacy bra she could feel the heat of his hand. When his thumb whisked across her nipple she arched her back and made a desperate sound.

The world was well lost to Sara. She melted against Rourke and gave herself up to the voluptuous pleasure. She felt on fire, her body quivering with a need she hadn't known existed just weeks ago.

At first the discreet cough registered only remotely. Not until the loud, "Ah-hem!" did she become aware that the plane had stopped, or that she and Rourke were no longer alone.

"We're all clear to deplane, Mr. Fallan," the pilot said from somewhere behind Sara.

She jumped, but Rourke tightened his hold and held her against his chest, shielding her body from the pilot's view. Sara moaned and buried her hot face against Rourke's shoulder.

He did not appear in the least discomfited. "Thank you, Dave. Tucker should be waiting. Please tell him that Mrs. Fallan and I will be right out."

"Yessir. Right away."

"You can sit up now," Rourke teased. "He's gone." He tried to ease Sara away from him, but she moaned and clung tighter. He chuckled. "C'mon, sweetheart. We can't sit here all night. Tucker is waiting."

"Oh, God. I'll never be able to face that man again."

Rourke grasped her upper arms and forced her to sit up, and Sara covered her crimson face with her hands. Grinning, he pulled up the bra strap he had dislodged and began to button her blouse. "Don't worry, he didn't see anything. Besides, we're newlyweds. No one will be shocked if we can't keep our hands off one another."

Sara lowered her hands and shot him an indignant look. *"I'm* shocked. I've never been caught in such an embarrassing position in my life. Oh, God, what must Dave think. We were so . . . so . . ."

"Licentious? Fill with unbridled passion? Hot to trot?"

"Yes!" She punched his chest. "And stop that laughing. It's not funny."

"Oh, but it is, sweetheart. You should see your face."

"Rourke!"

"I'm sorry. I shouldn't tease you." He straightened her blouse, brushed her pouting mouth with another kiss, and lifted her off his lap. "Come on. It's not the end of the world. And I promise you, Dave is the soul of discretion. Evelyn wouldn't have him on staff if he wasn't. Most likely he'll pretend it never happened, so just tip that regal head up and do the same."

"Easy for you to say," she grumbled.

It took every ounce of self-possession Sara could muster to step out of the plane, but the instant she spotted Jen waiting at the bottom of the steps she forgot her embarrassment. She could tell by the expression on her secretary's face that something was wrong.

"Welcome back, boss." Jen enveloped Sara in a hug the moment she was within reach.

"What's happened? Why are you here?"

"Well, gee. It's great to see you, too." She glanced from Sara to Rourke, and in a blink her offended look turned to a cheeky grin. "Gee, the honeymoon sure must have been hot. You two look great."

"Jennifer, behave. Don't think you're going to sidetrack me with your smart mouth. Something is wrong, and I want to know what it is. Right now."

"Oh, all right. I thought I'd at least let you catch your breath before I dumped it on you, but if you insist. It's Evelyn. She's back in the hospital."

The words hit Sara like a fist to the chest. She went utterly still, as stunned by her own reaction as by the news.

Rourke stiffened and took a step forward. "How bad?"

"Bad."

Evelyn saw the shock that came over Sara's face the instant she and Rourke walked into the room. The look was replaced quickly by compassion and sorrow, and she felt a twisting pain in her chest.

It would take so little to forge a link with Sara—a word, a gesture. Despite all that had been done to her, by Evelyn herself and by others, Sara had turned out to be a wonderful woman with a good heart, a born giver. She tried to be hardboiled and distant, but Evelyn knew that if she were to take the first step, Sara would meet her halfway.

Her hand twitched atop the covers. The need to reach out was almost irresistible. Gritting her teeth, she snatched her hand back and curled it into a fist. No. She could not.

"What the devil is this?" Rourke strode to the bed and snatched up Evelyn's hand, and her clenched fingers uncurled in his grasp and clung. "I swear, I leave you alone for a minute and you're in trouble. What're you doing back in here? I thought you were done with this place."

"I thought so, too, but it appears I was wrong."

Sara edged closer to the bed. "How are you feeling?"

"I've felt better." Evelyn hated the coolness in her voice. She hated even more the flash of hurt in Sara's eyes and the mask of indifference that quickly replaced it.

Rourke draped his arm around Sara's shoulders and pulled her against him with an easy familiarity that did not escape Evelyn's notice. Nor did the way Sara relaxed against him.

Evelyn bit back a smile. So . . . the marriage of convenience didn't last through the honeymoon. She had figured that a few days alone and the magic of Rio would do the trick, and apparently she had been right.

"What happened?" Rourke demanded. "You were in remission and doing great when we left here."

"The leukemia became active again." Evelyn shrugged. "Who knows why? These things are unpredictable. We were hoping the period of remission would last longer. That it didn't is an indication that it's particularly virulent, and that's not a good sign."

"What is Dr. Underwood doing about it?"

"All he can do is step up the chemotherapy a notch and pray we find a donor soon."

"Can we do anything for you? Is there anything you need?" Sara asked.

"Yes. You can check me out of here. If I'm going to die, I'm going to do it at home."

They argued with her. So did Dr. Underwood, but Evelyn remained adamant. John Underwood had been her friend and doctor too long not to know when he was beaten. After exacting certain promises and making arrangements for her to have a full-time nurse, he reluctantly signed the release papers.

Rourke and Sara accompanied Evelyn and her nurse in the helicopter. By the time they arrived at the ranch and got the two women settled in their quarters and retired to the room they would share, it was almost midnight. Sara was bone tired, but her emotions were churning too much to allow sleep. Not even a hot shower succeeded in relaxing her.

Standing at the window, she stared out at the rolling pastureland in the moonlight. She was grateful that the room did not overlook the back yard, and the charred remains of the guesthouse. She could not bear to look at it.

A shiver rippled through her as memories of that awful night slithered through her mind. How close she and Jen and Cindy had come to losing their lives. She crossed her arms and absently rubbed her elbows through the satin robe. She heard Rourke emerge from the bathroom, but she didn't move.

"What's the matter, sweetheart?" His arms slipped around her waist from behind and he snuggled his jaw against her temple. With a sigh, Sara relaxed back against his chest, savoring his warmth, his strength, the clean smell of soap that clung to his skin. It felt so good to have someone to lean on for once in her life.

Sara didn't answer for several seconds. She gazed at the sky and picked out the Little Dipper. Her throat felt as though there were a fist-sized rock lodged in it. "She's going to die, isn't she?"

She felt Rourke's deep sigh. "It looks that way."

Sara swallowed around the rock in her throat and blinked at the stars. Inexplicably, her chin began to wobble.

"That bothers you, doesn't it? No matter what you say, you do care about her."

"Oh, Rourke. I don't know." Her voice was a quavery whisper. "I'm so confused, I don't know what I feel." Resting her forearms on top of his, she absently rubbed his hands, fingering his knuckles and the new gold wedding band. Against the tender undersides of her arms she could feel the slight abrasive rub of the hair that covered his forearms. Through the satin robe and nightgown, she felt his heat, the solid wall of his firm chest. Her buttocks were nestled against his manhood. "I'm still angry with her. I don't know that I'll ever understand or be able to forgive her. She's made it fairly clear that she has no emotional attachment to me and wants none. She gave me away, and the only reason I'm here now is to save her company. Why should I care what happens to her?"

"But you do."

Sara rolled her head against his shoulder and struggled with the tightness in her chest. "I don't know. I don't want to care. But . . . I don't want her to die. She gave me life, and I've only just got to know her. I keep thinking that maybe . . . maybe if we had more time . . ." Sara folded her lips tightly together and fought to hold back the pain, but she could not.

"Oh, Rourke." Turning abruptly, she slipped her arms around his middle and buried her face against his bare chest. She pressed close and nuzzled her nose in the mat of silky hair. The towel knotted around his waist was all he wore. He skin was warm and still damp from the shower, and he smelled of soap and minty toothpaste. And male. Sara greedily inhaled the wonderful mixture into her lungs.

His arms encircled her and pulled her close. "It's all right, sweetheart. I know it's difficult. Hell, it's all such a tangle."

"A part of me hates her," she mumbled against his chest. "Most of the time I want to strike out at her. I want to lash her with cruel words and inflict pain—which isn't at all like me. But at the same time, I wish it wasn't that way. Does that make any sense?"

"It makes perfect sense," Rourke murmured, stroking her back and shoulders.

"I still don't know what I'm going to do with the stock. I can't promise not to sell it."

"It's your call."

Sara looked up at him. "You wouldn't be angry with me if I let the company go public? You wouldn't feel that I had betrayed Evelyn?"

The hand rubbing her back stilled. For an instant, Rourke looked uncomfortable. "No. I wouldn't be angry. The stock will belong to you, and you were up front with Evelyn from the start. You have to do what you think is best."

Sara studied his face for several seconds. Then she

lay her cheek back against his warm chest. Was she being a fool to put her trust in him? Was she making a horrible mistake, sharing her feelings, risking her heart this way? But, dear God, how could this be wrong when it felt so right?

Everything about Rourke pleased her, drew her— his strength, his intelligence, his patience, his inherent toughness and determination. The deep timbre of his voice, the way he looked, the way he moved, all touched something deep inside her. Everything that was masculine and manly about him appealed to her soft, feminine soul. How could it be wrong?

She clutched him tighter. "Oh, Rourke, love me," she whispered. "Love me."

He needed no second urging. In a move so sudden it made her cry out, he swooped her up in his arms and strode for the bed. Somewhere along the way the towel hit the floor, and within moments her robe and gown joined it. Rourke fell onto the bed with her, his mouth locked with Sara's in a devouring kiss that aroused her to a fever pitch.

Desire and a panicky need to banish her fears and doubts sent her spinning out of control. She was a wild thing, greedily taking, demanding his passion. She returned his kiss with abandon. Her hands roamed his body, groping, clutching.

They had made love many times in many ways during the last four days. Rourke was a superb lover, a sensuous man with a deep sensitivity for a woman's needs. So often he was perfectly content to go slowly, savoring each touch, each taste, letting the heat build gradually, stretching out the pleasure. Ordinarily, Sara loved that long, lazy route to fulfillment, but not now. Not this time.

She needed this. This fast, hot ride, the blessed oblivion of urgent, molten lovemaking. Only that searing heat could burn away the troubling thoughts and emotions that bedeviled her.

Rourke strung kisses down her neck, over her collarbone, her breasts. He drew her nipple into his mouth, and she cried out, her back arching off the mattress.

Searing heat. Searing need. The fire shot through her like a blinding light. Her fingers clutched his shoulders, almond-shaped nails digging crescents into his flesh. Her heart missed a beat, then took off at a gallop, racing, pounding.

The pleasure built, layer upon layer, until she could not bear it. "Yes! Oh, yes, Rourke!"

"Easy, baby. Easy." He shifted, gripping her hips, the muscles in his arms quivering as he lifted her. He thrust into her with one swift, sure stroke, sheathing himself deep. Their twin cries of ecstasy rent the sultry night.

Then they were moving. Fast. Hard. Desperate.

Head thrown back, her delicate body flushed and glistening, she took him deeper, drove him harder. She writhed beneath him, the delicious coil of pleasure drawing tighter and tighter.

The orgasm came quick. It slammed through them like a freight train. The impact was awesome, shattering. Sara splintered into a million pieces.

Braced up on his stiffened arms, Rourke threw his head back as a guttural roar tore through his clenched teeth. He stiffened, his back arched, his dark face clenched in exquisite agony. Then a shudder rippled through his big body and he collapsed on her.

Eyes closed, Sara ran her palms over his sweaty

back and gasped for breath. Their galloping hearts pounded against their ribs in a crazy syncopated rhythm.

Rourke rolled to his side, taking her with him. Sighing, Sara snuggled her head on his shoulder. Her body conformed to his like wax melting in the sun. Twining her fingers through the hair on his chest, she felt herself slipping into sweet oblivion and smiled.

No. No, this could not be a mistake. It felt too wonderful.

The next morning Sara and Rourke were in Evelyn's room, on the verge of leaving for Houston, when the housekeeper tapped on the door and informed Evelyn that Sheriff Petrie was downstairs and wanted to speak to her.

"He's probably come to give me the results of the investigation into the cause of the fire," she said to Sara and Rourke. "Show him up, please, Martha."

Sara picked up her purse and made a move toward the door. She had no wish to be reminded of the fire. "We really should be going, Rourke."

In the act of leaving, the housekeeper stopped and turned around. "Oh, but Sheriff Petrie wants to talk to you, Mrs. Fallan."

"Me? Whatever for? Did he say specifically he wanted to speak to me?"

"Yes, ma'am. He was real pleased when he learned you were here."

"How strange," Sara murmured, when the woman had gone.

Minutes later Sheriff Petrie ambled into the room accompanied by a younger man. The law man swept his Stetson from his head and murmured a greeting, tipping his head politely at the women. "I appreciate you seeing me so promptly, Mrs. Ketchum. I know you've been ill and I hate to bother you, but this is urgent. Oh, this is Detective Mike Calhoun of the Houston Police. He and I were partners before I left the department."

"You're a little out of your jurisdiction, aren't you, Detective?" Rourke said, as he shook hands with the officer.

Detective Calhoun's mouth hiked up on one side in a cocky smile. "A little. Thanks to Buford." He shot his former partner a sardonic look.

Sara sank down into a chair, an uneasy feeling trickling down her spine. Her eyes darted from the sheriff to the Houston detective. She could not imagine them as partners. A more unlikely pair she'd never seen. The sheriff was big and bearlike. His regulation attire seemed to be jeans, a western shirt, cowboy boots, and that battered Stetson he was twisting. He spoke with a country twang, he had the beginnings of a pot hanging over his fist-sized silver belt buckle, and a good-old-boy manner that Sara suspected hid a shrewd mind.

Detective Calhoun, on the other hand, had the slender, well-toned physique of a man who worked out regularly. If his knife-creased trousers and sport-coat were anything to go by, he also had a penchant for sharp clothes. He was brash and cocky and had hotshot city boy written all over him.

"I'm real glad to find you here, Miss Anderson. Me'n Mike were gonna go to Houston to speak to you as soon as we finished here."

"It's Mrs. Fallan now, Sheriff."

"Oh, sorry. I can't seem to keep your name straight, can I? I heard about your wedding." His glance shifted between Sara and Rourke. "Congratulations."

"Thank you," Sara replied politely. Rourke merely nodded.

"I assume this is about the fire, Sheriff," Evelyn interjected.

"Yes, ma'am. Leastways, that's part of it." Buford turned his hat around and shifted his feet. "The rest has to do with your daughter, I'm afraid. Tell me, Miss Ander—uh, Mrs. Fallan, do you have any enemies, or know of any reason why someone would want to harm you?"

"Why, no."

"What's this all about, Sheriff?" Rourke asked, frowning.

"Well . . . I hate to tell you folks this, but the fire at the guesthouse wasn't due to faulty wiring. It was arson."

Sara paled. "You mean . . . Oh, my God."

"Are you quite certain of this, Sheriff?"

Buford sent Evelyn a grimace of sympathy. "Yes, ma'am. There's no doubt about it."

"What does this have to do with Sara?" Rourke demanded.

"Detective Calhoun and I believe that whoever set the fire was trying to kill her."

Evelyn gasped and leaned back against the pillows piled in the chaise longue, her composure, for once, completely shattered. "Oh, dear Lord."

"That's preposterous. On what do you base your suspicion?"

"Well, to start with, I doubt Mrs. Ketchum would

burn down her own guesthouse and risk killing four people, one of 'em her own daughter, for the insurance. And it's unlikely that whoever set the fire was trying to kill Miss Potts or Mr. Neely. That leaves Mrs. Ketchum's daughter."

"That's rather flimsy, don't you think?" Rourke challenged. "What about a firebug?"

"Out here? Not likely. It seems fairly clear that someone wants her out of the way.

"I've been doing some nosing around. I found out about all the troubles you've been having, the sabotage at your Houston plant and the health spas you're building, so I contacted the authorities in Florida and California." He paused and swept them with a somber look. "It turns out the fire at the Palm Springs spa was started exactly the same way as the fire at the guesthouse—rags soaked in charcoal lighter. Crude, but effective."

Sara moaned and covered her mouth with her hand. Rourke shot the sheriff a quelling look, laying his hand on Sara's shoulder.

"Buford laid it all out for my chief and he thought the evidence was strong enough to warrant an investigation," Detective Calhoun put in. "Since there have been incidents at your Houston facilities, that involves HPD, too. Old Bu persuaded my chief that it would be best if we pooled our efforts and got me assigned to the case so we can work together on it."

Evelyn covered her face with her hands. Cold terror shivered down Sara's spine. Dear God. Someone wanted her dead.

Rourke squeezed her shoulder. "Take it easy, honey." He glared at the two lawmen. "I demand that you put all your men and available resources on this case immediately."

"Don't worry, Mr. Fallan, we're investigating. As a matter of fact, I'd like to ask you a few questions. I understand that you were here the night the fire occurred."

"That's right."

"And how is that?"

"Sara and I were here to discuss business with Evelyn."

"I see." Buford rocked back and forth on the heels of his cowboy boots and tugged at his bottom lip with his thumb and forefinger.

Rourke stiffened. "Am I a suspect, Sheriff?"

"Mr. Fallan, until I find out who's behind this, everyone's a suspect."

Chapter Twenty-Five

"You son of a bitch!"

Lawrence looked up from the newspaper he was reading in time to see his wife storm into the study and slam the door behind her with enough force to rattle the paintings on the walls. She was so furious her eyes were shooting sparks.

"Why, darling, what is it? What's wrong?" Rising swiftly, Lawrence went to her with his hands extended, but she knocked them away before he could take her into his arms.

"You *lied* to me, you bastard!" she screeched. "You promised you would get the money to renew my option on *Night Song.* You said not to worry, that you'd take care of it. Well, I just received a call from Harold. He told me that the option has only six weeks left to run." She was so furious she hit him three times before he could grab her arm. Cursing, Madelene jerked free and stomped to the window, then swung back. "I can't lose that option. Do you hear me? I can't! Morris and Stan are waiting like jackals to snap it up and cast another actress in the lead. So are at least three other studios. Damn you, this is all your fault! You promised me!"

"I tried, Maddie. I did everything I could, believe me. I talked to Sara. I even went to Evelyn, but they won't budge. I tried to find a loophole in the articles of incorporation, but there just isn't one. But don't worry, darling, there's still time. I'll figure something out. I'm working on a plan—"

"Screw your plan. I want some action and I want it now. Sell my jewelry, my car, the house. Anything! Just get me the goddamned money!"

"Maddie, Maddie. You can't be serious. Sweetheart, that would be committing financial suicide. You've earned millions over the years, but you've spent it all. The only real assets you have are a few pieces of good jewelry, your stock in Eve, and this house."

"I don't care! I have to have that part!"

A throbbing headache was building behind Lawrence's eyes. He massaged his temples with his fingertips and thumb. Maddie could be as willful and unreasonable as a petulant child. Especially when she was frightened.

He understood the source of her fear. His poor Maddie was mortally afraid of growing old and losing her looks, and along with them, her adoring fans. It hurt him that she didn't seem to know that there was so much more to her than just her stunning beauty.

Normally, Lawrence did whatever Madelene asked of him, catered to her every whim—because he adored her and because he didn't want to lose her. However, this fixation on playing the lead in *Night*

Song was becoming an unhealthy obsession. He was worried about her.

"Maddie. Darling," he said as gently as possible. "Maybe . . . well . . . maybe it's time you stopped trying to play romantic leads and moved on to more mature parts."

Madelene's eyes grew round. She stared at him as though he had suggested she slit her own throat. "What are you saying?"

"Well . . . that maybe you should take Morris and Stan up on their offer and accept the part of Victoria."

"The mother! You want me to play the frigging *mother?*"

"Darling, that role is the meatier part. You know that. And you're a tremendous actress. You could turn in an Academy Award performance with that role."

He might as well have saved his breath. Madelene was livid.

"You think I'm old, don't you? Well? *Don't* you?"

"No! No, my darling, of course n—"

"You're getting tired of me. Don't think I haven't noticed the way you look at other women. What is it? Have you found someone else? A younger woman?"

"Maddie, no! How can you even think such a thing? I love you."

"Do you honestly expect me to believe that, after you practically admitted you think I'm an old hag? An old has-been? Only fit to play mothers and dowagers and dried-up old prunes? Well, if that's the way you feel, just get out!"

"Maggie, darling. You don't mean that."

"The hell I don't. I'll be damned if I'll sit around

and wait for you to walk out on me." She poked her chest with a long crimson fingernail. "No one dumps Madelene Ketchum. No one, do you hear me! *I'm* the one who gives the old heave-ho around here. So just get out."

Lawrence stared at her, thunderstruck. In that moment he realized it had been Madelene's pride and almost pathological fear of getting old that had prompted her to leave her first four husbands. She had been afraid that as her looks faded, so would their feelings for her, and at the first sign of what she had perceived to be waning interest, she had called it quits before any of them had had the chance.

Now she was trying to do the same thing to him.

He ached for her, even while fear and sickness churned in his stomach. "Maddie, sweetheart, you don't really want to do this. Let me—"

"I said get out! *Get out!*"

"But Maddie—"

"Out!" She picked up a vase and hurled it at him. Lawrence dodged, and it crashed against the wall beside him.

"Get out of my house! I don't need you!" Snatching up a figurine, she sent it sailing. "I'll get the money myself! So go! Go, damn you!" She grabbed a heavy crystal dish and heaved it, then followed it up with a constant barrage, anything she could get her hands on.

Lawrence backed to the door, dodging the fusillade. He had never seen his wife in such a state. There was no reasoning with her. The only thing he could do was back off and give her time to cool down.

"All right. All right. I'm going," he yelled, raising

his arm to fend off another missile. "But we have to talk, Ma—"

"Get out!"

He ducked and scooted out the door as a china lamp shattered against the wall.

After the outer door closed Madelene threw three more items just to let off steam, but at the sound of Lawrence's BMW roaring down the drive, she threw herself face down onto the sofa and burst into tears.

For a while she indulged in the luxury of a good crying jag. Her sobs were piteous and heartrending, loud and noisy and blubbery. She cried for the little girl who, time after time, had been left behind, for the insecure adolescent who had braved the bewildering world of Hollywood to please her mother, for the woman who had never felt loved, who had only talent and pride and beauty to sustain her. And she cried, too, because now that beauty was fading.

Before long, the first overwhelming rush of grief had passed and she came to her senses and sat up. What had she been thinking? Tears made your eyes red and swollen and your skin blotchy. Disgusted with herself, she scrubbed at her cheeks with the heels of her hands, sniffed several more times, then stomped to the desk and snatched a tissue from the box in the bottom drawer.

She blew her nose several times, dabbed at her eyes, and forced herself to think. "All right. So Lawrence is gone. Good riddance," she muttered defiantly, stifling the stab of pain the words brought. She sniffed again. "There's no point in feeling sorry for yourself, either. It's not as though you didn't know it would eventually happen."

She paced back and forth across the room. What

she had to do now was forget about Lawrence and concentrate on something else. Like getting the money she needed. Or even better, getting someone else to put up the money and make the movie with her in the lead.

But who? She had already pitched the project to every producer in town.

All, that was, except one.

Madelene stopped and looked at the telephone. She tapped her chin with a crimson fingernail. She had not contacted Harry Weisfeld. He was sometimes willing to take a chance. For certain . . . favors.

She shuddered. Harry was the biggest lecher in Hollywood. It was rumored that he'd slept with almost every good-looking actress in town, from the stars to the lowliest bit players. It was also rumored that he kept a tally of his conquests in a book, and rated their performances.

So far, Madelene had avoided sleeping with the old creep. Not because of morals or scruples, particularly. Madelene liked sex, and she'd had her share of flings, between and even during her previous marriages, but they had all had been for her own pleasure. She'd never traded sex for money or professional favors.

Thanks to her mother's clout, she had started in the business as a child. By the time she'd become sexually active she'd been a star and hadn't needed men like Harry. Besides, he disgusted her. He was fat and old and hairy as a gorilla, except for his bald head. The very idea of having sex with him turned her stomach.

However, she was desperate now. Damn it, she

had to have that part. She would do anything to get it. Anything.

Before she could change her mind, Madelene ran to the desk and looked up Harry's private number in her address book. Snatching up the telephone, she punched the buttons, then drummed her fingernails on the desktop as she waited for him to answer.

"Yeah. Weisfeld here."

Madelene clutched the receiver tighter and forced a coy note into her voice. "Harry? This is Madelene Ketchum. How are you, darling? Good. Good. Listen, Harry, I have a business deal I'd like to discuss with you. I was wondering if maybe we could get together today?"

After the usual effusive and insincere greetings, Harry Weisfeld listened to Madelene's pitch without saying a word. He simply sat there with his pudgy fingers steepled beneath his chin and looked her over like a gourmet sizing up a new epicurean delight.

They were seated in overstuffed chairs in the bungalow behind his Beverly Hills mansion that he euphemistically called his office. In actuality, it was his private lovenest, right under his wife's nose.

When Madelene finished, he leaned over and patted her hand. She had to steel herself to keep from snatching it away.

"Maddie, darling. I must say, I'm impressed. How astute of you to recognize the book's potential so early and tie up the movie rights. Every studio head in town would give his right ball to get his hands on it."

"Yes, I know. But unfortunately, none of them are willing to meet *my* terms."

"Ah, yes. Well, it was very wise of you to bring the project to me."

"Then you'll produce it?" In her excitement Madelene forgot the first rule in Hollywood negotiating; never appear too eager and never let them see you sweat. She sat forward in her chair, her eyes alight with excitement. "Oh, Harry, that's wonderful. And I'll star in it, right?"

"You have my word that I'll sign you for the movie. Provided, of course, we can come to terms."

"Terms?" Some of Maddie's enthusiasm faded at the look in Harry's eyes.

"My dear, don't pull that naive crap on me. You knew when you came here that there would be a price to pay. You want something from me, first you must give me what I want, and we both know what that is, now, don't we?"

Madelene looked into his lustful eyes, and her fingers dug into the upholstered chair arms.

Harry cocked one eyebrow. "Shall I lock the door so that we can . . . shall we say . . . consummate our deal?"

She hesitated, then drew in a deep breath. "All right. If that's what it takes."

Smiling, Harry went to the door and locked it, then returned and took Madelene's hand and led her into the next room.

She looked with revulsion at the kingsized bed, but Harry led her past it to the mirrored closet doors on the opposite side of the room. He positioned her in front of them and stepped back.

"Now take off your clothes. Slowly, please." He

aimed a leering grin at her reflection in the mirror. "I like to watch."

You would, you fat creep, she thought, unzipping her dress. Jesus, if she didn't need that part so much she'd slug the worm for even suggesting this.

Even though she knew it gave Harry pleasure, Madelene took her time disrobing, drawing the process out as long as she could. With each successive article of clothing that dropped to the floor his breathing grew harsher and more ragged.

Maggie's slip slithered down and puddled around her feet. At the sight of her lacy black garter belt, Harry licked his lips. When she unhooked the matching bra and her full breasts spilled free, he began to moan and rub his crotch. By the time she stood naked before him he was almost salivating, his little porcine eyes gleaming.

Now that she had come that far, Madelene just wanted to get the whole ugly business over with. Fists clenched, she took a step toward the bed.

"Don't move," he snapped, making her jump. He snatched off his clothes with manic speed, and her revulsion grew. He was flabby and white as the belly of a fish, and his back was furry.

He rushed over to the dresser, pulled a foil packet from the top drawer, and ripped it open. He hurried back, rolling the condom on as he walked. "You can't be too careful these days," he said, grinning.

Especially not a tomcat like you, Madelene thought, but she was relieved. As much as Harry screwed around, there was no telling what he'd picked up.

Naked and fully aroused, he walked around her, looking his fill. She stood still as a statue, her fists clenched at her sides. He ran his pudgy hands over her breasts, and she wanted to scream. Cupping them, he bent his head and licked first one nipple, then the other. To Madelene's horror, they hardened into tight nubs. Harry grinned and suckled her nosily, and she found herself fighting nausea and pleasure at the same time.

Finally he released her breast and circled around behind.

"Hmm. Standing, I think. And from the rear."

"What? You mean right here?"

"Yes. That way we can watch ourselves in the mirror. Bend over, Maddie, love."

Reluctantly, she obeyed. Bracing her hands on her knees, she gritted her teeth and closed her eyes.

"No! Don't do that," he commanded, and her eyes popped open. "Damn it, I want you to watch. I want you to see me taking you."

He grasped her hips with both hands. She felt his sagging belly against her bottom and shivered. His cock nudged her moist flesh, rubbed back and forth. Harry reached one hand between her legs and played with the tender petals and moaned. He parted her with his fingers, then grasped his cock and positioned the head. "I've been wanting to fuck you since you were about fourteen," he growled in her ear, and rammed into her.

Madelene whimpered with pain and revulsion. She looked at their reflection in the mirror, and bile rose in her throat. Grunting like a pig, Harry pumped his hips at a furious pace, pounding into her again and again. His face was red and contorted, rigid with lust, and sweat poured from him.

It will be over soon. It will be over soon. It will be over soon.

Teeth gritted, Madelene silently repeated the words like a litany, in rhythm with the horrible, loveless sex act.

Then the part would be hers. She would play Helen, and her career would revive. She would be a star again, someone important and in demand, someone to be reckoned with in this goddamned town.

Then this hideous experience would be worth it.

Harry had more staying power than Madelene ever imagined. He seemed to go on forever. Finally he dug his fingers hard into her hips and drove himself into her with a vicious lunge, bellowing out his pleasure like a rutting bull.

Madelene hung her head and breathed deeply. Thank God.

Gasping, Harry pulled out of her, gave her bottom a pat and staggered over to the bed. "Whoowie, that was worth waiting almost thirty years for," he gasped, flopping down on his back. He shot her a gloating grin. "Gimme a few minutes and we can go another round if you want."

Madelene paused in snatching up her clothing to look at him. She did not even try to hide her revulsion. He lay sprawled on the bed like a blubbery whale, his white belly heaving, his limp penis lying against his leg, shiny and wet. The foul slug hadn't even bothered to remove the condom.

"Forget it. I've kept my part of the deal, now you keep yours." She had never dressed so fast in her life. In under two minutes she was fully clothed, except for her garter belt and stockings, which she left lying on the floor. She didn't think she could ever bring herself to wear them again. When she got home, she intended to burn everything she had on, but first she was going to take a shower and scrub herself for an hour.

Madelene picked up her purse and stepped into her shoes. "I expect you to get the contract ready and have it to me by tomorrow."

Harry laughed. "Sorry, sweetheart, but I've changed my mind about that."

She was almost out the door when his words halted her in her tracks. She spun around. *"What?* Why, you bastard. We had a deal!"

"C'mon, Maddie. Don't be foolish. You're twenty years too old for the part. Why do you think every producer in town has turned you down? Did you really think I'd risk my reputation by giving you the part? We'd both be laughed out of town. You're a good fuck, Maddie, but you're not that good."

"Why, you sleazy bastard. We had a deal. You promised you would sign me for the part!"

"No. Actually, I said I would sign you for the movie. Now, if you would agree to play the part of the mother . . ."

"Go to hell!"

Madelene glared at him and sputtered, so furious she could not speak for a second. Harry laughed, and she spun on her heel and stomped out, slamming the door behind her hard enough to knock it off its hinges. She was shaking all over when she climbed into her Jaguar. The bastard! The filthy, cheating, lowlife bastard! God, and she'd let him screw her like a bitch in heat. Ramming the car in gear, she stomped on the gas. Tires spun and gravel flew as the Jag took off at breakneck speed.

She was in such a state she drove the mile or so to her home like a maniac, but when she brought the car to a screeching halt in the drive, she had little or no recollection of the trip. The car had barely stopped rolling when she bailed out and ran up the steps.

She stormed into the house and slammed the door with all her might, but as it crashed against the frame she halted and stared at the pile of suitcases stacked in the foyer.

"So. You're back."

Her head snapped up. "Lawrence." Something about him put her on guard and sent a trickle of dread down her spine. He stood in the living room doorway, watching her. Belatedly, she noticed that his face was colder than she had ever seen it.

There was no way he could know, she thought, but she could not quite meet his eyes.

"How could you, Maddie?"

"What? I don't know what you're talking about?"

"You slept with Harry Weisfeld."

"Don't be silly. I haven't seen Harry in months."

"You're lying. I followed you. I watched you walk into the bungalow."

Guilt stabbed at her, and she used righteous indignation to subdue it. "How dare you? Where do you get off following me around?"

"You were upset. I was worried about you. I was afraid you'd do something foolish, so I parked across the street to wait for you to cool down. When you came barreling out of the driveway as though there was an emergency, I followed. I couldn't believe it when you turned into Harry's driveway."

Madelene gave him a sulky look. "You wouldn't help me, so I had to do something."

"Oh, no. Not this time. Don't try to twist this around and blame it on me. You made the decision to turn whore all on your own." He crossed the foyer, picked up two bags and headed for the door.

"Where are you going?"

"Away from here. Away from you. I can deal with your tantrums and your demands and your insecurities. I even find them endearing at times. But I can't take this. I won't take this." He paused and looked back at her, hurt and anger and a deep sadness in his eyes. "Goodbye, Maddie. I assume you got what you wanted from Harry. I hope it was worth it."

Chapter Twenty-Six

"Our sales in Germany are showing a steady increase. However, the Russian market isn't doing quite as well as we'd expected, but it's still too early to call. Over all, revenues are satisfactory." Sara turned to the next page of the financial report and adjusted her reading glasses.

"On the other hand, expenses at the spas are running thirty-seven point eight percent over budget. That will—"

"Please. No more," Evelyn murmured. "I'm just too tired right now."

Sara looked up from the papers and experienced a stab of concern when she saw that Evelyn's eyes were closed. Except for the tracery of blue veins on her eyelids, her skin was colorless. Even her mouth was white.

Sara bit her lower lip. She looked so fragile and weak. The very fact that she had called a halt to the briefing spoke volumes. Evelyn's first priority every waking moment was the company.

She had aged so much, Sara thought with a pang. These last few weeks since she and Rourke had returned from Rio, Evelyn seemed to have shriveled up. Her prominent cheekbones were now sharp, the hollows beneath them deep and shadowy, and her eyes seemed to have sunk deeper into their sockets.

"Are you all right? Shall I ring for the nurse?"

As though they were weighted with lead, Evelyn's eyelids lifted slowly. Her bony hand fluttered an inch or so off the cover, then dropped back. "No, I just want to sleep for a while. Why don't you go for a walk and stretch your legs for an hour or so? Then we'll continue."

"All right." Sara put the papers away in her briefcase, then rose and adjusted the covers around Evelyn's shoulders. "Would you like a drink of water or anything before I go?"

"No, thank you. You run along. It'll do you good to relax for a while. You've been under a lot of strain lately."

Sara nodded and headed for the door.

"Oh, and Sara?"

She stopped and looked back. "Yes?"

"Take Jennifer with you. I don't want you wandering about alone."

"Do you really think that's necessary? It's been eight weeks since the fire, and nothing else has happened. I'm beginning to think Sheriff Petrie was wrong."

"Nevertheless, I'd prefer that you not take any chances."

Sara would have liked to believe that Evelyn's concern was for her, but she knew better. She was simply worried about what would become of her company if something were to happen to her. Yet Sara could not totally suppress the surge of emotion that welled up in her chest. It was the same whenever Evelyn cautioned her.

Jennifer wasn't in the library, where they had set up a temporary office of sorts. Sara found her in the bedroom she used during their visits to the ranch, curled up on the bed with Cindy, taking a nap.

Loath to disturb them, she closed the door quietly and tiptoed down the hall and out the back door. She hesitated on the steps, glancing all around before heading for the corral, where newborn twin colts were gamboling around their mother. She had told Evelyn she wouldn't wander around alone, but there were three cowboys repairing fence on the other side of the yard and she would be in plain sight of the housekeeper, who was working in the kitchen.

At the corral she climbed up on the bottom rail to get a better view. The wobbly-legged colts promptly scampered behind their mother and peeked at her from underneath the mare's belly. Sara laughed.

She looked around. Gently rolling hills, dotted with huge ancient oak trees, undulated toward the horizon. Down by the stock tank tame mallard ducks were pecking through the tall grass, quacking softly. It was so peaceful here, so serene. Yet in all likelihood someone in this family was trying to kill her, perhaps someone who lived right here on the ranch.

Could it be Paul or Will? Or perhaps father and son were in on it together. Certainly Chad had the arrogance, but was he obsessed enough with the ranch to commit murder? Or was it sweet, charming Eric? Or Kitty? And, of course, there was always Madelene. God knew, Maddie hated her enough to want her dead. The truth was, it could have been any one of them. None of them had been happy about her arrival, and they all seemed to be desperate for more money.

Sara sighed and turned her attention to the colts. "Come here, pretty things. I won't hurt you," she called to the skittish youngsters.

While she was attempting to coax the colts closer Chad walked out of the barn and dumped a bucket of feed into the trough in the corner of the corral. The new mother ambled over to investigate, and Chad walked to where Sara stood on the fence.

"Well, well. If it isn't the blushing bride."

"Hello, Chad," she replied, refusing to rise to the bait. She had been around him and all of the other members of the Ketchum family several times since returning from Rio, but she had been careful not to be alone with any of them, Chad and Paul most of all. If someone in the family really was trying to kill her, Sara would put her money on Chad or his cousin.

Glancing around, she checked to be sure the cowboys were still there.

"So where's Rourke? He's been sticking to you like glue since you two got hitched."

"He's in Los Angeles on business."

"Ah, yes, business." Chad braced an elbow on the top rail. "Old Rourke's a real wheeler-dealer. I didn't realize just how much of one until he married you. He must be real happy, now that he's finally got what he's always wanted."

Chad was leading up to something. From the look on his face, Sara knew she wasn't going to like it. "And what is that?"

"What else? To be head honcho at Eve and have a

seat on the board. He's wanted that practically since the day he started to work for Evelyn."

The statement caught Sara off guard, and for an instant she could not hide her shock. When she had questioned him, Rourke had denied any ambitions in that direction. From the corner of her eye she saw Eric ride in the yard on a big bay stallion, but she was too busy trying to absorb Chad's charge to pay him any mind.

He grinned at her stunned expression. "It's common knowledge. If you don't believe me, ask anybody in the family. They'll tell you."

"You're mistaken, Chad. Rourke has known from the start that he was ineligible to take over for Evelyn."

"Yeah, the way things stand. That's why he wanted her to let the company go public. And believe me, lady, he wanted that as much as the rest of us. Then you turned up and he saw an easier way. God, he must've thought he'd struck the mother lode. You were his ticket to the top."

Surprise, disbelief, then anger followed one after the other in rapid succession. All she could do was stare at him.

"Knock it off, Chad." Eric dismounted and came to stand beside Sara, scowling at his cousin.

"Hey, I just think my stepsister has a right to know what kind of man she married, that's all." With just a hint of a smirk on his face, Chad stepped away from the fence, touched the brim of his Stetson with his forefinger, and ambled back to the barn.

Narrowing her eyes, Sara watched him go. Even from the back, Chad exuded an aura of toughness, remoteness. She studied that easy, hip-rolling stride and wondered what was behind the accusation. What did Chad have to gain by discrediting Rourke in her eyes?

"Don't pay any attention to him. He's just trying to get under your skin."

"Don't worry, Eric, I don't believe him."

She truly didn't, she realized, experiencing a rush of relief and elation. A month ago, she might have, but since their return from Rio, she had gradually learned to trust Rourke. He had done nothing to deserve anything less.

Rourke was attentive and affectionate, and very open with her. He was also a passionate and considerate lover. Ever since Sheriff Petrie's astounding revelation, he had been wonderful, worrying about her, hovering over her. He made her feel protected and cherished, which was a new and delightful experience for Sara.

She gazed out across the pasture and smiled. Rourke was, in fact, almost too protective. The business in Los Angeles was urgent, but he had not wanted to leave her alone. She'd had to put her foot down and insist that he make the trip.

Under his tender care, she had finally put aside her doubts and misgivings. What did it matter why they had married, or if Rourke was bound emotionally to Evelyn, so long as they were happy?

And Sara was happy—happier than she could ever remember being, despite the threat of danger. She got up each morning feeling like she was on top of the world. Just looking at Rourke made her heart flutter and being with him, sharing each day, gave her a soul deep pleasure so sweet it made her ache. She was so in love and so happy, at times she almost felt like pinching herself to be sure she wasn't dreaming.

It did bother her a bit that so far Rourke had not mentioned love, but that would come with time. She was sure of it. Passion as hot and consuming as the one they shared had to lead to love.

"What's that smile for?"

It took a moment for Eric's question to register. When it did, Sara blinked. "What? Oh. Nothing, really. I was just thinking of Rourke."

"Hmm. Lucky Rourke." Eric flashed his teasing grin. "It's too bad he beat me to you. I was giving serious consideration to sweeping you off your feet, you know."

"Why, Eric," she simpered, fluttering her eyelashes. "I had no idea."

"Yeah, well, before I had a chance to dazzle you with my charm, wit, and incredible good looks, that damned pirate hauled you before the judge and put a ring on your finger."

Sara gave a startled laugh. "Pirate? Rourke? Why, he's the most civilized man I know."

"Ahh, but beneath that polish, the man's got the soul of a buccaneer. Don't misunderstand me; I like Rourke a lot. He's a helluva businessman. He's smart and quick and sophisticated, but don't let those impeccable manners fool you; the man's tough as nails, and daring as any corsair who ever sailed the seas. When Rourke wants something, he goes after it, and he doesn't let anything stand in his way. No matter what he has to do or how long it takes, he'll keep on until he's captured the prize, and he'll relish the battle to get it. Trust me, put the man in a full-sleeved shirt, tight pants, and stick a cutlass between his teeth and he'd be right at home on the deck of a tall ship flying the skull-and-crossbones."

Eric heaved a dramatic sigh and assumed a woebegone look. "And now the dog has carried off the most beautiful maiden in the realm and ravished her."

Sara laughed. "Evelyn told me you were the creative type, but I never realized before just what a vivid imagination you have. I'll admit that Rourke is a determined man, but he's certainly no bloodthirsty pirate."

"Ah, well, spoken like a besotted woman. I should have known I couldn't talk any sense into you. Why is it you women always fall for rogues?"

"You mean men like you?" she teased.

Eric grinned and waggled his eyebrows at her, and Sara laughed again. "You're impossible. Go on, get out of here and see to your horse, you shameless devil."

"Okay, I can take a hint. C'mon, Dancer, let's go." Leading the animal toward the barn, he grinned at her over his shoulder. "Just remember, though, anytime you want to ditch that damned pirate, just say the word and we'll run away together to this little Caribbean island I know of. He'll never find us there."

"Go. Go."

Chuckling, Sara shook her head and watched him disappear into the barn. She was glad she had run into Eric. He was an outrageous flirt and any woman would be a fool to take him seriously, but his lighthearted humor never failed to lift her spirits. For a few minutes he had even made her forget how much she missed Rourke. And the inescapable fact that someone wanted her dead.

If Sheriff Petrie was right about that, she couldn't believe it was Eric.

She turned to go, and jumped. "Oh!" She gasped and fluttered her hand over her heart. *"Bri-aan!* For heaven's sake, don't sneak up on me like that. You scared the living daylights out of me!"

"Sorry. I didn't mean to. I know how much on edge you are, but I saw you leave the house alone and I thought I'd better keep an eye on you. Just in case."

"Oh, Brian, that's sweet." She touched his arm and smiled at him. Though the thought of Brian as a bodyguard was not particularly comforting, she was touched.

"I couldn't help but hear what Chad said."

"Now, Brian, don't start. Please. You know what Chad is like. He's still furious over Evelyn giving me the stock in Eve and he's just trying to stir up trouble."

"Even so, I think you should listen to him. If Rourke is using you, for whatever reason, I think you should at least be on guard."

"Brian, stop it." She halted and faced him squarely, her expression firm. "I don't want to go through this again. Ever since we married you've been taking digs at him and I'm sick of it. Can't you just be happy for me?"

"He doesn't love you, Sara."

The words struck home and she flinched, but she gritted her teeth and lifted her chin. "You don't know that."

"Has he told you he loves you?"

"That's none of your business." She pivoted on

her heel and resumed walking toward the house at a furious pace. Brian trotted to keep up with her.

"He hasn't, has he?"

"Brian, just drop it," she gritted out between clenched teeth.

"Did you know that he fired Helmut Schneider?"

"What?" She jerked to a halt and swung around, her face slack with shock. "That's crazy. He wouldn't do that, not without talking to me first."

"Well, he has. I just called the Berlin plant and asked to speak to Helmut. They were surprised that I didn't know he'd been dismissed. It happened over a week ago, when Rourke was in Germany."

"But . . . why would he fire the manager of our most profitable European plant?"

"Perhaps that's why. Maybe it was too profitable. We know that someone is trying to put the company in a financial bind. Removing effective management is as good a way as any to undercut profits."

Eric's mood was sunny when he entered the house after his ride . . . until he spotted the man standing before the fireplace in the living room. He jerked to a halt in the doorway and cast a frantic glance around, his heart pounding.

"What the hell are you doing here? I told you never to contact me at home."

At the hissed words, Keith Morrison turned from inspecting the painting above the mantel. He smiled, not in the least concerned. "Eric, love. How wonderful to see you. Actually, though, I'm waiting to see your father. I understand he's taking a nap, but your housekeeper said he should be waking up soon."

"Get out. Get the hell out of this house."

"Now, now, love, it's not as though I haven't been patient. It's been months, and all you've given me is a paltry ten thousand. A man's got to live, you know."

"Damn you, I told you I'd get the money, but you've got to give me more time. Half a million isn't easy to raise."

"Sorry, but I have a pressing need for money now. I'm betting your old man will be happy to cough up the cash rather than have the tabloids get their hands on the pictures."

"All right, all right." Eric glanced over his shoulder at the doorway. His father would be waking up any minute. Cold sweat popped out on his forehead and upper lip. He glanced at the door again and he raked spread fingers through his hair. "I can write you a check for fifty thousand. That's all I have right now. But I'll get the rest soon. I swear it."

"Mmm. Fifty thousand." Keith pursed his lips and tapped them with his forefinger. "Very well. But all you're buying is a month's time. If I don't have the rest of the half a mil by then, your old man gets the pictures."

She was late. But then, she always was. Rourke was already seated when she walked into Pierre's, the elegant little Hollywood bistro they had frequented many times in the past.

Sliding in beside him on the banquette, she smiled seductively and put her hand over his.

"Darling, how romantic of you to request our old table. I knew you still cared."

"Sorry to disappoint you, but this wasn't my doing. I'm afraid Pierre is the romantic." He smiled to take the sting out of his words. Madelene had tremendous talent and beauty, but she was driven by ego and was highly volatile. In a rage, she was unpredictable.

"Don't be mean, darling." Pouting, she toyed with the hair on the back of his hand. "I've missed you. It's been so long since we've been alone together. Much too long."

Sliding his hand from beneath hers, he reached for his coffee cup. "What is this about, Madelene? When you called you said it was urgent that you see me."

"Oh, it is. I've missed you, darling."

"Stop it, Maddie." He caught her hand, which she had somehow transferred to his leg, and placed it back on the table.

She made a moue and settled back, giving him a sultry look from beneath her lashes. "I remember what a wonderful lover you are. My best, really. We were great together. Don't try to tell me you've forgotten."

No, Rourke hadn't forgotten. His affair with Madelene had been brief and hot. In bed, she was insatiable and wild, a tigress. At one point, he had considered marrying her, but in the end he could not—not even to gain a seat on the board of Eve Cosmetics. Madelene was too self-absorbed, too needy. She used men up, sucked the life right out of them, then tossed them aside. In the twelve years he'd known her, he'd watched her destroy a whole string of lovers and husbands.

"I've always thought it was a waste of time to dwell on the past."

"But that's just my point; it doesn't have to be the past, darling. I made a terrible mistake when I broke off with you."

It had been Rourke who had broken it off, but he prudently did not point that out. Madelene's ego was monumental, and she was not above making a scene in public. He wanted to get through this meeting as quickly and quietly as possible. "Maddie, that was two husbands ago. It's too late to go back now."

"No, it isn't. I'm the one you should have married, not Evelyn's bastard. Sara is just like her. She'll never give up control of the business. Just look at how she's retained voting rights on the stock Evelyn gave her. If you were my husband, I'd turn it over to you. You would be in charge and you could run the business as you liked.

"Once Evelyn is gone and we all get our share of her fifty-one percent, we could let the company go public and all make a tidy fortune. Don't you see, darling? We belong together, you and I."

"Oh? What about Lawrence?"

Her mouth tightened, and for an instant Rourke thought he saw a shadow flicker across her face. "Lawrence and I are through. I never should have married him."

"I wouldn't know about that. But the fact remains that I am still married to Sara."

Madelene toyed with her water glass. "You know, darling, Texas is a community-property state. You do realize, don't you, that if something were to happen to Sara, you would inherit her shares in Eve?"

Rourke went utterly still. Slowly he turned his head and stared at her.

Chapter Twenty-Seven

Sara tried to concentrate on the figures in front of her, but she couldn't. She felt too restless.

Swiveling her chair around, she looked out the window of Evelyn's office. Houston was enjoying one of those rare spells of perfect weather that, according to Alice, came only briefly to the Gulf Coast each spring and fall.

The sky was a clear, deep azure blue, the air dry and crisp. Mums in yellows, rusts, and rich magenta splashed the manicured grounds with color. Raintrees nodded in the breeze like sleepy old men, their branches heavy with russet seed pods. Oak, pecan, and tallow trees blazed red and gold, in sharp contrast to the dark green pines.

It was too pretty a day to be cooped up inside, Sara decided. If Rourke were there she would twist his arm to play hookey. They could go for a picnic or a walk in the park, just the two of them. She grinned, imagining the argument he would give her; he was as much a workaholic as Evelyn.

Sighing, Sara arched her back and stretched her arms above her head. Rourke wasn't there, however.

Which accounted, in part, for her restlessness. She had grown accustomed to having him close by, and she missed him.

Since August he had hardly let her out of his sight. Only on two other occasions had he gone on a trip without her, and those had been emergencies. Even then, she'd had to argue with him to make him go.

Rourke worried too much. Sabotage at the spas was still a problem, but she had not had any close calls since the fire. It was more and more obvious that Sheriff Petrie had been wrong about the threat to her life.

Swiveling back around, Sara glanced at the telephone and pursed her lips. On impulse, she punched the intercom. "Jen, would you get Rourke on the phone for me? He's at Burns and Rosten in Dallas."

"Sure thing, boss."

Sara smiled to herself. Perhaps it was silly; he would be home tonight. But she wanted to talk to him, to hear his voice.

She knew she was acting like a giddy schoolgirl, and she didn't care. Never had she imagined that she could be so much in love with anyone. Or so happy. These past two and a half months with Rourke had been wonderful. He was everything she'd ever wanted in a man, everything she'd never truly thought she would find. She could kick herself for resisting him for so long.

She trusted him completely. The only time her faith in him had wavered even the slightest had been over the matter of Helmut Schneider, and that had been Brian's fault.

Sara smiled, remembering Rourke's reaction when she'd broached the subject. They had been in the bedroom at the time, preparing for bed, and she'd been watching him in her dressing table mirror for some sign of guilt or deceit, but Rourke hadn't so much as batted an eye.

"Sorry. I meant to tell you about that but it slipped my mind. By the time I got home from that trip, all I could think about was ravishing my wife." He paused in the act of unbuttoning his shirt and leered at her reflection in the mirror. "Which, if memory serves, I did a thorough job of."

The comment had made her flush, but she had persisted. "But why did you fire him? Especially without discussing it with me first?"

"There wasn't time. I discovered while I was there that Herr Schneider was taking kickbacks from suppliers. To keep profits high and cover his tracks, he was using inferior ingredients but billing the company for the good stuff. I gave him the boot on the spot."

Relief had flooded Sara, followed quickly by shame and remorse that she had doubted him, even for a minute. Perhaps it had been her conscience that had spurred her behavior that night. Sara only knew that as she'd watched Rourke shrug out of his shirt and shuck his trousers, she'd become so aroused she had felt as though she were on fire.

The memory of her behavior brought a rush of color to her cheeks and a feline smile to her lips. Rourke had been surprised by her boldness, but more than willing to be seduced. The night of passion that followed had left them both reeling.

The intercom crackled, jarring Sara out of the erotic memory, and she blushed as she reached for the button. "Yes, Jen."

"Sorry, boss, but the people at Burns and Rosten say Mr. Fallan isn't there. And no one there expected him today."

"What? But that can't be. Rourke had an eleven o'clock appointment with Claude Burns. Let me talk to them," Sara said, reaching for the telephone.

For the next ten minutes Sara talked with Mr. Burns and several others at Burns and Rosten, but with no better results. "I see. Well, thank you very much. Sorry to have bothered you."

She returned the receiver to its cradle, but kept her hand on it and stared into space. "How odd."

"Any luck?" Jen asked from the doorway.

"No. Rourke isn't there and no one there has seen or heard from him. Apparently he didn't have an appointment today." Sara shrugged and made a face "Oh, well, it must have been a mixup in communications."

"Yeah, you'll probably be hearing from Mr. Fallan soon. In the meantime, you got a call from the experimental lab. John Davis, that chemist who heads up the research team, wants you to meet him there at noon. There's something he wants to show you. Apparently it's urgent."

Glancing at the clock on her desk, Sara rose. "It's almost noon now. I'd better get going."

Before she could step away from the desk, the telephone rang. Jen started for it, but Sara waved her aside. "I'll get it."

The call was from the manager of their distribution center in Germany. By the time she had finished, it was almost noon.

Sara hurried out of the office and started across the complex. She could have taken a golf cart; many

executives and managers used them to scoot around
the vast complex, but the day was so lovely Sara
opted to walk. She would be a few minutes late, but
so what. There had to be some perks to being the
boss.

The sun on her face was warm and the cool breeze
carried a faint hint of woodsmoke and the nip of
autumn. Walking along briskly, Sara tipped her head
up and breathed in the crisp air and smiled. As she
approached the research lab, there was almost no one
about. This lab and two others had the same lunch
hour and all the employees were in the company
cafeteria.

Sara slowed, frowning. So what was John Davis
doing there at this hour?

She never saw the flash, nor did she hear the explosion. One instant she was walking toward the lab and
the next, as though a giant fist had slammed into her,
she was lifted her off her feet and knocked more than
twenty feet backward.

"I must insist that you keep this short, gentlemen."
The doctor gave Sheriff Petrie and Detective Calhoun a stern look. "Mrs. Fallan's injuries aren't all
that serious, but she's suffered a tremendous trauma.
She needs rest and time to recover from the shock."

"We understand, Doc," Buford said. "We just
need to ask a few questions."

"Very well." The emergency room doctor scribbled on a prescription pad, then tore the sheet off and
handed it to Sara. "This is for pain. If that shoulder
or those scrapes bother you or you develop a headache, take two every four hours."

He paused at the curtained entrance to the cubicle and gave the two lawmen another look. "Remember, keep it short."

When he had gone, Sara sat up and gingerly swung her legs over the side of the treatment table. She made no move to get down; she wasn't sure her legs would hold her. It had been almost two hours since the explosion, but she was still shaking. At least the woozy sensation had gone away and her ears had stopped ringing.

"Are you okay?" Sheriff Petrie stepped forward to help her, but she waved him off. "I . . . I'll b-be all right." She sat on the side of the table in the short hospital gown, her bare legs dangling, and gazed at the two men, dazed and frightened and pale as parchment. "You're going to t-tell me the explosion wasn't an ac-accident, aren't you, Sheriff?"

"Yes, ma'am. I'm afraid so. Since your factory complex is in Houston, HPD is investigating the scene. They're still there, and from what they've reported so far, it was a bomb—a crude homemade job, but effective. It destroyed your lab, I'm afraid."

"I see." Another wave of hard shivers rippled through Sara. She hugged herself tighter.

"Now, let's see if I've got this straight. You say the chief chemist called and asked you to come to the lab at noon?"

"Yes, that's right."

"But you didn't make it there by noon, did you?"

"N-no. I was late. I had an overseas c-call just as I was about to leave to k-keep the appointment. Also, I w-walked to the lab instead of taking a golf cart."

"A good thing for you," Detective Calhoun spoke

up. "Had you been two minutes earlier, we wouldn't be talking now."

Sara pressed her lips together and fought to control her wobbly chin.

The sheriff scowled at his friend. "Good going, Mike. Jeez, why don't you scare the lady?"

He turned back to Sara with an avuncular smile. "Don't pay any attention to this Irishman, Mrs. Fallan. He's kinda rough around the edges, but he means well. Now, then, are you sure the person who called you was this chemist, this . . . ." He flipped back through his notepad. "John Davis?"

"Yes . . . that is . . . I th-think so. I didn't actually sp-speak to him. My secretary took the call and relayed the message."

"That'd be Miss Potts, right?"

"Yes."

"Mmm." The sheriff scribbled some more in his notepad. "So it could have been anyone who made that call, right?"

"I . . . I suppose so."

"One more thing. Was there anyone—"

There was a commotion on the other side of the curtain. "God damn it, I want to see her now!" Rourke shoved his way past the policeman trying to detain him and burst through the curtain. "Sara."

"Oh, Rourke." She held out her arms to him, and he leaped forward and snatched her from the table.

"You're alive." His arms clamped around her, and he buried his face in her hair. "Thank God. Thank God."

The pressure of his embrace hurt her bruised back, but Sara didn't care. She burrowed against his chest, savoring his warmth, his familiar smell, his solid strength. "Oh, Rourke, it was so horrible. It happened so fast. If I hadn't been delayed by a phone call—"

"Ssh. Ssh. The important thing is you're all right. You are all right, aren't you?"

"Yes. I was lucky. The force of the blast knocked me about twenty feet, but I landed in some bushes and they provided some cushion. My injuries aren't serious."

He eased her away to see for himself. He was appalled by the scratches on her face and her bandaged arms, and the bruises that were beginning to blossom. His face darkened as relief turned to a dark, seething fury.

He pulled her back against his chest and glowered at the sheriff over her shaking shoulder. "What are you doing about this? You've had over two months to find out who's behind the attacks on my wife, and so far, nothing. I want to know why."

A uniformed policeman stuck his head through the curtain and motioned to Detective Calhoun, who stepped out.

"I don't blame you for being upset, Mr. Fallan, but believe me, I want this case solved as much as you do. I don't like attempted murder and arson in my county. Me'n Mike are following every lead and doing some digging, looking for a common thread that will lead us to the person responsible. We haven't turned up anything solid yet, but we will. It's just a matter of time.

"Technically, this particular incident is out of my jurisdiction. The HPD bomb squad is at the factory right now, sifting through the wreckage."

"You can add forensics to that." Detective Calhoun stepped back into the treatment cubicle and shot his partner a grim look. "Our guys found a body among the rubble. We're after a murderer now."

"Oh, my God." Pulling out of Rourke's arms, Sara turned and stared at the lawmen, her eyes wide with horror. "Who?"

"We don't know who the victim is yet, Mrs. Fallan."

"Oh, God. Oh, God. Oh, God." Sara felt the blood drain from her face. She sank down into the only chair in the room, her hand over her mouth. "But it was lunchtime. Everyone was supposed to be in the cafeteria, eating. The lab should have been empty."

"That's probably what our perp was counting on. But apparently you have a conscientious employee who decided to work through his or her lunch hour. Too bad."

"I demand that you put every available man on this case. I want whoever is behind this caught. And quickly."

"Take it easy, Mr. Fallan. I know you're upset, but believe me, we're doing everything we can."

"Would you mind telling us where you were when the explosion occurred, Mr. Fallan?" Detective Calhoun asked.

Rourke turned cold eyes on the younger man. "Of course not. I was in Dallas, meeting with a supplier. The wholesale firm of Burns and Rosten."

Sara's head snapped up. She stared at him, stunned.

"And how did you learn about the explosion?"

"When I got off the plane, I called the office from my car. Alice, Mrs. Ketchum's secretary, told me what had happened, and that Sara had been taken to the hospital. I came straight here. Look, is there anything else? Because if not, I'm going to take my wife home."

The sheriff flipped his notepad shut and slipped it into the pocket of his red plaid western shirt. "Sure, go ahead. We'll need her to sign a statement, but that can wait. I'm real sorry we had to put you through the questioning, Mrs. Fallan."

"Th-that's all right. I understand."

Rourke put a hand on her shoulder, and she flinched. He frowned, but when he spoke his voice was gentle. "Take it easy, honey. I need to talk to the sheriff. I'm going to step outside with him and Detective Calhoun, then I'll be back and help you get dressed. I won't be long."

Sara pressed her lips together and nodded, too shaken to speak. The awful trembling had returned, vibrating outward from the icy core of her being.

Outside the cubicle, Rourke motioned the two men down the corridor between the treatment rooms and out the swinging doors into the main hallway, well out of Sara's earshot. "Look, Sheriff, I don't want my wife to know this, but I wasn't in Dallas today like I told you. I was here in town making arrangements with a security firm for my wife to have round-the-clock protection."

"I see." The sheriff and his partner exchanged a look. "Why keep it a secret from your wife?"

"Because she's against it."

"Why have you waited until now to hire protection?" Calhoun asked. "You've known about the danger for two months."

"At first I thought you'd solve the case quickly.

Then the longer this thing dragged out, the more
convinced Sara became that you were mistaken.
Whenever I mentioned hiring a bodyguard she got
upset. Finally I decided I'd at least hire someone to
keep a watch on her from a discreet distance. I know
it's no guarantee, but it's better than nothing."

"Do you mind telling us the name of this security
firm?" the detective asked.

"It's Harrison Security. I met with the owner, Joe
Harrison. He and his secretary and perhaps three
others can testify that I was in their offices from ten
until approximately twelve. After that, Mr. Harrison
and I went to lunch at Maxim's. You can check with
the staff there, if you'd like."

"We'll do that." The sheriff fished his notepad out
of his pocket and scribbled down the information.
When he was done, he nodded at Rourke. "We'll be
in touch, Mr. Fallan."

Without a word, Rourke walked back down the
corridor. The two lawmen watched him until he disappeared into the cubicle then headed for the exit.

"Sheriff! Sheriff! Wait!"

Buford turned back to see Jennifer Potts hurrying
toward him from the opposite end of the hall. Alice
Burke was hot on her heels. The younger woman
looked frazzled and frightened. Her red-gold curls
stuck out in all directions, as though she'd been stabbing her fingers through them. She was so pale the
freckles on her nose stood out starkly. Concern
etched Alice Burke's face, but as always, she remained calm and in control.

"How is Sara?" Jennifer demanded breathlessly.
"Is she going to be all right? Is she seriously hurt?"
She paused and wrung her hands and glanced

through the windowed doors toward the cubicles. "Oh, damn. They won't let me see her," she wailed, fighting tears.

"Of course not, you silly child," Alice snapped. "This is a hospital and there are procedures that must be followed. You're not a relative, after all. Besides, what possible good could you be to Sara? You would only be in the way."

"Oh, stuff it, you old bitch," Jen flared, sending the older woman a scorching look. Ignoring her sputters, she grabbed Buford's shirt front with both hands. "You've seen her, Sheriff. Is she okay?"

"Take it easy, Miss Potts. Mrs. Fallan is going to be fine. She's a bit shaky, which is understandable, but except for a few cuts that required stitches, her wounds aren't serious." Gently he pried her fingers open and released his shirt, and she immediately transferred her death grip to his hands. Buford gave her fingers a reassuring squeeze and smiled. "Mr. Fallan is with her now. He'll be bringing her out in a few minutes and you can see for yourself."

The young girl's anxious gaze immediately flew to the curtained cubicle.

"Really, Jennifer, you shouldn't be bothering the sheriff this way. I'm sure he has more important things to do than to listen to your hysterical rantings."

"That's all right, Ms. Burke. As a matter of fact, Miss Potts is just the person I wanted to see." He gave the young woman's hands a pat and released them. "I wonder if you'd mind answering a few questions. Miss Potts?"

Jennifer dragged her gaze away from the other end of the corridor and blinked at him. "What? Oh! Sure,

sure. Whatever," she mumbled distractedly, glancing away again.

"I understand you were the one who took the call from the research lab. Is that right?"

"Uh-huh."

"Was the caller John Davis?"

"No. His assistant called and left the message."

"And this assistant, was it a man or a woman?"

Jennifer turned her head and looked at him, frowning, her attention fully focused on their conversation for the first time. "You know, that was the funny thing. I don't know. I couldn't tell. The voice sounded—I don't know—kinda muffled or something. I thought it was kinda weird, but it didn't seem important." Her eyes grew round as saucers. "Hey. That was the slimebucket who's trying to kill Sara, wasn't it?"

"Kill Sara?" Alice laughed. "Don't be so dramatic, Jennifer. Why on earth would anyone try to kill Sara?"

Buford hesitated, frowning. "May I ask how you knew about that, Miss Potts?"

"Sara told me. She's not just my boss, she's my best friend. She tells me everything."

"I see."

"What do you mean?" Alice looked from Jennifer to the two men, appalled. "Oh, dear Lord, You're not saying that someone actually *is* trying to kill Sara?"

"It appears so."

Jennifer bristled like a junkyard dog. "If I ever get my hands on that bastard, I'll—"

"Jennifer, really! Your language," Alice scolded, but the younger woman ignored her.

"Is there anything else you can remember about the caller's voice, Miss Potts?" Mike asked. "Any particular speech pattern? Anything at all unusual besides the muffled tone?"

She thought for a few seconds and shook her head. "No. I don't think so."

"Can you recall exactly what the caller said?"

"Let's see . . . it was, 'This is Mr. Davis's assistant. He would like for Mrs. Fallan to meet him in the research lab at noon. There is something he wants to show her. Please relay that this is an urgent matter.' Then I said that Sara was on the phone and I would give her the message."

Buford scribbled furiously in his notepad. Finally he slipped it back in his pocket and nodded at Jennifer. "Thank you, Miss Potts. You've been a big help. If you recall anything else, I'd appreciate it if you'd give me or Detective Calhoun a call."

"Sure. You can count on it. I want that asshole nailed."

Alice Burke made a disapproving sound. Fighting a grin, Sheriff Petrie headed for the exit.

"Well? Whaddaya think?" Mike asked, falling into step with Buford's long stride.

"Mmm, it's hard to say."

"Yeah, well, my money's on the husband."

The sheriff chuckled. "Why? Because you don't like the guy? And don't bother to deny it. You bristle like a porcupine whenever you're around him."

"Yeah, well, the guy's too smooth, if you ask me," Mike grumbled. "Hell, Buf, you did the background check on this guy. It all figures. At eighteen he's a poor logger right out of the East Texas piney woods. He scrabbles his way up the ladder for a few years, then latches onto one of the richest women in the country and the next thing you know, he's her right-hand man. A guy with that kind of ambition isn't going to be happy playing second banana forever."

"You don't know it happened that way. Maybe he deserved everything he got. Everyone we've talked with has said Fallan's as sharp as they come."

"Yeah, and they all also agree that he had his sights set on stepping into Mrs. Ketchum's shoes. First he tried to off the daughter just to get her out of the way so the rest of that bunch can inherit. They'll sell out quicker'n a speeding bullet, and old Rourke boy can buy in. Now that he's married to the daughter, he stands to inherit everything."

"You're reaching, and you know it. It'll take one helluva whole lot more than that to convince a grand jury."

"Look, the guy had a reputation as a ladies' man and as a confirmed bachelor, and a check of his bank accounts showed he spent a lot of money on women. Then all of a sudden he up and marries the boss's daughter. Why? Because she's his ticket into the presidency of Eve Cosmetics."

"C'mon, Mike. You've seen Sara. A man doesn't need incentives to marry a woman like that."

"So, he got lucky. But I guarantee you, he'd have married her if she'd been a bowzer. Trust me, this is a guy with his eye on the main chance. And if she dies now, he's sitting pretty."

"I don't know. If his story checks out, he has an alibi for today's attempt. And he has hired twenty-four-hour security for her."

Mike snorted. "Alibi, my ass. He's blowing smoke, and you know it. The attempts against his wife haven't been made in person. They were all booby-traps, set up to give the perp plenty of time to get out of the area. And having someone follow her around isn't any protection against that sort of thing. I'm telling you, Buf, he's our man."

"Mmm. Maybe."

"Take it easy, honey." Sara's hands were shaking so badly she could not unbutton her coat. Rourke pushed them away and performed the task himself. She shivered and stared at his shirt front, careful not to meet his eyes.

The instant she slipped out of the coat, Sara turned away and headed for the living room. Too upset to sit, she walked to the terrace doors and stared out.

"I think you ought to go to bed. Get some rest," Rourke said, entering the room behind her.

"I'm fine."

"No, you're not fine. You've had a rough day and—"

"I said, *I'm fine.*"

Several beats of silence followed. "Is something wrong, Sara? Something other than what happened at the lab? You've been acting cool ever since we left the hospital."

She turned around. He stood on the other side of the room, still and alert, watching her. This was the man she loved the man she'd made love with. Had he tried to kill her?

Sara felt as though she would crack apart any second, shatter into a million pieces. She loved Rourke, yet he frightened her. More than anything, she wanted to trust him. She *needed* to trust him, but how could she when he had lied to her?

She wanted to shriek at him that she knew he hadn't been in Dallas today, but she didn't dare let him know she was suspicious. She could, however, confront him with the other lie.

"Why did you marry me, Rourke?"

The question caught him by surprise. "That's certainly right out of left field. Why do you ask? You know why . . . partly, anyway."

"At least you admit there's another reason. That's something, I suppose."

"What is this all about, Sara?"

"When I asked you if, before I arrived on the scene, you'd had ambitions to step into Evelyn's position, you denied having any such plans, yet now I've been told that wasn't true. At first I didn't believe it, but now I'm beginning to wonder."

"Ah, I'm beginning to see. Which one of the Ketchums have you been listening to this time?"

"Does it matter?"

"I suppose not. And to answer your question, I believe what I said was, I wasn't eligible."

"So you did want the company to go public."

"Yes." He replied without hesitation. All the while he watched her, taut and alert as a jungle cat.

"I assume you planned to purchase a block of stock and leverage your way onto the board and into the president's chair."

"That's right."

"Which brings me back to my original question. Why did you marry me, Rourke?"

For several seconds he did not so much as blink. "Because I wanted you," he replied at last.

"You wanted me . . . or you wanted Eve Cosmetics?"

"Does it have to be one or the other?"

"No, I suppose not. But then, the question is . . . which one did you want most?"

Rourke did not appear to move, but a tic pulsed at the corner of his mouth. "At this point, I don't suppose you would believe me if I said I love you."

She gazed at him, torn. Her heart felt like it was being squeezed in a vise. She wanted to say "Yes! Yes, I believe you!" and fling herself into his arms. She needed so much to believe in him. But she could not. Her instinct for self-preservation, honed through years of abuse and disappointment, was too strong. "No. No, I don't think so."

Steeling herself to walk past him, she headed for the door, her chin high, her heart pounding.

"Where are you going?"

She stopped in the doorway and looked back at him. "Under the circumstances, I think it would be best if I moved back across the hall."

Chapter Twenty-Eight

Kitty hurried up the stairs to her apartment, mumbling under her breath. Of all the times to forget her allergy medicine. The play opened in just four days and she had a hundred things to do before then. She didn't have time to be running home in the middle of the day.

She let herself in and headed for the bathroom. Preoccupied, she was halfway across the loft living room before she heard the sounds.

Jerking to a stop in the middle of the floor, she froze, listening. They were coming from the bedroom. Her first thought was that she had walked in on a burglary, and for an instant she was too frightened to move. Then the sounds registered.

She pressed one hand over her mouth, the other against her stomach. No. No, it couldn't be.

But the soft moans were unmistakable.

Kitty took a step toward the bedroom, then another, and another, moving faster with each one as hurt and despair burgeoned. By the time she reached the door to the bedroom, she was almost running.

She charged into the room but skidded to a halt

three steps inside and stared at the naked couple on the bed.

The pain was excruciating. She felt as though her heart were being ripped out of her body. Miles lay sprawled on his back, his hands gripping Darla Holt's hips as she rode his erection.

The young actress had her hands braced on his chest, her head thrown back, eyes closed, rocking back and forth on her knees. Miles's lascivious gaze was fixed on Darla's bouncing breasts. With each undulation they panted and moaned.

"Oh, my God," Kitty whimpered, backing away. "Oh, my God."

Darla shrieked and Miles's head snapped around. "Kitty!"

"You . . . I . . ." Kitty shook her head and made a strangled sound.

Miles lifted Darla off his cock and shoved her away, scrambling to get up. "Kitty, sweetheart, now, take it easy. This isn't what you think."

She stared at him, incredulous. "Not what I think? Not what I *think!*" Something snapped inside her. "You cheat. You unfaithful . . . lying . . . *bastard!*"

"Now, love, you're becoming hysterical and it's really quite silly." He walked toward her naked, his expression rueful, like a naughty child caught with his hand in the cookie jar. "Let's discuss this in a civilized manner, shall we? This means nothing. It was just sex. One of those spur-of-the-moment thi— Kitty, wait!" he called, but she was already out the door.

Sobbing, she flew blindly across the living room, her vision distorted by tears. She snatched the door open and started to storm out, but something stopped her, and at the last second she brought herself up short. Holding onto the doorframe on either side, she threw her head back and gasped for breath, tears streaming down her cheeks. No. No. What was she doing?

She wasn't going to run away and lick her wounds. Not this time. All of her life she'd shrunk from confrontation and strife. She'd been sweet, docile little Kitty, meekly taking a back seat to everyone, allowing everyone to walk all over her. Especially Miles. Well, no more. This was *her* apartment. If anyone was going to leave, it would be Miles.

Drawing a deep breath, Kitty wiped her wet cheeks and turned back. From the bedroom came the frantic sounds of low voices as she paced back and forth.

The hurt was devastating, but Kitty couldn't remember ever having been so furious. She had loved him, damn it! And trusted him. She'd done everything for him—some things she hadn't wanted to do, even things she felt guilty about, like borrowing against her inheritance. And he'd betrayed her.

A year ago, even a few months ago, she'd have been destroyed by Miles's cheating, but during the past few months, as the play had begun to take shape she had gained confidence—in her abilities and in her personal worth. Damn it, she deserved better treatment. Especially from the man who claimed to love her.

"Kitty, love." Miles came striding out of the bedroom. He was still barefoot and bare-chested, his hair mussed and sticking out in all directions, but he had pulled on a pair of jeans and was hastily buttoning them. "Come now, sweetheart. There is no need for you to carry on so. It was nothing serious. What

you saw had nothing to do with us. You know that
I love you."

"How can you say that? How do you have the gall
to look me in the eye and say that?"

His mouth firmed. He actually looked insulted. No
doubt he'd expected her to cave in and accept his
excuses, as usual. "All right, perhaps I shouldn't have
fucked Darla. However, you're to blame, you
know."

"Me?"

"Yes. You've been so busy lately—rewriting dialog, consulting with the director, overseeing everything. You go to the theater early and usually come
home late. You have no time left for me."

Kitty gaped at his aggrieved expression. "Everything I've been doing has been for you! Dear God, I
went into tremendous debt just to put on this play so
you could have the lead. I'm working my rear end off
trying to make certain everything is perfect, so you
can be a smash. And you use that as an excuse to
screw Darla."

Miles's face tightened. "You're beginning to sound
like a shrew. I admitted to making a mistake, I've
apologized, now let's just forget the whole thing,
shall we?"

Darla sidled out of the bedroom, looking guilty
and bedraggled. Her clothes apparently had been
thrown on. Buttons were fastened crooked, her skirt
and blouse were askew, and she carried her pan-
tyhose over one arm and her shoes in the other hand.
"I'll . . . uh . . . I'll just be going now."

"I suggest both of you go."

"What? Come now, Kitty, you can't be serious."

"I want you out, Miles. Out of my apartment, out of my life, and out of my play."

"Now, Kitty, love, you know you don't mean that."

"I mean it. Take what you need with you. You can pick up the rest of your things at the theater in a few days."

"You're being ridiculous. If you will just calm down and listen to reas—"

"I said *get out!*"

"Now, see here—"

"Out! *Out!* So help me, if you and your little slut aren't out of here in five minutes, I'll call the police and have you *thrown* out!"

Darla scooted out the door like a rabbit.

Miles's face darkened. "Very well, I'll go. But you'll regret this. Your precious play opens in four days, remember? Without me in the lead it will flop and the creditors will be on your back. What do you think your dear stepmum will say when she finds out you gambled that she would die?"

Sickness and shame quivered through Kitty, but she stood her ground. "You're not the only actor in this town."

"Oh what? You actually think that pathetic excuse for an understudy can fill my shoes?" He snorted. "Dan Brussard isn't half the actor I am."

"I happen to think he's an excellent actor."

"Really? I doubt he could've carried off the role I've been playing these past eight months with you." A nasty grin curved his mouth. "I never loved you. I knew from the start that you were rich, and I wrangled an introduction in order to seduce you."

Kitty paled, and he smiled. He strode back into the bedroom, and she hurried after him. He tossed clothes into a duffle bag, then stomped into the bathroom. She trailed on his heels.

"But . . . you couldn't have known. I didn't tell anyone at the theater about my family. No one there knew."

Miles paused in the act of raking his shaving gear off the bathroom counter and threw his elegant head back and laughed. "Ah, poor little rich girl. You're so naive. That's what made it so deliciously easy." His expression changed to a sneer. "Everyone knew—the entire cast, the stagehands, everyone. Did you think you could walk around incognito by simply not announcing who your stepmum was?"

He hoisted the duffle onto his shoulder. Dazed, Kitty followed him back though the bedroom and into the living room. "So the whole time we've lived together, all these months, it's all been a lie?"

Miles paused at the door and looked at her. "A whopper. To tell the truth, I don't even find you particularly attractive, and you bore me silly, but you were a convenient meal ticket and a fairly good lay. And there was always the possibility that you could boost my career. It almost worked. Too bad you spoiled it for both of us."

Speechless with hurt, Kitty could only stare at him. Miles grinned at her shattered look.

"You'd best hope your mum croaks soon. Otherwise, you'll be in a tight spot. *Dark of the Moon* is going to be a disaster."

* * *

Alice tapped on the door of Evelyn's bedroom and stuck her head inside. "The helicopter is waiting, Mr. Fallan."

"I'll be right there." Rourke snapped his briefcase shut and stood up. Reaching down, he picked up Evelyn's bony hand from where it lay atop the satin comforter and winked. "Hang in there, beautiful."

"Wait, Rourke." Her feeble grip tightened slightly. "You will make it to Kitty's opening on Saturday, won't you? You and Sara. I'm counting on you both to go in my place."

"No problem. I'll be flying back from Paris that afternoon, and Sara will meet me in New York. Don't worry about it. This is Kitty's first play. We wouldn't miss it, would we, darling?" He glanced Sara's way, and she nodded.

"It's wonderful, isn't it? Her first success." Evelyn's eyes misted and a glowing expression came over her gaunt face. "Imagine . . . my little Kitty, a playwright. I'm so proud of her. I only wish I could be there."

Rourke glanced at Sara again. She had turned her face away and was staring out the window, her profile set. She would never admit it, but he knew the remarks hurt her.

"Don't worry. You will be soon."

Evelyn's lips moved in what could have been an attempt at a smile. "You always were a rogue with a charming line. Now go on, get out of here. It's a long way to Paris."

Rourke brushed her forehead with a kiss. "You don't mind if I steal Sara for a few minutes, do you?"

"Of course not. Go see your husband off, Sara. But hurry back. I want to talk to you."

Sara stood up without a word and preceded Rourke into the hall. They walked side by side in silence until they reached the top of the stairs, and he stopped her with a hand on her arm.

She looked at him, her gaze remote and calm. Inside she was quivering. She always did around Rourke, but now the reaction was as much from fear as attraction. It amazed her that she could experience both at the same time.

He searched her face. "How long are we going to go on like this, Sara? It's been a week. You avoid me whenever you can, and when I *am* around, you hardly speak to me. You won't even look at me."

She couldn't look at him then. It hurt too much. Crossing her arms over her midriff, she lowered her gaze to his shirt front. It wasn't fair that she should still want him, that his scent could still make her feel lightheaded. "I . . . I don't know."

"I miss you, Sara." He touched the side of her neck with his fingertips. "I want you."

Sara shivered and flinched back, turning her head aside. "Don't. Just . . . don't."

"We're never going to get this cleared up if you won't see me, won't talk to me."

Keeping her head averted, Sara did not answer. The seconds ticked by, and she felt his anger and impatience building, felt him stiffen and draw away, and the quivering deep in her core grew worse.

"Very well, if that's how you want it. I'll see you in New York on Friday."

"Yes. All right."

Rourke loped down the stairs. Halfway he stopped and looked up at her. "Sara . . ."

"Yes?"

"Be careful."

Cold trickled down her spine. She watched him hurry gracefully down the remaining stairs and stride across the foyer and out the door. Had that been genuine concern, or a subtle threat?

For the past week, her nerves had been eating her alive. She couldn't sleep, couldn't eat; she jumped at the tiniest noise. She'd had all the locks on the company apartment changed and a state-of-the-art alarm system installed. It didn't help.

All week she had expected Rourke to be arrested at any moment. No matter her fears and suspicions, she could not bring herself to tell Sheriff Petrie that Rourke had lied about his whereabouts on the day of the explosion, but the sheriff and Detective Calhoun surely must have learned of the deception when they checked out his story. Yet no charges had been brought against him nor, so far as she knew, had he even been questioned again. Sara didn't understand it.

She'd had no choice but to carry on as though she didn't suspect a thing, as though she were merely angry with Rourke for misleading her. After office hours, as much as possible, she avoided him, but that wasn't an option at the complex.

The only people Sara had told of her suspicions were Brian and Jennifer. Predictably, Brian was convinced that Rourke was trying to kill her, but Jen thought Sara had lost her mind.

"So he didn't tell you he wanted to take over the business . . . big frigging deal. I can't believe Mr. Fallan would harm you. The man's nuts about you. Any fool can see that. Why don't you just ask him where he was that day? I'm sure there's a perfectly logical explanation."

Sara, however, did not dare. What if Jennifer was wrong? Rourke would know she suspected him and be on guard.

By tacit agreement, neither Sara nor Rourke referred to their estrangement at the office. They carried on business as usual, working together like two strangers, treating each other with extreme politeness and formality.

They continued their visits to the ranch to keep Evelyn up to date. They went over reports together, met with clients and employees, dealt with bankers and suppliers. Now they were going to meet in New York and attend the opening of Kitty's play together. And stay together in Evelyn's apartment.

The prospect terrified Sara. She shuddered and rubbed her arms and headed back down the hallway.

Evelyn appeared to be sleeping when Sara entered the room, but her eyes opened as Sara approached the bed. Despite her gaunt features and sickly pallor, Evelyn's eyes were bright with intelligence, and they bore into Sara relentlessly.

"What's going on between you and Rourke?"

Surprise flickered through Sara. She and Rourke had agreed it would be best if they kept their separation a secret, especially from Evelyn. In her condition, she did not need the additional worry. They had thought they were being circumspect, but apparently they had not been cautious enough.

"Why, nothing. Everything's fine." Sara picked up the afghan that lay across the foot of the bed and refolded it, not meeting her eyes.

"Oh, really? Then why are you using separate bedrooms here? And why have you moved back into the company apartment?"

"You know about that?"

"My dear, everyone knows. Frankly, I'm surprised you thought you could keep it a secret. Rourke knows there is nothing that goes on in my company or in this house that I don't know about."

Alice, Sara thought. And no doubt, Mrs. Dodson. She glanced at the middle-aged nurse who was busily rearranging the tray of medicines on the other side of the room, pretending she wasn't listening. The woman was a born gossip.

"I see."

"Normally, I try not to meddle in other people's business, but I'm running too low on time to be diplomatic. So what happened?"

Sara gazed at Evelyn. Oddly, she was the only person in this nest of vipers whom Sara trusted completely, the only one she knew, with absolutely certainty, did not want her dead. In a way, it would be a comfort to confide in her, but she didn't dare. Evelyn would never believe such a thing of Rourke.

"It's nothing for you to worry about. We aren't divorcing, so Rourke can continue as president of Eve."

"Whether or not you believe it, my concern does go deeper than that. I want to know what happened between you two."

"Does it matter? Actually, it shouldn't have come as a surprise to anyone that the marriage didn't last. After all, it wasn't exactly a love match."

Evelyn looked at her for several excruciatingly long seconds, then hiked one eyebrow. "Wasn't it?"

* * *

On Saturday night, Rourke stepped from the limousine in front of the theater, resplendent in a tuxedo. Checking his watch, he cursed under his breath and strode toward the entrance. He was late. By now the audience would already be seated. He'd be lucky if he made it to his seat before the curtain went up.

He had hoped to arrive in New York early enough to have some time alone with Sara, but takeoff at Orly had been delayed and they'd had to detour around a storm over the Atlantic. He'd had to call Sara from the company jet to tell her he'd be late landing at JFK and would meet her at the theater. It was not exactly the evening he'd planned.

Rourke slipped into his front-row seat beside Sara seconds after the house lights dimmed.

"Hi. Sorry I'm late," he whispered.

Lifting her chin, she turned her head slowly and gave him what Rourke had come to think of as her patented "Nothing you say or do can touch me" look. Just as slowly, she turned her gaze back to the stage.

Rourke's jaw tightened. He had the feeling she'd have been happier had he not made it at all. He was about to make a sarcastic remark when Kitty stepped out on stage, looking nervous and lovely in a black sequined gown.

"Ladies and gentlemen, I have an announcement to make—a correction, actually. There have been a couple of last-minute changes to our cast, and your programs. Instead of Darla Holt, Janece Hudson will be playing the part of Marianne. And Dan Brussard will play the part of Wyatt Ashburn. Thank you."

Sara and Rourke exchanged looks of puzzled surprise. It was the first time in weeks she had let her guard down, even that much. "That's the lead," she whispered.

"Yeah, I know. I wonder what happened to Miles."

They had no chance to speculate. For the next two hours Rourke and the rest of the audience were spellbound by the action on stage. Given Kitty's retiring personality, he had not expected much, but he found himself drawn into a fascinating web of human emotions and a story that twisted and turned in a sinister tangle. Who could have imagined that Kitty had that kind of talent? Or imagination?

Perhaps the only person in the theater who had not become totally absorbed in the production was Sara. She tried. Staring straight ahead, she strove to concentrate on the action on stage, but she was too tightly wound. Ten minutes into the performance she was completely lost. She barely caught more than an occasional snatch of dialog.

With every fiber of her being, Sara was aware of Rourke sitting beside her, looking so darkly handsome and intent, so dangerous. Her nerves hummed like a high-voltage wire. Every time he shifted and his elbow touched her, she felt as though she'd received a thousand-watt jolt.

Backstage after the performance, Kitty was bursting with excitement and anxiety. Sara and Rourke offered their congratulations and praise and tried to reassure her that the reviews would be wonderful, but nothing they said had any effect.

"She was so wound up, I doubt she'll even remember that we were there," Rourke commented, when he and Sara were settled in the limo. "You'd think her whole future was riding on the success of this play."

"Perhaps it seems that way to her. A sense of accomplishment is important," Sara said with a shrug, and turned her head to look out the window.

She could feel Rourke's gaze fixed on her.

"Would you like to stop somewhere for dinner?"

She didn't take her gaze off the passing scenery. "No, thank you. I had an early meal before the performance."

The silence stretched out again. Rourke's growing impatience was palpable. This was the first time they'd been totally alone together outside business hours since the day of the explosion, and it was torture.

She knew he wanted to talk, to try lull her into trusting him again. After the brief spell of closeness they had shared, it was difficult to hold herself apart from him, but she had learned the hard way in life that the only person she could rely on was herself. For a while there, she had been so besotted she'd almost forgotten that.

Even now, part of her wanted to throw herself into his arms. She needed to feel his warmth, his strength, the delicious sensation of his skin gliding against hers. She ached for the special intimacy she had tasted only briefly. Even stronger, however, was her fear of letting her guard down and trusting blindly. No matter what her foolish heart told her, she could not afford to make a mistake. Her life depended on it.

They rode in silence for the remainder of the trip. The drive to Evelyn's apartment seemed interminable, but they finally arrived. Sara flinched when they climbed from the limo and Rourke put a solicitous hand at her elbow to lead her into the building. The slight tightening of his grip told her he had noticed, but when she peeked up at him, his face looked like it was set in stone.

They both murmured greetings to Oscar, the doorman, and Joe, the night guard, as they passed. Though it had been over six months since Sara had become a part of Evelyn's life, the two men still stared with stupefaction whenever they saw her.

During the elevator ride to the twenty-ninth floor, Sara kept her face impassive, but her nerves were screaming. She could sense a steely purpose in Rourke, and she knew a showdown was brewing.

The minute they stepped inside the apartment, Sara tried to make her escape.

"I'm tired, so I'll say goodnight."

She had barely taken three steps before Rourke stopped her. "I don't think so." He snagged her wrist from behind, and Sara let out a shriek as he jerked her to a halt and whipped her around, bringing her hard up against his chest.

"Stop it! Let me go! Take your hands off me!"

"Not a chance. This has gone on long enough."

Unreasoning terror had Sara by the throat. Her mask of indifference fell away, and she bucked and pitched and kicked like a wild woman. Where once the tensile strength of Rourke's lean body had thrilled her, now all she felt was threat. She felt caged within the circle of his arms and utterly helpless. Her heart pounded against her ribcage as though it were trying to beat its way out of her body. "Let me go!

Oh, please, please, don't do this!" she sobbed, even while she lashed out blindly.

"What the—Jesus!" Rourke struggled to control her. When he finally grasped her upper arms he shook her hard. "Damn it, will you . . . calm . . . down?" he gasped.

Caught in the grip of hysteria, Sara twisted from side to side, shaking her head, sobbing every breath. "Noooo! Noooo! Don't—"

"What the hell is going on out here?"

Rourke's head snapped around. Holding Sara at arm's length, he stared at the young girl standing in the open doorway, wearing a cotton nightshirt and bunny slippers and glaring at him as though he were Jack the Ripper.

"Jen! Oh, Jen. Thank God!"

"What the hell is she doing here?"

Sara tipped her head back, her eyes wide and wild. He stared at her white face. "My God. You're frightened of me."

"Let her go!" Jennifer tore across the room and pulled Sara from his hold. She shoved Sara behind her and glared at Rourke, bristling like a mother grizzly defending her cub. "You leave her alone."

Rourke's face hardened. "Get out of here, Jen."

"Like hell I will."

Rourke took a step toward the two women, and Sara gasped and tightened her hold on Jennifer.

"If you know what's good for you, you'll—"

The shrill of the telephone startled a cry out of the women and stopped Rourke in his tracks. He glared at the instrument for an instant, then strode across the room and snatched it up. "Yeah. Rourke."

Trembling, Sara clutched Jennifer and watched

him. Gradually, as she watched his expression change, her fear turned to anxiety.

After only a few terse sentences, Rourke slammed the receiver down. He sliced a hard look at the women. "Get your things together, we're flying home. Evelyn is critical."

Sheriff Buford Petrie strode into the squad room and plopped down onto the chair beside Mike's desk.

The young detective looked up from the file he was studying and grinned. "Hey, Buf. What's up?"

Buford tossed a folder on his desk. "Take a look at that."

"What is it?"

"I've pieced together every scrap of information we've got on the murder attempts. At one time or another all of the Ketchums and everyone else connected with Sara was close enough to have been responsible for at least one of the attempts. Of all the possible suspects, though, only a handful either had been present when each attempt occurred, or was close enough to the scene to have gotten in and out within the time frame."

"So?"

"So I played a hunch and checked with the airlines. It paid off. It seems that one person on the short list took redeye flights to both Sarasota and Palm Springs, the cities closest to the Eden projects, just prior to each incident at the spas. Each time, the suspect flew back the same night." Buford waved his beefy paw at the papers. "I've highlighted the name on the report."

Mike quickly scanned the pages and whistled through his teeth. "Hot damn, Buf, you nailed it."

"Yeah. At the very least, I figure we've got enough to get a search warrant. And we'd better do it fast. Evelyn Ketchum took another turn for the worse yesterday. It doesn't look like she's going to make it this time. The family and Evelyn's immediate associates have gathered at the ranch. If the motive is to get Sara out of the way before Evelyn buys it, then the suspect may panic and do something rash."

Mike slammed the folder shut and bolted out of his chair, reaching for his suit coat. "C'mon. Let's get that warrant."

Chapter Twenty-Nine

"Ho-ly shit. Would you get a load of this stuff?"

"Mmm." Buford bent over the table and nudged the dynamite cap and the coil of fuse line with the end of a pencil. "Looks like we got the makin's of a bomb, all right. Except for the explosive."

"Probably used all of it blowing up the lab. That bomb was a definite overkill. Made kindling out of the place."

Mike poked through the bookcase. Finding nothing, he moved over to the desk and began rifling through the drawers.

Buford worked his way around the room, checking behind pictures, under furniture, inside containers. He was replacing a chair cushion when Mike let out a whoop. "Hot damn! Pay dirt!"

"Whatcha got?"

Grinning, Mike handed him three sheets of paper. "Looks like copied pages from a book. Probably went to the library."

Buford scanned the pages and shook his head. "Well, I'll be damned." The sheets contained detailed, step-by-step instructions on constructing a dynamite bomb with a timed detonating mechanism.

He shoved the papers back into Mike's hands. "Bag it and the rest of the evidence. I've gotta get to the Ketchum Ranch, and fast."

Buford hadn't moved so fast since way back during his stint working robbery with the Houston force, when he'd run down a kick burglar on foot. In under five minutes he was in his patrol car, streaking west on I-10, siren blaring, accelerator floor-boarded.

Evelyn was dying. Staring out the window of her bedroom, Sara hugged her arms close to her body and tried to come to grips with that fact. Even if by some miracle they found a bone marrow donor, it was too late now. According to Dr. Underwood, the end was only days, perhaps hours away.

Sara wasn't sure what she was feeling. Her emotions were in so much turmoil she was numb. Anger, regret, hurt, fear and a host of other indefinable feelings formed a hard knot just beneath her breastbone.

For the past six months she had witnessed Evelyn's steady decline, but somehow she had never truly believed it would come to this. She had assumed they would find a donor and Evelyn would make a full recovery. Things like this weren't supposed to happen to people like Evelyn.

Sara realized now that subconsciously, she had also expected Evelyn would somehow do something to heal, or at least excuse, the pain her decision had caused. Instead, all Sara was left with was unresolved anger.

Still . . . she didn't want Evelyn to die.

Sara rubbed her burning eyes with her thumb and forefinger. She hadn't slept in over thirty-six hours. They had arrived at the ranch in the wee hours of the morning, and she and Dr. Underwood had sat with Evelyn until well past dawn. He was downstairs at that moment in one of the guest rooms, probably sleeping like a log. Sara was bone tired herself, but her mind would not allow her to rest.

They were taking turns. Kitty and Eric were with Evelyn now, and Madelene and Alice would take over in a few hours. Still, Sara felt she should be there. God alone knew why. Her mouth twisted in a wry grimace. No matter how hard you fought them, the tug of family ties were impossible to ignore.

Or then again, perhaps she really was simply a born caretaker, as Rourke had claimed. Whatever, someone had to stay with Evelyn in her last hours. No one, not even a mother who did not want you, should die alone.

Paul's wife was certainly no help. Monica got hysterical if you so much as suggested she sit with Evelyn. Apparently being around a dying person upset her delicate system.

Sara wandered aimlessly around the room. She wondered where Rourke was. Probably downstairs in the den with the rest of the family. He had hardly spoken to her since they received the call about Evelyn the night before. She didn't know if he was hurt because she suspected him, or furious that she had caught on.

Someone shouted outside, and a bell began to clang. The noise was followed by a sudden commotion downstairs.

Frowning, Sara walked back to the window and

looked out. From that angle she could see nothing, but she could hear the shouts coming from the barn area behind the house. What in the world?

Sara unlocked her door and looked out into the hall. She heard more shouts and doors banging. The telephone was ringing insistently, but no one bothered to answer it. Curious, Sara left her room and walked down the hall. Just as she reached the landing, Kitty and Eric burst out of Evelyn's room and tore down the stairs.

"Hey, what is it? What's going on?"

"The barn's on fire!" Kitty shouted over her shoulder without slowing down. "Stay with Evelyn, would you? I've got to get my mare out!"

"Of course," Sara shouted after her, but Kitty and her cousin had already disappeared down the central hallway toward the back of the house.

The telephone continued to shrill, but Sara ignored it. Wondering where Mrs. Dodson was, she turned to go into Evelyn's room and found herself looking down the barrel of a gun.

"Move, and I'll kill you where you stand."

"Answer, damn it! Answer the damned phone!" Sheriff Petrie snarled into his car phone. He cursed and slammed the instrument down.

Approaching the turnoff, he saw a column of black smoke coming from the vicinity of the house, and his heart kicked into high gear. "Oh, Christ! I hope I'm not too late."

He took the turn into the Ketchum Ranch at almost full throttle, putting the patrol car into a fishtailing, sideways skid. Letting up on the gas only slightly, Buford wrestled the car into submission, then floorboarded the pedal again. The car roared down the road, trailing a plume of boiling dust like a giant rooster's tail.

A quarter of a mile from the house, Buford spotted the crowd gathered around the smoldering barn. At his approach they turned, and an instant later Rourke broke away from the group and began to run. He reached the house at the same time that Buford's patrol car slid to a halt before the side veranda steps.

"What is it? What's wrong?"

The sheriff bailed out of the patrol car as though it were on fire. "Where's Alice Burke?"

"Alice?" Rourke looked around and scanned the group of people hurrying toward them from the barn. "I don't know. In the house, I guess."

"And your wife? Is she in there, too?"

"Yes. Why? Sheriff, wait! What's going on?"

Buford pounded up the veranda steps, drawing his gun on the run. "Alice Burke is our killer!" he barked over his shoulder.

Sara stared at the obscene black hole at the end of the gun barrel. Her heart clubbed against her ribs, almost suffocating her. She swallowed hard. "Alice. Wh-what are you doing?"

"I'm sorry, Sara. This isn't personal. I like you. I really do. But there's no other way. You have to die. Now, before . . ." She stopped and pressed her lips together, fighting back tears. "Before Evelyn does."

Sara clutched the banister so tight her knuckles

were bone-white. "Why, Alice? What could you possibly have to gain from my death?"

"I'm not doing this for me . . . I'm doing it for Chad." She waved the barrel of the gun. "Come on. We're going back to your room. You're going to write a suicide note. You'll say you're despondent over the breakup of your marriage and your mother's impending death, and you can't go on."

She gestured with the gun again. Sara gripped the banister tighter and shook her head. "No. No, I'm not going anywhere with you. If you're going to shoot me, you'll have to do it here."

Alice became agitated. "I'll do it. I'm warning you, I'll shoot you here if I have to." High-pitched and shrill, Alice's voice bordered on hysteria. She shifted from one foot to the other. The barrel of the gun wobbled, and Sara's heart jumped into her throat. "You don't think I'm serious, but if you don't move, I'll shoot you. I swear it."

"If you do, everyone will know it wasn't suicide and that you killed me."

"No, it—"

A door crashed open and Alice jumped. Her gaze darted around, her eyes wild.

Below, Sheriff Petrie and Rourke stormed into the foyer.

"Stop! Don't you come any closer!" Alice screamed.

The two men froze at the bottom of the stairs and took in the tableau on the second-floor landing. A look of horror came over Rourke's face. "Sara!"

He started to lunge up the stairs, but the sheriff restrained him. "Easy, easy."

"Damn it, let me go!"

"No. You wanna get your wife killed?"

"Put down your gun, sheriff!" Alice screamed. "Put it down or I'll shoot Sara now. I swear it!"

"Damn." Buford hesitated, his fingers clinching around the ivory handle of his Colt .45 automatic. From that angle, he didn't have a clear shot.

"Do it!"

"All right. All right." Buford held his hands out, palms forward, the Colt held loosely, the barrel pointed at the ceiling.

"God damn it, Sheriff, what're you doing?" Rourke snarled.

"The only thing I can do, under the circumstances." Never taking his eyes off Alice, Buford bent and carefully laid the revolver on the third step.

A door banged at the back of the house. Amid a chorus of raised voices, footsteps thudded toward them down the central hallway. Seconds later, the rest of the family, with Paul, Chad, and Eric in the lead, burst into the foyer.

"What the—"

"Holy shit—"

Their jaws slack, the three men jerked to a stop so fast the women careened into them from behind.

"What is it? What's going—oh, my God! She's got a gun!" Madelene shrieked.

Monica screamed.

Paling, Kitty wrung her hands and babbled over and over, "Oh dear, oh dear, oh dear."

Jennifer gaped, for once, too terrified to speak.

Looking sleep-tousled, Dr. Underwood stepped out of the back bedroom and headed down the hallway, buttoning his shirt on the way. "What in heaven's name is going on here? May I remind you there's a sick woman in this house? You people are making enough noise to wake the de—Dear God!"

Ignoring them, Buford spoke to Alice in a firm but calm voice. "Put the gun down, Ms. Burke. It's over. We know you tried to kill Mrs. Fallan twice, and that you caused the damage at the spas and at the Houston complex. You killed a man with that bomb, but a good lawyer could plea-bargain that charge down to manslaughter, since I don't believe you intended it to happen. But if you shoot her, it'll be first-degree murder."

"No." Alice shook her head. Her eyes had a deranged glow that sent a chill down Buford's spine. "No, don't you see? I'm doing the right thing. No one will punish me for that. Sara has to die."

Chad stepped forward. "Alice, what the hell do you think you're doing?"

"Chad." Alice seemed to glow from inside at the sight of him, her plain face transformed into something close to beauty. The abject adoration on her eyes was clearly visible to everyone in the foyer. "I have to kill Sara. I'm doing this for you, darling."

"Like hell," Chad roared. "Jesus! Are you crazy, woman? Put that damned gun down before you hurt someone."

"Oh, but you don't understand. I've seen Evelyn's new will. She's going to leave everything to Sara—all her stock in Eve, her other investments, everything. I can't let that happen."

"Damn it, Alice, you're not thinking straight. You can't do this."

"Oh, but I have to. Don't you see, with Sara out of the way, you'll get your rightful share of Eve Cosmetics. When Evelyn dies you can sell the shares and fix up the ranch, the way you've always wanted to. You said yourself, you need that money."

"Maybe so, but I wouldn't kill to get it. Now, put the gun down, Alice."

Her expression turned obdurate. "No. I have to do this. You know you won't be happy until you put Ketchum Cattle Company back the way it used to be. Once you do that, you won't have all these worries, and then you'll have time for me. Don't you see, darling, this is for both of us. This is for our future."

"Good God, Chad. Don't tell me you've been playing fast and loose with this poor woman." Paul shot his cousin a disgusted look. "I'm not exactly Sir Galahad, but even *I* wouldn't do that."

Chad had the grace to look guilty. "Jesus, I didn't know she was taking it so seriously," he muttered. "I thought it was just convenient sex—for both of us."

"Oh, good going, Chad," Eric snapped.

"If that isn't just like a man," Madelene said with a sniff.

"Shut up, all of you," Rourke ordered. "Alice, listen to me. If you harm Sara, you'll never have Chad. You'll go to prison. You don't want that to happen, do you? Put the gun down and let Sara go."

"No. No, I have to kill her. There's no other way. Why can't you all see that?"

She raised the gun a couple of inches and looked down the barrel at Sara. "I'm sorry." Her mouth set and her arms tensed.

"Nooooo!"

Emitting a roar like a bull, Rourke charged up the stairs. Alice jumped and swung the gun toward him.

"Rourke, no!" Sara didn't give herself time to think. Reacting purely on instinct, she lowered her shoulder and launched herself at Alice, slamming into her before Rourke reached the landing at the halfway point of the stairs.

The explosive retort of the gun drew screams and curses from the horrified onlookers. Sara felt a sting in her right arm, and inexplicably, her legs seemed to turn to mush.

"Saa-raaa!" Rourke bellowed, as she fell to her knees.

The force of the blow sent Alice stumbling backward, arms flailing. Her backside hit the railing and it broke with a crack almost as loud as the gunshot. For a suspended moment, as the section of railing and banisters fell to the marble floor of the foyer, Alice hung there, staring at Sara, her eyes round with surprise and horror. Then, as though in slow motion, she toppled over the edge.

Sara gasped and turned her head aside. The dull thud and the screams and shouts from below sent a shudder rippling through her. She swayed, and for a moment she thought she was going to faint.

"Sara. Oh, God, Sara." Suddenly Rourke was there, pulling her into his arms.

"Rourke." His name shuddered from her like a prayer of thanks. He clamped her against his chest and rocked her, and she clung to him, crying, gasping for breath. She buried her face in his neck and burrowed against him. From what seemed a long distance she heard him curse as she began to shake.

"Oh, Rourke. Rourke," she gasped and sobbed all at once. "It was so aw . . . awful."

"It's all right, baby. Take it easy. You're safe now," he crooned, running his hands over her. "Are you all right? She didn't—" His hand encountered the stickiness on her arm. "My God, you're bleeding. You've been hit!"

Sara was shaking so hard she couldn't tell him it was only a graze, that she didn't think it was serious. It would have been a waste of time in any case.

Rourke swooped her up in his arms and strode for her bedroom. "Dr. Underwood! Get up here! Sara's been shot!"

Rourke laid her on the bed as though she were made of spun glass. He stayed bent over her, his arms braced on either side of her body. Feature by feature, he examined her face, his vivid blue eyes frantic and dark with emotion. He touched her cheek with trembling fingertips. "Sara."

"All right, let's see what we've got here," Dr. Underwood said, brushing Rourke aside. Going to work with brisk efficiency, he cut away Sara's torn sleeve and examined the wound. "Mmm, doesn't look too bad. Just a graze, really. Another quarter inch to the left, though, and the bullet would have torn muscle instead of merely gouging out a furrow of flesh."

He looked up at her over the tops of his glasses as he worked. "That was a brave thing you did, young woman. Brave, but reckless as hell, and dangerous. You could have gotten yourself killed! You must love this husband of yours very much."

Sara started, her gaze jumping to where Rourke stood, gripping the footboard of the bed. His eyes burned into her like twin blue flames.

He did not move the entire time the doctor treated and bandaged her wound, nor did his intent gaze leave her face. Every line of his taut body vibrated with emotions held firmly in check.

"Use this salve and change the dressing every day

and you should heal nicely. If you have any trouble, call me. Otherwise, come into my office in a week." Dr. Underwood snapped his bag shut and stood up. "I imagine your nerves are pretty jangled. I can give you a sedative, if you like."

"No. Thank you. I'm fine."

When he had gone, the air in the room pulsed with tension. Leaning back against the pillows, Sara plucked at a loose thread in the bedspread and stared at her fingers as though she found the task fascinating. Now that the crisis had passed, she was swamped with guilt. "I . . . I owe you an apology. I'm sorry I suspected you. I should have known better."

"Yes, you should have. But never mind that now. Was he right?"

"Who?" Sara asked, but she knew.

"The doctor. Do you love me?"

"Rourke . . . that really isn't—"

"Do you, Sara?"

She looked up and met his intent gaze and caught her lower lip between her teeth. "Yes. It's true." Something flashed in his eyes and he made a move toward her. Sara quickly held up her hands to stop him and said in a rush, "But that doesn't change anything between us."

"How can you say that? Sara . . . darling, I love you, too. Can't you see that?"

"Do you?" Her lips twitched in a wan attempt at a smile. "I'd like to believe that, but how can I? No matter what you say, I'll always wonder if you want me because you love me, or because I'm a convenient means to an end. For someone as ambitious as you, marriage is a small price to pay in return for the presidency of a company like Eve Cosmetics."

"Damn it, Sara—"

"Sara!" An urgent knock accompanied Kitty's frantic call. Immediately the door opened and she stuck her head inside. "Sara, it's Evelyn. The doctor says this is it. Hurry."

Before she finished speaking, Sara was on her feet. She swayed a bit and had to grab the bedpost to steady herself as she stepped into her shoes, and Rourke immediately protested.

"Where do you think you're going? Get back in that bed. You need to rest."

"No. I'm going to be with her. Now, get out of my way."

She brushed past him and hurried down the hall. Cursing, Rourke followed on her heels.

Everyone was there, even Paul and Chad. Kitty and her sister stood on either side of the bed holding Evelyn's hands, but when Sara eased into the room, Eric nudged Madelene aside and ushered Sara into her place.

She had not expected it to hurt so much, but as she gazed down at the woman who had given her life, she felt as though an iron fist were squeezing her heart. Evelyn's once beautiful face was reduced to skin and bone, the eyes sunk deep into her skull, her skin white and waxy.

Hesitantly, Sara picked up Evelyn's hand. It was cold and lifeless and pitifully bony. Evelyn's eyelids fluttered open. Her eyes were cloudy and glazed, and Sara knew she could not see.

"S-Sa-ra?"

"I'm here."

"I . . . I'm s—sor—ry." The words came out on a

whispery sigh, so soft Sara almost did not hear them. Sara held her breath and waited for more, but Evelyn's eyes drifted shut. She drew two more shallow breaths. Then she was gone.

Chapter Thirty

Three days later, in the Ketchum cemetery about a half a mile behind the ranch house, they buried Evelyn beside Joe.

Hundreds of people attended—business associates, movie stars, politicians, Eve employees from the executive suite to the assembly lines. Even the governor came. And, of course, the media.

Once again Sara had to endure the glare of publicity about her mysterious appearance, speculation as to who her father was, and endless references to her uncanny resemblance to her mother. Along with the articles, several newspapers and magazines even ran their pictures side by side.

At the graveside, Sara suffered through endless condolences, feeling like a fraud. It was not grief that put the stoic look on her face, but anger.

After the service, as soon as the last of the mourners had left, the will was read in the front parlor of the ranch house. As Alice had predicted, the bulk of the estate went to Sara. Evelyn left two hundred thousand dollars in cash to each of her stepchildren, and fifty thousand each to Eric and Paul. She willed the ranch house jointly to all five of the younger Ketch-ums. To everyone's surprise, all Rourke inherited was Evelyn's diaries.

Sara was prepared for a negative reaction from the family, and they did not disappoint her. With the exception of Kitty and Eric, they were outraged.

."This is absurd. You won't get away with this," Paul threatened, and Chad, Madelene, and Will mumbled agreement. "We're going to challenge this will."

"On what grounds?" Rourke asked.

"She exerted undue influence over a dying old woman who wasn't in her right mind."

"Evelyn?" Rourke laughed. "You'll have a tough time proving that one."

"Mr. Fallan is right," Charles Kirkland, Evelyn's attorney, interjected. "Evelyn was in complete charge of her mental faculties right up to the end, and certainly so when she had me draw up this will last spring. You will find that it is ironclad. She made sure of that."

Paul and Chad were not deterred. However, a meeting with their own attorney a few days later convinced them the document was inviolable and that to contest it would be a waste of time and money. They had no choice but to accept defeat and wait and see what Sara would do.

She knew they all wanted to sell their stock and were waiting anxiously to see she if she would keep the company in the family or sell out. The October board meeting was scheduled for one week after the funeral. The day before the meeting, Sara was still trying to make up her mind when Rourke paid her an unexpected visit.

Though he lived right across the hall, since the reading of the will, Sara had not returned to the office and she had not seen him. When she opened the door to him, her heart gave a little jump.

"Rourke."

"Hello, Sara. May I come in?"

"Of course." She stepped back and held the door open wide, and when he walked past, her senses were assailed by his nearness. His dark good looks made her ache, and her stomach went woozy when she breathed in his scent. Dear Lord, she had missed him so much.

She led him into the living room, her skin prickling with awareness. She expected him to sit beside her on the sofa, but he chose one of the chairs on the opposite side of the coffee table. For the first time, Sara noticed that he had his briefcase with him, and her spirits sank. So this was a business call. She sat up straighter and tilted her chin. "What did you want to see me about?"

"Before I get to that, would you tell me something?"

"If I can."

"As I'm sure you know, tomorrow at the board meeting, Paul is going to make a motion that Eve go public. I'd like to know how you're going to vote."

"I see." Sara smoothed an imaginary wrinkle from her skirt. "I haven't fully decided."

"But you're leaning toward going public, aren't you?"

"So what if I am?" She jumped to her feet and walked with jerky steps to the terrace doors. Folding her arms tight across her midriff, she whirled around and glared at Rourke. "Give me one good reason why I should abide by Evelyn's wishes? She gave me away. Sentenced me to a life of hell, ignored me until she needed me, and all she has to say is, 'I'm sorry.' I'm *sorry?* Is that supposed to make everything all right? Well, it doesn't!"

She spun back and stared out the glass, blinking back tears. Her heart was beating as though she'd run a mile. "Why shouldn't I take the money and run?"

"That's your prerogative, of course. But before you make a firm decision, I'd like you to do me a favor."

"What?"

Rourke snapped open his briefcase and withdrew three books, two cheap clothbound volumes, and one of rich leather. "These are three of Evelyn's diaries. I've marked several entries that I would like you to read."

Sara stared at the journals, tempted and repelled at the same time. "I don't know, Rourke. Those are private."

"It's all right. Evelyn included a letter with the diaries instructing me to use my own judgment about showing them to you. There are many others that you will probably want to read later, but these are the most significant to you right now."

He laid the books on the coffee table and stood up. "All I ask is that you read them before you make your decision." He started to leave, but he stopped in the doorway and looked back at her.

"I love you, Sara. I know that you doubt that. I realize it must look to you as though I'm just saying I love you in order to keep control of Eve, but that's not true. I want our marriage to continue because I love you, and I can't stand the thought of a life without you. I'm hoping reading the diaries will prove it to you." He turned and walked out.

How could Evelyn's private diary entries possibly convince her of Rourke's feelings? As the door clicked shut behind him, Sara stared at the three diaries. Were the answers to her question in there?

It was what she wanted, what she had been hoping for, but now that the time had come, she was leery of what she might learn. For a long time, she simply stared at the journals, excitement and dread coiling together in the pit of her stomach.

Finally, she picked the books up and carried them into her bedroom. To give herself time to work up her courage, she laid them on her bed and went through her nightly routine. When she was showered and in her nightgown, she propped up in the bed and opened the oldest of the diaries. It was labeled the year before she was born. The first place marked was May eleventh.

Sara leaned back against the pillows and began to read Evelyn's girlish handwriting, her chest tight with anticipation.

I'm so excited, I feel as though I'm going to burst at any moment! Larry Bainbridge asked me for a date . . .

A little under two hours later, Sara closed the second cloth diary. Still holding the book propped against her knees, she absently rubbed her fingers over the frayed cover and stared into space.

Raped. She closed her eyes and pressed her lips

together against the rush of painful feelings. She had not expected that.

Finally, she understood her mother and the forces that had driven her young life. In the writings she had glimpsed the naive, love-starved girl Evelyn had been, felt her pain and disillusionment, the humiliation she had suffered, not only at the hands of Larry Bainbridge, but also at those of the college administrators. How awful it must have been to be alone, penniless and scared, with no one to whom you could turn.

The heartrending outpourings of Evelyn's soul made Sara ache for her mother's lost innocence and sympathize with her horror and rage at the outcome of the violence that had been perpetrated against her. Sara felt keenly her mother's anguish over what to do with the unwanted child, her worry that she would not be able to give her love, and her determination that Sara not suffer the same loveless childhood she herself had endured.

It was hardly comforting to know that she'd been conceived not in love, nor even passion, but through a vicious act of violence, but at least now she understood why Evelyn had given her up. Sara could not find it in her heart to blame her. In her place, she knew she would probably have done the same.

Though it hurt, she even understood why Evelyn had not wanted to get close to her these past six months.

Sara exchanged the cloth diary for the leather-bound one and propped it against her knees. She fingered the gold lettering. The year was the current one, and she realized that it had been written in large part since she'd come back into Evelyn's life. Her hand trembled as she opened the book to the single bookmark.

The entry had been written the night Evelyn had made her decision to try and find her. The next one was her reaction to Sara after their first meeting.

For the next hour, Sara read the diary straight through. Her mother's meticulously honest writings touched her deeply. Evelyn had not made excuses; she had never blamed anyone else or whined. She had done what she'd felt she had to do and had accepted responsibility for the outcome, right or wrong.

She was amazed at her mother's strength and sharpness and unyielding determination. Another woman might have crumpled had those things happened to her.

Evelyn's handwriting got shakier and harder to read as the months passed. When Sara reached the end, she was surprised to find that the last entry, made two weeks before Evelyn's death, had been written by someone else, and that it was addressed to her.

Dear Sara,

Nurse Dodson is writing this for me as I no longer have the strength. I know now that there is no hope; I am dying. By the time you read this—if Rourke decides that you should—I will be gone. I sincerely hope that learning the truth will not hurt too much. It is my hope that these books will help you to understand why I did what I did, even if you are not able to forgive me.

These past six months I tried very hard not to be drawn into any sort of emotional relationship with you. To be brutally frank, I did not want to feel anything for you. I certainly did not want to love you, and I fought against it every day. I suppose, had I admitted I cared,

I would have had to accept that I did not do the right thing in giving you away.

I must confess, I was not completely successful. I suppose it's true, what they say; blood is thicker than water. Your intelligence, your ability, your gritty determination—even that stubborn pride of yours and your defiant refusal to let go of your anger toward me are worthy of respect. You, Sara, are a daughter any mother would be happy to claim, and I must admit, I am very proud of you. I wish with all my heart that things could have been different for us.

As my time grows short, I see more clearly what is truly important. I've come to realize that your happiness is the most important thing to me—more important even than the business to which I have devoted my life.

Sara, as you know, I would like for Eve to stay in the family, but I understand that you must do what is best for you. I leave the decision to you.

One last thing: I pray that you and Rourke will work through whatever problem you are having and be happy together. Nothing would please me more than for my daughter and the man I love like a son to build a life together. I know that he loves you, Sara. As I do.

Swallowing the lump in her throat, Sara ran her fingertips over the page. She could barely see it for the tears in her eyes.

She glanced at the clock on the bedside table. It was after three in the morning . . . too late to knock on Rourke's door.

She didn't care. Her emotions were too raw, too stirred up for her to wait until morning. She tossed back the cover and without bothering with robe or slippers, hurried through the apartment and across the hall.

"You knew if I read those diaries I would keep the company, didn't you?" she said, the instant he opened the door. He was wearing his robe and his hair was mussed, but Sara had a feeling he had been waiting for her.

"I was fairly certain you would."

"Yet if I had let Eve go public, you could have purchased stock. That's what you've been wanting for years. As a shareholder, you wouldn't have needed to stay married to me to have a seat on the board or to step in as president."

"I know." Rourke watched her, his gaze intent. "You once asked which I wanted more, you or the presidency of Eve. Now you know."

Her mouth began to quiver. His image blurred as tears banked against her lower eyelids. "Oh, Rourke."

She launched herself against his chest and his arms clamped around her like a vise. "I'm sorry. I'm so sorry, my darling," she sobbed. "Forgive me for ever doubting you."

With a desperate sound, Rourke lifted her off the floor and buried his face against the side of her neck. "I love you. I love you. I love you," he murmured over and over, as though once started, he could not stop.

Sara clung to him, her arms wrapped around his neck, her fingers raking through his hair. She scattered hectic kisses against his temple, his jaw, his ear, all the while sobbing with relief, with joy.

"Love me, darling," she pleaded. "Please, love me."

Rourke made a low sound and clamped his mouth to hers. Kicking the door shut, he turned and strode into the bedroom with her hanging in his arms.

When Sara and Rourke walked into the board-room the next morning, they were surprised to find Lawrence in his usual chair. He had come to Evelyn's funeral, but they had not expected to see him there.

"I thought he and Madelene were calling it quits," Sara whispered under her breath.

"That's what she said," Rourke whispered back.

They had barely exchanged a greeting with Mad-die's husband and taken their seats when she and the others walked in. Madelene stopped in her tracks when she spotted Lawrence.

"What are you doing here?"

"I am a member of the board of directors. I'm here to look after your interests."

"Don't put yourself out on my account. I can manage just fine without you, thank you very much."

"No doubt that's true, but as long as we're married, there's no need. Sit down, Maddie."

Maddie glanced around at the others. They were already seated and waiting anxiously for the meeting to begin. Just as eager to get the meeting started, she swallowed whatever sharp retort she might have made and sat down beside her husband.

"I know that you all are planning to put forth a motion that would dissolve the articles of incorporation and put the company's stock on the open market," Sara said, the instant she had called the meeting to order. "In the interest of saving time, I'd like to make an announcement. After due consideration, I have decided that Eve Cosmetics will remain a family-owned company. You may put the matter to a vote, of course, but let me remind you that I now control fifty-five percent of the stock."

The faces around the table revealed hopes demolished. Grim-faced, Chad rose and stalked out without a word. Madelene's hopeful expression crumbled and she put her face in her hands and began to weep softly. After an initial start, Kitty merely shrugged.

"Well, I guess that's that." Looking old and defeated, Will sagged in his wheelchair.

"Oh, God. Oh, my God." Holding his head in his hands, Eric began to shake as though he were in the grip of a chill.

Paul was mute for an instant before he erupted. He shot out of his chair so fast it tumbled over backward. "You can't do this to me! Damn you, I *need* that money. I have to have it. Don't you understand? It's a matter of life and death. If I don't get the money, I'll soon be floating face down in Buffalo Bayou."

"What the hell are you talking about?" Will demanded.

"I'm talking about a gambling debt!" his son shouted back. "I owe three hundred thousand to Bruno Scagliala. He's a bookie with mob connections. If I don't pay up soon, I'm dead meat."

Sara and everyone around the table gaped at Paul. Her gaze went to his thumbs, which were still in casts, and she sucked in a sharp breath. "That's how your thumbs got broken, isn't it? You didn't have an accident on a drilling site. That gangster broke them, didn't he?"

"He had his goons do it. Bruno just watched. And

he'll watch them blow my brains out without batting an eye if I don't pay up."

"Good grief, Paul. I can't believe you'd be so stupid as to get mixed up with lowlife like that," Maddie snapped, and the others joined in with a barrage of criticism. Finally Sara banged her gavel to shut them up.

"This isn't getting us anywhere." She aimed a no-nonsense look at Paul. "Normally, I think everyone should take the consequences of their actions, but they're too severe in this case. I will cover your debt, Paul, provided you agree to get help for your gambling problem."

"Fuck you, lady! I don't have a problem."

"Paul, anyone who lets a bookie get his hooks into him for three hundred thousand definitely has a problem."

"Rourke's right, son," Will said. "Take Sara's offer and get this monkey off your back."

Paul looked ready to commit mayhem. A vein pulsed in his temple and his face turned a purplish red. He sent a furious look around the table that finally settled on Sara. "Keep your damned money. I don't need it! Damn bunch of busybody holier-than-thous." Cursing them all under his breath, he stormed out.

They were all a bunch of ninnies. Wimps. He didn't need their help. He muttered insults and curses at Sara, his father, and every one of his relatives all the way down in the elevator. His righteous anger carried him all the way to the side entrance, but when he stepped out into the parking lot, he stopped cold, and the blood drained from his face at the sight of the three men leaning against the hood of his car.

"Hello, Mr. Ketchum," Bruno said pleasantly. "We've been waiting for you."

After Paul's abrupt departure, a thick silence filled the boardroom.

"How did this happen?" Sadly shaking his head, Will made an anguished sound. He looked as though he'd aged twenty years in the last five minutes. "I don't understand. Why didn't he come to me? I would have understood. I would have found a way to help him. He's my son, for God's sake."

"Don't be too hard on yourself, Uncle Will. You can't help someone who won't admit he has a problem." Kitty stood up and stretched. "I don't know about the rest of you, but I see no reason to continue this meeting."

"You certainly don't seem too upset about Sara's decision," Madelene flared, as she and the others followed Kitty to the door.

Her younger sister shrugged. "I'll admit, I'm disappointed. I could use some extra capital. But I can't complain. The reviews on my play were smashing. I've got a hit on my hands."

"Congratulations," Maddie offered grudgingly. "How nice for you."

"Now, Maddie, there's no reason to be nasty to your sister. Kitty has worked hard for her success."

"You mind your own business, Lawrence," Madelene flared. "What're you doing here, anyway? I'm not going to be an heiress and my career is obviously over, so why are you still hanging around?"

"You career doesn't have to be over, Maddie. Not

if you are willing to go in a different direction, as I suggested."

"You mean play character parts? No, thank you."

On the verge of leaving, Kitty hesitated. Finally she made a face and turned back to her sister. "Lawrence is right, Maddie. Like it or not, there's just not much call for glamorous forty-one-year-old heroines in the movies these days."

"I'm thirty-six!"

"Oh, please, Maddie. This is me you're talking to, remember? I'm ten years younger than you and I'm thirty-one."

Maddie sniffed and shot her a furious look.

"Look, if you're willing to give it a try, there's a plum part for you in my next play. Thanks to the success of *Dark of the Moon,* it's already scheduled to go into production."

Madelene tried to hold on to her anger, but she was obviously tempted. She shot Kitty a sulky look. "Why are you offering me a part? What do *you* care what happens to me?"

"Because you're my sister and I love you. And I happen to think that you're an enormous talent."

"Really?"

"Yes, really. So what do you say?"

Maddie bit her lower lip. "I don't know. I've never done Broadway before."

"So what? You've got the talent. And once you establish yourself as a serious stage actress, no telling what kind of offers will come your way."

"Kitty's right, darling. I think you should go for it."

"I don't know. It . . . it's scary."

"I know. But you can do it, darling. I know you

can. And I promise I'll be there for you, all the way."

"Really? You'd do that? After . . . after what I've done? Why?"

"Because I love you, Maddie." Lawrence sighed and looked resigned. "And because I've discovered that I'm miserable without you."

She searched his face, her eyes wide with amazement. "You do, don't you? You really do love me."

"Of course he loves you. Good grief, Maddie, where have you been these past three years?" Laughing, Kitty flung her arm around her sister's shoulders and led her toward the door. "Come on, you two. You've got a play to read."

Eric looked searchingly at his father. "Dad . . . Did you mean what you said? About standing by Paul, no matter what?"

"Certainly, I meant it," the old man snapped. "What did you think? You and Paul are my sons, for Chrissake."

Will backed his wheelchair away from the table and maneuvered toward the door. After a brief hesitation, Eric jumped up and took the handles of the chair. "Here, let me push you out. There's, uh . . . there's something I want to talk to you about, Dad. You're probably not going to like what I have to say, but I hope you'll hear me out. You see . . ."

When they all had gone, Rourke and Sara looked at each other across the conference table.

"Alone at last," he murmured in a sexy growl.

Sara fluttered her eyelashes. "I thought they'd never leave."

He rose and came around the table and took her hands, pulling her to her feet and into his arms. He bent and kissed the end of her nose, then took her mouth in a long, lingering caress that made her toes curl. When she was lying weak against him, he broke the kiss and grinned down at her. "Let's go home, Mrs. Fallan."